Three-Ways

A Detectives Seagate

and Miner Mystery

Volume 4

MIKE MARKEL

Three-Ways

A Detectives Seagate and Miner Mystery

Volume 4

ISBN-13: 978-0692228678
ISBN-10: 0692228675

Prologue

She stood on the concrete pad outside his apartment, squinting as the headlights swept past every few seconds, even now, a few minutes before midnight. She shielded her eyes and peered through the picture window into his small, unlit living room. Then she glanced down the row at the other four apartments. One picture window was outlined by a rectangle of light.

The apartment next door was dark. She knew the unit was occupied, but she didn't know who lived there or what hours they kept. Since his apartment was the end unit, there was only that one neighboring unit.

She stepped onto the pebbled black rubber mat, one side torn away so that it read Welcom, and put her ear to the door. She waited a moment, listening for any sounds from inside the shabby one-bedroom unit in the old flat-roofed, one-story brick building four blocks from campus.

She knocked, three taps on the battered wooden door. A few seconds later, she heard his muted footsteps. A light came on in the living room and the door opened. "I didn't expect you," he said. She did not reply. He adjusted the belt on his dark green terrycloth bathrobe.

"Please." He stepped back, sweeping his arm, gesturing for her to enter.

She walked in and placed her bag on the small pine table near the door. Her eyes scanned the humble furnishings: a threadbare blue couch, two mismatched upholstered chairs, a black plastic entertainment center with a TV, a pile of a dozen DVD cases, and a portable stereo system with small speakers built-in. A few books lay on the wooden coffee table, one of them open at the spine. Off in the corner was the tiny kitchen, just a small refrigerator, a narrow range, a white enamel sink chipped down to the black steel, and a few feet of speckled Formica countertop.

Her gaze settled on the three sets of dirty dishes and glasses on the small round kitchen table with its two matching dining chairs.

He said, "Is there something in particular you needed?"

She looked at him and began to unbutton her short cotton jacket. She watched him as his eyes were drawn to the blue and yellow silk scarf knotted loosely at the neck of her sheer silk cream blouse with its top two buttons open. Removing her jacket, she watched him stare at the outlines of her nipples shifting against the silk. Her jacket rustled as it slid off her shoulders and fell softly onto the carpet.

He smiled as she removed her clothing deliberately. First the blouse, and then the skirt and the panties. She left the blue and yellow scarf knotted at her throat. She slipped out of the low heels and followed him into the bedroom.

He untied the belt on his bathrobe and let it drop to the floor. He retrieved the two pillows, one on the floor, the other askew in the middle of the queen-size bed, and arranged them neatly, one on top of the other, centered at the head of the mattress. He tossed aside the rumpled top sheet.

She said, "Is there wine?"

When he turned to face her, she was pleased to see that he was already erect. "Out in the living room," he said. He followed her to the bedroom doorway so that he could see her glide through his apartment. Although she could feel his eyes on her, she moved confidently, her posture tall and straight.

She saw the half-empty bottle of white on the coffee table, surrounded by three glasses: one empty, two with a few sips left in the bottom. She walked into the kitchen, confident that he would watch her rise on her toes and stretch to get two clean glasses from the top shelf of the cabinet to the left of the sink.

He watched her come back toward him, the bottle in one hand, the two glasses, crossed at the stems, in the other. She kept her arms at her sides as she walked, knowing how much he appreciated the way her breasts swayed in rhythm with her gait.

By the time she was at the bed, he was already in position, on his back, his fingers interlaced behind his head on the stacked pillows. She glanced down at his penis to be sure he was ready.

She placed the two glasses next to each other on the night stand and half-filled each one. She put the bottle down next to the glasses.

Slowly she sank onto the mattress, swinging one leg over him and settling on her knees. "Are you sure you can—so soon?" she said, the question a casual compliment. She knew the answer.

Unlacing his fingers and resting his arms at his side, he said, "Come closer and we'll see."

She bent at the waist, lowering her trunk until her palms rested on the mattress on either side of the stacked pillows. She felt his erect penis touch the inside of her left thigh. She pulled the thigh away and watched him smile. Her breasts were three inches above his face.

He lifted his head, slowly, and she pulled her breasts away. He laughed gently, and she smiled a little bit.

His hands came up and grazed her hips, his fingers lightly running up her flank and tracing the undersides of her breasts. He heard her begin to sigh.

His fingers slid down her sides, slowly, across her hips, then inward, toward her sex. She gasped when the fingers began to caress the folds of her vagina. He raised his head and kissed one nipple, and then the other.

She closed her eyes and reached between his legs, taking his penis and guiding it to her sex. She heard him moan. She held it steady and lowered herself onto it, the both of them beginning to breathe deeply.

They moved slowly in rhythm for a minute.

"Now?" she said, opening her eyes to gauge his response. He nodded silently.

As she untied the loose knot in her yellow and blue silk scarf and removed it from her neck, his hands came up and lightly stroked the underside of each breast.

She rocked up and down gently, pausing at the top of the movement when only the tip of his penis was inside her. She reached behind her and let the scarf trail across his scrotum.

"Now." He opened his eyes and lifted his head off the pillows.

She stopped rocking to concentrate on the task. She slid the scarf under his neck and adjusted it so that each end was the same length. She noticed his eyes fixed on her breasts as they swayed above his face.

He moaned softly as she knotted the scarf at the front of his throat and began to tighten it. She started to rock again, feeling his penis get even harder as she tightened the scarf.

His eyes began to close, his moans of pleasure becoming longer and lower. Steadily she tightened the knot at his throat.

His moans turned to groans and his hands lifted off the mattress as she pulled at the knot. After a few moments his eyes opened wide, and his hands reached up toward his throat. He appeared to be trying to shout, but he couldn't produce a sound. His fingers grasped at the scarf, but it was too tight against his throat. His eyelids began to close, as if he were falling asleep. The skin on his cheeks began to pale, then turn a faint blue. His hands fluttered in the air for a moment before falling to the mattress. He was no longer breathing.

Her face contorted as she pulled hard on the knot one last time, increasing the pressure and maintaining it for several long moments. She felt the bulge of his penis increasing inside her, exciting her more, even though he was now lifeless. Beads of perspiration formed on her upper lip as she rose and fell on his erect penis for another minute, until she climaxed. She paused, the sensation flooding her body.

She let go of the scarf, placed her hands on the mattress, near his shoulders, and began to rock back and forth again, her breasts almost grazing his still face. She lifted her hips, exposing the tip of his penis, paused, and then fell onto it, violently. She knew this time it would take only a few thrusts. Then, when it was over, she paused, breathing deeply, her eyes closed, her head bowed, letting the pleasure radiate through her body.

"What you did was wrong, Austin."

Gently she lifted herself off him. Standing next to the bed, she looked down at his beautiful, motionless body, his muscular chest and arms, the slim waist, and that wonderful, hard penis.

She untied the knot in the scarf and removed it from around his neck. She stroked the silk, trying to remove its creases. She tied the scarf loosely around her neck and walked over to the dresser with the mirror on top, leaning against the wall. Looking at her image, she smoothed the scarf again and, satisfied, walked into the living room, where she put her clothes back on: the panties, the blouse, the skirt, and the shoes.

She walked over to the coffee table, bent down, and with her forearm swept all the glasses onto the soiled grey carpet. They didn't break. She crushed one of them under her heel. Then she walked into the kitchen and swept the soiled dishes off the counter and onto the linoleum floor, where they broke with a satisfyingly clatter.

She went back into the living room and kicked the coffee table over, then lifted a dinette chair and swung it, shattering the table's glass top. She worked her way methodically across the small living room, upending, knocking over, and breaking every object in her path.

She was breathing heavily now from her exertions. She picked up her jacket from the floor and put it on, retrieved her purse from the small table near the door, and paused. She walked back into the kitchen and grabbed a paper napkin from the counter. She went to the door and rubbed the napkin across the knob twice as she left the apartment. She pulled the door shut and wiped the knob on the outside, and then put the napkin in her purse. She glanced down at the four other units in the brick building. There were no lights on in the unit next door. She walked at a moderate pace toward her car, which she had parked a block away.

Chapter 1

I'd gotten the call from headquarters a little before seven, which was twenty minutes before I was hoping to wake up. According to the sergeant, the body of a young man was lying on a bed in a shitty little apartment in a rundown five-unit brick building on a mixed commercial/residential block near campus. He was on his back, completely nude, with a huge erection. The death looked suspicious, the sergeant reported. I was curious.

The yellow tape was already up when I got there at seven-twenty. The edge of the sun was just visible, a yellow-pink smudge in the east against a pale blue sky. It was forty-five degrees. By five this afternoon, it would climb another twenty degrees. Spring is my favorite time here in the middle of Montana. In late April, you'll still wake up to frost, but you get a definite feeling the worst is over, that the plants and trees had somehow made it through another ungodly winter, that things would start to grow, that life would go on.

Not for the poor bastard in the apartment, of course, him lying there nude, mast up.

I have mixed feelings about starting a new case. I don't like it that someone got killed, of course, especially a young person. I'm a cop, but I'm still a person. More cop than person at this particular stage of my life, but still technically a person. On the other hand, I didn't miss the presentations to junior-high kids about why they shouldn't pop Mommy's Percocet.

The cars in front of the brick building told me who was already at the crime scene. The blue Mitsubishi belongs to my partner, Ryan Miner. Ryan is a handsome, well-adjusted, happily married father of two point five kids. He's been my partner for more than a year, which here in Rawlings has worked out to four or five murders. I've tried as hard as I can to dislike Ryan because he represents everything that I hate. Not the Mormon part. I don't give a crap how you try to figure out the Big Picture, or if you even try. That's your business.

It's that he is a superb detective: smart, strong, cheerful, totally committed to the job. Earlier this year, this asshole took a shot at us. Ryan pushed me out of the way and took the bullet himself. It ripped up his intestine pretty bad, and for a few days he was pretty close to checking out because the rest of your body apparently doesn't like it when all the shit leaks out of your large intestine. But the doctors blasted him with weapons-grade antibiotics, removed the torn-up part of the intestine and sewed the two ends together, and hooked him up to a colostomy bag while the whole thing healed.

After a couple months they stitched his plumbing back together and he was healing pretty fast, being young and otherwise healthy, but then he screwed it up by pushing too hard. He used to be a big-deal athlete in college, and he could Krav Maga a guy onto the ground before I could get my pistol out of the holster. I think he was surprised and a little offended when that bullet didn't just bounce off him, so he started back into training before his doc okayed it and ended up ripping his gut, which set him back a few weeks. Now he's got this cane that his doc makes him carry around to remind him he almost goddamn died, so maybe he should try harder not to be an idiot by re-injuring himself more often than necessary.

The first few weeks after he was shot, after they got his infection under control, the scary part was he couldn't remember people's names and had trouble thinking of the right word. But he's at about eighty percent of his old self now, which puts him at about a hundred-and-fifty percent of me. He sets the bar so high I just walk under it. Don't even have to bend.

The busted, rusted minivan belongs to Harold Breen, our Medical Examiner. I love Harold. He's morbidly obese, with a perpetually sweaty scalp, stubble in his chin folds, and a belly sticking out of his plaid K-Mart polyester sport shirt because the bottom button popped off the first time he put it on. Harold has been with the department almost twenty years, longer than me. I don't believe he's ever blown an autopsy, screwed-up a court appearance, or gotten pissed at an alcoholic detective because she contaminated a body. And he never forgets that the stiff on the steel table used to be limber.

The 1968 Beetle, hand-painted in swirly black and white like a Holstein cow, belongs to Robin, our Evidence Tech. She's been with us four or five years. Those years have transformed her from a tall, freckled, strong-boned athlete with baby fat to a tall, freckled, strong-boned athlete without baby fat. She wears all kinds of jeweled hardware on her face—in her nose, up and down her ears, in her eyebrows. She frequently changes the color of the streaks in her blond hair, the only rule being that the color must not appear in nature. She curses more than me, which requires significant effort, and effortlessly drops the word *pubes* into quite a few sentences that would have been perfectly fine without it.

"Enjoy," said Officer Truman, opening the cheap wooden door with a metal "5" screwed into it. Right away I was hit by a funky smell, equal parts cheap white wine and hard sex. My gaze swept the room. The dead guy was a worse housekeeper than me. Scattered across the floor were busted glasses, dishes, framed pictures, and all kinds of books, wooden drawers, throw pillows, lamps, chair cushions, and a stereo, a TV set, a pizza box, and a few broken wine bottles. A glass-topped coffee table was on its side, one of the four legs snapped off, the glass in a thousand pieces on the grey-brown carpet. To tidy up, you'd start with a snow shovel.

Robin or one of the uniforms had already laid down the metal plates that we walk across at a crime scene. You see them more outside than inside, but the living room was so full of busted crap that Robin hadn't had a chance to tag and bag it all. I hopscotched across the plates toward the bedroom. From its doorway I saw Ryan's broad back and Harold's broad front.

Ryan was standing by the side of the bed, hands on his skinny hips, his cane hooked on his wrist, the tip dangling in the air. As usual, he was wearing a real nice suit, dark, with a bright white shirt, button down. Today's tie was striped, some reds and a blue. He turned when he heard me. "Good morning, Karen," he said.

I nodded. "Still a little early to call it that," I said, "but, okay, good morning."

Harold Breen was kneeling next to the bed, his big frame blocking my view of the stiff. "Hello, sweetheart," he said, without looking up.

"Good morning, handsome." I glanced around the tiny bedroom. There was a cheap dresser with an unframed mirror sitting on top, leaning against the wall, a small closet with accordion doors, and the queen bed covered in a plain white fitted sheet.

One of the uniforms had covered up the vic with the top sheet. Harold had pulled the sheet down to the vic's waist and was looking at him. On the night table to the left of the bed was an almost empty bottle of white wine next to two half-full glasses.

I bent down to look at the glasses. I could see faint prints. It didn't look like anyone had drunk anything from the glasses.

"Robin been in here yet?" I said.

"No," Ryan said. "No touching, please."

"How come this room's okay and the living room's all busted up?"

Ryan smiled. "We're going to have to devote some thought to that, Karen."

"Don't you hate that?"

"No, actually." Ryan treated my crankiness like caffeine: he was fine with others indulging, but it was against his religion.

I walked around to the other side of the bed, carefully avoiding two Trojan wrappers, a pair of sex handcuffs covered in phony fur, and a foot-long black dildo as thick as an oar handle. It was a deluxe model with a set of balls molded into it and a couple leather straps attached to it. In the world of dildos, black is a more common color than you would imagine, given the demographics, I mean. I've never discussed the issue with black guys, so I don't know whether they think it's racist or just a compliment. I could see both points of view.

Having worked Vice, I'm familiar with all kinds of weird-ass toys, but in the typical bedroom it's mostly vibrators. I crouched down next to the dildo. There was some dried sticky stuff covering the first six inches or so of it. So either the dead guy partied with lesbos or he used the strappy dildo on his girlfriend because he didn't have a strapless bargain model. Or he figured out how to strap it on his own ass so he could drill two girls at the same time, each back-and-forth doubling as a forth-and-back. I don't even know if that's possible. I made a mental note to ask my ex-husband.

I stood up and looked down at the vic's face. He was a good-looking guy. I put him in his early twenties, with a long, straight nose, full lips, and strong cheek bones. Dark hair, thick and wavy, swept back, not parted, like he was moving forward and his hair was blowing back in the breeze. He had a moustache and goatee, carefully trimmed. The whole look said, Yeah, I'm a handsome

son of a bitch, and I'm willing to make the effort. You're
welcome.

"Jesus," I said as my gaze landed on the sheet covering his
tent pole a couple feet south. "That's all him?" I said.

Harold turned to me. "You want to see?"

I sighed. "I have so little in my life, Harold."

He knew my story. He nodded in agreement, then pulled back
the sheet.

This was one significant dick. It was circumcised, sticking
straight up in the air seven or eight inches, couple or three inches
across. His balls were as big as a good-sized Golden Delicious.

I'm not that into size as a measure of anything important, but
any woman who looked at that package and didn't think, "Oh, my
Lord, you have outdone yourself"—well, that woman would be
dead, blind, or … no, there's no third possibility: dead or blind.

"You done, Karen?" Harold said.

I was somewhere else. "Excuse me?" I said after a moment.

He lifted an eyebrow. "I asked if you're done."

"I guess so."

Ryan said, "Did you notice anything interesting?"

I looked at him. "You're kidding, right?"

"No hair," he said.

"What?"

"I said, 'No hair.' He's got no hair on his chest or his
stomach. And no pubic hair."

I hadn't noticed. "You mean like he's got some kind of
disease or like he shaved it all off?"

"My guess, Karen," he said gently, seeing that I hadn't
completely re-focused my attention, "since he's got hair on his
head and his face and his legs, is he liked to shave."

"Guys shave down there?"

"Not most guys, at least guy cops and guys who go to my
gym, but apparently some guys."

"This is very interesting," I said. "Maybe I should look again down there."

Ryan nodded. Harold ignored me.

"Okay," I said, shaking the images out of my head, "so who was this guy?"

"He was Austin Sulenka, age twenty-four, apparently some kind of student here at Central Montana. He has a Montana license, with this place listed as his home address."

"How did he die, Harold?"

The Medical Examiner looked up at me. Then he pointed to the vic's neck, which had a pink band about an inch wide, as well as a big red-speckled bruise over the Adam's apple. "My guess is asphyxia. He was strangled. Or he strangled himself."

"During sex?"

"I think he was having sex, what with him being nude and on his bed."

"Plus the rod," I said.

"The rod might be nothing." He shook his head. "Could be a death erection. We used to see that quite a bit at hangings."

"Well, I'll be. So someone could have staged the scene to look like he was getting laid?"

"I'm only a doc. That's for you two to figure out. I'm just saying it could be a death erection."

"Wait a second," I said. I leaned my head down toward it, studied it for a few seconds, then walked around to the other side of the bed to examine it from another angle.

Ryan was looking at me. "I could ask Robin to print you an extra set of pictures."

"Very funny," I said. "Just wanted to see if this dick's seen any action lately."

"And?"

"Yes." I was a couple inches away from it, and I didn't want to bother trying to find my glasses in my big shoulder bag. "I do believe it has."

"Yeah?"

"If he was just jerking off, there'd be some balled-up tissues around, or some sticky stuff on his crotch or his legs or on the ceiling or the windows or something, but it wouldn't be all over the shaft where his hand was. This dick's got a clear high-tide mark on it." I paused. "Ryan, did you find whatever it was strangled him? It wasn't a set of hands, right?"

"No, I didn't find a cord or a belt or anything on the bed. Harold, can you tell if it was a set of hands?"

Harold shook his head. "If it was just hands, we'd see a pattern, particularly where the thumbs pressed in. No, it wasn't hands. The petechiae in front says it was a cord or rope or something like that. It was knotted, broke the blood vessels."

"So," I said, looking at Ryan, "this wasn't auto-asphyxiation, like he was jerking off, right?"

"Unless he used a noose, so he could strangle himself with one hand and jerk off with the other, he would need three hands: two to tighten the cinch around his neck and one to jerk off."

I noticed a tiny smile on Ryan's face, which probably meant he was making fun of me. I didn't mind. It was early; the shift hadn't officially started. Anything dumb I say before eight AM doesn't count. "He probably wouldn't have trashed his own living room."

Ryan put on the mock-thoughtful expression he used when I was particularly slow-witted. "So you find the trashed-living-room anomaly more troubling than the three-hand-masturbation paradox?"

"I have no idea what the hell you just said."

Chapter 2

When I caught up with Robin, her head was in the guy's bathtub. She always does the bathrooms first. She thinks stiff towels, hairy drains, and stray specks of vomit that missed the bowl tell the most interesting stories. Usually, I'm afraid I agree with her, but with this guy, I got the feeling there'd be no shortage of biologicals in every room.

"Hey, Karen," she said, looking up from the tub drain and giving me a big smile. She wiped her brow with the sleeve of her white jumpsuit. She had on her paper booties. She was a stickler on methods.

"Are we having fun, Robin?"

"I can't speak for you," she said cheerfully, "but I could spend a whole day just in the shitter."

"Oh, yeah?"

"Look at this," she said, sweeping her arm to take in the tiny bathroom. "Four different wet towels on the floor, two others hanging on the shower-curtain rod. Enough pubes to stuff a small pillow. There's birth-control pills, tampons, douches, pink plastic razors, makeup, body spray, perfume. Shit, there's enough girlie crap here to outfit a women's dorm for a year. Plus all the guy crap—lotions, creams, skin softener, rubbers, three kinds of razors. You might as well work another murder this week, 'cause it's gonna take me two days just to collect and label the stuff in this place."

"Okay, I'll see what I can do," I said. "Where are you so far?"

"I've photo'd the whole apartment, but I haven't bagged and tagged any of the stuff."

"Can Ryan and I go over the living room?"

"Go ahead. I'll need another hour in here, at least."

"All right, thanks." I snapped on a pair of gloves and walked out to the living room, where Ryan was already rummaging around. "You find his wallet yet?"

He waved it at me. "Yup. It's got his license, credit cards, all his plastic. Plus about forty bucks."

"Okay, let's see if we can identify some of his fuck buddies from this landfill, then we'll do a canvass and meet back here. Sound good?"

"Absolutely." He was bent over, leaning on his cane, sifting through the papers, photographs, and assorted busted junk all over the floor. There was stuff everywhere, but most of the papers seemed to be clustered around the desk in the corner of the room.

We spent about ten minutes looking through the scattered remains of Austin Sulenka's life. Ryan moved to the desk and fired up the guy's laptop.

"Looking for anything in particular?" I said.

"Trying to figure out who this woman is." He held up a photo of the vic with a good-looking woman, long medium-brown hair, big smile aimed at the camera. They were in a canoe, bright sunshine reflecting off the water. "I'd nominate her as his favorite girlfriend," he said, fanning a bunch of photos of her like playing cards.

"Good," I said. "Tell me what you figure out."

It took him the better part of thirty seconds. "Name's May Eberlein. Graduate student in English, just like Austin." Ryan was pointing to a gallery of a few dozen pictures of her in the picture folder on the vic's computer.

"How'd you get her name?"

"His Facebook page." He clicked a button and pulled up Austin's wall, then swiveled the laptop so I could see it head-on. He clicked on the photos, and there was her name beneath a big set of photos.

"She's the only one he tagged?"

"Seems so," he said, back at the keyboard. "He's got lots of photos of other guys and girls, but May seems to be his true love."

"Okay, let's bring the laptop in."

He nodded. "Haven't found a phone yet," he said. "Be on the lookout for that, okay?"

"Yeah." I was scanning the layers of debris. "Who called this in?"

"The woman in Unit 4, next door."

"You got a name?"

Ryan pulled his notebook out of his inside suit jacket pocket. "Jessica Allen," he said.

"Okay, let me start with her. You start working the other three units, okay? Then we'll meet back here."

He nodded and I left the apartment. What passes for morning traffic in Rawlings was starting to pick up. The gas and diesel fumes from the street that passed within fifteen feet of the little apartment block were a pleasant contrast to the funk in the stiff's place. Because of the traffic noise, I knocked hard on the door to Unit 4.

Footsteps came clomping toward me. The door opened. "Ms. Allen." I pointed to the gold shield on the chain around my neck. "Detective Karen Seagate, Rawlings Police Department. You got a minute to speak with me about this?" I pointed next door.

A car honked behind me so loud I jumped. I turned around to see a guy in a Saturn flipping off a woman in a Honda. Good morning, everyone.

She shook her head as she looked out onto the street. "Yeah, sure," she said. Jessica Allen was about forty, tall, thin, and tired. Her body had started to go concave, shoulders slumping forward, chest pulling in. She was smoking a cigarette, her bleached blond hair tied back in a rubber band. Her skin was pale, a cluster of zit scars running up both sides of her neck toward her cheeks. She was wearing a sweatshirt, no bra, and plaid men's flannel pajama bottoms.

"You phoned the police about an hour ago, right, about Austin?"

She closed the door behind me. "That's right." She motioned for me to sit at her small kitchen table. "I'm making some coffee. Want some?"

"Sure," I said. "Thanks." She turned toward her counter. "What made you think something was wrong?"

"I was walking Richard to the bus stop like I do every morning," she said. "I glance in Austin's living-room window. Usually he's got the shade closed—you know, when he's partying—"

"He partied a lot?"

She raised an eyebrow. "Big time."

"Anyway, go ahead," I said. "You're looking in his window."

"Yeah, and I see what you guys saw: the place was trashed. So I phoned him, no answer. I knock on his door. Nothing. He's not an early riser, you know what I mean? I just got this bad feeling. So I called the cops."

"There's no manager here who could've opened the place up—I mean, in one of these five units?"

"No, there's nobody here."

"So, you said he partied last night?"

"Yeah, it was about eleven-thirty, maybe midnight. Started hearing a real ruckus, stuff flying, crashing."

"How long did that last?"

"Just a few minutes."

"You didn't think maybe something was wrong?" The refrigerator cycled on, the hum filling the small kitchen area.

"Not really," she said. "There was stuff going on earlier in the night. I could hear girls' voices, some laughing."

The coffeemaker started gurgling. Jessica Allen poured the coffee, then grabbed a quart of milk from the refrigerator. There were sugar packets in a shiny container on the table, like you see in diners. "Austin parties three or four times a week. Guys, girls. There could be ten people in there. They start up any time, go for a few hours, rest up. Then start up later and go a few more hours." She pointed toward her living room. "His place is the exact same size at this. Of course, he could get a lot more people in there 'cause he's got some in the bedroom, some in the living room, if you know what I mean."

"Yeah," I said. "I think I get the picture. You say there were guys and girls, right?"

"It was mixed, you know. There'd be guys there in the afternoons, weekends, watching football, guy shit. But at night, for the partying, there were girls and guys. I could tell sometimes there'd be two or three sets of people humping away."

"You could hear it?"

"Through these paper walls?" Jessica Allen tapped an ash off her cigarette into a plastic restaurant ashtray. "You see that bed in the living room?" I nodded. "That's where I have Richard sleep. Can't have him with me in the bedroom 'cause that wall's up against Austin's. The noise used to wake Richard up two or three times a night. You know, I try to get him down by nine. That's just when Austin's getting into high gear over there."

"Did you ever ask him to keep it down?"

Jessica Allen took a pull on her cigarette and shrugged. "Every once in a while I send Richard off to my ex's and I make some noise myself, you know what I mean? Besides," she said, "it's not like I got a lot of housing options. I make three bucks an hour working Sally's Diner, plus tips. Economy this bad, a lot of people cut back on the tips. My rent's late half the time. I'm lucky I got this place. It's four seventy-five, utilities included. Not gonna find a better deal in this school district."

"Okay, so getting back to last night. You hear some crashing around eleven-thirty, midnight. Lasted a few minutes."

"That's right."

"Then, you hear anything else?"

"No, it goes quiet."

"Did you hear anybody leave? Did you see anyone?"

"No, I don't keep track of comings and goings. Like I said, it could be a bus depot in there."

"Let me ask you, did Austin have one girl he partied with more than the others?"

She shook her head. "I think he was just a pussy hound."

I put a photo of May Eberlein on the kitchen table. "How 'bout this girl? You seen her before?"

Jessica Allen looked at the photo, then nodded her head. "That girl can take a photograph, know what I mean?"

"She's good-looking."

"Yeah, I think I've seen her. Maybe, I'm not sure."

"Do you know who she is?"

"Sorry." She shook her head. "Might've run into her once or twice, but, tell you the truth, only real thing me and Austin had in common was that wall over there."

"So," I said, "you and Austin never partied?"

She exhaled a stream of smoke. "Just between you and me?"

I nodded. Jessica Allen could have been from my neighborhood when I was a kid. She asked me if I'd keep it quiet, I said I would, and that was good enough for her.

"Only once. It was maybe a year ago, year and a half. He'd just moved in. We ran into each other. One thing led to another, you know how it is."

"Yeah," I said. Which was true.

"So I find myself at his place. We're drinking, a little smoking. We're both half wasted. He shows me what he's got." She paused.

"Yeah?"

She was kind of smiling. "He's a good-looking guy and all, but you wouldn't believe the sword he was carrying."

I smiled, too. "I've just been next door."

Jessica Allen nodded. "All right, then."

"And he knew how to use it?"

Jessica Allen's left eyebrow went up, and then she frowned. "Yes and no," she said.

"How's that?"

"He was real athletic, and he knew where my spots were. But …" She paused. "He didn't even pretend I was in the room with him. It was more like I was his first waitress, if you know what I mean, although I can't believe I was. Or his first woman with a kid. His first something. You know, like he kept a checklist?" She shrugged her shoulders.

I've known a lot of guys who do that. No women, though. "So it was just that one time?"

"Yeah," she said. "We didn't have anything in common. I couldn't understand half the things he said. All about old books, you know, which I don't know anything about."

"But no hard feelings?"

She stubbed out her cigarette as she knit her brows. "No way. He banged me hard, which I appreciated. But I'll be honest. I'm not looking for a guy." Her eyes drifted off and she was silent for a moment. A small smile crept onto her face. "But sometimes, when I'm in bed, I can still see that sweet dick."

Chapter 3

Ryan and I met up back outside Austin's apartment. "I interviewed Jessica Allen," I said. "She doesn't really remember May. But she did screw Austin once."

"Really?" Ryan said. "See her as a possible?"

"Not at all," I said. "She's an adult. She's got a kid, no money. She's fifteen, twenty years older than him. She bangs guys once in a while, but I didn't see any interest in getting involved with one guy. Especially a guy like that, a college guy who talks about old books. Think she was mostly curious. Said he was a good lay. Technically, I mean."

"Technique is important." Ryan shook his head. "Did she say why she didn't call it in when the furniture started flying last night?"

"Apparently, wasn't the first time furniture hit the wall. Plus, she wants to stay on good terms with everyone. She's late with the rent sometimes, so she tries to be easy to get along with."

"And you buy her story?"

"Completely," I said. "What'd you get?"

"Nothing," he said. "One of the units was unoccupied. Another one, nobody home. A third one, an old man with hearing aids and an oxygen tube. He wouldn't have heard someone tossing his own apartment."

"I'm gonna ask for a couple of uniforms to do the rest of the canvass. Did you look around behind the apartments?"

"There's five numbered parking spots. Beyond that, the parking lot for the bank. Across the street, a vet clinic and an insurance agent."

"Nothing with anybody there about midnight, right?"

"I asked the woman at the vet's. They're open seven days, but nobody's there after six on Sundays."

"All right," I said. "Want to talk to the chief?"

"See you back there," Ryan said.

We got in our separate cars and drove to headquarters. I carded my way into the back door, walked down the hall, and made it to my desk, nose-to-nose with Ryan's in the middle of the detectives' bullpen. I glanced at the floor next to his chair. His black leather briefcase, like a professor's, was already there, so I walked past the break room and the incident room, down the hall to the chief's office. Ryan was sitting on the couch in the outer office.

"Morning, Margaret," I said. Margaret started when the new chief did, about a year ago. She's always at her desk, always looking intently at her computer screen. Every few seconds there's a burst of typing. I've never seen her standing up, never seen her walking, never run into her in the bathroom. If I had to pick her out of a lineup, they'd have to put five thirty-year-old women at desks, staring at computers. I think I could recognize the top of her head, her chestnut hair straight and sleek, parted neatly a little off the center.

Her eyes still on the screen, she smiled briefly and nodded. "The chief will see you now."

Robert Murtaugh was working at his desk. He got up, hitching his pants. He's about fifty, fifty-three. I've heard he's in the weight room downstairs at six-thirty AM sharp. He's one of those guys who lives according to a routine, and it shows. His face has the lines you'd expect for a guy his age, and the hair is going salty, but the body is toned and muscular. Must make it easier to be a chief if you look like you could run a hundred yards without doubling over and puking. But he's not doing it for looks or even as part of the job. It's more that he's figured out he has to do it this way. He's a former drunk, like me, and he's learned you can't just do whatever you want or you'll be dead in a few weeks.

"What have you got?" the chief said.

"Austin Sulenka, age twenty-four." Ryan was looking down at his skinny notebook. "Sometime last night. He's a graduate student in English at CMSU. He's lying on the bed, nude, looks like he was strangled."

The chief was frowning. I've learned it doesn't mean he's pissed or unhappy with us. It's just his expression when he starts to collect the pieces we're going to have to assemble into a jigsaw puzzle.

"We did the initial canvass," I said. "He was a good-looking guy. Apparently liked to screw as many women as he could. Lots of parties."

"You thinking this was a sex game? Auto-asphyxiation?"

"We don't think so," Ryan said. "Harold said the broken blood vessels look like strangulation." Ryan looked at me to continue.

"Plus, the apartment was trashed," I said.

"'Trashed' as in everyone was drunk, or as in someone was looking for something?"

I shrugged my shoulders. "If they were looking for something, they wasted a lot of time breaking stuff they didn't need to break. Robin's said she'd need the better part of the day just to catalog it all. Right now, we can't tell if the place was trashed before or after the murder. It could have been a home invasion, or someone killed him and wanted to make it look like one. Or maybe someone was really mad at him."

"Hmmm." The chief looked troubled. "Okay, how do you want to go at it?"

"Looks like he was killed in his apartment," I said, "a little five-unit brick building on Liberty, near campus. One unit is empty. We interviewed a couple of his neighbors. One other wasn't home. We'd like two uniforms, a couple hours, to finish the canvass."

"Sure, what else?"

"We thought we'd follow up with a woman named May Eberlein, who appears to be his main girlfriend. And go over to campus, find out what kind of student he was. See if we can figure out who'd want him dead. Sound good?"

He nodded. "Keep me in the loop."

"Absolutely," Ryan said as we left his office.

Back at our desks, I asked Ryan to call the university and get an address on May Eberlein.

We drove over to the east side of town, a quiet residential area. I was hoping we could get to her before she left her place for the day.

"You sure this is right?" I said. "2414 Marshall?"

We were parked under a big old sycamore. This was a nice section of town, two-story colonials and Craftsman bungalows from the thirties and forties. Manicured lawns, sidewalks. The kind of neighborhood that would have a lemonade stand on every block in July.

"That's what it says."

We walked up to a weathered picket fence and opened the gate, then followed the brick path to the steps leading to the porch. I opened the screen door and used the knocker on the dark green wooden door. A few seconds later, a woman opened it. She was about seventy, wearing a plaid dress, little fake-pearl earrings, a pin of a butterfly up near her neck.

I had my shield around my neck. "Good morning, ma'am. I'm Detective Seagate, my partner Detective Miner. Is there a May Eberlein lives here?"

The woman looked concerned, her brow furrowed behind her metal-rimmed round glasses. "I hope there's nothing wrong."

"No, just a few questions for her. Does she live here?"

"Yes, she does," the woman said. "She rents the upstairs apartment." She pointed around to the east side of her house. "Take those metal stairs," she said.

Ryan gave her a nice smile and decided to chat her up. "Is May a good tenant?"

"Oh, my goodness." The lady folded her hands in front of her chest. "May is such a nice girl. I feel so lucky to have her."

"Is that right?" Ryan said.

"Some of my lady friends have given up taking girls in, you know, with the way they dress, and the smoking. They say they won't bring men in, but you turn your back ... well, I don't have to spell it out."

"But May doesn't give you any trouble," Ryan said.

"To be honest with you, I feel a little safer living in this big house all by myself when I know she's upstairs. May is a delight. And such a pretty girl. Well, you'll see." She smiled my grandmother's chipmunk-cheeked smile.

"Thanks very much, ma'am."

I riffled the buds on the junipers growing tall around the side of the house as we walked along the path to the black wrought-iron stairs leading up to May's apartment. "May's very pretty. You be pretty, too, okay?"

"You know I can't *not* be pretty, Karen."

I knocked. The footsteps were rapid, like she was in a hurry. The door opened quickly. May was tall, maybe five-ten, a hundred and ten pounds. She was wearing a dark blue silk blouse, a placket hiding the buttons. She had on pale blue corduroy slacks, no socks or shoes. She held a mascara wand in her hand. She'd been working on her right eye. Hadn't gotten to the left one yet.

"Yeah?" she said, like people with detective shields around their necks climb the metal stairs and knock on her door all the time.

I introduced us.

"What is it?" she said. "I'm kinda in a hurry."

"Are you May Eberlein?" I said.

"That's right." Her face showed the frustration of us taking up her time.

"We want to ask you some questions about a case we're working on."

"I'm running late." She glanced at her watch. "I teach in fourteen minutes. Can we do this some other time?"

"You know, Ms. Eberlein, ordinarily we'd stop back later to accommodate your schedule, but we really need to talk with you now. Is there someone you can call to put a note on the board or whatever that you'll be a few minutes late? We could talk here. No need to go down to police headquarters."

I've found that last sentence helps people find the time to talk with us now.

She frowned big, like she'd been told since she was little that it was adorable. "Stay right there." She hurried back into her apartment, picked up her cell from an end table, and made the call. I couldn't make out everything she was saying. I caught "cops" and an annoyed "I don't know." The light from a lamp behind her was silhouetting her body. Through her blouse I could see she didn't have any fat on her. Not anorexia-thin. Talbots-thin. I was her height and weight when I was her age, but she had better boobs than I had then. Much better than I have now.

"Okay." She strode back to us. "What do you need?" She just stood there at the door.

I turned to Ryan, signaling for him to take over. "Ms. Eberlein," he said, turning on his smile. "It'll only take a couple of minutes. Do you think we could come in?"

She scoped him out quickly. She didn't like the cane, but then she considered the whole package. Her posture relaxed, and her hand came up to brush her long, light brown hair back behind her ear. She had on turquoise and gold earrings, maybe three-hundred bucks.

"Yes, I'm sorry," she said, returning his smile. Between the two of them, they must have had a hundred big, beautiful white teeth. "Come in."

It was a small apartment, with the living room, maybe ten by fifteen, dominated by a couch and two matching upholstered chairs, sitting on thick cherry legs, suffocating beneath a busy Victorian floral pattern made to look like needlepoint. Definitely a furnished apartment. "Sit down," she said to the two of us. "How can I help you?"

"We want to ask you a couple questions about Austin Sulenka," I said.

"What questions?" She pursed her lips. She was the kind of girl who displayed every emotion because every one of them looked good on her.

"Can you tell us what your relationship is with Austin?"

She nodded her head like she knew where this was going. "What did he say our relationship is?"

"Well, we'd rather hear it from your perspective," Ryan said, then flashed his smile.

"Austin is … how do I say this?" She paused. "Austin has been a rather big disappointment."

"How so?" I said.

"No, let me change that. Knowing Austin has been a positive experience for me, I mean, for me in my life. But yes, I'll stick with what I said: Austin has been a big disappointment."

"Tell us more," I said.

She glanced at Ryan, then turned back to me. "You know how, when you meet someone, you're aware that they might not be what they seem? But," she extended her palm toward me, "if you've had any experience with men, you think your radar will help you understand what they really want, what they're really like." She addressed Ryan. "No offense, Detective, but men can be …" She wrinkled her nose, like she was about to say something unpleasant, but something that needed to be said. "Sort of stupid." This harsh truth out of the way, she turned back to me. "Men think we don't know they mostly just want to sleep with us."

She was playing me, but I was pleasantly surprised to make the category of people men would want to sleep with. It had been a while. I nodded gravely, May's sister in the struggle.

"Well, I knew Austin's reputation. In fact, I'd seen him in action with a number of the other girls. So I thought I was ready, you know, when he got to me. But then, what I learned was that I was not prepared for him. I thought I understood him, that we had a real connection." Her big, almond-shaped grey eyes got even bigger. "But I found out … I found out," she said, her palms up in a gesture of sad resignation, "that it was just my turn." She put her hands back in her lap and looked down. She brushed an invisible speck of something off her slacks and then looked up, first at me and then at Ryan, as if she expected one of us to praise her for having admitted that Austin taught her a painful but necessary lesson.

"Did you break it off with him?" I said.

"Yes, I did." She held her head up high. "As I said, it was a valuable learning experience for me."

"When did you break it off, Ms. Eberlein?"

"About a month ago."

"When did you last have any contact with Austin?"

She looked toward the ceiling. "Last week, Thursday or Friday, around the department. In the mailroom."

"So you didn't see him socially, this weekend?"

She frowned. "What is he saying about me?"

I looked at her. "Ms. Eberlein, we need to tell you some bad news." I put on my serious expression. "Austin is dead."

Her body went stiff, then her hands came up to her face. "Oh, my God," she cried out, almost shrieked. "Oh, my God, that can't be." She started to gasp for air, like she was going to pass out. She clutched at her chest. "No, that can't be," she said four or five more times, and then she started to cry, out of control.

Ryan pushed down on his cane, lifting himself out of his overstuffed chair, trying to figure out if she was in some kind of medical trouble. I had my hand on my phone in case I needed to call for help. But after half a minute she got her breathing under control. She looked kind of ghoulish, a river of black mascara trailing down her right cheek. "What happened to him?"

"We're not exactly sure," I said.

"What do you mean?"

"We haven't conducted the autopsy yet, but he appears to have died of asphyxia." I wanted to see how she responded to that.

"You mean, like carbon-monoxide poisoning or something?"

"No, there were marks around his neck, like he was strangled."

She looked confused. "Are you saying he was murdered?"

"That's our best guess, right now."

She was slack-jawed, looking back and forth between me and Ryan. "I can't believe what you're telling me."

"I'm sorry, Ms. Eberlein, that's all we know at the moment. We think he died last night or very early this morning."

"This is unbelievable." She started crying again and looked up at me. "I just can't process what you've told me."

Ryan and I sat there a few moments. "Ms. Eberlein," I said, "we have to ask you this next question. You understand. Can you tell us where you were last night, between eight PM and, say, two?"

She looked at me, horrified. "I was here. Right here. I was preparing for my classes this morning."

"Was there anyone here with you? Anyone who can corroborate that?"

"You don't believe me? You think I might have killed Austin?"

"We don't think anything, Ms. Eberlein." I shook my head. "It's just a standard question we have to ask everyone who knew Austin."

"I was alone. Maybe Mrs. Brauchner was downstairs."

"The landlady?"

"If she had her hearing aid in, maybe she heard me." May started crying again.

"Can you think of anyone who might've wanted to hurt Austin?"

Her head was in her hands again. She was crying harder now. She shook her head.

Ryan and I stood up. "Okay, Ms. Eberlein, sorry to have to give you this news. We'll be in touch if we need to talk to you some more." I walked over to her, my card in my hand, but she didn't look up. I put it on the table next to her chair. "My card's got all my numbers on it."

We left her to her grief, real or otherwise.

Chapter 4

Down the black metal stairs, back to the cruiser. We'd just switched over to Dodge Chargers. This one, only a few weeks old, still had that new-car plastic smell. The sun reflected off the black hood, shining right in our eyes. I put down the visor and cracked the front windows a little to let some of the plastic fumes out.

"Well?" I said to Ryan. "What do you make of May?"

"That she is quite attractive?"

I looked at him.

"You asked me what I make of May."

"I have an idea, Ryan. Let's play a game. Pretend we're police detectives. We're working a case together. We want to figure out who killed Big Dick. We just spent ten minutes with his main girlfriend, a willowy young lady named May. Your partner is a middle-age recovering drunk who's desperately searching for any reason to keep going, and for now she's trying out Just Doing Her Job. Do you think you could help her?"

Ryan frowned, then nodded his head slowly as if he was giving the question some deep thought. "Well, if that's the game you'd like to play, here's what I would say."

"Wonderful," I said. "I look forward to your response."

"Well, I'm pretty sure May is quite attractive."

I sighed. "Ah, shit."

"Give me a second, Karen. I'm being serious. The fact that May is quite attractive is about all I'm willing to say at this point."

"Why is that, Ryan?"

"No, let me modify that. May is quite attractive, very self-centered, used to getting her own way and confident she always will, and she's had many boyfriends."

"Yeah, well, that all goes with 'quite attractive.' I was hoping you might have some thoughts on—I don't know—whether she strangled Austin Sulenka."

He shook his head and put on his I'd-like-to-help-you face. "I'm sorry. That's all I've got at the moment."

"Explain."

"In general, I tend to believe the stuff a witness says before she knows the guy is dead more than what she says after. But with May I don't really believe any of it. If she didn't kill him—and didn't know he's dead—all the business about how disappointing he is because he wasn't the wonderful fellow he said he is, all that might be true, although the part I really believe is that she learned a lot about her own limitations in that she didn't realize he was just out to have sex with her. A girl that attractive, she's been fending off guys since she was twelve, so obviously she thought she was good at it. Maybe she met her match with Austin, and that's what made the biggest impression on her."

"And if she did kill Austin?"

"If she did kill him, then everything she said is baloney. She knew we'd be by to interview her. She's got the mascara brush in her hand, she's rushing off to teach her class, she broke up with him a month ago, only runs into him around the office, but the news of his death is still shocking, mainly because she knew nothing about it since she's moved on. Still, Austin's death diminishes her even though she doesn't have sex with him anymore because no man is an island."

"'No man is an island'?"

"John Donne. Seventeenth-century English poet," Ryan said, nodding. "They were English majors."

"You had me worried there. I thought for a moment you were gonna concentrate on the case."

He gave me a big grin. "I was just having a little fun with you. I am concentrating on the case."

"Prove it," I said. "What should we do next?"

"All right. Next we should stop by the English Department and interview the chairman."

"Why?"

"So he can tell us all about Austin and May and several other fun people we don't know about yet."

"And how do we find out if May is a liar?"

"Well," Ryan said, gazing up at the roof liner two inches above his head and theatrically rubbing his chin, "when we get back to headquarters, you start to head off to the ladies' room, then you pause, turn back to me, and say, 'Ryan, you mind getting the chief to sign off on pulling Austin's phone records?' and I say 'Absolutely, Karen, great idea.'"

"Did your big sisters beat the crap out of you a lot?"

"Quite frequently." Ryan frowned. "Never did figure out why." Then he showed me his big grin.

"But that idea I'm gonna have: checking his phones to see if he's been in touch with May? You gotta admit that's a great idea, no?"

He wrinkled his nose like May did. "Good, not great. Kind of obvious, actually. I was being generous, what with you having so little in your life."

"Which way is the English Department?"

"In the Humanities Building," he said. "On University Drive."

The Humanities Building is a three-story brick-and-glass rectangle from the Sixties. The English Department was up on the third floor. I didn't recognize the place, although all the departments that aren't built around labs or art galleries or something special blend together in the few remaining fragments of my mind. The faculty offices ring the perimeter, with classrooms and meeting rooms in the windowless core of the building. We walked into the main department offices, where we were greeted by a chirpy forty-something woman wearing jeans and a sweatshirt with the CMSU logo on it.

Since Ryan looked up the English chair's name when we were driving over, I let him introduce us and ask if he was in. The secretary scurried off to knock on the guy's door and announce us. I heard the phrase "two police officers."

A man in tan chinos and a navy sport jacket came out of the inner office briskly, wearing a concerned expression. "I'm Jonathan Van Vleet." He waved us in. He was a distinguished looking guy, about forty-five, with a long, slender face. His hair was mostly white, thinning on top, about halfway through the transition to bald. He was working on a goatee, also white, in preparation. He wore stylish eyeglasses, tortoise-shell plastic frames, round, arty-looking.

"I'm Detective Karen Seagate, my partner Detective Ryan Miner."

"Pleased to meet you," he said, but he didn't look at all pleased. He pointed to the two chairs set up in front of his wide wooden desk. He had two monitors on his desk, one showing a letter, another a spreadsheet. When we were settled in, he said, "I'm afraid to ask."

I nodded. "I'm sorry to tell you this, Dr. Van Vleet, but we've got some bad news about one of your students."

His shoulders seemed to relax a little bit, as if he was relieved it wasn't his family. "Go ahead."

"This information hasn't been made public yet, but we wanted to tell you and ask for your help. One of your grad students, Austin Sulenka, was found dead this morning."

He was silent for a while. His eyes closed slowly and his cheeks seemed to droop. "What happened?"

"We're not exactly sure, sir. The autopsy hasn't been conducted yet. We don't know if it was some kind of accident or murder."

"Is that all you're permitted to tell me?"

"He apparently died of asphyxia, but we're not sure how it happened."

He nodded his head. "What would you like to know?"

"Could you start with the basics? He was a graduate student, right?"

"Give me a second while I pull up his records." He hit a few keys, waited a bit, hit a few more. "Okay. Austin was a graduate student, in his fourth semester with us. He was a teaching assistant."

"Translate that for us, would you? What kind of degree was he getting? How close to finishing was he?"

Van Vleet looked at the screen a moment. "He was getting a Master of Arts in literature. A teaching assistant teaches two sections of first-year writing each semester and takes three graduate seminars. In exchange, he gets free tuition and fees and a little over ten thousand dollars a year."

"So he would have graduated this month?"

He put up his palms in a slow-down gesture. "It's a little more complicated than that. He would have completed his courses, but to graduate he would have to successfully defend his thesis."

"I've heard that phrase. Not sure what it means."

"Each MA candidate proposes a thesis—which is a research project of about a hundred pages—to a committee of three graduate faculty members. When it's complete, they read it, then the four of them sit down for the defense. That's a meeting where they ask the student questions about the thesis. If the committee votes yes, the student is awarded the degree. If the committee votes no—well, actually, they rarely vote no. Most of the time, they vote 'not yet.' They send the student back to revise it and schedule another defense, maybe the next semester."

"Do your records tell you whether he had done the defense yet?"

"No, I don't have that information."

"Who's the committee?"

"You'll want to speak to his adviser, Suzannah Montgomery. The adviser is the chair of the committee."

I glanced at Ryan to be sure he was taking notes.

"What do your students do after they get an MA in literature? Do you know what Austin's plans were?"

"No, I don't know. Some of them, less than ten percent, go on to get a PhD at another university. We don't have one here. They want to be professors, and that's the admission ticket. Almost half stay on here as adjunct faculty or go someplace else to do that—"

"What's that mean?"

"An adjunct faculty member works semester-to-semester, course-by-course. At most universities, including here, they teach first-year writing, maybe an intro to lit. But the pay is insulting—twenty-four hundred per section, no benefits. And no security. If the section doesn't make, they don't get paid."

"So they're second-class citizens."

"I'd call them fourth-class citizens because they're so much lower than the regular faculty, but since there aren't any other groups in between, officially I guess they're second-class." He shifted in his chair, like he'd just said something witty. Apparently, he'd gotten over the dead grad student. "The idea was they were meant to fill in the holes when we didn't have tenure-track faculty to teach a particular course, or when a regular faculty member was sick or on leave or sabbatical. But since adjuncts are so cheap, their role has expanded exponentially, especially in the last decade.

They now teach ninety-five percent of the first-year writing and most of the intro courses. Yes, we have a two-track system. The adjuncts do the bulk of the teaching; the regular faculty do some teaching but almost all the research."

"But you don't know what Austin was planning to do?"

"You'll have to ask Suzannah."

"Do you have access to any performance evaluations? I assume you have his grades?" I pointed to his computer screens.

He nodded, moused around for a moment, then turned back to me. "On the basis of his grades, Austin Sulenka was a mediocre student. His GPA was 3.14, with a couple of C's that he repeated, a lot of B's, and a couple of A's."

"That's mediocre?" I would have thrown myself a party if I'd ever gotten those grades when I was in college. I saw Ryan turn toward me and give me a look.

Van Vleet nodded. "An excellent grad student is 3.8 or better. A very good one is 3.5, 3.7. You're supposed to be disappointed if you didn't earn an A in a grad course."

"Aside from grades, what can you tell us about what kind of student he was?

"*De mortuis nil nisi bonum,*" he said.

I just looked at him.

Ryan spoke. "No one should speak ill of the dead."

I looked at Van Vleet. "Is that what you just said?"

"Darn tootin'," he said, granting Ryan a small smile for having passed the audition.

I wasn't smiling. "The way I'd look at it, Professor, you want us to catch whoever did this, right?"

"Of course, Detective." He sat up straighter in his chair. The pussy. "I just want to be sure I'm speaking in confidence. I really don't want anything bad about Austin to end up in the media."

"You have my word on that, Professor. What do we need to know?"

"What you need to know is that Austin was … an asshole."

"'Asshole' is such a broad term. Can you give us an example?"

"Okay, how about sleeping with one of his students?"

"That violates policy?"

"The policy is a lot less clear than I would like. On the one hand, Austin is officially a student. Students sleep with other students all the time, of course. But he's also the instructor of record for the two courses he teaches. If he were a faculty member sleeping with one of his students, he would face dismissal. All TA's are given paperwork that explains the university's policy: that it's inappropriate. But there are no officially stated penalties. He received a reprimand and was told that if it happens again he's out."

"How far did the student take the complaint? Did she go beyond the department here?"

"She took it to the dean of students. They have their own disciplinary procedure."

"Is that Mary Dawson?" Ryan asked. He remembered her name from a case a few months ago. I remembered a face, sort of.

"That's right," Jonathan Van Vleet said. "She can fill you in on that."

"Is that the kind of thing makes you call him an asshole?"

"That's just the most obvious example. I mean, if you're a teacher and you don't see two or three good reasons you shouldn't be screwing an eighteen-year old in your class, you're either too stupid to work in a university or you're an asshole."

"Give me another example."

He nodded. "He was in one of my seminars. An undistinguished student—no doubt about that. Didn't prepare for the classes, wrote lazy papers, *et cetera*. What he was really there for was the girls."

"The other grad students?"

"They couldn't take their eyes off him. He'd sit there, a bemused look on his face when anyone actually talked about literature. I'm not a prude. I don't have any problem with the grad students hooking up. Hell, my wife and I met in grad school. But when you're in class, when you're studying—we'd like you to take it seriously. Or at least pretend to. It makes us feel we have a purpose in life, you know? Ten o'clock at night, go meet up with the other students at a bar downtown, do whatever you want … but my faculty take their jobs seriously, and I do, too. It's insulting to all of us when we get a student who thinks this is a Club Med for people who like books."

I nodded. "Okay, he was an asshole. Can you help us with anyone who'd want to hurt him?"

Van Vleet shook his head. "I just don't know him well enough. He might've been an asshole in other ways. And since I imagine he cycled through the grad students, he could've pissed off one or two of them—or maybe their boyfriends. But I really don't know."

"All right, Professor. Sorry we had to bring you this news. But we appreciate you giving us all this information. You've been very helpful." I handed him my card. "You call me if you think of anything else that could help us with what happened?"

Ryan and I made it back to the Charger. "Austin Sulenka seems to have been an asshole," I said, turning over the big engine.

"Yeah, I got that." Ryan winced as he twisted to fasten his seat belt.

"So is Van Vleet," I said.

"What? Just because he drops a Latin phrase about how you shouldn't speak ill of the dead, then calls his dead grad student an asshole?"

Chapter 5

We crawled along the congested roads on campus. I honked at a kid, his face in his phone, wandering in front of the Charger. It would take us as long to cover a half mile on campus as five miles on city streets.

"That appears to be the consensus," Ryan said. "Austin was an asshole. If two interviews are enough to form a consensus."

"You're not buying it?"

Ryan paused a moment. "Not quite yet," he said. "Take May Eberlein. She said Austin wasn't what he appeared to be. But why should we believe he misrepresented himself? Maybe he was straight with her that he wasn't into monogamy. She'd broken a lot of normal guys, so she saw it as a challenge to domesticate him. Then, she would drop him. Game over. But she failed. Rather than admit that to us—"

"Or to herself."

"That's right, rather than admit that to us or to herself, she feeds us this story about how the whole experience was so educational. To her, admitting to being naïve is less humiliating than admitting that she wasn't sufficiently bewitching to break him."

"Okay," I said. "Possible. How about sleeping with one of his students? Let's hear you spin that one."

"Well, that one's a little more challenging—"

"No shit, as in, whatever the girl's motives were, whatever her actions were, unless she somehow managed to yank his dick out of his pants against his will …"

"Agreed." He nodded. "No matter what she said or did, it was his responsibility, as the adult, not to pursue her. Even if she stopped by his office, closed the door behind her, and took off her clothes, it's officially his fault. And if he instigated it by exploiting the power differential, then he's really at fault." Ryan shifted in his seat. I could see his injury was still bothering him.

"So we agree he was an asshole."

"If it's true he had an affair with a freshman in his class, then yes."

"All right," I said. "Good. When we get back, let's get his phone records and see if he was drilling any of his freshmen."

"And catch up with his adviser." Ryan pulled his notebook from his inside jacket pocket and opened it up. "Suzannah Montgomery."

"Yeah, let's see if he was drilling all the women in Rawlings."

I pulled into a spot behind headquarters, and we made our way to the detectives' bullpen.

"Ryan, you ask for permission to get his phones, will you, and I'll see what I can get from the dean of students about him screwing his student."

He nodded, hooked his cane over the back of his chair, and headed off toward the chief's office.

I went to the university site and got the number for Mary Dawson, the dean of students. She had helped us a few months ago on a case involving the murder of an exchange student. I decided not to tell her Austin Sulenka was dead. She wasn't close enough to the victim or high enough in the university to merit an early heads-up. I punched in her number.

"This is Mary," the cheerful voice on the phone said. I remembered from our last case that she was the approachable dean.

"Dean Dawson? This is Karen Seagate, Rawlings Police Department," I said. "Don't know if you remember me, from the Maricel Salizar case, earlier this year?"

"Oh, yes, Detective, I do remember you," she said. It started out friendly, then she must have figured out I probably wasn't calling to catch up on old times. "I hope you're not calling with another case."

"Unfortunately, I am calling in relation to a case, but I can't really tell you about it at this point."

She sighed into the phone. It wasn't that she wanted to dish about students. It was that she really took it hard when one of them got in trouble. She was genuinely busted up about that other case we worked on. I could tell it, from her face when we talked. "How can I help?"

"Here's what I need," I said. "We were just talking with Jonathan Van Vleet in English. He said you could fill us in on a situation earlier this year about an inappropriate relationship between an English teaching assistant and a freshman woman."

"Ugh," she said.

"Ugh?"

"Yes, that was a nasty episode. What do you need to know?"

"Well, I need the name of the woman, and how it turned out."

"Hang on a sec," Mary Dawson said. "Let me get that file." She was back in twenty seconds. "The TA was Austin Sulenka, the student was Tiffany Rhodes. She was in his English 101."

"And she claimed he had an inappropriate relationship with her?"

"That's right. She claimed it, and he admitted it."

"How'd it turn out?"

"The committee voted to reprimand Mr. Sulenka and put an official letter in his file."

"Any penalty for the girl?" I looked up when I heard Ryan coming back from the chief's office. I hit Speaker on my phone.

"The way these things work, there's almost never a penalty for the student."

"Yeah, that makes sense," I said.

"But in this case, it took all we had not to discipline her."

"Why's that?"

"The TA argued—and we believed him—that she was fully complicit in the relationship, that she admitted she initiated it to improve her grade, and that the only reason she came forward is that she got a lower grade than she thought she deserved in the course."

"She actually said that?"

"You'd be surprised at some of the things students say. They have no idea how they sound. Her attitude was that she was working really hard on the course—"

"By sleeping with the teacher?"

"And therefore, when he didn't live up to his end of the bargain—which involved the B she thought she deserved … well, you get the idea."

"Do you have contact information on this sweet young thing?"

"Yes," she said. She read me Tiffany Rhodes' address, spelling out all the names. I looked over at Ryan, who was writing it down. "And there's one other thing you might want to follow up on."

"What's that?" I said.

"Tiffany had a boyfriend, don't know whether he's still in the picture. His name is Brian Hawser." She spelled it out. "You need to look him up in your own system."

"What'd Brian do?"

"Brian vandalized some of Mr. Sulenka's property, and I think he threatened him. The judge issued a restraining order on him. He was to stay at least one-hundred feet away from Mr. Sulenka."

"Very interesting," I said. "Any more chapters in this story?"

"I'm hoping not." Mary Dawson sounded weary. "I've told you everything I know from the university's perspective. Just between the two of us, nothing would make me happier than to learn that Mr. Sulenka has decided that grad school just isn't for him and that Ms. Rhodes and Mr. Hawser have transferred to another university."

"Well, Dean Dawson, I'm afraid that's not what you're going to learn. But I appreciate you giving me that information."

"Goodbye, Detective."

I hung up and looked over at Ryan. "Can you punch in Brian Hawser and get an address?"

He hit some keys, looked at the screen, and then looked at his notebook. "He and Tiffany are roommates."

"She's living with this guy and sleeping with her professor?"

"Don't look at me," Ryan said cheerfully. "That wasn't how I did extra-credit assignments. Besides," he said, "we don't know she and Brian were living together at the time."

"You're saying she starts doing her professor, Brian Hawser rides up on his white horse, defends her honor by keying Austin's car or whatever, they fall in love, sign a lease, live happily ever after?"

Ryan smiled. "No, I bet she was doing both the guys at once. I'm just saying we don't know the facts yet."

I shook my head. "You're not as much fun as you used to be."

"I got shot, you know." He smiled.

"Heard you got a commendation for that."

"I did. It was totally worth it."

"That's what I assumed."

Ryan looked down at this notebook. "Okay, now we have Austin's girlfriend, May Eberlein, who we've already interviewed; plus his adviser, Suzannah Montgomery; his student, Tiffany Rhodes; and her boyfriend, Brian Hawser. Anyone else?"

"Not at the moment," I said. "Let me call Robin and see how she's coming with the forensics." I speed-dialed her cell.

She picked up. "Yeah, Karen."

"Robin, just wanted to see what you've got."

"I'm still at Austin's. I did a quick survey of the apartment. I've pulled a few dozen prints. There're some good ones on the wine glasses and the bottles. The sheet on his bed has some ejaculate, as well as quite a bit of what looks like vaginal fluid. There's vaginal fluid on his dick, and some more on the dildo. But I'm not seeing what he was strangled with."

"When'll you be able to start typing that stuff?"

"I'm gonna need a couple more hours here. I'll be back after lunch. You want to authorize DNA on the biologicals?"

"Yeah," I said. "We gotta know who was nailing who. Plus, run the prints. Maybe we'll get lucky."

"Okay," Robin said.

"Talk to you later. Thanks."

"No, no," she said. "Thank you. It's been a long time since I've seen this much sticky stuff at one address."

I ended the call. "Did the chief okay getting Austin's phones?"

"We should have them later today," Ryan said.

"Okay, good. Why don't we see what we've got on Tiffany and Brian?"

Ryan tapped away at the computer for a few moments. "Tiffany Rhodes has a couple of traffic misdemeanors and a DUI."

"What'd she get on the DUI?"

"Her BAC was only .09, so she was able to plead down to a wet reckless. One day in jail, points, five-hundred bucks."

"Did we take her DNA?"

"No," Ryan said. "Just prints."

"Any other charges on her?"

"No."

"Brian?"

"Brian has the usual misdemeanors plus the restraining order on Austin. It was December 19." Ryan was reading off the screen. "He drove over to Austin's place, took a baseball bat to all the glass on his car. Austin wasn't home at the time, but the neighbor—hey, it's your waitress friend in Unit 4—she heard it and called it in. Couple of uniforms pulled him over, gave him a BAC. It came back .17. He admitted to the vandalism."

"What'd he get?"

"It was his first felony. Two weeks. Points. A thousand dollars. Plus," Ryan said, looking up at me, smiling, "we took his prints and DNA."

"Very good," I said. "Can you make a note to get that to Robin?"

Ryan nodded. "Done."

"That RO, was it civil or criminal?"

Ryan looked back at the screen. "It was criminal. Austin was okay with a civil Order of Protection, but the DA insisted on a criminal RO because of the DUI. Brian pled to criminal mischief, with fourteen-hundred dollars in restitution to Austin."

"Did the criminal mischief carry any additional time?"

"One week extra. Brian said he's already paid tuition for this semester, and the judge kept the sentence light in exchange for the plea."

"Is the RO still in effect?" I said.

Ryan looked at the screen again. "It's indefinite. So if we find Brian's prints over at Austin's apartment, we'll be able to push him pretty hard on it."

"Let's stop by the chief's office and tell him we're gonna look at Brian and Tiffany, then we go stop by their place, okay?"

He looked puzzled. "Think he'd have a problem with that?"

"It'll just take a minute," I said. I knew we didn't need to inform the chief about every interview or lead. The real reason I was checking everything with him was that he gave me my job back a year ago. I wasn't officially on probation, but I wanted to show him I could do the job. Really, show myself I could still be a good cop.

We walked over to the chief's office. "Quick question for the chief," I said to Margaret. "Thirty seconds?"

She picked up the phone, pushed a button, and relayed the message. The chief stepped out of his office and raised his eyebrows.

"The grad student case?" I said.

The chief nodded.

"The vic was screwing one of his students. She complained officially. Her boyfriend got liquored up and vandalized the vic's car. The judge issued an RO and gave him some jail time. We want to interview the girl and the boyfriend. You okay with that?"

"We have the boyfriend's DNA, then?"

"Yeah."

"Well, that's what I would do," the chief said. He nodded and waved his hand, meaning go ahead.

Which I took to mean, Thanks for checking with me, but relax. Run the case. I'll tell you if I've got a problem.

Chapter 6

It was about five hours since we discovered Austin Sulenka's body. I've always liked to finish as many of the initial interviews as I can within eight hours, or at least before the local TV newsboys and girls start looking all pouty about the murder. My thinking is that by five-thirty or six, word's gotten out, and it's a lot tougher to tell who already knew about it because they saw it on TV—or because they did it.

But maybe I'm just fooling myself about getting better info before the murder goes public. After all, the more I think about May Eberlein rushing off to class, I really have no idea whether all her boo-hooing about Austin was real. I'm not all that bright, but I think I'm a pretty good liar. And if I killed someone, I'd be sure to have my response all worked out—right down to the props, such as the mascara brush in my hand—for when the cops stopped by to chat.

"You want to talk about a strategy for questioning them?" Ryan said. We were driving out toward the solidly lower-middle-class neighborhood near campus where Brian Hawser and Tiffany Rhodes lived.

"How do you mean?"

"Well, if only one of them is there? Both of them?"

I thought about it for a second. "I think I'd just play it by ear. Let's tell them it's about a legal formality. Something about Brian's RO."

"We just want to know if he's still in compliance. That sort of thing?"

"Yeah, that'll be fine."

We parked at 2400 Christopher Place, a two-story apartment complex, maybe five or eight years old. Each unit on the ground floor had an ugly cement pad patio. On the second floor, each had a tiny balcony, mostly crammed with oversized barbeques and bikes chained to the chipped painted-aluminum railing. The unpainted wooden stockade fence that bordered the property had grey crescents where the sprinklers had weathered it. The lawn was spotty and full of weeds.

"What's the number?" I said.

"204."

As we climbed the concrete and steel steps, I glanced over at Ryan, who was carrying his cane but not putting any weight on it. That was good.

We made our way down the exterior hallway on a dirty indoor-outdoor carpet with a checkerboard pattern. I knocked on the door and hung my shield around my neck. The door opened.

"Brian Hawser?" I said. He nodded. "Detective Karen Seagate and Detective Ryan Miner, Rawlings Police Department. You got a minute to talk with us?"

He scratched at his cheek. I'd put the beard at three or four days. Medium brown, like his hair. The hair was cut short on the sides, just long enough to comb on the top. He had a ski-slope nose, the curse of the formerly cute little boy. His brown eyes looked alert, wary more than intelligent. He wasn't hiding his scowl.

He ignored my question about whether he had a minute to speak with us, but he moved back a little to let us in. He was a big guy: six-two, two-thirty. I'd say high-school lineman, not quite beefy enough for the college team. His washed-out grey tee shirt said Property of Central Montana State University, which meant it wasn't. He had on old gym shorts, no shoes or socks.

"What's this about?" he said.

"Just following up on the restraining order," I said. "It's four months now. We want to talk with you, see if everything's going okay."

He looked at me, expressionless. "Yeah, everything's going okay. I don't go near that prick." He paused. "Anything else?" Like he was running the interview.

"We have to write up a report, Brian. We're gonna need to talk with you a little bit more about it. You think we could sit down?"

He paused, then stepped back. Ryan and I walked into the living room. It had a fake-leather brown couch, the kind where the back cushion in the middle folded down and you put your drinks in round cup holders. He had been playing a computer game on his TV. He walked over to the couch, turned off the game, picked up the can of Coke from the cushion, and flipped it back into place. I took that to mean we were to sit there. Brian walked over to a red cloth upholstered chair next to the TV set and sat down. He sat there, still, his big forearms on the arms of the chair.

"Since my partner and I weren't involved in the case that led to the restraining order, we just wanna make sure we understand what happened."

He didn't say anything, just sat there. Having had some experience with cops and judges, he knew we were going to do what we were going to do, so there was no sense trying to stop us. On the other hand, there was no need to help us or pretend we were friends.

"You were charged with malicious mischief for vandalizing Austin Sulenka's car, is that right?"

He nodded, just a little.

"And you got a DUI that night, too?" I had a notebook in my lap. I looked up at him. This time he didn't bother to nod. "Our records say you're keeping up with the restitution payments to him."

"That's right," he said.

"When we write up our report, we get to recommend to the court whether the restraining order stays in place. You know, whether we think there's still a danger that you might come after Mr. Sulenka …" I let it hang there.

"Not gonna go after him." The words were clear, but he wasn't giving me and Ryan any reason to believe them.

I nodded and made some doodle marks in my notebook. "What the judge likes to see is that you understand how you got into trouble." I looked at Brian Hawser.

"Busting up the asshole's car," he said.

Ryan said, "I think what my partner means is that we want to be able to write that you understand that what you did was wrong and that you're not going to do it again."

Brian Hawser looked at Ryan. "So I'm not supposed to think he's an asshole."

"We understand you've got some resentment against Mr. Sulenka," I said, "but from a legal point of view, it was all you. You're the one took the baseball bat to his car."

"I didn't take him apart." Brian Hawser shifted in his seat. "Which he deserved."

He was working it over in his mind, getting himself more pissed off. Which we like to see. It helps us understand how hard to look at him for killing Austin.

I said, "Brian, I think we need to keep the situation with Tiffany separate from the situation with the vandalism of Mr. Sulenka's car. I mean, for the purpose of this interview with you."

He looked at me, a mean look on his face. "The way he treated Tiffany? You expect me to say he wasn't an asshole?"

"Why don't we talk about Tiffany for a little bit, get that out of the way. Then we can get back to the restraining order so we get a statement we can put in our report." I paused. "By the way, Tiffany's not here, right?"

"That's right. She's on her way back from Billings. Visiting her parents."

"Okay," I said. "I understand why you think the guy's an asshole. Tell us what happened."

"I'm not gonna tell you." He shook his head. "Except to say that he took advantage of her. Slept with her, then gave her the C anyway." He held his jaw high, like that was all I needed to know to conclude Austin was an asshole.

"Gave her a C anyway?"

"Fuckin' right. Tiffany's not one of those rich girls gets everything handed to her. She's had to work for everything she's ever gotten. She's taking fifteen credits, working twenty-nine hours a week as a collection agent for a bank—the twenty-nine is so she's officially part-time and doesn't get benefits. We don't have enough money as it is to get by without loans. She knew she wasn't gonna do better than a C in the class. She told me how he was sniffing around all the girls. All the ones who weren't real pigs, I mean. Tiffany could tell it. She made a decision."

"She told you she was gonna do it?"

Brian shook his head. "She didn't want me to know."

"How'd you find out?" I said.

"I saw her e-mails, thought she was e-mailing this guy more than necessary. Then I read some of them. I went to her. She explained why she did it."

"How'd you feel about what she did?"

His brows furrowed, like he was thinking of an answer. "I wouldn't've did it that way."

"What do you mean?"

"She didn't need to screw him. She should've gone to the teacher, threaten to go to the English Department, tell them he was coming on to her." He nodded his head, warming to his plan. "She would've gotten the B without having to do him."

"Hmm," I said. I nodded sympathetically, like that would have been a better plan. "So, how did it get to the disciplinary committee?"

"Asshole gave her a C. Tiffany admitted what she did, and she was willing to take the consequences. She said, it's not like she was the first girl to use sex to get a better grade."

Not knowing quite how to respond, I gave him another "Hmm." He seemed to be interpreting it the way I wanted. "What's your relationship with Tiffany now?"

"It's fine. She made a mistake. Everyone makes mistakes."

"What's your future? I mean, you and Tiffany."

"Not sure. Me and Tiff hooked up back in Billings, couple years ago. I can see us together for a long while."

"Brian, there's something else we have to tell you."

His expression looked cloudy. "Yeah?"

"Austin Sulenka is dead."

Now his expression got mean. "He's fuckin' dead?" The tiny gears in his head turned a little bit. "So all this stuff about writing a report to the judge—all that was bullshit?"

"Basically, yeah." I nodded my head, my sad expression saying I was sorry to have done it.

"You don't have any right to do that." He was leaning toward me, half getting out of his chair. His fists were clenching and unclenching.

Ryan noticed it and stood up, slower than he used to but still fast enough. "You want to take it easy, Brian," Ryan said, leaning on his cane as he stepped toward him. "In fact, we have every right to do exactly that. What *you* want to do at this point, Brian, is keep your cool. Answer the questions honestly. Help us see you as not involved with killing Sulenka. You think you can do that?"

Brian looked at Ryan, then looked at me. He sank back into his chair, but now we really weren't friends.

I said, "Can you tell us where you were last night between eleven PM and, say, one?"

He waited a couple of beats. "I was right here. I ordered a pizza, played some games, watched some Netflix, went to bed around midnight."

"Can anyone vouch for that?"

"Like I fuckin' told you, Tiffany was home in Billings."

"So that's a no?"

He shook his head. Now Ryan and I were assholes, just like Austin. "That's a no."

"Austin Sulenka's apartment is crawling with fingerprints," I said. "Are we gonna find your prints there?"

He shook his head no. "I know what a restraining order means. If I was gonna kill him, I'd've did it that first time."

I nodded. "All right, Brian, is there anything else?" I stood up. Ryan did, too.

"One thing," he said. "Him being dead, that mean I don't have to keep paying him back for the car?"

Chapter 7

Brian Hawser slammed the door pretty hard. Ryan and I walked down the hall, down the stairs, over to the cruiser. We got in.

"So, Ryan, explain this to me. What Austin did wrong is, he gave her a C even though she screwed him?"

He shrugged his shoulders. "Guess it's a breach of contract."

"I don't know," I said. "Maybe she was a lousy lay, and that nullified the contract."

"Now you're way beyond my area of expertise," Ryan said.

"You believe him: we're not gonna find his prints at Austin's place?"

"Yes, I do. But that doesn't mean he didn't do it. It might just mean he knows how to put on a pair of gloves."

"The way he acted when I told him we really stopped by to talk about the murder, I could see him getting in Austin's face, trashing the place."

"Me, too," Ryan said. "The question is, Is he caveman enough to kill Austin for what he did to Tiff?"

"Brian's a rough boy. Fully capable of carrying a grudge against the guy who was fucking his girlfriend—"

"Don't forget, he's also paying Austin for having trashed his car," Ryan said.

"Yeah, that might be pissing him off more."

We were sitting in the Charger, trying to figure out the next move after interviewing Brian. A fat grey cloud passed in front of the early afternoon sun, throwing a shadow across our car. It reminded me we could still have some cold days before our short summer. "And Brian's fully capable of beating the crap out of him. Or strangling him. Agree?"

"Agree," Ryan said. "But with Tiffany in Billings, I'm having trouble seeing how Brian gets into Austin's apartment. And even more trouble figuring out how Austin gets nude and gets strangled."

We were both silent a minute. "There was no forced entry into Austin's apartment. No way Austin's sitting in his shitty apartment, Brian knocks on the door, Austin lets him in. So the only scenario that makes sense is either there's other people in the apartment—and someone lets him in—"

Ryan was shaking his head. "That means whoever Austin was screwing—or about to screw—just leaves, and Brian strangles him and trashes the place."

"It isn't working. With Tiffany in Billings, Brian isn't killing Austin."

"So we cross Brian off?" Ryan said.

"No," I said. "We figure out if Tiffany was in Billings."

"We phone her parents' house?"

"That could work," I said. "But what if the mother's as creepy as Tiffany? No guarantee she'd be straight with us."

"Okay. Your turn."

"It's Monday afternoon. If you were still in college, where would you be?"

"I'd be in class."

"That's right. You were a good boy."

"Let me get her schedule," Ryan said.

"She's here in town," I said. "I know it."

Ryan took out his cell and phoned Mary Dawson at the university. She wasn't in, but he asked the secretary for help. Ryan explained that we needed Tiffany's class schedule for today and tomorrow. "Okay," he said as he finished writing down what the secretary said, "thanks a lot for the help."

It was starting to come into focus for me. "If Tiffany was home in Billings, Brian didn't kill Austin," I said. "But if Tiffany was here in Rawlings, couple of ways they could've done it. Tiffany gets into Austin's place, leaves the front door unlocked, starts screwing Austin. Puts a cloth around his neck, Austin's big dick starts throbbing good. All of a sudden, Brian appears and strangles him. Then Brian and Tiffany trash the place—"

"Because they're both pissed at him."

"Exactly," I said. "Or—you're gonna like this one. Tiffany tells Brian she's going home for the weekend, see you Monday. Brian's eating pizza, playing computer games, scratching his balls. Meanwhile, Tiffany's scratching Austin's balls. Fucking him up one side, down the other. She knows he likes strangulation games. She plays along. Then she tightens the knot. Then trashes the living room just because she can."

"Because he gave her a C in English?"

"Because he fucked her in exchange for the B, *then* gave her a C. Or she fell in love with him, or she caught him nailing some other shitty student. I can think of a dozen reasons she'd want to kill him. Keep in mind, she's eighteen, and she's fucking Brian Hawser. How smart can she be?"

Ryan nodded, then looked down at his notebook. "Tiffany is supposed to be in Anthropology 215," he said, looking at his watch, "right about now."

"Let's take a drive."

It took ten minutes to roll over to campus. I was tired. It had been a long day, and I hadn't sucked in as much caffeine as I normally do, but I was excited. I love thinking through the what-if's. And this was my kind of case—I don't know anything about literature, but I do know quite a bit about stupid behavior involving penises.

I parked the Charger in a metered spot outside the Social Sciences Building. I put down my visor to show the Official Police Business card.

"Room 320," Ryan said. Normally, Ryan would take the stairs in any building in Rawlings. But since he got back from rehab, he was willing to take the elevator if it was three floors or more. We walked down the hall to 320. Ryan looked through the thin rectangular window in the door.

When I caught up with him, he said, "Twenty-five or thirty students in the class."

"You know what she looks like?"

"Not yet," he said.

"You know how to get her picture?"

He smiled. "I know how to get anyone's picture." He walked over to a small student desk in the hall and pulled his tablet from his briefcase. It took him fifteen seconds to get on Facebook. He held up the tablet for me to see the picture. Tiffany was a round-faced girl, plain, still packing a little baby fat. She had dark hair, straight, parted down the middle, and thick black plastic-framed eyeglasses.

Ryan stood up, walked over to the door, and looked in. "She's in the second row, off to the side. I say we get her now."

"Before she gets a chance to talk to Brian?"

He nodded. "I got it," he said, and walked into the classroom. I watched him go over to the instructor, a forty-something woman in blue jeans and a bone-colored cable-knit sweater that came about halfway down her thighs. The professor pointed to Tiffany, who got out of her chair and walked up to the front. She looked a little confused but not scared. Ryan led her out of the classroom.

"Tiffany, I'm Detective Ryan Miner, Rawlings Police Department. This is my partner, Detective Karen Seagate. We need to talk with you a couple minutes about a case we're working on."

I'd grabbed Ryan's briefcase. I gestured to a small round table in the hall about thirty feet away from the classroom. "Let's go sit over there, Tiffany," I said. "We'll only be a few minutes, then you can get back to your class."

She nodded. I watched her follow Ryan toward the table. She was wearing flip-flops, jeans with rhinestone designs on the back pockets. She was about five-seven, with a soft, rounded body twenty pounds over her ideal fighting weight.

"You got your phone with you?" I said to her after we got settled at the table. She opened her backpack, pulled it out, and waved it at me. She had on a V-necked tee shirt with a pretty deep V. "Is it on?"

She shook her head. "The professor's real anal about that. We can't just put it on vibrate. Have to turn it off. 'I want your undivided attention for fifty minutes,' it says on the syllabus. What might help is saying something interesting every once in a while." Tiffany shook her head to show her disdain.

"Okay, Tiffany." I didn't feel any pressure to say something interesting. "Your name's come up in an investigation. We just need you to answer a few questions, then, like I say, we'll let you get back to your life, okay?"

She shrugged.

"Can you tell us where you were last night, late, after nine?"

She didn't answer right away. "Last night?" Her eyes fluttered upward. She was thinking. "I was at home."

"Here in Rawlings?"

"No, my parents' home. In Billings."

"When did you drive back?"

"This morning. I wanted to make this class."

She didn't look like she was that into anthropology. "This an important class?"

"No, it sucks, but the professor's strict about attendance. Miss four classes, you lose points. I've missed my three."

I nodded and smiled at her. "I remember those days."

Tiffany looked impatient. "What's this about, anyway?"

I nodded and put on my serious expression. "The case we're working on involves Austin Sulenka."

Tiffany Rhodes shifted in her chair. "He find another student to screw?"

"No," I said. "He's done screwing. He died earlier today."

She pulled back, stunned. "Shit," she said. "What happened to him?"

"We're not sure, but we think he was murdered."

"Shit. I can't believe what I'm hearing."

"Why is that, Tiffany? You got into a pretty nasty situation with him. Like you just said, there could've been another girl."

Her expression turned defensive. "I got into it with him because what he did to me was wrong. But I never thought of hurting him. I mean, physically."

"Sometimes there are boyfriends."

She shook her head. "If you're talking about Brian, I know what he did was wrong, and he's paying off the damage to Austin's car. But he never laid a hand on him, and he never would."

"What was your relationship with Austin Sulenka? I mean, since the disciplinary hearing and the restraining order on Brian."

"After that?" she said. "No relationship. I'm taking the next English course right now—it's a requirement. But I don't hang out in the English Department. I haven't even spoken to him. Saw him a couple times on campus, you know, in the distance. One time, coming out of the library. But he didn't see me, I didn't acknowledge him. Like I said, no relationship."

"You have any ideas about who might want to hurt him?"

"I'd be surprised if there wasn't all kinds of people who'd want to hurt him. But I don't know any. And I know *I* didn't hurt him."

A young guy walked by, staring at the three of us. I couldn't tell whether it was that Ryan and I looked out of place or that Tiffany was displaying some serious cleavage.

"All right, Tiffany," I said as my partner and I stood up. "This is my card. You get in touch with us if you think of anything can help us understand who might've done this."

She looked at me as she took the card. I thought I saw her eyes a little shiny. "Listen, I know me and Austin got into this big thing with the disciplinary bullshit and all. I thought what he did to me was wrong, and I wanted the university to make it right—which they didn't." She held up her palms, the gesture saying justice doesn't always win. "But I never had anything against him personally. And I never would've hurt him. I mean that."

I nodded. "You can go back to your class, Tiffany."

She slung her backpack over her shoulder and started walking back toward the classroom. She put her hand on the doorknob but stood there, motionless, a long while, her head down, her back to us. Finally, she opened the classroom door and walked in.

Ryan and I sat back down.

"She's lying," I said.

"About what?"

"Not quite sure about all the details, but she's lying about her relationship with Austin."

"How do you know?" Ryan said.

"She called him 'Austin.' Not 'Sulenka,' not 'the teacher,' not 'the professor.' Not 'that asshole.' He was 'Austin.'"

"I hadn't caught that," Ryan said. "But now that you point it out …" He paused. "There's a bunch of ways to check her story. Let me start by finding out if she was in Billings this morning."

He pulled out his notebook and jotted a few words. "I'll get her Billings phone and call Mom and Dad about that."

"We could check out the rest of her Monday classes. See if she just got here for the anthropology course. Do you mind if we head downstairs to that coffee place in the lobby? I'm running on fumes."

"Sure." We stood up and headed down the hall to the stairs. Ryan found a booth near the back of the Coffee Hut. It had half-a-dozen palm fronds hanging on the walls, and two unlit tiki torches up at the entrance, like it was decorated by a couple of eighth-graders with a half hour and a budget of twenty bucks. As Ryan put his stuff down and took out his phone, I peeled off toward the counter.

Couple minutes later, I came back with a large coffee and a bottle of water for Ryan. Him being a Mormon, I know what he drinks: basically nothing. I put the two drinks down and went off to get some cream and sugar. When I got back, he was thanking someone on the phone.

"That was easy," he said as he ended the call. "I couldn't get the teacher from her ten o'clock biology class, but her economics teacher from nine o'clock said Tiffany's participation in this morning's class shows she's making some real progress."

"Is that so?" I stirred the second creamer into my coffee. I'd already put in the three sugars.

"So, with Billings two-and-a-half hours down the road, either Tiffany got up around four this morning—"

"Or she was here last night," I said.

"I don't think we need to phone her parents."

I lie all the time. Always have. But even when I was Tiffany's age, I think I knew it was dumb to lie about shit that was so easy to check. I shook my head and took a sip of the coffee. "No, I don't think we need to do that."

Chapter 8

"Margaret, do you know if we've got the phone logs yet from Austin Sulenka? The grad student?" I waited while the chief's assistant checked. She told me no, they wouldn't be available until tomorrow morning. "Okay, thanks," I said and ended the call.

Ryan looked at his watch. "It's about three. Long as we're on campus, want to try to track down Suzannah Montgomery?"

I nodded. We walked over to the Humanities Building, about a hundred yards across the quad. I pulled my jacket close as the wind picked up. It was still in the fifties, but a lot of the students were trying out their summer looks, with shorts showing off their pasty white legs, and goose bumps up and down their arms.

Back at the English Department on the third floor of the Humanities Building, I walked up to the receptionist. The department chair, Jonathan Van Vleet, must have told her about Austin Sulenka biting it this morning, so she wasn't so chirpy this time when she recognized me and Ryan.

"Yes, Detective, can I help you?"

"Can you give me a room number for Suzannah Montgomery?"

She looked at a sheet of paper taped to the counter. "She's in 325, but she's not there now."

"Know where we can reach her?"

"She's in the conference room: 333." She pointed across the hall. "She's doing a thesis defense. Melissa Harmon."

"How long will that last, do you know?"

She looked at her watch. "It started at 2:30. They'll probably be finishing up in fifteen or twenty minutes."

Ryan said, "Do you know if defenses are public?"

"Yes, I think they are." She brightened up a little. She was the kind of person enjoyed helping people get where they needed to be. "Just go ahead and walk in."

Ryan gave her a big smile. "Thanks very much."

We turned and walked out into the hall. "Is that gonna freak out the student?"

"I don't think so," he said. "My guess is she's already fully amped. If we don't make any sudden movements, she should be okay." He pointed to the detective's shield around my neck. "You might want to put that away."

I took it off and dropped it into my big shoulder bag as we headed toward the conference room. "You been to one of these before?"

"I saw a couple of master's defenses—a brother and a sister," he said. "And I did an undergraduate version of a defense on a senior project at BYU," he said.

"Hey, I did a senior project, too," I said.

"Yeah?"

"It was a math project. I needed to calculate what grades I needed in my last sixteen credits to pull up my GPA to 2.5 so I could graduate."

He smiled. "Good for you."

"I nailed it." I turned the knob on the conference room door. "Ended up with a 2.51."

The room was big, I'd guess forty by forty. Up at the front was a long conference table, with a student and three professors sitting at one end. The rest of the space was taken up with about thirty lightly upholstered arm chairs arranged in rows. There were three other young people, probably other graduate students, scattered across the rows.

"Excuse us," I said as the conversation stopped and all eyes looked up at me and Ryan coming in and sitting next to each other near the back.

The conference room doubled as a storeroom. The perimeter was filled with mismatched file cabinets topped with cardboard boxes full of file folders. There were a few bookcases filled with what looked like old yearbooks and professional magazines. Up near the front, off to the side of the big table, was a battered wooden podium with the seal of Central Montana Junior College, which the school hadn't been in more than a quarter century.

Written on the whiteboard at the front of the room was "Melissa Harmon Thesis Defense 2:30." Melissa was a heavy-boned early twenties girl with a shock of curly red hair tied back and pinned down, a little too much rouge and bruise-purple eyeliner, and a freakish smile frozen on her face. She wore a conservative royal blue pantsuit over her big frame. Stacks of books five high were arranged on the table in front of her, like she'd set them up to withstand the attacks of the three professors. Which made sense, since they call this thing a defense.

I looked at the three professors: one old guy and two women. The guy was wearing a dark suit. He was maybe sixty, white haired with a pencil moustache. He was leaning back in his chair, doodling on a legal pad, looking up occasionally and raising an eyebrow, but mostly focused on his watch. My guess was he was there to sign—or not sign—a piece of paper after the defense.

The younger woman professor was doing most of the talking, so I assumed she was Suzannah Montgomery. She was forty, auburn hair pulled back tight and braided. She wore no makeup, but she smiled brightly and laughed every once in a while when she said something she thought was witty or funny or something.

I didn't get any of her jokes. They were all talking about a book by someone named Chopin.

I leaned over to Ryan. "Are they talking about the composer?"

He shook his head and whispered, "No, it's an American writer. Kate Chopin. No relation."

I nodded, unsure whether my question was smart or stupid. Ryan is very good about never making me feel ashamed about how broadly ignorant I am, especially about stuff you were supposed to learn in school. If you think about it, though, there's no reason to be ashamed for not knowing who the hell Kate Chopin was, and whether she was the composer's wife or daughter or whatever. Really, what you should be ashamed about is thinking that knowing who the hell Kate Chopin was makes you better than someone who's never heard of her. That isn't Ryan. He realizes he's lucky to have had the time and the opportunity to find out who the hell Kate Chopin was.

The other woman professor looked late forties, with a pleasantly lined face and a spiky Rod Stewart haircut with two or three shades of blond streaks. She was full of dangly silver earrings with geometric designs that looked Native American, a bunch of silver necklaces, one with a crucifix, and two wrists' full of bracelets, including chains, bangles, and a really nice Cleopatra five-row piece that was two or three inches wide. This woman didn't say much, but when she joined in she was lively and animated, the silver jangling as she gestured.

The talk went on for a while. I didn't understand a damn thing anyone said, except that it had something to do with a famous book this Kate Chopin wrote that's been turned into a movie a couple times. The grad student was working hard to make it sound very important that we all understood how this one movie emphasized one thing in the book, but this other movie focused on some other thing. And she was way excited about how someone wrote some show about the book and put it on in Minneapolis and it was a major breakthrough because it had music and dancing in addition to the story from the book.

I was kind of moved by how charged up Melissa was about this whole thing, until I realized she probably wasn't. Most likely, all I was seeing was adrenaline. But maybe there was some real connection to what she was blabbing about—or had been, some time ago. As you get older, it gets harder to remember what it was that got you excited about a goal when you were young. Melissa was still young.

After a few more minutes, the jangly professor asked the student to leave the room. The three professors stood up and huddled together in a corner of the room. They were deciding her fate. It took all of thirty seconds. There was a lot of head nodding. Then, they broke the huddle, and the jangly professor went to the door and told the student to come back in. Melissa looked like she was about to drop a major brick. She sat down.

The jangly professor gave her a big smile and told her she'd passed the defense. Melissa almost jumped out of her chair and immediately started crying and hopping around on her toes and hugging each of the three professors. The other grad students filed out as Ryan and I stood up. The old guy professor left, too, and then the younger one with the braid.

Melissa and the silvery professor went in for another hug. They held it for a long time, talking to each other with low voices. The professor rubbed the student's shoulders, like she was massaging out the stress.

Finally, they broke the hug. The professor noticed me and Ryan. "I'm sorry," she said with a happy smile, "is there something we can do for you?"

"Are you Suzannah Montgomery?" I said.

"Yes." She was still excited for the student, still happy. "I am."

"We need to speak with you," I said. "I mean, when you're done here."

"Okay, sure." She turned to Melissa. "I'll see you at seven? My house?"

The student was still smiling, still bouncing, still crying. She wiped at her eyes, further wrecking her makeup. She looked like a clown who'd been over-seltzered. She couldn't speak, but she nodded enthusiastically, then gave the professor one more hug and bounded out of the conference room.

Suzannah Montgomery came over to us. "I just love to see this." She was beaming. "So young, so excited."

"Dr. Montgomery, my name is Karen Seagate. This is Ryan Miner. We're detectives, Rawlings Police Department."

Suzannah Montgomery's smile started to unwind until only a little bit remained. "Is there something wrong?"

"We need a couple minutes to talk with you."

"Of course," the professor said. Now the smile was all gone, like she knew we were going to tell her something shitty. She sat down at the conference table and gestured for us to sit, too.

"I'm sorry about barging into your defense, Professor, but we wanted to catch you before you left for the day. I'm afraid we have some bad news."

Her face began to contort in fear. "Is it Adam?"

"No, no, I'm sorry," I said. "It's about a student."

She sighed with relief, her eyelids closing slowly. Whatever it was she was afraid we were going to tell her about Adam, whoever he was, it was real bad.

"One of your graduate students, Austin Sulenka. He was found dead early this morning."

She flinched and her hand came up to her mouth. "Oh, no," she said. "Oh, my God. What happened?"

"We're not exactly sure. He died of asphyxia, in his apartment."

"He choked on some food?"

"We think he was strangled."

"Are you saying he was murdered?" She was motionless, her silver jewelry silent.

"Yes, Professor, that is what I'm saying."

She began to cry. She reached into her bag and pulled out a pack of tissues. She wiped her eyes, then her nose. "That poor boy," she said. "That poor, poor boy."

I waited a few seconds as she tried to pull herself together. "Can you tell us about your relationship with Austin?"

She shook her head sadly. "Officially, I was his adviser. He was a student in three of my seminars, and he was working on his thesis." She paused. "Strangled?"

"Yes," I said. "The autopsy hasn't been done yet, but all signs suggest that it was strangulation." I waited a beat. "You said 'officially' he was your student. Is there an 'unofficially' you can tell us about?"

"You saw him?" Suzannah Montgomery said.

"Yes." I saw all of him. "We did." I wondered how much of him she'd seen.

"You know, then, that he was an extremely attractive young man." She started to weep again. "What everyone saw was this tall, muscular young man. The hair, the cheekbones. But that wasn't Austin." She wiped at her eyes again.

"What was Austin, Professor?"

"Austin was a scared little boy. His father abandoned him and his mother when he was just a child. She died of cancer several years ago. He had no siblings, no close friends, no real family. It was a classic case of a person who looked self-confident and assured but who was exactly the opposite."

"Can you tell us a little about his interactions with the other professors, the other graduate students?"

"I know that some of the faculty didn't care for him. He could be an indifferent student. And I did see that from time to time in my own seminars. But I attribute that primarily to his restlessness. He was really quite distracted. He didn't love literature the way some of our more serious students do. He read well, although perhaps not widely enough. Yet the … the weight of his personal demons kept him from becoming fully engrossed in his studies. I am convinced that, with the right education, the right support, he could have become a significant talent." She paused, shaking her head and wiping at her nose with a tissue.

"And the other graduate students?"

"Well, I think some of the grad students had the same feeling about him that some of the faculty did: that he wasn't serious, wasn't engaged."

"And the females?"

She smiled sadly. "I think you can guess the answer to that question. He was very popular with the females. A true Byronic hero. Very handsome, very troubled. Therefore irresistible."

"Did he treat the girls well?"

She closed her eyes for a moment and shook her head back and forth, as if to dismiss the question as too simple. "Did he break some hearts? Yes, I am certain of that. But did he intend to do so? No, I don't believe that he did. It would be wrong to describe him as a cynical ladies' man, just collecting trophies. That was not Austin at all. The way I would describe it, when he selected a girl, he focused on her intently. He lavished her with attention. Of course, she would fall for him—quickly and completely. But, inevitably, when he discovered that she would not be able to satisfy his hunger—his very deep needs, I should say—he would turn away, just as suddenly. I suppose that could be interpreted as cruelty. But I would characterize it as honesty."

"Can you help us understand his relationship with May Eberlein?"

She shook her head. "May is in British, so I've never had her in a seminar. I do know that they were together for a time, and, of course, that she is quite attractive, almost an *Elle* girl." She smiled, as if that described May's limitations as much as her beauty. I got the feeling she had thought of that line some time ago. "But I do not believe I have ever had a conversation with her, and therefore I cannot tell you anything about her relationship with Austin."

"Can you help us with that episode earlier this year, that student in Austin's freshman class?"

She frowned and nodded her head. "Yes, well, that was *quite* the topic of discussion around here for some weeks. I know that what he did was wrong. Under no circumstances should an instructor become involved with a student who's taking her or his course. The power differential is real and substantial. And I do believe he came to realize that."

"You don't think he knew it was wrong when he was doing it?"

She shrugged, her palm fluttering in the air, her bracelets jangling. "I really can't say. I don't believe Austin's mind worked in that way. Yes, I suppose he did, on an abstract level. But how many of us are able to think clearly and objectively about the ethical implications of what we are doing, the reality in which we are immersed? That is not how we are made. We are shaped by our experiences—all that we have endured and survived, all that is occurring in our environment at the moment. If you were to ask Austin to write an essay about the topic, I am confident he would have provided a sensitive and thoughtful response. But in the midst of the situation, with a young girl smitten with him, a young girl sexually knowing and willing—in that situation, I'm not sure it's reasonable to expect that he would act in any way other than he did. They were attracted to each other sexually. The atmosphere was electric, and they acted on their impulses. I suspect ultimately it's as simple as that."

"You don't think it was, you know, that the girl was just a piece of ass?"

Suzannah Montgomery furrowed her brow and looked at me for a long moment. "I know nothing about the girl, Detective, and therefore I'm in no position to comment on whether she was, to use your phrase, 'a piece of ass.' But to describe Austin's motivations in that way would certainly mischaracterize him, as well as caricature everything that was sweet and honorable in him." She stood up, grabbed her bag, and strode out of the conference room like I'd just said something insensitive.

Chapter 9

"'A piece of ass'?"

"Hey," I said, "I might not know what the hell a Byronic hero is, but I can smell bullshit from three feet away. 'The atmosphere was electric'? Come on. His dick got hard, she spread her legs, he fucked her."

Ryan smiled. "I believe Professor Montgomery might conclude that you lack the soul of a true poet."

"Listen, college boy, I know why men screw women."

"Yeah, yeah, I got that," he said cheerfully, raising his palms in a gesture of surrender. "And I understand why you said it that way. You threw her off her game, and that's good."

"If she wants to think of him as a lost little boy who eases his pain by sticking his ten inches into any nearby cooch, that's fine with me. But I'm gonna trust my own instincts on this one. The smart money says he was a pussy hound, just like the waitress lives next door said."

We were sitting at the big table in the conference room in the English department. Ryan stood up and walked over to the stacks of books the grad student had left behind. He picked one up and looked at the cover, then opened it up.

"Thinking of reading about Kate Chopin?" I said.

"I'm thinking of talking to the grad student." He looked up at the whiteboard to get her name. "Melissa Harmon."

"To figure out what kind of crazy Suzannah Montgomery is?" I said.

Ryan nodded. "Stay here," he said. "I'm going to see if I can track her down." He left his cane behind as he walked over to the door and disappeared into the hall.

I stood up and drifted over to the books. They were from the university library, all about this Kate Chopin woman. I'd gone to my university library half a dozen times to do research on writers, but it had been twenty years and a three or four lifetimes ago. I tried to remember who or what I was writing about, but it was all gone, like almost everything else from those five years that had anything to do with education.

I envied Melissa Harmon, just going to classes, writing papers, teaching freshmen about what a sentence is, and a paragraph. Low stress. If the thing in your life that's pumping acid into your stomach is a bunch of professors asking you questions about stuff you know better than they do because you've been studying it for six months—well, that's not a bad gig. Not bad at all.

I heard the door open behind me. I turned, expecting Ryan. But it was Melissa Harmon. She stopped abruptly when she saw me looking at her books.

"Excuse me?" she said. Not hostile, just surprised.

I gave her a nonthreatening smile. "I'm sorry. Just looking at the books."

"Have we met?"

"No, we haven't," I said. "My name is Karen Seagate. I'm a detective with the Rawlings Police Department."

Her eyes got wide, then narrowed. "Why were you at my defense?"

"Take a seat, Melissa, would you?" She sat. "The man that was with me, he's my partner, Ryan Miner. We were here to talk with your adviser. About a case we're working on."

Ryan walked in. "I can't find—" When he saw her, he walked right over and turned it on. "Melissa, I'm Detective Ryan Miner." He gave her a big smile. "I want to congratulate you on your defense."

"Glad to meet you," she said, standing up. She relaxed right away and returned his smile. "Thank you. I'm really glad it's over." She laughed awkwardly.

"Sit, please," Ryan said, and the two of them sat down. "I studied *The Awakening* in college, but I didn't realize it had been adapted so often. That must have been a lot of fun to study."

She adjusted the chair so she could face him directly. "It was. It really was. I'm so glad you got something out of what I was … you know, the part of the defense you heard."

"It was excellent." He nodded. "I'm going to have to re-read it, now that I've got a better sense of what Chopin was doing."

Melissa Harmon was wearing a grin as big as Ryan's. She had cleaned up her smeared makeup, and she looked a lot more pulled together. She wasn't a bad looking woman, but she was overweight and moved like a linebacker. And she hadn't figured out what to do with her super curly red hair. You could tell she put a lot of effort into making it behave. But right now, basking in the attention of a handsome devil like Ryan—who said he liked her work on this writer—she was free of the self-consciousness that probably weighed her down like a backpack full of rocks. She looked happy—a lot happier than when she was wearing that frozen smile during the defense. And I was happy for her, even though I knew that Ryan was just working her.

Ryan glanced at me to see if I wanted to lead the interview. I raised my chin a little bit, telling him to keep going. We had never talked about it directly, but we'd gotten into the rhythm of letting him work the young women, particularly the vulnerable ones.

"Melissa, you must have been a little surprised when you saw me and Detective Seagate at your defense."

She nodded her head and smiled. "If I'd known you were detectives, that really would've freaked me out."

"Like we were going to arrest you if you made a mistake, right?" The two of them laughed. "Actually—" he said, putting on his detective face and turning to me, "did you get a chance to explain the case we're working on?"

"No," I said. "I didn't."

Ryan turned back to Melissa. "It's an investigation—nothing to do with you—but Suzannah Montgomery's name came up, and we were hoping you could give us a little information …"

She put her arms out. "If I can help."

"Tell us about your relationship with Suzannah Montgomery."

"Suzannah is terrific. I just love her. She's so friendly and enthusiastic. I mean, you saw how happy she was for me when I defended? That was genuine. And she's like that with all the students she directs. No, let me change that. She's like that with all the students—period. I've taken, like, three or four seminars with her, and she's always the same: she wants us all to succeed, to love literature—sure—but the most important thing for her— the thing that's been most important in my personal development—is she wants us all to be happy."

"How do you mean?"

"Not in a superficial, greeting-card sense. But in terms of how we approach life: our relationships, our careers, everything. How we live every moment of the day. She sees literature as a way to— this is a phrase she uses all the time—to open up our hearts, make us more receptive to the possibilities of love, to see those possibilities in other people, and ultimately to see it in ourselves."

Ryan was nodding his head. "Is that why you wanted to work with her on your thesis?"

Melissa laughed. "No," she said. "That was because Frances Hamblin wouldn't take me."

"Frances Hamblin?"

"She's the queen of American literature here at CMSU. She's a terrific scholar. All kinds of grants, books, conferences, you name it."

"What do you mean she wouldn't take you?" Ryan said.

"It was nothing personal," Melissa said, but the way she shifted in the chair and put on her plastic smile told me it still hurt. "Because she's so successful, every MA student wants to work with her—anyone who wants to go on and get a PhD in American, I mean. She takes four students at a time, and I didn't make the cut."

"There was some kind of competition?" Ryan said.

"Not officially," Melissa said, pushing down on a red curl that had escaped from the tortoise-shell clip on the right side of her hair. Her hand trembled slightly. "But looking back on it now, now that I'm almost done, I can see there *was* a competition. It started when the faculty got us all together at a little party before our first semester began. They were asking us about why we wanted to study literature, what we wanted to do for a living, who our favorite authors were, that sort of thing. At the time, we all assumed it was chit-chat, but now I'm convinced it was the start of the audition. Then, in the classes, of course, she was evaluating each of us all the time. So when it came time for us to ask a professor to chair our committee, I think Professor Hamblin already knew who she was going to take."

"So if she works with you, it's easier to get into a PhD program?"

Melissa tried to smile. "She picks up the phone and makes a call."

"But you've been happy working with Suzannah Montgomery?"

"Oh, absolutely," she said. "She's been so supportive. It's not like Professor Hamblin won't talk with me or anything like that.

In fact, she gave me the topic for my thesis—the Chopin thing. That play I mentioned, in Minneapolis, based on *The Awakening*? She'd seen it when she was in Minneapolis one time at a conference and was telling Suzannah about it, and Suzannah passed it along to me. Professor Hamblin is very generous in that way."

"How well do you know Austin Sulenka?" Ryan said.

The abrupt shift caught her by surprise. She paused a moment, then said, "Austin and I ..." She paused a moment to think. "We've worked together on two or three projects." She nodded. "He's okay, I guess. He does his share of the work but nothing more. No, he's good. No complaints. I really don't know him that well." But her expression said she had indeed given some thought to the topic of Austin Sulenka.

"I imagine you've been in a lot of courses with him, right?" Ryan said. "He's in American, too, right?"

"That's right. He's doing something with Poe. Not sure exactly what. We don't ... we're not close, socially."

"And May Eberlein?"

"Yeah, those two. They're in the same circle. But she's in British. Don't know what period or anything."

"I don't know how close all the English grad students are," Ryan said, "but do you know if Austin and May are still a couple?"

"Brangelina? Yeah, I think they are. I don't really know. There's two groups in the department, basically. I mean the girls. Those that Austin hooks up with, and the rest." She paused, a wistful look coming over her face. "I've been so busy, with my courses, and the thesis—I really don't have the patience to keep track of who Austin's sleeping with." But it was clear from the way she said it—the way her eyes drifted off into the distance when she said *sleeping with*—if she didn't want him to fuck her, she really wanted him to want to.

Ryan picked it up, too. He nodded, like a father telling his gawky fourteen-year-old daughter she shouldn't worry, that she'd find the right guy. "So," he said with a little bump on it, to get her mind back on track, "what's next for you, Melissa?"

She put her smile back on. "I'll probably stay on here, at least for a while. Teach first-year. Maybe I'll get an American survey." She was nodding her head, telling us—trying to tell herself—it would be okay.

"No PhD program at the moment?"

"I don't think so." Her posture sagged a little. "Suzannah isn't connected to the programs, you know, like Professor Hamblin is. I'm going to try to mine the thesis for a couple of articles. I'm sure I'll be able to get something in one of the journals for grad students, or an online journal. But, to be honest, I'm not sure I have what it takes get a PhD. When I've got a topic, I can do okay with it, but … I just don't have the kind of mind that comes up with ideas like that. Certainly not like Professor Hamblin. Not even like Suzannah."

Ryan smiled. "I've got a sister, PhD in English. I've got to tell you: when you were doing the defense today, you reminded me a lot of her. Don't sell yourself short. If you want a PhD, go after it."

Melissa sat up taller in her chair and gave him a genuine smile. "That's really nice of you to say."

If Ryan had asked her to marry him, she'd have said, "Yes, please. Would this afternoon work for you?"

Ryan stood and picked up his cane off the conference table. I stood, too. "Can I help you get these books back to your office?"

"No, thanks, that's fine," she said. She scooped them all up. I counted twelve books. She was a big girl.

"Thanks for talking with us, Melissa." Ryan slipped his card into the pages of one of the books, up near her chin. I got the door for her but stayed silent, not wanting to break the spell.

After she left the conference room, I turned back to Ryan. "You dawg."

He gave me his innocent, confused-boy look. "Just interviewing the young lady to understand more about our murder victim."

"Don't bullshit me, Ryan." I was smiling. "That girl's down in her office right now, writing Melissa Miner in her notebook."

"She's a good kid. All she needs is a little attention. Then watch her blossom."

"Okay, let's do the counseling some other time. What did you get from your new girlfriend?"

He thought for a second. "Well, there seems to be a class system among the students. The really smart ones get to work with the active scholars, like Frances Hamblin. The others work with the ones who are really nice, like Suzannah Montgomery."

"Which lines up with what Jonathan Van Vleet told us about Austin Sulenka," I said. "He wasn't a serious student, so he ended up with Suzannah."

"And the active professors are the rainmakers. They give away topics for the kids to write about," Ryan said. "And they help their students get into PhD programs."

"And the Melissas end up—what's the word for the contractors who teach for shitty pay?"

"Adjuncts," Ryan said.

"So Austin was gonna end up an adjunct, teaching freshmen."

Ryan shrugged. "We'll never know."

I looked at my watch: 3:45. A little more than an hour before most people would learn about Austin's death. "Melissa said she got her thesis topic from Frances Hamblin. Wanna see if we can track her down?"

"Since Frances Hamblin knows Suzannah Montgomery, maybe she'll tell us if Suzannah was one of his girlfriends."

"Maybe she'll tell us if *she* was one of his girlfriends."

"Frances Hamblin?" Ryan laughed. "With all her books? The articles, the conferences? Why would she be interested in a mediocre grad student like Austin?"

"Oh, Ryan. Poor Ryan. So handsome, so buff, so dumb."

Chapter 10

The secretary told us Frances Josephine Hamblin's office number but said she wouldn't be in because it isn't Wednesday.

"She part-time?"

"Professor Hamblin teaches one course, Wednesday night, and she comes into the office late Wednesday afternoons." The secretary didn't say, "She makes five times what I make, and I have to haul my sorry ass in here by eight AM, five days a week." She didn't have to. Her left eyebrow said it.

"One course. Really?" I put enough sauce on that last word to show her I was a working stiff myself. "Could you give us her address?"

She wrote it down on a slip of paper, along with a phone number. "She asks that you call first. She doesn't just answer the door."

"Want me to call her?" Ryan said as we headed down to the Charger.

"No," I said. "I'd rather surprise her. If we lean on her doorbell, she'll answer."

We got in the car and Ryan looked up the address on Google. "It says 2914 Blue Stem," he said. "That's behind the gates, isn't it? In Ravensmere?"

"No idea," I said. "Just get me there."

It took us less than ten minutes to make it through the patchy traffic and up to the gate, which I opened using the year-plus-pound password that was standard throughout the city. Blue Stem turned out to be one of the four streets that snaked around the tennis courts and the pool and bordered the Rawlings River and the Greenpath. Behind the gate, every one-acre lot had a two- or three-story mansion that went for a million or two. Each house had a theme. One looked like a ski lodge. Another was phony Tudor. The next had Greek columns over the two-story entryway. One looked like a giant bird, with two symmetrical wings that swept up and out, away from the main part of the house.

There were no fences between the lots. I remember reading about that when the development went up about fifteen years ago. All the owners had to grow the same kind of grass, so one lawn would flow into the next, like a fairway at a golf course. The kind of golf course that officially admits black people but for some reason never has admitted any. The whole place was truly puke-worthy.

We parked at the curb at 2914 Blue Stem and walked up the flagstone path toward the house. It was two stories, with a jagged roofline, which made the thing seem to go on and on, like a British manor house that was built in 1300 but expanded six times since. Stones the size of breadboxes stuck out of the stucco in a random pattern at the corners, for no apparent reason. The doorway was double-wide. On either side of the doors were thin frosted-glass panels with flower motifs and the initials RJH in the glass.

"Your father's a professor, right?" I said as we waited.

"That's right," he said.

"You grow up in a place like this?"

He pointed at the garage with dormer windows above each of the four bays. "Closer to that."

I waited about half a minute, then leaned on the bell again so it rang repeatedly.

Professor Frances Josephine Hamblin opened the door. She was wearing a nasty scowl. "I heard you the first time."

"Professor Hamblin?" I said, giving her a smile that made it clear I wasn't going to respond to her comment.

She was in her mid-sixties, a cappuccino-colored black woman with white hair, curly but not quite an Afro. She was tall and thin, but her posture was stooped, and she leaned on a shiny black wooden cane with a silver handle. She wore black wool slacks, pleated, and a black silk blouse than hung limp over her thin torso. No jewelry. "Who wants to know?"

"That would be me." I fished my shield out of my bag and hung it around my neck. "Detective Karen Seagate. My partner, Detective Ryan Miner. Can we have ten minutes?"

"What about?"

"We're working on a case. We thought you could help us with some information."

"Show me an ID."

Most people are good with the gold shield. I retrieved my wallet from my big shoulder bag, opened it to the picture ID, and handed it to her. She looked at it, then looked at me, sniffed dismissively, and handed it back to me.

"Would you like to see mine, too?" Ryan said, with enough sarcasm for me to get it but not so much that Frances Hamblin would.

She looked at him, top to bottom, taking in his drugstore aluminum cane, and turned to me.

"Make it quick," she said as she stepped back to permit us to enter her house. *Invite* wouldn't be the word. "I'm very busy."

"We appreciate that, Professor Hamblin," I said. Of course you're busy: you have your course to prepare for later this week. "We'll be fast." We stood on the black-veined marble tiles in the double-height foyer. Off to one side I could see some kind of sun room, dominated by a gleaming mahogany grand piano. Off to the other was a sitting room built around a huge fireplace with a marble mantelpiece and all kinds of nice chairs that I wouldn't have minded trying out. She didn't invite us into either of the rooms.

"We were talking with a graduate student, Melissa Harmon," I said. "She just defended her thesis." Professor Hamblin furrowed her brows, as if she was trying to place the student. Her eyes were ringed with raised black spots. I said, "Big-boned woman. Red hair."

She waved her hand in a circle, telling me to get to the point. Now I understood the furrowed brows: she was trying to think of why she should give a shit.

"She mentioned that you came up with the idea for her master's thesis." Frances Hamblin just shrugged. "About a play. Something about Kate Chopin. You saw a play in Minneapolis."

She nodded. "Yes, I remember the play. Don't remember giving the idea to the student."

"Melissa said you gave the idea to Suzannah Montgomery, who gave it to her."

She stuck her chin out. "A pedestrian topic. Perfect for giving away."

I looked over at Ryan, signaling him to jump in. "Why is that, Professor?" he said.

She looked at him, mildly annoyed at having to explain the obvious. "Because it doesn't get us any closer to the text. How others have interpreted the book over the last century? Frankly, who cares?" I couldn't place her accent. It reminded me a little of the Kennedy brothers.

"That's interesting—" Ryan said.

"Young man." She turned to him, the tip of her cane clicking as it came down on the marble floor. "When I said 'Who cares?'

that was a rhetorical question. I meant to suggest that I certainly don't, and therefore I'd like you to come to the point. As I said a minute ago, I am very busy."

"All right, Professor," I said, "we were hoping you could tell us a little about Suzannah Montgomery."

"I could tell you quite a bit about Suzannah, but at the moment I don't know why you want to know about her, and therefore I wouldn't know where to begin. Tell me what this is about—or let me get back to my work. Please, choose the latter."

Since the news of the murder was going to be broadcast within the hour, I decided to tell her. "We're investigating a possible homicide, a graduate student named Austin Sulenka."

"Austin Sulenka …" she said, tipping her head. "A graduate student here?"

"Yes, Professor, in American literature. He was about to finish his MA. He was working with Suzannah Montgomery, something about … what was it about, Ryan?"

"Edgar Allan Poe," Ryan said.

She frowned and shook her head.

"He was in a couple of your seminars," I said. "Tall, good-looking. Long dark hair, goatee."

Frances Hamblin's expression was a combination of confusion and impatience. "I have no interest in what he looked like. I don't know whom you're referring to." She paused. "You say he was one of Suzannah's advisees?"

"Yes, that's right," I said.

"So why are you bothering me about this?"

I'd forgotten: the dead kid isn't your responsibility. We shouldn't be taking up your time. Maybe no man is an island, but this old bitch hadn't gotten the memo.

"We're trying to determine who might want to hurt him. We were hoping you could tell us something about him."

"Well, another hope dashed, young lady. I work with my graduate students. She works with hers. To my recollection, she has never mentioned him to me." She looked at Ryan, then at me. "Will that be all?"

"Can you tell us a little about Suzannah Montgomery? She's been here six or seven years, right? You must have gotten to know her."

"Detective, my relationship with Suzannah Montgomery, such as it is, is of no relevance to your investigation, I assure you. She is my colleague in the English department. I see her at the various department functions and meetings. She asks me how I am, and I reply conventionally. I ask her how she is, and she replies in kind. I serve on her grad students' committees; she serves on mine. It is a fully satisfactory relationship, one of my better ones with my colleagues." She paused. "She was very solicitous when my husband passed away four years ago, for which I will always be grateful. Will that suffice?"

"Professor Hamblin," Ryan said. "I apologize in advance for what I am about to say." She sighed, and a scowl settled in. "When I was in college I read your book on slave narratives. This was at Brigham Young. I don't have to tell you about the sad history of my church's relations with African Americans. Your book helped me understand that history better—and helped me re-think my relationship with my faith in a very fundamental way."

"Yes, your church, as you choose to call it, has left quite a lengthy trail of shame, not least in its relations with African Americans." I took this to mean she was giving Ryan ten more seconds to say something interesting or get out of her foyer.

"Yes, Professor. I'm quite certain that I will never be able to think about my church's role in the nineteenth—and even the twentieth century—without considering the context of its relationship with African Americans, and, by extension, the native peoples."

I had no idea what Ryan was up to, but since Frances Hamblin hadn't started jabbing at us with her cane I was willing to sit back and see where he took us. She nodded her head, telling him to continue.

"It would be a real privilege if you could tell us—just very briefly—what you're working on now."

She stared at Ryan a moment. "Have you read any Melville?"

"Just *Moby-Dick*. *Billy Budd*. A handful of the stories."

"You haven't read *The Isle of the Cross*?"

Ryan looked sheepish. "Sorry, ma'am, I've never even heard of it."

"Very good." Frances Hamblin nodded. "You're correct. You haven't. Only a few dozen people in the world have. And nobody has read it, with the possible exception of Nathaniel Hawthorne."

"It's unpublished? A Melville novel?"

"That's right." She held her gaze. "An unpublished Melville novel."

Ryan was shaking his head, like he couldn't believe it. "You've seen it? Where is it?"

She smiled. Ryan had gotten the old snot to smile. She had a full set of beautiful teeth. She pointed over her left shoulder. "It's in my study."

"I can't believe what you're telling me."

"I found it quite hard to believe, as well, last summer, when I discovered a holograph manuscript in a box of unrelated papers in a local historical society in Gloucester, Massachusetts."

"This is unbelievable," he said.

"I have been looking for this manuscript for more than thirty years, and I believe I have found it. If I am correct …" she said, pausing for emphasis, "and I *do* believe I am, this will constitute one of the greatest discoveries in literary studies in the last fifty years."

"What are you planning to do with it?" Ryan had an expression on his face that I'd never seen on him, a mix of awe and excitement. He had this crazy old professor going, and it was almost working on me.

"I'm going to Harvard this summer to meet with a group of Melville scholars, where I will present my case that this is indeed the manuscript that Melville was 'prevented' from publishing—"

"I'm sorry, Professor, did you say 'prevented'?"

"Indeed I did."

"What do you mean?"

She smiled again. "I have no idea. Or, to be precise, I do not yet have an idea what Melville meant in his letter to Hawthorne stating that he was prevented from publishing it. But I will be presenting my preliminary conclusions to the community this summer."

"If you're right—I mean that this is Melville's book—will you then publish it?"

She nodded. "It will be my final—and my greatest—project."

"Professor Hamblin, I cannot tell you what an honor it was to hear about this enormously exciting discovery. This is just so thrilling." He shook his head at his own inarticulateness. "I'm just speechless. Thank you so much for sharing this."

She nodded, almost a bow. "It was my pleasure talking with you, young man."

"Karen," Ryan said, turning to me and giving me a big smile, "let's let the professor get back to her work. And Professor Hamblin," he said, taking a card out of his jacket pocket and handing it to her, "again, my sincere thanks. If you need a research assistant, would you please keep me in mind?"

She smiled and nodded. "I do appreciate your gracious offer," she said, "but I don't believe I will have any trouble securing a research assistant."

"Have a good day, Professor," Ryan said to her as the door closed slowly behind us.

We walked back to the Charger and got in. I turned the ignition so I could lower the windows. The sun was streaming in, heating up the black plastic seats.

I looked at Ryan, my brows furrowed. I didn't say anything.

He looked back at me for a long moment. "Is there something you'd like to say, Detective?"

"I'm just wondering," I said. "How long do you think you could be charming? I mean, before you make yourself vomit?"

He rubbed his chin for a moment. "Well, let's see, I became charming sometime in 1996, I believe it was, and I've been charming every moment since then—by the way, have I mentioned that you're looking quite well? Very strong, confident, well-rested." He gave me a big smile.

"All that horseshit about that book—anything to do with who killed the grad student with the Moby Dick?"

"Uh, no," he said, "I don't think so. Frances Hamblin lives on Planet Hamblin, and I don't think she has much to do with Suzannah Montgomery—and I'm sure she had nothing to do with Austin Sulenka. As long as the university doesn't make her work with dull grad students like Melissa Harmon or Austin, or do too much teaching, she's happy. She's all about her research."

"So you believe she doesn't know who Austin was?"

"Yes, I do believe that. I wouldn't even assume she could pick Suzannah Montgomery out of a lineup."

"And the Melville book? That's a big deal?"

"If you care about Melville, I guess. Otherwise, no. Personally, it does nothing for me. But the professor was so egotistical, I just wanted to see if I could get her to open up a little. For most people, there's one sure-fire topic."

"Themselves?"

"Have I mentioned how well you're looking these days, Karen?"

"Are you interested in how she can afford that house?"

"Not particularly," Ryan said. "She could have gotten some money from her publications—I'll check to see if she's written a big textbook or something—but I doubt if it would be enough for that place. Or she married well. Her husband could've been an oil man out in the Bakken. Maybe Van Vleet could tell us, or Suzannah Montgomery."

I thought for a moment. "Let's call it a day. We'll get Austin's phone records tomorrow morning, and maybe Robin will have some prints for us."

Ryan smiled. "Absolutely. This is fun, huh?"

"To quote you, 'not particularly.'"

"Oh, come on. You just learned there might be a new Melville book coming out. You read *Moby-Dick*, didn't you?"

"The first five pages. Then I skimmed the CliffsNotes."

"Why'd you give up?"

"All the blubber."

Chapter 11

The Hispanic lawn guys who kept the expensive houses in Ravensmere looking expensive were quitting for the day, gathering up their big water jugs and rakes and edgers and steering their riding mowers up the steel ramps onto the trailers hitched to their pickups.

"You let me know if you see a homeowner working on his house," I said as we drove toward the gate that would automatically swing back to let us re-enter the world of the ninety-nine percenters.

"I'm not sure you understand how the economy works," Ryan said. "The homeowners aren't home now. They're at the office earning a million bucks so it can trickle down to the workers, nine dollars every hour."

"Are you a socialist, Ryan?"

"Not as much as Jesus, but more than a Christian politician."

My cell rang. I reached around and fished it out of my big shoulder bag on the back seat. It was Jorge Espinoza, our IT guy. He had a preliminary report on what was on Austin Sulenka's laptop.

I looked at my watch. It was twenty to five. "Can you give us five minutes to get there?"

"Of course, Karen."

We made it back to headquarters and hurried downstairs to Jorge's den. He had two small, windowless rooms. One was a noisy closet with super air-conditioning, filled with steel racks holding all the servers and routers. The other was a ten-by-ten bare-walled cell with fluorescent tube lights overhead, a desk and chair, and a worktable full of desktops, laptops, and tablets, some working, some cracked open like black plastic lobsters.

"Thanks for getting in touch," I said as Ryan and I squeezed into the small office.

"No problem," he said. He was about thirty, tall and thin. He favored Hawaiian shirts, cargo shorts, and rubber flip-flops, regardless of the season. "You wanna hit the light?" he said to Ryan.

Ryan turned it off as Jorge powered up a small projector, throwing an image of a directory on the tan wall of his office. "Here's a mirror of the hard drive." He passed me a memory stick, which I passed to Ryan. "Just want to give you a big picture on what's going on."

I recognized the image on the wall as Austin's main directory, the My Documents view. "He's got Windows 7, so there's Pictures, Movies, Music, and Documents. The Movies directory is empty, the Music directory is full of what looks like bootleg music files from a Russian server, and the Pictures directory is full of photos."

"What kind of pictures has he got?" I said.

"It's him with girls, some older women, some outdoor scenes. Nothing surprising. Some nudes of a really fine young woman." That would be May Eberlien. "And he's got a folder full of porn."

"Anything interesting there?"

"No," Jorge said. "It's all women, all of legal age. No kids, no animals. But he did like Japanese women."

I shrugged. "Okay. What are you seeing in the documents?"

"It's all school work. Papers from courses, stuff like that. He was trying to get some papers accepted at conferences. He's got a folder for conferences and one for journals."

"Boring," I said. "So you didn't see anything that tells us who killed him?"

He gave me a sympathetic smile. "Sorry, no. But there might be some interesting things out in the cloud."

"Yeah?"

"His browsing history shows that he's been some places you'll want to check out. He's got an account at A1-TermPaper, which sells term papers to students. He's got an account at Central Montana First National Bank. A PayPal account."

"Can we see what he was up to?"

"Not yet," Jorge said. "He used Mitto."

"What's that?"

"It's a site that stores all his passwords," Ryan said.

"I already put in a request through the chief's office to unlock the Mitto account. Margaret said they'll have to figure out whether they need separate authorizations to look at his financials. She said she'd have an answer tomorrow morning."

Ryan held up the memory stick. "Did you check his system for malware?"

"I cleaned it up before I imaged it."

I turned to Ryan. "That all you need?"

"This is great." He nodded to Jorge. "Gracias," he said.

Jorge waved his hand. No problem.

"Thanks a lot, Jorge," I said. "We'll get back to you if we have any questions."

Ryan turned the light back on and we headed upstairs. He was leaning on his cane. I noticed that he gets tired late in the afternoon. That didn't happen before he got shot. "Okay, Ryan, call it quits for today?"

"Kali's going to be out with the kids till six-thirty. I'm going to take a quick look at Austin's computer."

"Knock yourself out." I headed toward the break room, where I bought some calories from a machine and wolfed down the doughnut half from the box on the counter. The two ends were squashed, like a guy had just ripped it in two with his fingers. But I didn't have time to get home, cook a regular dinner, and make it to my seven PM AA meeting.

So I was still eating crappy food all the time, but at least I had the drinking mostly under control. When you've got six or eight major bad habits going at the same time, you start with the one that's most likely to kill you the soonest. For me, it's liquor. I've been going to the meetings now for almost a year. The deal I had with the chief was that I had to get my card signed, seven days a week for three months, or I was gone.

So now I don't have to go to any more meetings. But I'm still going. I'm done feeling like I want to throw up at the meetings. I can stand in front of the room and talk to the other drunks about any of the topics that come up. I'm reasonably comfortable blah-blahing about how my drinking made me selfish, busted up my family, hurt everyone in my life, and all the rest. I know it did all that, I've got the stories to prove it, and I'm on board the AA train.

I do wish I could get past the "recovering alcoholic" bit. I'd like to be recovered already. But since I still can't smell Jack Daniel's without wanting to drop everything I'm doing and have just one small glass or four, maybe I haven't actually recovered. The thought that I'm going to be like this for the rest of my life sucks, actually, but not as bad as nailing strangers at a bar and passing out six or seven times a week.

I was at the stove, around eight-thirty, when my cell rang. I'd ditched my land line a little while ago, but I hadn't yet gotten into the habit of keeping my cell with me at all times, like the kids do.

I turned off the stove and followed the ring tone into my bedroom.

"Detective Seagate, this is Tiffany. Tiffany Rhodes?"

It took me a second to remember who she was. Then I pulled it up: the freshman who screwed Austin, then got pissed at him because he gave her the C she deserved.

"Yes, Tiffany. This is Detective Seagate." I didn't know why she was calling. I threw in a "How ya doin'?"

She didn't answer that question. "Do you have a minute? I mean, to talk?"

"Sure," I said. "What's on your mind?"

"I'm sorry to call you so late, but I wanted to talk to you. You want me to wait until tomorrow morning?"

"No, that's fine. Let's talk now."

"Okay, thanks," she said. Then there was a long pause.

"You still there, Tiffany?"

Nothing. Then, "Yeah, I'm still here. It's just hard for me to say what I have to tell you."

"Listen, Tiffany, just say it. You won't get in any trouble if, you know, you want to change anything you told me and my partner earlier. It happens all the time. As long as you're being truthful with me now, I promise you, you won't catch any shit for it."

I knew what she was going to tell me: she was in town Sunday night.

"It's about Austin," she said. "I wasn't telling the truth when I told you I wasn't still seeing him."

"Yeah?"

I should start to feel a little better about myself. Once each blue moon I get something right.

"I was thinking about what I said to you. Some of my girlfriends know I was still seeing him. I didn't want you to find out from them."

I decided not to mention how this was a shitty reason to tell the truth. "Well, you're doing the right thing, Tiffany. Being honest with me now."

"I was here in Rawlings last night. I wasn't at home in Billings."

"Okay, tell me about last night. Where were you last night?"

"I was with a girlfriend. I mean, I slept over at this girlfriend's apartment."

"You weren't with Austin?"

It took her a little while to answer. "I was with him early in the evening. Around seven, seven-thirty."

"Where was that, Tiffany?"

"At his apartment," she said. "We were at his apartment."

"You had sex with him at his apartment around seven or seven-thirty."

"That's right." Tiffany's voice was soft, like she was ashamed. Which surprised me. I didn't see her as the kind of girl ever felt ashamed.

"Was there anyone else with you and Austin?"

"What?" Her tone was halfway between confused and pissed. "What do you mean?"

"Simple enough question: was there anyone else in the apartment with you and Austin? Another guy? Another girl?"

"No," she said. Her tone was clipped. "What do you think I am?"

I decided to pass on that one. "I'm not here to judge you or anything you did. I'm just trying to figure out who killed Austin Sulenka."

"No, there wasn't anyone else there, and no, I didn't kill Austin."

"Okay, so you were there with Austin for what—a half-hour or so?"

"That's right. Then I left."

I headed back out to the kitchen and turned the stove back on, low. "Is there anyone who can put you there, anyone who saw you leave?"

"I don't think so. Me being there wasn't something I want everyone to know."

"So when you left, Austin was in good health, right?"

"He was fine."

"And tell me about the apartment. What kind of shape was the apartment in?"

"I don't understand what you mean."

"I mean, was everything the way it always was? You know, the furniture?"

"He's not the neatest guy in the world, but yeah, it was normal."

"Where did you go then, around seven-thirty?"

"To my girlfriend's place."

I asked Tiffany for the contact information on the girlfriend. I went over to the counter where I keep a pad and pen. I wrote it down, but there was probably no point in checking it out. If Tiffany was lying to me now, she'd have already worked out the alibi with the girlfriend.

"Help me understand your relationship with Austin."

"It's kinda complicated," Tiffany said.

"I got time." I heard the key turn in the lock on my front door. I walked out to the hallway and saw Mac come in. He's good—doesn't call out or anything. He just walks in and tries to find me. I drifted back to the kitchen and stirred the cheapo fried rice with chicken and pea pods.

"That thing with the disciplinary committee," she said, "all that part was real."

"You mean you were pissed at him about the English class?" I didn't want to say she was pissed at him for giving her a C after she fucked him. Words can be so hurtful.

"Yeah, I didn't want to see him or hear from him again—ever."

"So what changed your mind?"

I heard her sigh. "Do you know how it is, sometimes you know a relationship is … that it's not working, it's wrong, but you can't really stop thinking about the guy?"

That question I definitely wasn't going to answer. But I knew she was telling me the truth. "Go on."

"I just missed him."

"The sex?"

"Not the sex," she said. "Well, yeah, the sex was part of it. But not the biggest part. It was … ever since I've been little … I've never been the best-looking girl, or the smartest, or anything like that. I'm just … I'm just what you saw when we talked today. I've never had a guy like Austin. He was good in bed, and he really looked good, but that's not what I'm talking about. He was just a cut above the kind of guys I'm usually with."

"You mean better educated?"

"Better educated, sure. That's part of it. But it wasn't a status thing. I know what class I'm from, and I know I'm never gonna be, like, a glamorous girl or rich or anything like that. But with Austin … just being with him, having him want to be with me. I don't know, somehow it made me feel a little better about myself. Do you know what I mean?"

I could have told her she's an idiot, that the only possible reason Austin was doing her was he was slumming, or he got his rocks off on dumb girls idolizing him, or he appreciated her two quite substantial tits. But at her age, I would've thought just like she did. "Yeah, I do know what you mean."

"Are you going to arrest me or something?"

"No."

"Are you going to tell Brian?"

"Tiffany, you said you went from Austin's apartment to your girlfriend's apartment, right?"

"Yeah."

"So you didn't go back to your own place—the apartment you share with Brian?"

"No, I didn't come here."

"You've done this before: tell Brian you're in Billings when you're really with Austin?"

"A few times," she said. "Maybe five or six."

"And Sunday night, did you have any contact with Brian after you'd been with Austin? Did you phone him? Just sneak into your own place to get clean clothes? Anything like that?"

"No, Brian didn't know I was with Austin. He thought I was in Billings."

"But obviously, Brian knows where Austin lives. That's where he trashed Austin's car. How do you know he wasn't across the street, saw you go into Austin's place, come out a half-hour later?"

"The way I know is, he'd have come after me with a baseball bat if he saw that."

"So you're saying Brian is a violent guy, that he could've hurt you—or Austin."

"No," she said, her voice a little shrill, "that's not what I'm saying at all." She took a moment. "I'm saying if Brian knew I was involved with Austin he couldn't have played along like everything's normal. If he wants to say something, no way he can keep from talking. It was hard enough for Brian when he found out that me and Austin were, you know, together last semester. If he'd found out I was still with Austin, he'd've went batshit. There'd be all kinds of shit happening."

"Like him strangling Austin."

Tiffany started crying. "No, you've got that all wrong. Brian's not that kind of guy. He wouldn't hurt Austin, and he wouldn't hurt me. He would've broke up with me, for sure, but he wouldn't hurt anyone. I'm sure of that. You have to believe that."

"All right, Tiffany, where are you now? You at your place?"

"I'm in my bedroom."

"Where's Brian?"

"In the living room, watching TV or something."

"Do you think he can hear you, I mean, crying?"

"No," she said. "I don't think so."

I glanced up at Mac standing in the kitchen doorway. I nodded to signal that everything was okay. He came over to the stove and picked up the spoon to stir the Chinese food. He waved his hand to tell me he would take over. I squeezed his arm and went back out to the living room.

"You want me to come over to your place now," I said to Tiffany, "or send a patrol car?"

"No," she said, still crying. "That'd just make it worse. He'd know something's going on, and he wouldn't be able to let it go."

"Okay, you change your mind, call me right back, okay?" I heard her mumble something but I couldn't quite make it out. "Tiffany, do you have anything else you want to tell me?"

"No," she said. "You promise you won't tell Brian about me calling you?"

"I'm not gonna tell Brian. This phone call never happened," I said. "But you need to understand something. Even if everything you told me now is true, that doesn't provide an alibi for Brian—"

"You gotta believe me, Detective. Brian would never do that."

"Yeah, you told me that. But that's not an alibi. You don't know where he was yesterday around midnight. Because, like you said, he wasn't with you. So I'm gonna have to treat him just like everybody else: until I can rule him out, he's in. Do you understand me?"

Tiffany started crying harder now. "He's gonna find out I called you, I just know it."

"Pull yourself together, Tiffany. The only way he's gonna find out is if he hears you crying and you tell him you called me. So if my partner and I come to your place sometime to interview you and Brian, you act like we never had this conversation, right?"

She didn't say anything.

"I asked you if you understood me, Tiffany."

"Yeah, I understand you."

"If you screw that up because you're trying to protect Brian, that's gonna make me think he was involved in killing Austin—and maybe you were, too."

"I didn't kill him," she said. "I'm telling you the truth. I swear."

"Yeah, okay," I said. "Clean yourself up, go watch TV with Brian or he's gonna wonder what you're up to."

"All right," she said. The line went silent. She didn't sound like she thought everything was all right, and I wasn't at all confident, either. A girl that weak—I didn't know what it would be, but I had a real strong feeling something bad was going to happen to her.

Chapter 12

It was a couple minutes after eight AM when I made it to my desk. Back before I was fired, I used to aim for around eight-thirty, quarter-to-nine, because the old chief never pulled in until closer to ten and Ryan always had something productive to do until I pulled in.

Now I aim for eight sharp. Not because the new chief is going to check on me but because that's the deal: eight hours at one-hundred percent. I want to see if I can do what I say I'll do.

But I lost ten minutes this morning talking with Mac about how this wasn't a good time to talk. We're at a delicate point in our relationship. He's seen me in action for a few months now, so he has some idea of my more-obvious bad habits, and I've hinted at some of the less-obvious ones. It's not that I think it's important to be honest in a relationship or anything sensible like that. It's that I like him and therefore want to give him every opportunity to run like hell. Which would of course be easier and probably better for me in the long run. And certainly better for him. I've learned to set the bar low.

I hung up my jacket on the coatrack in the corner of the detectives' bullpen and made my way over to my desk. "What you got there?"

Ryan was leaning back in his chair, his calves up on the metal shelf that slid out from above the desk drawers. He was studying some paper. "Same thing you've got there," he said, pointing to my desk.

I sat down and picked it up. It was six pages, showing the last four months of Austin Sulenka's phone log. "Anything interesting?"

"Well, he was a chatty young man." He flipped through the pages. "Twenty or thirty calls a day."

"To anyone interesting?"

"I think so," he said. "May Eberlein told us she broke up with him, didn't she, a month or so ago?"

"That's what she said."

"And that she didn't see him socially this weekend, right?"

"Said she ran into him late last week in the department. She wasn't involved with him anymore because he was … what was that phrase she used?"

Ryan winced a little as he lifted his legs off the shelf and sat up straight. He leafed through the skinny notebook on his desk. "She was 'disappointed' in him."

"That's right," I said. "Because she figured out mostly he just wanted to bang her."

"So how come they had five calls last weekend, one longer than fourteen minutes?"

"Because it took a long time to explain how much he disappointed her?" I said.

"Even if they were in a course together and working on some project, they wouldn't be talking like that," Ryan said.

"What else you see?"

"I see him calling Suzannah Montgomery, his thesis adviser, every week or so. Which makes sense," he said. "He was probably in some kind of rhythm, giving her chapters of his thesis every so often."

"What else?"

"I see him calling Tiffany Rhodes, the skanky freshman. Couple of times a week, including the day he died. What's with that?"

"She called me last night." I sat down and pulled the phone records out of the envelope.

"She called you," Ryan said, putting down his copy. "What for?"

"To tell me she'd lied to us earlier. She was still doing Austin."

"In God's name, why?"

I smiled. "Because he made her feel good about herself."

He just shook his head. "What do you mean: by comparison? Because Austin was even skankier than she is?"

"I don't think so," I said. "It's kind of a class thing. She's always been with guys like the moron Brian. She knows that's the kind of guy she's gonna end up with, but she saw Austin as, you know, an intellectual."

"So she's living with Brian and carrying on with Austin behind his back? For months?"

"Hey, I'm not her life coach. I'm just telling you what she told me."

"And the night Austin died?"

"The night he died, they screwed. Not that much. Maybe a half-hour, around seven o'clock. At his apartment."

"Any witnesses put her there?"

"She was offended when I asked her that. No, it was an intimate encounter. Just the two of them."

"And Brian didn't know about that?"

"She swears no. She's nailed Austin at his place five or six times."

"So she's got no alibi for Austin's murder," Ryan said.

"Neither does Brian."

"You buy her story that she was cheating on Brian," Ryan said, "or you see the two of them working together and killing Austin?"

"Actually, there's two ways that could've happened. Tiff and Brian put their pointy heads together, she gets Austin nude, Brian strangles him—"

"What's the motive there?" Ryan said.

"Austin broke up their happy relationship. It's revenge. And it takes him out of the picture. Or, they're making it up as they go along. Brian finds out Tiff's doing Austin, goes over to his place, catches them together, throttles him, trashes the place. Then they get together, work out their stories. Neither one rats out the other."

"And that makes sense how?" Ryan said.

He's usually much brighter than me, but I have a more sophisticated understanding of skeevy losers. "Easy: Austin's swinging dick is too big for Tiff to resist. That's why she's still screwing him, even after he reneged on the B in the class. So the only solution is to take him out so she and Brian can live happily ever after."

"You like either of those motives?"

"Nope. I think Tiffany was telling me the truth last night. She was just all squishy about Austin. He was her dream vacation from Brian."

"How can she be romantic about a pathetic guy like Austin?"

"Ryan, you ever been a dumpy eighteen-year-old girl with a one-hundred IQ?"

He tilted his head, considering my question. "Not to my knowledge," he said.

"Well, I'm just telling you how I read her last night."

We were both silent for a minute. Ryan said, "I'm not seeing a good way to work on these two."

I shook my head. "Me neither." Then I remembered Ryan was going to look at Austin's computer. "Hey, did you get a chance to go over the drive Jorge gave you?"

"Yeah," he said. "It's consistent with what the English chair told us: he's not that sharp a student."

"How do you get that?"

"He tried. Proposed papers to deliver at conferences, sent in articles to journals. Every one of them was rejected."

"Can you tell if that makes him a dunce? Maybe he's competing against professors?"

"Some of the conferences and journals were for the professors. The big deal is the annual conference for the American Literature Association. There are some grad students there, but mostly PhD students, not MA students like Austin. But he was shut out of some smaller conferences, and even some journals on the Web that are made for grad students. So I'm not sure I'd call him a dunce. I'd say he didn't get a chance to fulfill his scholarly potential."

"That's sweet," I said. "Okay, he was a dunce. Why don't we go brief the chief? He might have an idea how to proceed."

The bullpen was starting to come to life. One of the other day-shift detectives, Hanson, had just come in. He was off to get some coffee. His partner, Gupta, was already talking with a sergeant about a case. Staff people slalomed around the desks, picking up and delivering documents. The phones started to jangle.

When we got to the chief's office, Margaret looked at the lights on her phone and told us he was on a call. "It'll just be a minute," she said, motioning for us to sit on the couch. Her eyes snapped back to her screen.

Thirty seconds later, she said, "Detectives, the chief can see you now." We got up and walked over to his office. I knocked.

"Come," his voice said.

I opened the door. Chief Murtaugh was seated at his desk. "You got a minute on the grad student?

He waved us in and invited us to sit.

We got settled. "We're looking hard at this couple of undergrads: Tiffany Rhodes and Brian Hawser. They live together—"

"I remember." The chief nodded.

"She had the affair with the vic, which went to a disciplinary hearing at the university. The boyfriend bashed-up the vic's car, earned himself an RO."

The chief nodded again.

"She phones me last night, tells me she was lying when she told us she didn't want anything to do with the vic anymore. She was still doing him. In fact, she did him the night he died—at his apartment."

"The boyfriend know about this?" the chief said.

"She swears no."

"Have you got the forensics back on the vic's apartment?"

"Probably later this morning," I said.

"Hmm." The chief was stroking his bottom lip. "We have the boyfriend's prints and DNA, right, from his DUI and the vandalism?"

"Yeah," I said.

"But not hers."

"Just her prints," Ryan said.

"When I talked with her last night," I said, "I made it clear that she didn't have an alibi and neither did her boyfriend, so we weren't prepared to rule either of them out. What we're working on now is whether the boyfriend tracked her down in the vic's apartment and killed him, or whether she's still lying to us and she lured the vic into bed so her boyfriend could kill him."

"That would be risky, wouldn't it? She could end up dead."

"She's not a deep thinker."

The chief didn't say anything. "Nobody else you like at this point?"

"The vic had a girlfriend," I said, "another grad student, who said she broke up with him a month ago but who's been phoning him a little more than we'd expect. But we like Tiffany and Brian more because we know Brian's got a temper."

"Okay, so her DNA will be all over the vic's apartment, but we don't have her on file. And we don't know whether Brian left anything there."

"When we interviewed him yesterday he told us we're free to look. He seemed pretty confident we wouldn't find anything," I said.

"That could've been a bluff," the chief said. "If you asked him for a sample, his reaction might tell you if he was there."

"Since she's already admitted to being there that night, there's no reason to ask her for a sample. And we've already got his," I said. I didn't want to say, "So what's the point of getting their DNA?"

"True," the chief said, "but he might've forgotten that. We want them to know we're looking at them hard. If we increase the pressure, they might start to jockey for position. Ask both of them at the same time," the chief said.

"Tiffany might be smart enough to play along, since she knows her DNA won't implicate her any more than what she told me last night," I said. "Worse come to worst, she can admit she was still screwing Austin. Which is legal."

"But Brian wouldn't be able to explain his DNA being there," the chief said. "The only explanation would be that he was there to kill Austin Sulenka. Or he ended up killing him. So Brian doesn't have any other option. He has to claim he's innocent and hope he didn't leave any traces there."

"We ask them at the same time and watch what happens," I said. "If he starts shitting bricks, we know he was there. And he'll try to figure out a way to put it on Tiffany."

"Once Brian realizes he might be on the hook for the murder," the chief said, "the two of them will turn on each other. She'll try to put it on him because he already has a conviction and the RO, and he'll say it was her. She was showing Brian how much she loved him—she was willing to kill Austin just to win Brian back. That's what you're really doing here: trying to split them up so that each one starts calculating how to get the best deal if their story falls apart."

"Are you worried he might hurt her?"

He nodded his head. "That's a possibility." He thought a moment. "When you talked to her last night, did you tell her we could help her out?"

"Yeah, I said I could come over or send a patrol car."

"What did she say?"

"I don't think she said anything, but she heard me."

"Here's how I look at it. She's eighteen, right?"

"Nineteen, I think."

"And she's the one you like for the murder," the chief said. "She and her boyfriend. Unless we can split them up, we're never going to get anywhere. Let's say we don't get any forensics putting Brian there. She stays with her story that she was involved with Austin, that she'd never hurt him. Brian stays with his story that he wasn't there. And we can't make an arrest. We've got to make her decide whether to trust Brian or us. If she's scared of Brian, she's got your phone number." The chief looked at me, then at Ryan. "Does that make sense?"

I looked at my watch: 8:21. I turned to Ryan, "Let's go talk to them now. Maybe they haven't left for the day."

I felt a little better now that the chief okayed the plan to pressure her to flip on Brian. Like the chief said, if the two of them stuck to the game plan, we wouldn't be able to make a move. But that theory made sense only if Tiffany and Brian were bright enough and calculating enough to sit down and agree to a plan—and then stick to it. What I was seeing, though, was that the two of them were quite stupid—and they were just making it up as they went along. If we pressured her to work with us and Brian figured it out, Tiffany would be in real danger.

The chief was right about one thing: they were both officially adults. We had offered Tiffany protection if she thought she needed it. That was the right thing to do. But we had no responsibility to go easy on her just because she was in over her head. It was all her doing. Our job was to solve the murder of Austin Sulenka. If she killed Austin or knew that Brian did—or they did it together—this was our best shot at breaking it open.

Then it hit me that maybe I felt a little better that the chief okayed the plan because it wouldn't be all on me if Tiffany got hurt. I felt my stomach lurch, which I always do when I realize I'm bullshitting myself.

Chapter 13

"Got the swabs?" We were driving over to Brian and Tiffany's apartment.

"Right here," Ryan said, tapping his briefcase.

We parked out on the street, walked up the stairs to the second floor, then over to number 204. I knocked hard.

Ryan put his ear up to the door and listened for a moment. "There's someone in there."

I put my shield around my neck. The door opened.

Tiffany was wearing a pair of men's boxers and a tee shirt, no bra. She rubbed her eyes. "What do you guys want?" She was half asleep, too groggy to say it either hostile or polite.

"Good morning, Tiffany," I said. "Did we wake you up?"

"Shhh," she said. "You'll wake up Brian. What do you want?" Now she was starting to tune in, maybe remember she'd called me last night.

"We want to wake up Brian."

"What for?" She looked confused.

"We want to get DNA samples from the two of you."

She came out into the hall, closing the door most of the way. "Can I talk to you in private over here?" she said, pointing down the hall.

"That's okay, Tiffany. Detective Miner knows you called me last night. You can say whatever you want in front of him."

"I thought we had an understanding, you know, when we talked last night. If Brian finds out I was still involved with Austin, that's the end of us."

"Yeah, I understand that, Tiffany, but my boss tells me we gotta move this along. You and Brian breaking up—that's more of a problem for you than for me."

"But I told you in confidence I was at Austin's place."

"That's not how it works, Tiffany. You told me you'd lied to us earlier yesterday. Which, by the way, is a felony. Obstruction of justice." That's probably a stretch. But it got her attention. "I'm not interesting in messing up your relationship with Brian, but my top priority is figuring out who killed Austin Sulenka. You can tell Brian anything you want about where you were Sunday night. I'm fine with you telling him you were with your parents in Billings. But right now I've got you over at Austin's place four or five hours before he died—with no alibi for when he died. And I have no idea where the hell Brian was."

"Are you gonna tell Brian I was at Austin's place?"

"I don't know what I'm gonna say. Like I said, I'm not interested in you and Brian—unless one of you, or both of you, killed Austin. If you didn't do it, you might wanna start thinking about how to make me believe you."

The door opened. Brian was wearing boxers and scratching an armpit. "What the fuck do you two want?" He had a nasty scowl on his face.

I gave him an official smile. "Good morning, Brian. Hope we didn't wake you?"

"I said, 'What the fuck do you two want?'"

"Hey, babe," Tiffany said. "I'm sorry we woke you up."

He gave her a pissed-off look, then turned back to me.

"We want your DNA, Brian," I said. "Yours and Tiffany's."

"You got some kind of warrant?"

I shook my head. "No, we're asking you to volunteer it."

"Now, why would we want to do that?" Brian stepped out into the hall and walked up to me.

"How about we go inside the apartment, Brian, so we don't wake up any of the neighbors?"

He stared at me for a few seconds, then turned and walked back into his apartment.

When the four of us were inside, I closed the door. "Here's where we are, Brian. We've got a lot of forensic evidence from Austin Sulenka's apartment. We need to rule you two out. Simple as that."

He shook his head. "I don't believe you."

I looked confused. "What do you mean?"

"You're playing some kind of game. If you had any evidence I was over at that fucker's place, you'd be arresting me right now, not waking me up to ask me some bullshit favor. Why the fuck should I do you a favor? And Tiffany? What are you asking her for? There's no way in hell she'd be over there."

Out of the corner of my eye, I could see her, her eyes big, trying to figure out how to play it. "Are you sure of that, Brian?"

"Sure as I'm standing here right now." He put his chin out, defending his girlfriend's honor.

"Sure as you were last semester when you found out she was fucking Austin?"

His face contorted in rage, he started to move toward me.

"No, no," Ryan said, stepping in and putting his finger on Brian's chest. "You move one more inch toward the detective, I'll take you down."

Brian Hawser looked at Ryan's cane and smirked. He thought about it a second, then stepped back.

"Look at it this way, Brian," I said. "You weren't at Austin's apartment, no reason not to give us your DNA. Tiffany wasn't there, no reason for her not to give us her DNA."

"You're forgetting one thing," Brian said.

"What's that?"

"I don't trust you."

"Now you're just hurting my feelings."

"Once we give you our DNA, what's to stop you from planting it on something from his apartment?"

"Well, when the prosecutor files the case, he signs off on it," I said. "You know, swearing to tell the truth, the whole truth, all of that. Besides, you're kinda missing the point. We don't work on commission. We have no reason to pin this thing on you just because you're a scumbag. Which obviously you are. We're interested in nailing you if you did it. That's all."

"You telling me you don't lie all the time to frame someone for a crime they didn't commit?"

"Like that time we arrested you for DUI when you hadn't been drinking? Or for smashing in Austin's car when you didn't do that, either?"

He was shaking his head like there's no point even talking to someone as stupid as me. "You know how to make the evidence say whatever the fuck you want it to say."

"Okay, Brian, you think what you want to think. I'm not gonna spend any more time talking about how cops fabricate evidence. My partner and I came here to ask you and Tiffany for your DNA. I'll just tell my chief you said no. Okay?"

He nodded.

"And how about you, Tiffany? We gonna make up evidence putting you at Austin Sulenka's apartment?"

She was looking back and forth from me to Brian. She was trying to figure out what to do, but she wasn't thinking fast enough. She seemed like she was going to start crying.

Brian said, "Don't do it, babe. If they had anything on you, they'd have brought you in to the police station. Don't cooperate. They get your DNA, you'll never know what they do with it."

"You know I wasn't there, babe," she said. "You know I was home. Let me just give them the DNA and it'll be over."

He folded his arms over his chest and half turned away from her. Now she started to cry and rushed over to him, putting her hands on his meaty forearms. "You know I wasn't there," she said between the tears. "They can't say I was there if I wasn't. Please, babe."

He jerked his arms, breaking her grip on him. He didn't say anything. And at that moment, I knew she was going to go along with him.

She turned to me, wiping the tears away. "You know I didn't kill him. I can't give you the DNA." She walked back into the living room and collapsed onto the couch, her head in her hands.

"All right, Ryan, let's go," I said. "We gotta figure out where Brian was late Sunday night." I walked over to the couch. Tiffany heard me come over and looked up. "You, too, Tiffany. Sunday night. Around midnight."

Tiffany was crying, out of control, as Ryan and I walked past Brian and left the apartment.

"Well," I said as we walked down the steps. The air was cool and dry. It was going to be a nice day. "That didn't get us anywhere, did it?"

"How do you mean?" Ryan said.

"Ten minutes ago, we didn't know whether Tiff and Bri had anything to do with killing Austin. And now, ten minutes later, we still don't know."

"True," Ryan said, "but like the chief said, the point was to put the game in play. Which I think we did."

"What do you expect is gonna happen next?"

He smiled as we got in the Charger. "I haven't had quite enough time to figure it out, Karen."

I turned the engine over, and we buckled our belts.

"It appears Tiffany is more frightened of losing Brian than she is of us," Ryan said.

"Yeah," I said. "I got that."

"So nothing happens next. Brian's happy because he persuaded Tiffany not to cooperate with us. Tiffany's happy because she's persuaded Brian that she's not hiding anything from him. Nothing happens until we get the forensics from Robin. If it turns out Brian was over at Austin's place, we arrest him, question the both of them, and we'll know who killed Austin from who decides to deal with us first."

"But if we can't connect Brian to it," I said, "that still doesn't tell us whether Tiffany was freelancing. Her DNA will be all over his apartment—and his dick. She could have fallen in love with Austin, found out he betrayed her in a particularly humiliating way, and strangled him."

"That's very true," Ryan said.

I pulled over to the curb. "Doesn't that bother you?"

"That she might have fallen in love with a guy like Austin?"

"No, Holmes," I said. "That we can't tell if Tiffany killed him."

Ryan turned to me and smiled. "Not particularly. Look at it this way, Karen. Do you think we're dealing with a serial killer?"

"What?"

"I asked you a simple question: Do you think whoever killed Austin is going to kill again?"

"Like, guys with big dicks start dying left and right?"

"Well, it could be guys with big dicks, or guys who sleep with girls in their classes, or guys who are writing theses about Edgar Allan Poe. Don't get hung up on his big dick. I'm asking you an abstract question. Do you think whoever killed Austin is going to kill again because of some characteristic Austin shared with other potential victims, or do you think it was personal: the killer wanted Austin to die?"

"Why do you do this to me, Ryan?"

He laughed. "Okay, so you think it was personal. The killer wanted Austin to die for some reason."

I just looked at him.

"That's what I think, too, Karen. You see my point?"

"No," I said. "I didn't realize you had a point. Should I expect it soon?"

"It's really very simple. If the killer were going to kill again, the fact that we didn't get any closer to determining if the killer was Tiffany Rhodes would be disappointing."

"Because we're giving her more time to kill again."

"That's right. But if you think the killer wanted to kill only Austin, the time element is not crucial, unless we're concerned that the murderer is going to leave town—and head for Billings, for instance. But that doesn't worry me. We'd track her down in Billings."

"How about the city's resources? Doesn't it bother you if the city of Rawlings spends more time catching the killer?"

"Only if it costs the city more than it should have cost— because we made some mistakes, for example. But since we're on salary, if it takes us three days rather than two days, it probably won't cost the city an extra dime."

"All right, how about this: wouldn't you rather arrest the killer today rather than tomorrow. You know, just to be done with it?"

"Well," he said, tapping his chin, "I guess there is some value in showing the citizenry that we're extremely good at what we do."

"It improves their confidence in us?"

"Exactly," Ryan said. "But just between you and me, I'd rather it go three days than two."

"Why is that?"

"Because it's fun," he said. "Plus, we get to have more chats like this one."

I just shook my head. "All in all, I think I'd rather be talking to Brian."

He laughed. "You've got a crush on me. You know you do. Admit it."

"You're delusional, you know that?"

"We'll get her—whoever she is. Or he. But you have to let the case develop at its own speed. You have to let it unfold—"

"If you say 'like a flower,' I swear you're off the case." I put the blinker on and headed back into traffic.

"Like a delicate flower."

Chapter 14

"I think you might find this interesting, Karen." Harold Breen lumbered toward me as Ryan and I walked into his lab. Robin, the Evidence Tech, was on the other side of the lab, studying a folder.

"What's that, Harold?" I kept my distance. Not from Harold. From Austin Sulenka, resting in peace on the steel table.

"Asphyxia was one of the first therapies suggested for erectile dysfunction."

"You strangle yourself to get wood?"

"Executioners noticed that a lot of guys who were hanged got an erection, and some of them even orgasmed. Further study showed that this type of orgasm wasn't exactly what asphyxiophiles are looking for—"

"What did you just say?"

"An asphyxiophile is someone who likes to get strangled to achieve greater sexual pleasure. As I was saying, when guys orgasmed when they were hanged, it was due to a complete muscle relaxation, which is not what happens with the sex games, but that's when scientists first made the connection between asphyxia and sexual pleasure."

I wish people would stop trying to educate me. "So how did Austin Sulenka die?"

"Austin died of hypoxia. Too little oxygen. The carotid arteries, on either side of the neck, were constricted, reducing the blood flow to the brain. The brain died, which made the rest of him die."

"Is there any doubt about the medical cause of death?"

Harold shook his head. "No, it was clear." He thought for a moment. "Let me say that better. The proximate cause was hypoxia, the loss of oxygen to the brain. This was caused probably by a combination of two ultimate causes: asphyxia and ischemia. When he was strangled, he was asphyxiated. No air into his lungs. But he also suffered ischemia, the loss of blood flow to the brain. I don't know if it's possible to determine the causality, in terms of whether the blood wasn't carrying enough oxygen when it got to the brain or whether the blood was sufficiently oxygenated but couldn't get to the brain."

"But in terms of what killed him?"

"In terms of what killed him, he died because his brain didn't get enough oxygen because someone strangled him."

"You're sure of that?"

"One-hundred percent." He walked over to the body on the table. He pulled back the sheet covering Austin's body and pointed to his neck. "These little red marks around his neck, the petechiae, are burst capillaries caused by physical pressure. When I open up his neck, I'm going to see bruising and trauma to the neck. Probably damage to the voicebox, too, and the hyoid bone."

"Is this murder, suicide, or an accident?" I said.

"I'm just telling you the mechanism of death. Robin can talk about the manner."

"It's homicide," she said.

I stood there, waiting for her to say more. "I appreciate your conciseness."

"You want more?"

"If you don't mind."

"Every year in the U.S., about five-hundred people, maybe as many as a thousand, mostly guys, die from accidental strangulation. They're jerking off, they've got ropes or cords, or they put plastic bags on their heads, or they suck chemicals from a spray can. The loss of oxygen and the build-up of carbon dioxide in the brain cause a semi-hallucinogenic state that increases the intensity of the orgasm. Guys who are really into it say it's as good as cocaine, and just as addictive."

"So it could've been an accident. You said it was homicide." I was getting a little impatient.

"Absolutely. Even though guys set up all kinds of escape mechanisms, the fact that they're flying solo means that sometimes they lose consciousness and can't activate them."

"But you didn't find any bags or cords or spray cans, right?"

"True, but one of the things that happens a lot is that the scene is disturbed post-mortem. Someone comes in, sees the corpse, and removes the paraphernalia. That's possible here."

"All right. Let's go through this. Could it be suicide?"

"Intentional? Very unlikely. Guys who do this are trying to feel pleasure. They're not trying to kill themselves. If he wanted to kill himself, he'd drive his car into a tree or take a handful of pills."

"But with Austin, if it was an accident, someone came by later and removed the evidence."

"Yeah," Robin said. "And trashed the living room."

"That's why you like homicide."

"Not really," Robin said. "I don't know who trashed the living room or why, but I like homicide because of the vaginal fluids on the sheets and on his dick and on the dildo."

"He wasn't alone when he died."

"That's my guess. It's possible he drilled a couple girls earlier that evening, then decided he needed to get his rocks off again, which he did with autoasphyxia, killing himself by mistake, then someone came by later and removed the plastic bag and any fetish outfits he was wearing."

"What?"

"Gaspers don't put a produce bag over their heads and jerk off into a couple of tissues. They make a whole evening out of it, complete with role playing and costumes. They're Nazi storm troopers with riding crops or Princess Leia or Batman. You know, they get into it."

"Actually, I don't know, but I appreciate the information. Okay, so someone could've cleaned up the bedroom and removed his Catholic schoolgirl uniform. And then decided to trash the living room, for good measure," I said.

"Sure, just to give you something else to figure out." She smiled. "The reason I think Austin was murdered is that his dick was covered in vaginal fluid. Plus the sticky dildo. I know he was a young guy and all, so he could have teed it up probably four or five times a night, but if he was nailing one or more women, I don't see him yanking it himself afterwards. With that face and body—and that package—if he was yanking it, he was one sick dude. My bet: someone else—or several someone elses—wanted him dead. He was already in bed or they got him into bed, then they strangled him."

"Okay, Robin, thanks very much for all that," I said. "What do the forensics say?"

She looked down at the clipboard in her hands. "I've got two sets of forensics: prints and DNA. I collected and ran forty-two sets of prints—"

"Forty-two?"

"Yeah, well, he wasn't exactly a neat freak, and he had a lot of people over," Robin said. "There were eleven different sets of prints—full and partial—on various wine glasses and dishes. Plus prints all over the kitchen and on the bathroom counter and toilet handle. Total: twenty-seven different people left their prints in that place."

"Please tell me you got Brian Hawser."

She shook her head. "I'll tell you that if you want, but either he was never in that apartment or he was wearing gloves."

"Shit," I said.

"One semi-interesting thing: there were no prints at all on the doorknob, on the inside or the outside."

"No usable prints?" I said.

"No, it was wiped clean, with a cloth or something. The last person who left the place didn't want us to read her prints."

"Or wanted us to think we could identify her prints," I said.

Robin just shrugged. The gesture said "whatever."

"So," I said, "with forty-two sets of prints, twenty-seven different people, you don't have anything for us?"

"You say it like that, makes me feel you don't respect my work." She put on a pouty face. "You understand I ran all twenty-seven through every database I've got. It's not really my fault Austin Sulenka wasn't screwing someone in the database."

I rolled my eyes at her. "And the DNA?"

"I got one guy: Austin Sulenka. He was coming all over the place, especially in his bedroom, but also in a couple places in the living room, on the carpet and on the couch. But he's the only guy I could identify—from his own DNA. There were three other male ejaculate samples I could retrieve, but I can't tell you who they were."

"Females?"

"He screwed at least two different women on his last night on Earth."

"What do you mean 'at least two'?"

"I got two sets of epithelial cells off his dick. Two women. But I think there were others he might've showered off."

"Can you give me any names?"

"No, I can't. No match in any of the databases for either of the samples."

"Why do you think there were others?"

"Austin had two sets of sheets: one on the bed, one in a closet near the bathroom. The sheets on his bed had markers for four different females. One of them was a real squirter."

I sighed. "Should I ask?"

"I was kind of hoping." Robin gave me a big smile. "A small number of women, maybe ten percent, tops, ejaculate when they orgasm. We think the fluid is produced by the Skene's gland, which is an itty-bitty thing near where the urethra enters the vagina."

"Can you tell me who the real squirter is?" I said.

Robin shook her head. "Sorry. The female ejaculate is mostly acid and water. It doesn't have any DNA in it."

"Robin." I was trying to be as patient as possible. "Why are you telling me about the squirter, then?"

"Well, I thought if you found out that one of your suspects was a real squirter, chances are she was the squirter at Austin's."

"How would I find that out, Robin?"

"That could be a number of ways. It can scare the shit out of the woman or the guy she's with. So maybe it came up in one of your interviews. Or you could see it when you're doing an interview."

"It's visible on the sheets?"

"It sure is, although it's easier to see under UV light."

"Well, that's very helpful—"

"But mostly I just wanted you to know about it because it's cool." She gave me a big smile. "It's called she-jaculation."

"All right, Robin," I said. "This has been very educational. To summarize, we are now certain that Austin Sulenka was present in his own apartment." I turned to Ryan. "Let's go." I turned to the Medical Examiner. "Thanks, Harold."

Ryan and I started walking out of Harold's lab.

"Kathy Caravelli," Robin said.

I stopped and turned. "Excuse me."

"I said 'Kathy Caravelli.'"

I walked over to her and touched her upper arm. "Robin, why did you say Kathy Caravelli?"

"She's the one who likes the black dildo."

"Who is she?"

"She's an artist. Downtown. She used to be in the Air Force. Airman First Class, Retired."

"She left some DNA on the dildo?"

"She was shedding epithelial cells like crazy that night. And a couple of pubes."

"Can you tell me how she spells her name?"

Robin handed me a sheet of paper.

"Just to be sure I've got this, Kathy wasn't one of the women riding his dick?"

"I can't say, but I didn't find her DNA on his dick."

"But you can't rule her out," I said.

"There were condoms all over the apartment. You can't rule out anyone. I'm fairly sure it wasn't me." She cocked her head and raised an eyebrow, like I should think hard about where I was Sunday night.

"As always, Robin, a pleasure to talk with you."

She offered me her big white smile. "You're welcome, Karen."

Chapter 15

I phoned the Air Force Personnel Center at Randolph Air Force Base in Texas, which is the information center for discharged Air Force personnel. After spending twelve minutes falling off quite a few branches on their phone tree, being shuttled from one wrong office to another and hearing many, many Air Force recruitment jingles that didn't make me want to enlist, not even a little bit, I was pleased when a female human got on the line.

I explained why sending a written request for Kathy Caravelli's service records had its disadvantages when you're trying to work a murder case. The woman listened, thought about it some, and settled for taking my contact information and the name of my police department so she could look it up and see if I exist. We ended the call, me thanking her profusely three times for her willingness to do something she obviously wasn't required to do. Thirty seconds later I got an e-mail from her, with a copy of Kathleen Caravelli's service records attached.

Kathy Caravelli did her training in helicopter maintenance and repair at Robins Air Force Base in Georgia. She served two tours in Iraq, one in maintenance and one in standby search-and-rescue. In February 2010, she received a Purple Heart for injuries sustained while participating in a rescue mission near Tikrit in which her helicopter was hit by enemy fire. She was separated from the United States Air Force in 2010 with the rank of Airman First Class.

"Listen to this, Ryan," I said. "'The Sikorsky Pave Hawk helicopter was hit by an aerial improvised explosive device, which showered the helicopter with metal shards. The rear rotor disabled, the helicopter was forced into a hard landing, killing two wounded soldiers who had just been evacuated from a forward operating base, and injuring AFC Caravelli and two other Air Force airmen.'"

"Does it say how badly she was injured?"

I scanned the report. "She broke her back. Airlifted to Germany, then to the U.S., where she did three months of rehab. She received two service decorations."

"Pretty impressive," Ryan said.

"What do you have on her?"

"She is the proprietor of Caravelli Fine Arts Studio, which is located out on Amberson. Her personal Facebook account shows she's in a relationship with May Eberlein."

"Whoa. Our May?"

"That's what it says," Ryan said. "Let me see if May's page shows her in that same relationship." He clicked around some. "May's got her information shielded from everyone but her friends."

"What exactly does 'being in a relationship' mean, anyway?"

"I guess it can mean whatever you want it to," he said, "but I thought it meant a romantic relationship."

"Wanna take a drive out to Amberson?"

"Sometimes you ask such silly questions, Karen." He grabbed his suit jacket off the back of his chair and slid it on, picked up his cane, and off we went.

Amberson Parkway is a four-lane, mixed commercial and residential, although these days it's a lot more commercial than residential. It's full of businesses that couldn't afford the rent downtown. There were a mom-and-pop pawn shop, a small tailor shop, and a couple of payday-loan joints, as well as businesses that need a little space, like RV places and a small used-car dealer whose selling point is "no credit no problem."

Nestled among these ragtag businesses was Caravelli Fine Arts Studio. We pulled into the lot, which was really just a dirt driveway partially covered with pea gravel in front of a fifty-year-old two-story clapboard house that could've used a coat of paint. Off to the side was an unattached two-car garage with the Caravelli Fine Arts Studio sign above the garage door. The garage was ringed with scruffy shrubs and scraggly plains grasses. The garage door, including the row of windows near the top and the handle someone once used to raise and lower it, was painted grey, like the rest of the garage. Next to the big grey door was an entry door with a hand-painted "Come In" sign on it. A little bell jangled as we opened the door.

The floor was plywood, almost completely covered in dried paint drips. The walls were lined with cheap do-it-yourself shelving of all different makes and materials, attached to the studs in the garage. The shelves sagged under the stacked paint cans, piles of wood stripping, rolls of canvas, and assorted crapola: hubcaps, busted bird feeders, wheels from wheel barrows or tricycles, all kinds of plastic, metal, wood, and concrete junk. I couldn't tell if Kathy was a hopeless packrat or she was going to use this stuff in her art projects.

Ryan and I followed a jagged path through tables overflowing with painting materials, jars of brushes, and plastic bins filled with putty knives, spray cans, squeegies, plastic bottles, rollers, and busted picture frames. We made it into the center of the garage floor, which was illuminated by a couple of big skylights. The plywood sheeting on the uninsulated garage roof was stained by watermarks leading down from the corners of the skylights. In the middle of the floor was a large easel, holding a painting maybe four feet by three. Kathy Caravelli looked up as she heard us walking toward her.

She was about thirty-five, with short-cropped brown hair with a patch of grey right in the middle, above her broad forehead. She wore silver-rimmed round eyeglasses that looked military issue. Her purple tee shirt and blue denim overalls were baggy and paint-covered. She brushed at her face with the back of her hand, smearing some blue paint on her cheek in the process. "Hey," she said. No smile.

"Are you Kathy Caravelli?" I said. She nodded. "I'm Detective Karen Seagate, Rawlings Police Department. My partner, Detective Ryan Miner."

She looked at Ryan, then back at me. She nodded. "I guess this is about Austin?" She put down a thick brush on a table next to her easel and faced us, hands on her hips.

I glanced at the painting she was working on. It was full of dark blues and black and red, with big, broad strokes. It was definitely a painting of a horse. Or maybe a building or a bowl of fruit. Whatever it was, it was pissed.

"Yeah, we're investigating the murder of Austin Sulenka," I said. "We were hoping you could help us with his relationship with his girlfriend, May Eberlein." The way her mouth turned down at the edges told me she wasn't thrilled by my choice of topics. "Can you tell us how well you know May?" I'd decided not to ask her directly about her Facebook thing about being in a relationship with her. In general, it's best to come off as dumb and unprepared. Gives them a little more room to start lying to us.

"She's a friend." Kathy scratched at her shoulder. "I met May about a year ago. I had this exhibit at one of the galleries downtown."

Out of the corner of my eye I saw Ryan drift off toward some handmade wooden racks holding canvases stacked upright like books on a shelf. The canvases were stapled onto wooden frames.

I didn't say anything. Kathy took this as a cue to say some more. "She stopped by during one of those First Thursday nights in the summer," she said. "She liked some of my paintings, we started talking. We struck up a friendship."

Ryan walked over, carrying a canvas about four feet wide and two feet tall. It showed a nude woman stretched out on a blanket in front of a riverbank. It looked like the Rawlings River, the same kind of shrubs and trees in the background, although I don't know any place on the river where you can get nude like that for a couple hours without drawing some attention.

Especially if you looked like the woman in the painting. She was young, early twenties, with long, thin limbs and medium dark hair. All she had on were big gold hoop earrings and pink lipstick. Her expression was hard to read. She didn't look happy or unhappy. I'd call it uncomfortable. She was lying on her side, one arm up, her hand supporting her head. Her other arm was draped over her stomach. Her breasts were good-sized for such a thin girl. Her nipples were a medium brown, and the pubic hair was shaved into a thin line. If it was a mugshot with the person's name on it, it couldn't have been more obvious: it was May Eberlein.

"Is this part of your friendship?" Ryan said.

She turned to him. "She's sat for me a number of times. If you've seen her, you understand why any artist would want to have her as a model."

"Are you in a sexual relationship with May Eberlein?"

"I don't see how that's any business of yours." She shifted her weight and crossed her arms in front of her chest.

"Kathy, let's be clear about what's going on here," I said. "We didn't stop by for a friendly chat, and we have no interest in your personal life. Reason my partner asked that question is it has something to do with the Austin Sulenka case. You gonna answer the question now, or you wanna go to police headquarters and sit in a metal cage for six or eight hours, then answer it?"

"Yes."

"'Yes' you're gonna answer it, or 'yes' you're in a sexual relationship with May Eberlein?"

"May and I are lovers."

"So May is bisexual."

She looked annoyed. "My relationship with her is recreational. We get together sometimes. We have sex. But we're not BFFs. What she does with other guys or women—I really don't know, and I really don't care. I'm not into labels, and I'm not into possession."

"You ever have a three-way with May and Austin?"

"Yes."

"Sunday night, at his apartment?"

"Yes."

"Around what time?"

"I'd say, maybe eight to ten."

"Did you and May go over to Austin's place together?"

"No, she was already there when I got there. Like I said, around eight."

"Do you know when she got there?"

Kathy shook her head. "That didn't come up."

"You know if May and Austin had already had sex when you got there?"

"She was wearing a tee shirt, looked like it could've been his. No bra. And panties. So maybe they'd already screwed. He was in a bathrobe. Can't tell what that means. Maybe he'd just taken a shower. Or maybe he thinks he's Hugh Hefner."

"So the three of you had sex."

"Yeah, that's right." She paused, jutting out her chin. "You want the details? You know, what parts went into what holes?"

"Maybe some other time." I thought for a second. "So you finished up around, what? Nine? Ten?"

"I don't know. Nine, ten. I didn't notice the time."

"You and May leave together?"

"No, we had our own cars. I left. The two of them were still there."

"What did the apartment look like when you left?"

She looked at me, confused. "Just like it looked when I got there. Wine bottles, glasses, dishes on the counter. Is that what you mean?"

"Yeah," I said. "So you partied in the bedroom?"

"Mostly."

"Okay, so you left. Did anyone see you leave?"

"No idea."

"Where'd you go then?"

She swept her palm out to tell me she was here. "I did some painting."

"Ten o'clock at night?"

"Why not? Sex clears my head, frees me up. I paint at night all the time."

"Can anyone put you here ten o'clock Sunday night?"

"I live alone."

"Did you hear from May or Austin after you left that night?"

She shook her head.

"You know why anyone would want to hurt Austin?"

She thought for a moment. "I didn't really know Austin that well. I'm sure there's some things he did must've pissed someone off—"

"Such as?"

"No idea. I'm just saying people piss other people off. But my relationship with him was pretty straightforward. I never partied with him alone. Only with him and May. I know he was a grad student, like May. But we didn't do a lot of talking, if you know what I mean."

"Since you were friends with May, maybe you could read something in their relationship?"

"You'd have to ask her."

"What were they doing when you left Sunday night?"

She thought a moment, half closing her eyes. "When I left Sunday night, I think he had his tongue in her pussy."

Chapter 16

"Can you tell me if May Eberlein is teaching or in class?"

Now that the news of Austin Sulenka's murder was a day old, the chirpy secretary had dialed back her enthusiasm by at least half. Now she was the loyal, efficient problem-solver. She opened a three-ring binder and shuffled around in the pages. "She's got office hours. In the bullpen."

I put my palms out.

"Sorry." She pointed toward the stairwell in the corner of the building. "Room 103."

"Thanks," I said. Ryan and I headed downstairs for our second chat with the very attractive May Eberlein.

The bullpen was a big, long room full of cubicles, with an aisle going down the middle. Like a corporate setting, but shabbier, and with more posters of Che Guevara, Pee Wee Herman, and Jay-Z than you see in a typical IBM cube farm. Half the cubicles were empty. In a few of the others, grad students were working or wasting time at their computers. May Eberlein was talking to a student. They were leaning over a printout of a paper, May sitting at her steel desk, the student, a Hispanic girl, on a cheap plastic chair pulled up next to May's.

May looked up and recognized me. Her eyes darted to the side to see if she could make out Ryan's shape through the wavy glass partition that separated her cube from the center aisle.

She didn't see Ryan because I'd left him in back in the hall. I
wanted to lead this next interview to amp up the unpleasantness
for her.

Her expression said this was a really bad turn of events. "I'll
… uh … I'll be right with you." She pointed to the printout on
the desk. "I'm in conference. It'll just be a few more minutes."
She gave me what passed for her minimal official smile, but she
was too young and too good-looking to smile in a hostile way. It
was one of the things I could teach her.

I nodded my head, turning to walk out of the bullpen.

"She in there?" Ryan said when I got over to him.

"Oh, yeah. She'll be right out."

"She phoning an attorney?"

"No," I said. "She's 'in conference.' Talking to a student."

"There's no back door, right?"

I smiled. "I think we should take her in for this one. What do
you think?"

"I would." He nodded. "If Kathy Caravelli wasn't making the
whole story up, we've got at least two or three different motives
for May or Kathy to throttle him. We need to get a little better
read on these two women."

The Hispanic girl came out of the bullpen and started walking
down the hall. "That's her student," I said softly.

A moment later, May stepped into the hall. She squared her
shoulders, put on a bland smile, and walked over to us. She was
wearing black leather boots, with a moderate heel, cranberry jeans,
and a white cotton blouse with a ruffled neckline. I recognized
her gold hoop earrings from Kathy's painting. "Detectives," she
said, nodding to me and then to Ryan. "I'm sorry," she said, "I've
forgotten your names."

"Seagate," I said, thumb to my chest. "And Miner. We need
to talk. Now."

She looked at her watch. "I still have office hours for another forty-five minutes."

"No, you don't." I pointed my chin toward her cube in the bullpen. "Leave a note on the glass."

She walked back in. Even when she was off her game, she walked tall, with long strides, like she was on a runway.

"You're a meanie," Ryan said to me.

She was back in twenty seconds.

"We need to talk to you again. About Austin Sulenka."

She looked back toward the bullpen. "It's not that private in there. Could we go someplace—"

"Go back and get your things, May. We know someplace private."

This time, she came out with her bag and a jacket slung over her arm. Her expression was a blank.

"Let's go," I said, leading her by the elbow.

We made it out to the Charger. Ryan opened the rear door for her and got her in the back seat, pushing her head down so she wouldn't bump it, which I thought was a nice touch. Nobody said anything as we drove to headquarters.

I carded us in at the rear entrance. We walked down the hall toward the two interview rooms. I looked through the window on Interview 1, which we used for interrogations. It was empty. I walked in first, followed by May and Ryan. I motioned for her to sit at the table, then took a chair opposite her.

Her eyes followed Ryan as he walked over to the video controls on the wall. She picked hard at a cuticle. We had her attention.

I spoke the identifying information: the time and the names of the people in the room. "Ms. Eberlein." The last name added to the chill in the room. "Where were you Sunday night, around ten PM?"

"I told you this yesterday." She sounded annoyed. "I was at home. Preparing for my Monday classes."

I sat there, silently. Staring straight at her, I counted to ten. "Ms. Eberlein, I am very aware we asked you this yesterday. I remember it very clearly, and Detective Miner took notes." I paused again. "What do you think it means that I'm asking you again?"

She didn't say anything, but she looked down at her hands on the table.

"I'll answer my own question. It means, if you lie to us one more time, I will arrest you for the murder of Austin Sulenka."

She flinched and looked up at me. "That can't be. No."

"Yes," I said. "Lie to me. Watch it happen." She sat there, and a tear rolled down her face. "Take a moment," I said. "Think it through. This is your last chance to get it right."

There we sat, the three of us, our hands folded on the battered steel table with a set of long bars, one on each end. A set of cuffs was attached to each bar.

May swallowed. "I was with Austin that night."

"Thank you, Ms. Eberlein." I paused. "Was there anybody else there with the two of you?"

She closed her eyes and held them shut for a moment. "Kathy Caravelli was there with us."

"What were the three of you doing?" She looked at me, then at Ryan, then back at me. "Don't mind him," I said. "He's not even paying attention."

"We were getting together," she said.

"Getting together?" I raised an eyebrow. "Can you be more specific?"

"Do I have to?"

"Depends. When would you like to go home?"

She looked at me. "We were drinking," she said. "White wine. I had sex with Kathy and then with Austin."

"You had sex with Kathy, then you had sex with Austin?"

She was crying with both eyes now, and she was blushing. "That's what I said." Her voice was soft.

"When we interviewed you yesterday—you told us you were preparing your classes—did you lie because you're embarrassed by the sex?"

"Obviously, I'm uncomfortable talking about it. But I lied because I didn't want to implicate either myself or Kathy."

"If neither of you killed him, how would it implicate you?"

She shook her head. "I don't know. I just know that I didn't kill him and that Kathy didn't kill him."

"Tell me how you know that."

"I know that because Kathy left his place about ten-thirty, and I left about eleven. And when I left, he was very much alive." She looked up at me. "That's how I know."

"Problem I'm having is, you can't really prove it. Nobody saw him alive after that. And you do, you know, lie."

"I'm not lying now. Kathy didn't kill him. Neither did I. Why would either of us want to kill him?"

"That's a really good question. But first I want to make sure I understand what you say happened. Let's start with the three-way, which, as you explain it, was really a couple of two-ways. Tell us again about the sex."

"Kathy and I had sex. Austin watched. Then Austin and I had sex."

"How did that work?"

"I don't understand your question."

"Kathy's bisexual, no?"

"No." She shook her head. "Kathy's a lesbian."

"She didn't have sex with you and Austin?"

"That's right. She had sex with me. Austin watched. Then Kathy watched me and Austin having sex." She paused. "That's how I know she couldn't kill Austin."

I was confused. "She couldn't kill him because she didn't have sex with him?"

"She couldn't kill him because she couldn't touch him. She found him repulsive."

"She couldn't overcome her repulsion just once—just enough to strangle him?"

She shook her head. "Not even once."

"Okay, so you and Kathy go at it. Any toys?"

She looked at me. "Austin had this … this thing."

"A big black dildo, with a strap?"

She nodded, her eyes focused on the battered steel tabletop.

"Ms. Eberlein, you're one of three people nude in a room. You fuck her while he watches. Then you fuck him while she watches. And you're too refined to say the word *dildo*?"

She looked at me, and for the first time I saw an honest emotion. If I had to name it, I'd say hatred. Which was a little unfair, seeing as it wasn't me put her in that bedroom.

"So, Austin got off watching you screw Kathy with your black dildo."

She said, "Do you want me to respond?"

"Yes, please," I said. "Is it true that Austin knew Kathy didn't want to have anything to do with him, but he got off watching you two anyway?"

"That's correct," May said. "Austin didn't want to have sex with Kathy, but he liked to watch. If you're curious about how I know that he liked to watch, he got an erection. And sometimes he masturbated while he watched us." She brushed her hair back behind her ear. If I wanted details, she'd give me details.

"And Kathy liked to watch you and Austin?"

"Yes. She would masturbate with the dildo while she watched. Austin also had a vibrator. A small one, with batteries. Sometimes she would use that at the same time."

"All right, Ms. Eberlein. Thank you for that information. Now, let's turn to what happened after all the sex. You say Kathy left around ten-thirty, correct?"

"Yes."

"Why did she leave? You said you and Austin had sex. Didn't Kathy want to stay for that?"

"She and Austin got in a fight. He called her a dyke. Said she was pathetic. That sort of thing."

"I don't get it. She already found him repulsive. So he called her names. Why would that upset her?"

May Eberlein got up and walked over to the wall with the big one-way mirror. She stood there, looking at her reflection in the glass, her back turned to me and Ryan. "It was because of me. I didn't stop him. I just let him say that stuff."

"You didn't defend her."

"That's right," May said. "I was planning to stop seeing her— tell her she couldn't hang with me and Austin anymore—"

"Wait a second. You used to see Kathy on your own? Just the two of you?"

"Not that much anymore. It started with me sitting for her. But I didn't want to do that anymore. It had run its course."

"So you didn't say anything to Austin when he started calling her names."

"I thought it was the kindest way to tell Kathy this had to stop."

"By calling her a dyke?"

May nodded. "I'm not an idiot. I understood it was cruel. But Kathy was in way too far. With me, I mean. I thought it would be best to get her to, you know, see me like she saw Austin." She turned and faced me.

"So how would you describe Kathy's actions when she left Austin's apartment?"

May came back to the table and sat down. She put her head in her hands. "She was crying. She ran out of the apartment, slammed the door. I looked out the window. She was running toward her car."

"Did she say anything when she left?"

"She called us assholes, said we deserved each other.'"

"Did you say anything to her?"

May shook her head. "No."

"Did Austin?"

"He laughed at her."

"Do you think she heard Austin laughing at her?"

"I don't know." She closed her eyes. "Might've."

"Then you and Austin had sex?"

She nodded.

I turned to Ryan. "Do you have any questions for Ms. Eberlein."

Ryan was sitting there, his head bowed. "No."

"Would you get an officer to drive Ms. Eberlein back to campus?"

Ryan nodded, stood up, and left the interview room.

I announced the time and stated that we were concluding the interview. Then I walked over to the video controls and shut the system down, glad to be done, at least for the moment, with the lovely Ms. Eberlein. We'd finally gotten her to tell the truth about who was fucking who, but she was still lying. She wanted us to believe she acted like a bitch to Kathy to make Kathy hate her. That was bullshit. I think May acted like a bitch because she was a bitch.

Chapter 17

"You in there, partner?" I said.

Ryan was sitting next to me in Interview 1, hands on the table, fingers interlaced, tapping his thumbs together slowly. A couple seconds went by, then he looked up at me. "I'm here, Karen," he said softly. "Just barely."

"What is it?" I said. "All that talk about screwing make you uncomfortable?"

"What's wrong with those people?"

"Well, one of them was strangled, so he's dead." Ryan looked at me, his expression as close to disdain as I've ever seen on him. "The two women?" I exhaled, my palms up in the air. "No idea what's going on with them."

"I understand," he said. "You're young, you're trying to figure things out. Who you are, who you want to be with—"

"Whether you're straight or gay."

"Whatever," he said. "I'm fine with all that. But these three—there doesn't seem to be any relationship between sex and love at all. I mean, it's almost like they're using sex as a weapon against each other." He sighed. "Am I totally missing something?"

"You know, Ryan, if you want to understand what these folks are up to, I think you're talking to the wrong person. But it's possible—technically, it's possible—that there's some kind of … I don't know, some sort of love or maybe affection or kindness, some type of hunger for closeness or something. Listen, I can't explain what we're seeing here. All I'm saying is, maybe Kathy really is in love with May. Maybe May was in love with Austin. I really don't know. And Austin? Shit, I have no idea what—if anything—Austin was in love with, except maybe his own reflection in a pool."

"I'm sorry," Ryan said, sitting up straight as if to shake off his mood. "I'm getting off track here, wasting our time. It's not our job to figure out why they live the way they do."

"You're right. We just have to figure out how Austin Sulenka died. We gotta start with the idea that all this screwing is consensual. Whatever else this sex is, it's not rape. So let's just figure out who had a reason to kill him, and take it from there."

Ryan nodded. "This one's going to turn on motive. Since he would apparently screw any woman who'd have him, there was no shortage of opportunity. And means was easy, too: a shirtsleeve would do it. As long as the woman had enough upper-body strength to pull a cinch tight around his neck, she's in play."

"Yeah," I said, "except that we don't know he partied only with women. The waitress next door told us there'd be three couples humping away at one time in the apartment. Who's to say one of those guys didn't throttle him—"

"Because Austin was doing his girl."

"That would be a very conventional attitude." I nodded. "Or Austin was doing a better job of screwing his girl. Boys can be competitive, right?"

"Okay, so how do you read May's latest story?" Ryan said.

"You mean the creepy part about how she'd do Kathy, then she'd do Austin?"

"Leaving the creepiness aside, do you believe it? How Kathy found Austin repulsive?"

"Sure," I said. "Except for that amazing rod, I think I'd find him repulsive, too."

"I mean, when May says that shows Kathy couldn't have killed him."

"Well, no," I said. "That could be May's way of pointing us to Kathy."

"But that doesn't necessarily mean Kathy didn't do it," Ryan said. "It could be May letting us do the detective work."

"Because she can't bring herself to say Kathy did it?"

"May is afraid that Kathy killed him, so she's laying out a motive for us to follow up on."

"Or May killed him," Ryan said, "but she's worried her good looks might be a detriment as she sits in prison the rest of her life."

"Let's not forget Austin nailed the freshman moron around seven. He did May around ten. He died maybe midnight. Plenty of time for one more girl—"

"Or for Tiffany's knuckle-dragging roommate, Brian, to come back and kill him," Ryan said.

"Or Kathy."

We weren't getting anywhere. There were too many people could've killed Austin, too many who might've wanted him dead, too many willing to lie to us.

"Ryan, who drove May back to campus just now?"

"Officer Winthrop. Why?"

"Get her on the radio, would you? Ask her to meet us at our desks when she gets back."

He got up and left Interview 1. I headed down to the break room. It was about eleven-forty, close enough to lunch time. I got the lasagna leftover I'd brought in this morning. I nuked it, watching the time on the little screen count down. I took the plastic out of the microwave, burned my fingertips on it like I do every damn time, and carried it back to my desk.

"Winthrop should be here in a couple of minutes." Ryan was eating a sandwich at his desk. "Want to tell me why you want to talk to her?"

I put down my fork. "I'll tell you if you want. Or I could not tell you." I took a sip of cold coffee left over from when I came in a few hours ago. "Up to you."

Officer Winthrop came walking over to our desks. Ryan smiled. "Guess I'll find out now."

"Debbie," I said, "thanks for coming over." She nodded. "When you drove that tall girl back to campus a couple minutes ago, where'd she tell you to drop her?"

"The parking lot next to the Humanities Building," she said. "Why?"

"Just trying to figure out what she's up to," I said. "Did you notice what kind of car she got into?"

"She just asked me to pull over at the entrance to the lot. I didn't see her get in a car."

"Okay," I said. "Thanks a lot."

"No problem," Officer Winthrop said. She turned and left.

"Well," Ryan said, "I listened, but I don't yet understand."

"Get your jacket," I said. "We're going for a ride. You don't understand women, do you?"

"Apparently not," he said cheerfully as he put his half sandwich back in the baggie and slid it into a side pocket of his jacket.

We left the detectives' bullpen, made our way out to the Charger, and headed over to Amberson Street.

As we turned onto Walnut Street, Ryan said, "She's going to visit Kathy?"

"Of course she is," I said.

"Even though she just told us we ought to be looking at Kathy for strangling Austin?"

"No, *because* she just told us that."

We pulled into the gravel parking area in front of the old grey house, thirty yards from the garage. A fire-engine red Suzuki shitcan was sitting in front of the studio.

"Read the plate and run it, would you?" I said to Ryan. He has really good vision. He pulled his notebook from his jacket pocket, wrote down the plate number, and swiveled the computer toward him. He hit a couple of keys, then a couple more.

"Well, how about that?" he said. "Eberlein, May." He turned and gave me a big smile.

"Want to come with me?" I shut down the cruiser.

"Not sure," he said, putting on a suspicious face. "What do you have in mind?"

"Gonna look at a couple women going at it."

"You're kidding."

"Was I kidding when I told you where May would be headed?" I got out of the cruiser and started walking toward the studio. I looked back and gave him a wave that said, Suit yourself. After a moment, I heard his car door close softly and his footsteps crunching the gravel as he caught up with me.

He started heading toward the entrance door, with the Come In sign on top of it. He stopped when he saw I wasn't walking with him. I shook my head and motioned for him to come with me.

"You're serious," he said when he caught up with me. "You want to look in a window?"

"If you walk in the door, they're not gonna screw, now, are they? Sheesh." I shook my head, making fun of his slow thinking. "And don't crunch the gravel." I led us around toward the east side, where I remembered there was a window.

A scraggly Rose of Sharon sat right in front of the window. On the inside of the window was some steel shelving with paint cans and jars of brushes partially blocking the view. Which would help disguise us.

I brushed the lower branches of the shrub out of the way so I could get in close to the window. I turned back to see what Ryan was up to. He looked conflicted. I know he didn't want to look at the two women, but he also didn't want to miss whatever it was they were doing. After all, it was part of the case.

I waved my hand for him to stop being such a pussy and step up to the window. He shook his head but came up next to me.

The window was smeared with dust, dried dirt, and bird shit, and there were all kinds of spider webs on the inside, but we could easily see Kathy, with her back to us, and May, facing her.

Kathy was frumpy and potato-shaped in her painting clothes. She had her hands on her hips, her head cocked. She looked like a mom listening to her kid explain how the lamp got busted. May was talking with some energy, her hands pumping, palms out in a you-gotta-believe-me gesture.

Then May stopped talking for a moment. Kathy shifted her weight, crossing her arms over her chest. Then they started talking again, first one, then the other. After a minute, their body language softened. Gradually they started to move closer to each other. May put out her hand and touched Kathy's shoulder, seemed to rub it. Kathy looked down at the paint-splattered floor. May reached out her other arm and put it on Kathy's shoulder. She drew the older woman in for a hug.

"I guess I was wrong," I said softly to Ryan. "Here comes the kiss-off. 'I'll always remember the good times the three of us had together. You, me, and the enormous black dildo.'"

The two women were both crying now, wiping at their eyes. May was rubbing Kathy's back. The hug ended as the women pulled back. They were still for the longest while, looking into each other's eyes. Slowly their heads came together, and they kissed.

"I'm not so sure," Ryan said.

The kiss continued. Kathy put her hands on May's hips. Her hands slowly slid up May's sides until she reached her breasts. Kathy began to caress May, who lifted her head and arched her back. Her eyes were closed, her mouth opened. She was beginning to breathe deeply.

Kathy began undoing the buttons on May's blouse. May stood still, her arms at her sides, as Kathy removed the blouse and then reached around behind her to unhook her bra. Kathy let May's blouse and bra drop to the floor.

Kathy unbuckled May's black leather belt and unbuttoned her slacks. Slowly she slid them over May's hips. May put her hands on Kathy's shoulders and lifted one leg, then the other, so Kathy could remove the slacks and her leather boots. May was now nude. Kathy and May kissed again.

"Okay, I'm out," Ryan said, turning and walking toward the Charger. I turned back to the show. Kathy began caressing May's breasts again. Now Kathy was kissing May's neck. Kathy lowered her head and began to kiss May's breasts. May now had her hands on Kathy's shoulders. May's head was back, her eyes closed. She opened her stance. Kathy was kissing May's stomach and her flanks.

I backed away from the window and started walking toward the car. Ryan rolled down his window as I leaned down.

"What are they up to?" he said.

"They're fucking."

"Seems like kind of a complicated relationship."

I shrugged. "Kathy's really into May's body, and May seems to be fine with that. But a relationship? Can't tell if there's any more to it than that."

"What do you want to do now?"

An eighteen-wheeler rumbled past us on Amberson. I waited for the noise to die down. "Let's stay here, wait for May to come out and see us. I want her to know we're looking at her and

Kathy. Eventually May's gonna have to decide which side she's on. She's gotta either give Kathy up or understand that we're coming after her."

"You're assuming they didn't kill Austin together."

I shook my head. "I'm not assuming anything, Ryan."

"Then you want to interview Kathy again?"

"Yeah, I think so. She's infatuated with May—at least that. Whether she'd be willing to kill Austin over it I can't quite tell yet. But we need to put a little more pressure on her, too. Sound good?"

"Well," Ryan said, "if I had a better idea, now's when I'd offer it." He gave me a sad smile.

I nodded, then walked around to the front of the cruiser and hopped onto the hood. I checked my watch. It was just about noon, the sun directly overhead, throwing the tiniest shadow of me onto the black paint on the hood. I looked off toward the garage, where a couple of squirrels were chasing each other around the trunk of an old elm that shaded the roof.

Seventeen minutes later May came walking out of the garage, looking into her big leather bag. She headed in the direction of her red Suzuki. Suddenly, she looked up, saw me, and stopped. We stared at each for a few seconds. She put her bag over her shoulder and started walking over to me. I didn't move.

"What are you doing here?" she said.

"Came to interview Kathy Caravelli. Saw she was busy."

May shook her head. "There's a bell on the door. We didn't hear you."

"That's right," I said. "I didn't come in the door."

"You're a pervert, you know that?"

"I'm a cop." I shrugged my shoulders. "Just trying to figure out who killed Austin Sulenka."

She nodded. "Wasn't me. Wasn't Kathy."

"I'm not sure who it was," I said.

May Eberlein stood there, holding my gaze. "You're never going to be able to prove it was me or Kathy."

"When people say things like that, usually means they're done pretending they didn't do it."

"In this case it means you can't prove it because it didn't happen. You've got Kathy's DNA, but she's admitted she was there with me and Austin. And I've already told you I was there, too. So you don't even need my DNA." She smiled. "If you had any evidence that either Kathy or I killed him, you'd have arrested one of us—or both of us. The fact that you haven't done that?" She tilted her head. "You can't prove it because there's no evidence because it didn't happen. So I suggest you get yourself some lesbian porn, lie back, rub your pussy hard, and leave me and Kathy alone." She pointed her chin to Ryan, sitting in the passenger seat. "Let Clark Kent figure out who killed Austin. He seems less easily distracted than you."

She turned and started walking back to her car.

I got in the driver's seat of the Charger.

"You two have a nice chat?"

I nodded. "She said some hurtful things."

"Really?"

"Suggested I'm a lesbian."

"I bet she attracts a lot of lesbians."

"She's very attractive, but she has a nasty side."

"She give up anything?"

"She did say we'd never prove it was her or Kathy, but then she was quick to point out that it was because neither of them did it."

"Okay, well, you wanted to put some pressure on her. Sounds like you did that."

I nodded. "Let's go talk to Kathy again."

We walked over to the garage, in through the door, and down the jagged junk aisle. Kathy was fully dressed, sitting on a stool in the middle of the lighted rectangle beneath the skylight.

She looked up and recognized me and Ryan. Her expression got cloudy, as if she was trying to figure out if we had just run into May and, if so, what we had said.

"Hi, Kathy," I said. "Got a minute?"

She nodded. She didn't get up from the stool or look around for something for me and Ryan to sit on.

"We wanted to ask you about something May told us."

She motioned with her head toward the door. "You mean just now?"

I shook my head. "We did chat a minute ago, but I mean earlier today. She said what happened the night Austin died is you left real angry. Austin called you a dyke, maybe some other names. You were crying, seeing as how May didn't come to your defense or anything. You called them assholes, said they deserved each other." I paused and looked at her, waiting for her to respond, but she didn't say anything, and her expression was a blank. "Is that what happened?"

"People say things," Kathy said.

"I'm aware of that. I asked you if that's what happened."

"I don't remember. Austin had a big mouth. He might've said some stuff. I might've said some stuff."

"So it wasn't that big a deal?"

"I've had people shooting at me. People calling me a dyke? Not that big a deal."

"Not such a big deal that you'd go back to his place later that night and strangle him?"

Kathy shook her head, giving me a look like I was out of my mind. "Not even close."

"So it wasn't that you realized May was willing to give you up—if she had to make a choice, I mean, between you and Austin?"

"Look at me. I'm a busted-up old lesbian packing fifty extra pounds. No way a woman looks like May is gonna choose me over a guy like Austin. I was a novelty for her. I know that. That's all I was. I got some good paintings out of it. And some good sex. It didn't go anywhere. It's over. May wasn't the first straight chick I screwed. She won't be the last."

"All right," I said. Ryan and I turned and walked out of the garage. After Ryan shut the door behind him, I saw him peel off and head toward the window at the side of the garage. A minute later, he caught up with me.

"What's she up to?"

Ryan walked toward the cruiser. He opened the passenger door and looked at me over the roof of the car. "She's crying. Out of control, curled up on the floor."

Chapter 18

I eased the Charger out into the traffic on the four-lane headed back toward headquarters. Neither of us said anything. We were trying to think of what we could do next.

"How do you read Kathy's crying jag?" Ryan said.

"Well, that's obvious," I said. "She's very upset because we humiliated her when we caught her screwing May at noon in her studio. Or she's very upset because the episode must have humiliated May, who she loves. Or May broke it off with her, and she's therefore very upset. Or saying those things to us about how she knows she can never really get a good-looking woman like May made her realize she's kinda pathetic, so she's very upset."

"Okay, great," Ryan said. "I'm going to write that down. She's very upset."

"Did I miss any other possibilities?"

"I remember once, I was maybe ten, I asked my father about why one of my older sisters was crying. He waved his hand, said something about how it was about a romance. It would be very intense, he told me, but it wouldn't last that long, and there was no sense trying to figure it out."

"Tone's a little sexist, but I think he had the basic story right." I drove a little more. "We've hit a wall, partner. Without any more forensics, there's nothing more we can do."

"Unless someone gets an attack of conscience," Ryan said. "Or thinks there might be more forensics and decides to cut a deal with us."

"I'm not seeing it. Let's set up a board in the incident room and draw some lines. Something might jump out at us."

We got back to headquarters, hung up our coats, and walked over to our desks. "Gather up the photos of the players, will you?"

"Let me just check this message first." Ryan's phone was flashing. He picked it up and started writing on a slip of paper. Then he hit a button and hung up. "It was Jorge. He got authorization to tap into Austin's username and password on Mitto."

"That include his financials?"

"Yup," Ryan said.

"Let's take a quick look now," I said. I wheeled my desk chair over next to Ryan, who was already logging in as Austin.

"He's got an account at TripleXXX.com." Ryan clicked their main page. "That's four dollars a week."

"Next."

"An account with Sunrise Fertility Center."

"He's a sperm donor? You gotta admire his stamina."

"And BioSure Plasma Services." Ryan looked at their site. "He sells them plasma. We'll check it on his bank account."

"Anything else?"

"Something going on at A1-TermPaper.com."

"He's buying his term papers? No wonder he's a dunce."

"We'll see when we look at his bank statement," Ryan said. He tapped the keys some more and got into the bank. "He's got a checking/debit account. No savings account." We both looked down the list for the last year.

"There's his rent," I said, "start of each month. There's his groceries, once a week. Seems normal enough."

"He's not buying term papers. He's selling them."

"Look at that." I looked at all the credits from A1-TermPaper. "There's fourteen payments. Why are some of them forty bucks, some of them eighty?"

"My guess is it's forty dollars per paper. Sometimes he's selling them two at a time." Ryan furrowed his brow. "No way he's got time to write shitty papers."

"He's selling the shitty papers his students are writing." I smiled. "So he's screwing Tiffany two different ways."

"Not just Tiffany. This way he can screw the guys, too."

"What's he got going at Sunrise Fertility Center? That's two hundred a month. They're paying him two hundred to jerk off?"

"That would be to jerk off four times in the month."

"Where you seeing that?"

"That's how I got my first Mitsubishi."

"You wanked your way through college?"

"No, my parents paid the tuition and other expenses. I wanked my way into my first Mitsubishi."

"And Bio Life Plasma Services?"

"Looks like he gets sixty bucks every three or four weeks," Ryan said. "So you don't have to ask, that would be twice a week for the sixty."

"What's this?" I said. "Scroll up a little." Ryan showed me Austin's activity going back a year. "He's donating money to United Cerebral Palsy."

"I see seven hundred bucks in this last year," Ryan said. He ran his finger down the screen. "And four hundred to the Children's Fund at the hospital."

"So he's giving away all the money he's making on the plasma and the sperm, right?"

"That's what it says," Ryan said.

"I didn't see that coming," I said. "We're gonna have to figure out why a grad student who was going noplace was giving money away."

Ryan nodded. "You bet."

"Okay," I said, "let's get our stuff and set up a board in the incident room.

Ryan nodded and slid some folders into his briefcase. We walked over to the incident room, which was just off the main corridor. There were a few old desks, some phones and computers, street maps with pushpins on the walls, and three or four whiteboards on wheels.

Ryan put all his stuff on one of the desks while I wheeled a clean board out so we could work on it. "Give me Austin," I said. Ryan handed me a picture of the victim. I grabbed a roll of tape and taped the photo in the middle of the board. Then I wrote his name in marker on the white border at the bottom of the photo.

"Give me the dumb freshman girl." He passed me a photo of Tiffany Rhodes. I put her off to the side, wrote her name on it, and drew a line connecting the two photos. "And her idiot boyfriend." I taped the photo of Brian Hawser next to Tiffany, connected them with a line, and drew a dotted line between him and Austin Sulenka.

Ryan handed me a photo of May Eberlein. I put her in Austin's orbit and drew a line from her to Austin. Next I put up Kathy Caravelli, connected her to May, and drew a dotted line to Austin.

"Who're the other players?" I said.

Ryan looked down at his notebook. "There's Jonathan Van Vleet, the English chair." I wrote his name off to the side. "Suzannah Montgomery, his adviser." I wrote her name underneath Van Vleet. "Frances Josephine Hamblin, the Melville scholar." I wrote it.

"Anyone else we've interviewed?"

"Melissa Harmon, the new MA."

I wrote her name. "That it?"

"That's all we've got so far." He looked at the board. "Let me draw a timeline."

I handed him the marker. He drew a horizontal line. He made a mark on the left end and wrote a "7." He made another mark, to the right, and wrote "10." Then a third mark, and a "12."

"Okay, he was with Tiffany at seven." He wrote her name above the mark. "We don't have her DNA." He wrote "No DNA" after her name. "Around ten we have May and Kathy." He wrote "No DNA" after May's name. He paused.

"After Kathy's name," I said, "write 'DNA on dildo.'" He paused and looked at me. "Write it down, Miss," I said.

He wrote it, and then wrote "Murder" above the "12." We both looked at the timeline.

"Robin said there were two different sets of DNA on his dick, right?"

"That's right," Ryan said.

"But neither of them is Kathy. So write 'DNA1 and DNA2 on dick' above 'Murder.'"

He shook his head but wrote just what I said. We stood there, looking at the board. "Next to Kathy, change 'DNA on dildo' to 'DNA3 on dildo.'" He did it.

"Since May and Kathy both say May had sex with him around ten, we could say May is DNA1," Ryan said.

"So that means DNA2 is either Tiffany Rhodes—"

"Which means Austin didn't wash up after she left before eight."

"That's right," I said. "Or DNA2 is a fuck buddy we haven't identified yet."

"If we had Tiffany Rhodes' DNA, we'd know the murderer is Tiffany, May, or Kathy—"

"No, we wouldn't," I said. "It could be Brian, the boyfriend. Hell, it could be the waitress next door."

"But we can't even make a list of suspects until we figure out if there's another player we haven't identified yet."

I walked over to the table, picked up the phone, and dialed the chief's office. "Margaret, this is Seagate. Yeah, I'm in the incident room. Could you see if the chief could give us two minutes?" I waited a few seconds. "Terrific," I said. "Yeah, the incident room. Thanks." I hung up.

A minute later, the chief walked in. "What have you got?"

"We need a third set of eyes. Help us see if we're missing something."

"Sure," he said. He waved his hand, telling me to go ahead. I really like that about him. I think he misses working cases.

I walked over to the board and pointed to the horizontal line. "This is Sunday evening. Seven PM, Austin Sulenka is screwing Tiffany Rhodes."

He looked up at the photographs. "She's his student."

"From last semester," Ryan said. He pointed to the picture of the boyfriend. "Brian Hawser knew she was involved with Austin as late as January of this year, but he still doesn't know she was involved with him as late as the night of the murder."

"That's the dotted line?"

"That shows a relationship we don't yet understand," I said. "Brian had the restraining order from trashing Austin's car. Tiffany tells us Brian doesn't know she was still screwing Austin, but maybe the two of them plotted to kill Austin, or maybe they just stumbled into killing him. Or Brian did it on his own, and Tiffany's protecting him."

"But we don't have her DNA? That's what 'No DNA' means?"

"Yeah," I said. "Around ten o'clock, May Eberlein and Kathy Caravelli are over there. Kathy's the lesbian from the Air Force.

May straps on the big black dildo and pokes Kathy. Then May takes off the dildo so Austin can poke her. We've got Kathy's DNA on the dildo, and two other, unidentified sets of girl DNA—"

"On Austin's dick," the chief said, reading off the board. "Presumably, one set is May Eberlein. And the other?"

"That's where we are now, Chief," I said. "Could be Tiffany from earlier, or another girl." We were silent for a moment. "Unless we can get some more DNA, we can't say if Austin was screwing someone we don't even know about."

"This other list?" the chief said, pointing to the names.

"Those are people we've interviewed," Ryan said.

"English department chair. He got any motive?"

"No," I said. "He told us Austin was an asshole for screwing the student and being a general dickhead. But no."

"Suzannah Montgomery, his adviser? You like her?"

"I don't," I said. "She's got a vagina, but she's at least in her mid-forties. Not particularly attractive. What do you think, Ryan?"

"I don't see Austin going for cougars when he could get young women as good-looking as May." He shrugged his shoulders. "But we don't really understand him. Maybe he was, you know, a sex addict. But, Karen, you remember how Suzannah got all huffy when you suggested he might have nailed the freshman just because she was a piece of ass?"

"Yeah, but I think she's just the protective type. And it was real soon after he died."

"Frances Josephine Hamblin, the Melville scholar?" The chief turned to me. "She have a vagina, Karen?"

"Yeah," I said, "but she's had it about sixty-five years."

"Who's this Melissa Harmon?"

"She's another grad student, an uggo. He wouldn't do her. Anyway, she's in love with Ryan."

The chief looked at Ryan. "Should I ask?"

"Ignore Karen," Ryan said. "I was polite to Melissa. She appreciated it. That's all. There's no evidence she was ever in contact with Austin."

"You've looked at the phones?"

"Yeah," I said. "That's how we found out he was still screwing the dumb freshman."

"And May, too," Ryan said.

"That's right," I said. "May tried to tell us she'd broken up with Austin a month ago, but the phones said they were still in touch."

"Why'd she lie?"

I exhaled. "Could've been a couple of things. I think it hurt her feelings that Austin was such a pussy hound—her being a real looker, and all—or maybe it was she was kind of embarrassed about doing the les while Austin looked on, beating his meat. I think that was it."

The chief nodded. "Anything else I can do?"

"The one thing we'd like to know: there's two sets of female DNA on Austin. One's probably his girlfriend, May Eberlein. The other one could be Tiffany Rhodes, who we think he screwed at seven o'clock. He didn't screw anyone else—at least, anyone we know of—until ten o'clock." I looked at Ryan, then at the chief. "I'm not a guy," I said, "but wouldn't you, you know, hose that thing down between sessions?"

Ryan put his palms up. "You're asking the wrong guy."

I turned to the chief.

He just smiled. "I think Mr. Sulenka would want to clean himself up a little. But what do I know? I don't make a habit of watching live lesbian sex."

"So," I said, "if we could get DNA from Tiffany Rhodes and May Eberlein, we'd at least know if he nailed any other women that night."

"Assuming he didn't use a condom with her," Ryan said.

The chief nodded. "Did you ask those two for their DNA?"

"They both refused," I said.

The chief walked over to the desk and sat on the corner. "Just trying to think of a story you could tell them to scare them into volunteering it." He shook his head. "Since we don't have a weapon, I'm not coming up with anything. They've already admitted they were with him that night."

"Can we compel them?" I said.

"I don't think so, but let me ask Larry." He was referring to the prosecutor, Larry Klein. Chief Murtaugh stood up. "I'll get back to you," he said. "Did you get a chance to check his financials?"

"Yeah, we took a quick look, a few minutes ago. Thanks for that."

"Anything pop out?"

"Not really," I said. "He was selling his plasma and sperm—and I think he was selling his students' term papers—but he was also donating money to United Cerebral Palsy and the Children's Fund at the hospital."

His head pulled back. "He didn't have cerebral palsy, right?"

"No, he sure didn't."

"Someone in his family?"

I turned to Ryan. "What did Suzannah Montgomery tell us about him, Ryan?"

"I'll have to check, but I think she said the father left and the mother died of cancer."

"That's what I remember," I said.

"It might be important. Run it down," the chief said.

Chapter 19

"Thanks for coming over, Larry," the chief said, gesturing for the prosecutor to sit.

"I'm glad you called me," Larry Klein said. "Needed an excuse to get out of the office for a little while."

Larry Klein has been the prosecutor about as long as I've been a cop. He came here from Philadelphia, a small, wiry guy with grey eyes that dart all around as he's talking with you. He always wears a black suit and tie and a white shirt over a sleeveless undershirt. I've worked with him on cases maybe eight or ten times. He gives straight advice in simple English, and he'll spend as much time as you need, which I appreciate because sometimes the law doesn't make any sense to me. But he never says anything personal—about me, about himself, anyone. I don't know, for example, if he has a family, if he's straight or gay, or why he left Philadelphia.

I'm okay with him being all business, me not being willing to tell people all that much about myself. But his level of reserve is quite unusual in Rawlings, where we're pretty outgoing, although most of what we say to each other most of the time is bullshit. In both senses of the word: waste of time, plus mostly untrue.

All the judges really like Larry Klein, probably because he knows the law inside out, but also because he never talks them into doing something stupid that will come back and bite them on the ass. For that reason, the judges don't try to second-guess him, and cops don't, either. If he agrees to file for a warrant or a court order for you, you'll almost certainly get it. If he starts to shake his head a little and suggests there might be a problem with that, you should ask him what he would do, thank him for his time, smile, and turn on your heels. Then you should do what he told you to, because you're not going to get what you wanted—and you probably shouldn't.

It's not that he resents explaining the law to you. He seems to enjoy that. But he doesn't appreciate it if you want to waste his time bitching about how the law is stupid or out of date or contradictory or something. He tells you—once—that he didn't write the law, which is your cue to move on. And he really won't tolerate you telling him he's wrong and you're right. He isn't, and you aren't. I've seen other detectives try to do it. He just turns around and walks away in his little black suit.

Larry sat down in a soft chair, his left ankle tucked up under his right knee. The chief motioned for me and Ryan to sit on the couch against the wall. We got settled.

"As I said on the phone, Larry, Karen and Ryan wanted some help on a case. I told them I wasn't sure if we could do what they wanted, but that I'd ask you."

Larry nodded and adjusted his thick black-framed glasses on his thin, pale face. He looked like he'd gone a couple days without a shave, but that's how he always looks by ten in the morning. He turned to me. "What ya got?"

"Austin Sulenka, the grad student. Died Sunday night. Choked. We got two sets of female DNA on him, and two women said they had sex with him that night. We've asked one of them to volunteer for a buccal swab. She refused. Haven't asked the other one yet."

"Okay." He shrugged. "So what's the question?"

"Can we force them to give it up?"

"No."

"Just like that?"

"Just like that." He shifted in the seat. "The crime's good. Murder, I mean. The Supreme Court says we can compel DNA from anyone we arrest, but Montana says no, not unless they're offenders—that is, convicted—or already arrested for a serious crime."

"So, can we arrest one of them, get her DNA, then release her?"

"No. I won't file for an arrest warrant as a means of compelling them to give DNA. You don't have probable cause on the two of them, right?"

"Well, we got a pretty good sense it's one of the two."

"No, I mean you're not thinking the two women conspired to kill the grad student."

"That's right. We think it's probably one or the other."

"Well, then, definitely no," Klein said.

"How's that?" I said.

"If you can convince me the two women conspired to kill him, I'll file the papers for you. One woman lures him into an alley, the other hits him on the head. But if you think it's probably one or the other, that's a textbook case of *not* having probable cause. Because if it's Woman A, then it can't be Woman B. And the reverse. You need to choose a woman, get the evidence to show probable cause, and I'll get you an arrest warrant. Once she's in the system, show me why you need the DNA."

"That's the only way to get the DNA?"

He put up his hand. "You've only got three ways to argue it." He raised a thumb. "You can compel an offender or arrestee to provide DNA if you have probable cause she committed the crime." He raised his index finger. "Or if you have reasonable suspicion that she did it." He raised his middle finger. "Or if you have reasonable suspicion the DNA will produce material evidence in a case where you already have probable cause. Without one of those three, you're violating the Fourth Amendment, as well as the same thing written in Montana statute."

"But if I could match only one of the two women to the DNA evidence on the vic's body," I said, "that could provide material evidence."

"How's that?"

"We're trying to see if there was another woman involved—I mean, other than the two we're looking at already."

He shook his head. "It doesn't work that way. You can't compel evidence to broaden your suspect list. You can compel evidence only if you already have probable cause. Which you don't have, right?"

"Where we are, Larry," Ryan said, "is we've got two women with motives, and we can place them each of them at the scene at the right time. But we want to see if there was a third woman. If the two women don't match up to the DNA on the victim's body, we know we have to expand the investigation."

"Nope," Larry said. "You said the victim was strangled, right?"

"Yeah," I said.

"You got DNA on the weapon?"

I shook my head. "We don't have a weapon."

"So where's the DNA?"

"It's on his dick. Two women have admitted to screwing him. But we think there may be more than that."

"If you can't put the DNA on a murder weapon, you don't have anything. Screwing him doesn't even make 'reasonable suspicion.' In fact, unless you've got other actions that show the two women both wanted him dead," he said, raising an eyebrow, "the fact that they screwed him suggests that they were friends."

"I can give you motive that each of the women might have wanted to kill him."

"I said 'other actions.' I didn't say motives. If motives were enough, you could arrest me every time something bad happens to a judge."

"These women were with him within a few hours of his death," Ryan said.

"Show me a video of one woman leaving his place right before he died. Prove to me it was impossible for someone else to have gotten in and strangled him. And prove to me it was impossible for him to have killed himself. Prove he wasn't a gasper with a plastic bag—then prove that someone didn't stop by and remove the evidence. Prove all those things and we'll talk about compelling that woman to give up her DNA. Right now, what you have is a guy who got laid a lot—and, oh, by the way, you think he was strangled but you're not really sure if it was one of the women did it."

I glanced over at the chief, who was looking down at his hands, which were intertwined in his lap. Ryan was tapping a fist against his jaw. I looked at Larry Klein. He wasn't gloating or preening or anything. His forehead was covered with deep wrinkles, like he was sorry to have to spell it out for us but that he felt it would be useful for us to see where we really were in the case.

"Larry," I said, "doesn't it make sense that it's gonna speed up our investigation if we know we should be looking at only these two women, or there are other suspects?"

"Of course," he said. He put his hands on the chair arms and lifted himself off the chair slightly so he could switch legs. "But the purpose of the law isn't to make it easier for you to catch the bad guy. It's to make it harder."

I put out my hands in confusion.

"The law protects people from unreasonable searches and seizures. That doesn't mean it's unreasonable for you to want to know whether that person was at the crime scene. Obviously, you'd like to know that. It means that the search is reasonable only if you have probable cause to believe that person killed that other person."

"That's not exactly a level playing field, is it?"

"Not supposed to be. It's tipped in favor of the defendant. If I prosecute someone, I have to make the case that this particular person did it, beyond a reasonable doubt. You got two women—or two dozen women—screwing this guy the night someone throttled him. Choose a woman, make a case that she did it—not that she or someone else had a reason to do it, but that she *did* do it—and I'll get you a court order to compel her to give us her DNA. But you think one of those two women did it because they screwed him that night?" He shook his head. "I can't bring that to a judge."

"Isn't there something in the law about 'exonerating innocent suspects'?" Ryan said.

"Yeah," Klein said. "If Woman A is serving a sentence for killing a guy, and you can show probable cause that Woman B killed him, I'll get you a court order to compel Woman B to give up her DNA, whether she's already in prison or she's the mayor's wife. But I still want probable cause."

Ryan leaned forward. "The fact that at least one of these women would be helping themselves out by cooperating with us—that doesn't make a difference?"

"Being stupid's not a crime," Klein said. "We don't have the prison space."

"Shit," I said to Klein.

"Shit, indeed." He put up his hands. "Anything else I can not help you with?"

I gave him a sad smile. "No, I think you've sandbagged us enough."

"Excellent." He stood, buttoning his black suit jacket. He shook hands all around and left.

I turned to the chief. "When Ryan and I came in, you told Larry you didn't know whether we could compel the two women to give up the DNA."

He nodded. "Yeah, I said that."

"You have a doctorate in criminal justice, right?"

"That's right."

"So you already knew, didn't you?"

"I've been in Montana less than a year." He gave a little shrug. "There might be some loophole I don't know about."

"I don't believe you." I smiled. "You had him come over and explain it so we wouldn't think you were shutting us down. So we'd be pissed at Larry."

"Interesting theory." I could almost make out a smile.

"That's what you were doing, right?"

"Like the prosecutor said, 'Show me probable cause.'"

Chapter 20

"Well, that was somewhat embarrassing," Ryan said as we made our way back toward the center of the building and headed into the incident room.

"What's that?"

"Larry Klein explaining to us how we can't compel the two women to give us their DNA." Ryan put his briefcase and cane down on a desk.

"I don't see it that way." I put my bag on a table in the center of the room. "That's Larry's job. We're supposed to ask for help. And he's supposed to explain what we can do and can't do. We should be embarrassed if we decide not to ask him and it turns out he could've helped us with the case."

"Okay," Ryan said. "But what I get from him is we're not any farther along now than we were a day and a half ago."

"Austin calls Kathy Caravelli a dyke around ten-thirty or eleven." I sat down in a cheap plastic chair at the desk. "May doesn't call him out on it. Kathy leaves. So, assuming Kathy didn't come back and strangle him—with May there or not—May is the last person sees Austin alive."

Ryan stood there, looking at the whiteboard. "Yeah?"

"How're we gonna check out May's story that she went home?"

"Ask her landlady?"

"The one with the hearing aids? Who probably took them out when she went to bed around nine, nine-thirty?"

"We could canvass the scene," Ryan said. "There might be some teenage boy across the street with binoculars who keeps a log of when May enters and leaves her apartment."

"Might as well," I said. "Write that down, would you?"

"And the same for Kathy Caravelli?"

"I don't see anyone tracking her comings and goings, but, yeah, I guess we should."

Ryan wrote it down in his notebook.

"It's ten-thirty or eleven. Austin's apartment. He watched the two women going at it. Then he nails May. Then—we don't know how it got around to Austin calling Kathy a dyke—but she leaves, pissed off. So it's just May and Austin. He lies back on the mattress, she gets on top of him, strangles him with … it could be anything."

"Sure, a sleeve of a blouse. A jacket. Anything. Gets dressed. Walks out, wiping her prints off the doorknob."

"Because Austin called Kathy a dyke?" I said.

Ryan shrugged. "I don't see that. Now, if he'd been humiliating Kathy for a long time, and May had been telling him to stop. Or if he'd done something to Kathy beyond calling her names—maybe. For May to get worked up enough to want to kill him, she'd have to be totally committed to Kathy."

"Which would make me wonder why she's still screwing him," I said.

"Exactly. Whatever crimes Austin committed, they'd be against May, not against Kathy. Maybe he'd humiliated May by sleeping around. She might've found out he'd nailed Tiffany earlier that night. She could've smelled it on him."

"Or May called Kathy and told her to come back," I said. "She comes back. The two women kill him."

"Or Kathy decides to come back to tell Austin off. May's still there. She lets Kathy back in. Kathy kills him. May watches. The two women walk out, wiping the doorknob."

"Jesus Christ, we're just spinning our wheels." I shook my head. "We've got motives, means, and opportunities for May, for Kathy, and for the two of them together, either premeditated or spur-of-the moment."

"The only thing we don't have," Ryan said, "is probable cause."

I was looking at the timeline on the whiteboard. "Tiffany fucked him around seven, right?"

"That's right."

"Then she went to a girlfriend's house."

"We never did follow up on that," Ryan said.

"Go back to the chief's office, get authorization to get some uniforms to canvass Kathy's place and May's. I'll call Tiffany."

Ryan nodded and walked out of the incident room. I got my cell from my shoulder bag and called Tiffany. She picked up right away.

"Tiffany, Detective Seagate. We need to talk with you again."

"Oh, God, what about? I told you everything I know about Austin."

"Yeah, I know. We need to talk with you more about Sunday night, after you were at his apartment."

"I went to a girlfriend's place. I told you that already."

"Yeah, that's what we wanna talk to you about."

"What else do you wanna know?"

"We need to talk in person. Where are you? Your apartment?"

"Yeah."

"We can be there in ten minutes."

"No." Her voice was high. "Not here."

"All right," I said. "Where?"

"The Starbucks on Fourth."

"Okay," I said. "Ten minutes. You got that?"

She didn't answer. She just ended the call. People can be so rude.

Ryan came back into the room. "The chief said okay. The canvass will be done by end of shift today."

"Good, thanks." I stood up. "Let's go talk to Tiffany."

We drove over to the Starbucks. There were no spots, so I parked in a private lot where you put money in an envelope in a box on a pole. I put down the visor with the Official Police Business sign visible.

We walked into the coffee place. I breathed in the smells—the coffee, the steamy cream, the cologne from the two business guys in suits at the table right near the door. Paul McCartney was singing from the speakers in the ceiling. Ryan and I scanned the place. No Tiffany. We threaded our way to a table near the back and sat down to wait for her.

"She gonna pull a runner?" The coffee smelled real good. I was tempted.

"If she does, we know who killed Austin," Ryan said.

"I'm not sure we'll ever know," I said. "Screw it. I'm getting a coffee. Want something?"

He shook his head.

I grabbed a paper cup and pumped some of the regular coffee and put two dollar bills on the counter. As I was getting the cream and sugar, Tiffany walked in, looking pissed-off.

She wasn't quite pulled together. She had on jeans and a tee-shirt, half tucked in, with a light cloth jacket, unzipped. Her hair was uncombed. She squinted, then frowned some more when she spotted us near the back. She navigated between the tables, turning sideways now and then to squeeze through. A couple of young guys sitting off to the side watched her tits bobbing their way to our table.

Ryan stood up when she arrived. She looked at him, confused.

"Thanks for coming, Tiffany," I said.

She sat down, and Ryan did the same. She just looked at me. Paul McCartney stopped singing, and some Sixties music I didn't recognize came on. The espresso machine was hissing and whooshing, sending clouds of steam into the air.

"You told us yesterday you were at Austin's apartment around seven, that you stayed there around a half hour or so."

"That's right."

"And then you drove over to a girlfriend's apartment. You didn't go to your own place. That correct?"

She nodded. The frown lines coming down from the sides of her mouth were going to become a problem in a few years.

"What's her name?"

"Emily Johnston."

I glanced over at Ryan, who was writing it in his notebook.

"What's her phone?"

Tiffany leaned over and pulled her phone from her pocket. She turned it on, hit a button, and held it up to me. I pointed my chin to Ryan. She held it up for him to write it down.

"When we talk to her, she gonna tell us you were there all night, watching a movie, you went to bed around midnight in the spare bed in her bedroom, and she swears you didn't leave till the next morning?"

Tiffany looked at me. "She's not gonna say that."

"What's she gonna say?"

"She's gonna say we ordered in some pizza, then a couple guys from her building came by to hang out."

"Hang out?"

"Yeah." She looked down at her hands for a moment and then back up to me. "Hang out."

One of my goals in life is to figure what the hell it means to hang out. I've asked my son about a hundred times, after he's told me that's what he'd been doing for the last day or three when he'd been off the grid, but he can't seem to explain it, either. "What exactly does that mean?"

"They came over. We were talking. You know, hanging out."

Ryan said, "If we bring Emily in to headquarters to make a formal statement, is she going to tell us the four of you were together in the same room, then the two guys left, then you and Emily went to bed?"

Now she turned to Ryan and shared the fuck-you expression that I thought she reserved for me.

"Come on, Tiffany." I was getting a little pissed myself. "Is Emily gonna tell us you never left her place until Monday morning?"

"How the fuck should I know what she's gonna tell you?" She shifted in her wooden chair.

"Okay," I said, standing up. "Let's go down to headquarters, have you make a formal statement."

She put out her hands. "What do you want me to say?"

"I want you to tell us the truth. Have you got an alibi for Sunday night, around midnight?"

She looked out over my shoulder, then pulled her gaze back toward me. "What happened was, Emily and this guy went into her bedroom."

"When was that?"

"I don't know. Around nine."

"How long were they in there?"

She shook her head. "Till maybe ... I wasn't looking at my watch. Eleven?"

"So you were out in the living room? With this guy? The two of you?"

She looked up at me and stuck her chin out. "That's right."

"What's this guy's name?"

"I don't know."

"When we track him down, what's he gonna say you were doing?"

"Fooling around."

"You had sex with him?"

"That's none of your fuckin' business."

"Let's get this straight, Tiffany. I don't give a shit about you fucking Brian and Austin and this guy you don't even know his name. As many times as you want. You can fuck one of them at a time, two at a time, or all three together. The only thing I care about is if you stopped by Austin's place around midnight and strangled him."

She shook her head. "The two guys had some weed. I was completely wrecked. I think I sucked him off. I might've fucked him. I can't remember. Maybe the other guy, too. So, if you're asking me if I have an alibi, the two guys will say I was there at Emily's place. I know I couldn't've drove over to Austin's, the shape I was in. Wouldn't have even tried. I got a DUI last year, and my parents were all up my ass about it. I'm not an idiot.

"Besides," she said, "I was over at Austin's place earlier. If I'd wanted to kill him—which I didn't—I'd've did it then." She looked at me, then at Ryan. "You two geniuses ever consider that?"

I nodded my head. "We'll be in touch if we want to talk to you again."

"Can't fuckin' wait." She stood up, pushed her phone into her jeans pocket, and crashed her way through the tables and chairs at the Starbucks.

I looked at Ryan. "Well, genius, did you ever consider that?"

Ryan smiled. "To tell you the truth—"

"Yes, that would be a refreshing change."

"The fact that she could've killed Austin earlier doesn't mean she couldn't have killed him later."

"You mean she knew Austin would probably be nailing someone later on, so she wanted to contaminate the scene more by getting more DNA on his dick?"

"No." He shook his head. "Tiffany lives in the present tense. Two guys come over with some weed, she smokes it, starts giggling. Next thing you know, she's got her clothes off. No, I don't buy her reasoning because it simply doesn't logically follow that she didn't kill him later because she didn't kill him earlier."

"Well, you put it that way …" I rubbed my forehead. "What the hell did you just say?"

He laughed. "All I said is she doesn't have an alibi. It might be true that she could have killed him at seven, but maybe the conditions weren't right. Or maybe she didn't want to kill him then. She just wanted to screw him then."

"Okay," I said. "But you're saying you think she didn't kill him at all, right?"

"That's right. It's not that she couldn't have killed him. It's that she didn't want to kill him. She doesn't hold a grudge— especially if there's a dick involved."

I nodded. "Yeah."

"You want to track down the guys with the weed?"

I thought for a second. "Not at the moment." I drank a few gulps of coffee. We sat there, silently, for a little bit.

"We haven't checked to see who her current English teacher is, have we?" Ryan said.

I nodded. "You thinking it might be May?"

"If it turns out to be May, that would be interesting. Otherwise, I don't see any reason to keep going at Tiffany. My gut tells me that what makes Tiffany such a skank is what *doesn't* make her a murderer."

"Like when she said she wouldn't have driven over to Austin's because she was wrecked?"

"That's right," Ryan said. "Her parents were all over her about it. Morally, she's an eight-year-old. She thinks in terms of rewards and punishments. She stays out of trouble, she incurs no punishment. She kills someone, she risks the biggest punishment of all."

"No more dick?"

"Sure, no more dick."

"Can you look up and see if May is Tiffany's teacher?"

He reached over and fished the tablet out of his briefcase. "Give me a minute." It was more like forty-five seconds. "No, Tiffany's instructor is Haley, Jennifer, not Eberlein, May."

"We're running out of women to track down." I looked down at the dregs of the coffee in my paper cup. "Maybe Haley, Jennifer was nailing him, too."

"What about Suzannah Montgomery?"

I looked up at Ryan. "I thought you said she was too old."

"No," he said, "she wasn't doing him. But she's the one who told us about his father running out and his mother dying of cancer, right? Maybe she can help us with why he was donating to cerebral palsy."

"Okay, let's go back to campus and see if we can track her down." We stood up and squeezed our way between the tables. I tossed my cup in a garbage can near the door. "Maybe I'll get a chance to ask her if she was nailing Austin, too."

He pointed with his chin to two young women working the machines. "How about the baristas? Want to ask them if they were nailing him, too?"

Chapter 21

We walked the thirty yards to the lot where the Charger was parked. I started it up and we made the five-minute drive to campus, where we parked in the lot at the Humanities Building.

"What's her office number?" We were on the third floor.

"It's up here," Ryan said, pointing down the hall. "314."

I looked in the window in her door. The lights were on, and the computer screen was lit, but she wasn't in. I tried the door; it was locked. "Let's go to the main office, see if they know where she is."

The department secretary greeted us. "Can I help you, Detectives?"

"We're looking for Suzannah Montgomery. She's still on campus, but she's not in her office."

The secretary put on a pained expression. "Suzannah had to rush home."

"Yeah?"

"It's her son, Adam. He had a seizure."

"Does that happen a lot?"

"I think it does. He has cerebral palsy. Sometimes it's mild, and his caregivers can handle it. Other times it's severe. He panics and starts screaming." She shook her head. "It's just terrible."

"Is Professor Van Vleet in?" Ryan said.

The secretary turned to him, wearing a confused look. "Let me see if he's available." She walked toward the chair's office, tapped on the door, and stuck her head in. She was back in ten seconds. "Yes, he can see you."

Jonathan Van Vleet was standing at the door to his office. "Come on in," he said, gesturing for us to sit.

"We're sorry to barge in like this," Ryan said as we sat down. "But your secretary was just telling us about Suzannah Montgomery having to go home to take care of her son."

"I didn't know he was having a problem," Van Vleet said. "What Suzannah does … she's just terrific with that boy."

"Adam has cerebral palsy, is that right?"

"Yes, he's the sweetest little boy." Jonathan Van Vleet paused. "Is there something I can help you with, I mean, related to Suzannah?"

"We were hoping she could help us with our investigation," Ryan said.

Van Vleet tilted his head, telling Ryan to continue. I didn't know where Ryan was going, but I know him well enough to get out of the way when he wants to lead an interview.

"We wanted to ask her if she could help us by suggesting the names of any other people who Austin Sulenka associated with."

"Did you have a chance to talk with that freshman, the one he was involved with last semester?"

"Yes," Ryan said. "Yes, we did. That was very helpful. And we've talked with his former girlfriend, May Eberlein, and a few other people."

"Presumably, you've hit some kind of barrier."

Ryan nodded. "We can't go into any details—I'm sure you understand—but we're trying to find out more about his associates."

Van Vleet put out his hands. "I'm sorry, I really can't tell you any more than I've already told you about Austin. He and I weren't close."

"One of the things we learned about Austin is that he donated money to United Cerebral Palsy. Were you aware of that?"

Okay, I thought. Now I knew where Ryan is going.

Van Vleet looked puzzled. "No, I didn't know that." He ran his fingers through his beard, like he was still getting used to it. "You mean he gave them a small donation, twenty-five dollars or something like that?"

"He gave them quite a bit of money. Many hundreds of dollars, in regular donations every few months. In fact, he used to sell his plasma and sperm to bring in extra income."

"That's a side of him I didn't know."

Ryan held his gaze but said nothing. He was waiting.

Then, the bulb went on in Van Vleet's head. "Do you think he was donating that money because of Suzannah Montgomery's child?"

Ryan shrugged his shoulders. "It could be," he said. "Does that strike you as unusual?"

Van Vleet sat back in his chair. "Yes, it certainly does. And I'd add extremely generous."

"Professor Montgomery's child is about how old?"

"I'm just guessing. Ten or twelve."

Ryan nodded his head but didn't say anything for the longest time. "Do you think there might have been a relationship between Austin and Suzannah Montgomery? I mean, something that went beyond the adviser-student relationship?"

Jonathan Van Vleet stood and walked over to the door. He closed it, then pushed on it to make sure the latch had caught. Back in his chair, he frowned. "Don't you think that's a bit of a stretch? I mean, from his donating money to a charity?"

"Well, it suggests that maybe they were social friends." Ryan paused. I could tell he was setting up the interrogation. "Does Suzannah bring her son to campus much?"

"No," Van Vleet said. "I've never seen her do that."

"It's possible, then, that Austin has been to her house. You know, for a cookout or something. It stands to reason Austin might have met her son there."

"Yes, of course, Suzannah's a very outgoing person. She's friendly with all the grad students—and a number of our undergraduates, too. And she does have a lot of social events at her house. In fact, she's volunteered her house for a number of our Fall socials for the department."

Ryan nodded his head again.

Van Vleet looked uncomfortable. He ran his hand through his beard. "I'm sorry, I thought for a moment you were suggesting that they might have had some kind of intimate relationship." He offered an embarrassed smile.

Ryan was doing a good job. It's best to let the interviewee connect the dots himself. That way, he doesn't automatically reject the idea because it came from a cop.

"We really have no idea, Professor. It's only been a day and a half since we began the investigation."

"I have to tell you: I haven't seen any indication that something like that might have been going on."

Ryan nodded. "Like you told us yesterday, a relationship like that would violate the terms of her contract."

"Oh, absolutely. She could be fired. Immediately. In fact, I would expect it."

"So you don't know of any relationships like that here on campus?"

"No," he said. "Nothing like that. There are personal relationships—marriages, in fact—between faculty and their *former* graduate students. For the most part, however, the former students have finished their programs and left the university. Certainly they are no longer students who might be subject to exams or thesis review by the faculty member." He was using his official tone. "The regulations on that are crystal-clear."

"We do know, however, that Austin was carrying on an inappropriate relationship with a student."

Van Vleet put up a hand and tilted his head. "Yes, yes, that is very true. But I ask that you consider he was twenty-four years old, just a few years older than the student. He was relatively new to the profession. Hadn't had a chance to think through his responsibilities. I remember, when I began my own career, now many years ago, that it was a very heady experience walking in front of that classroom. All those faces looking at you. Some of the girls—you could see from their body language, their expressions—they saw the instructor as … how should I say this? … a kind of authority figure, but—no, that's not the term I'm looking for. It's not like they saw the instructor as a police officer. More as if the instructor had earned the right to open doors for them—"

"What kind of doors, Professor?"

"An English teacher simply comes across as more refined, more cultured. He can introduce the students to literature, the arts, humanities." His forehead was starting to shine a little bit. "It's tied up with the gender roles in our culture, in a way."

"How do you mean?"

"The older male introduces the younger student to the habits, the perspectives, the ways of doing that the student needs to understand in order to become proficient in the … the whole enterprise of college."

"Wow," I said. "It does sound kind of sexual, the way you put it."

Van Vleet turned to me. "I am not condoning the relationship between Austin and that freshman, mind you. I want to be very clear about that."

"Of course not." I shook my head. What a preposterous idea.

"And some students are fully aware of this dynamic—the symbolic sexual initiation. I wouldn't be surprised if that student was exploiting it, in fact. Her admission, in the disciplinary hearing, that she wanted a higher grade could be seen as an admission of that. I'm saying, simply, that while Austin's actions were inappropriate, that sort of thing has been going on as long as women have been in the academy. That doesn't excuse it, of course."

"That sexual dynamic," Ryan said, "do you think it occurs in the other direction: a female instructor and a male student?"

"Yes, I think it does. The power relationship is the same, even though the gender roles are reversed. But in a way, it's essentially the same thing: a more-knowledgeable, more-experienced teacher initiating a less-knowledgeable, less-experienced student."

"But I imagine there is a difference. After all, a graduate student is older than an undergraduate. The whole notion of *in loco parentis* no longer applies."

"That's very true," the professor said. "But the same dynamic could be at work."

Ryan can do a lot of things I can't do. Getting a professor to stumble so far into a theoretical discussion that he forgets what he's trying to do and ends up telling us what he really thinks—he's much better at that than I am.

"You say you've been over at Suzannah Montgomery's house," Ryan said. "For department functions?"

"Yes," Van Vleet said. "Many times. For department functions, as well as informal dinners. My wife, Lauren, and I consider Suzannah and Aaron personal friends."

"What can you tell us about Aaron?"

"He's a wonderful man. He founded an organization called Rivers United. It's an environmental group."

"Oh, yes," Ryan said. "I've heard of it."

"I think he's an architect by training, but the environmental stuff has kind of taken over his life. He did well enough as an architect to be able to pursue the activism almost full-time, I believe."

"And the relationship between Suzannah and Aaron?"

"Well, given the obvious caveat that one person cannot ever truly know another person—or that person's relationships—my impression is that their marriage is quite strong. I know he takes his role as father very seriously. Raising Adam requires a considerable amount of time and patience, and I believe he takes that commitment very seriously. They both do, Aaron and Suzannah."

"My father is a professor," Ryan said. "I know that the hours can be tough, particularly when you have graduate seminars, thesis committees, reference letters. All of it."

Van Vleet nodded and smiled sadly. One comment that everyone seems to agree with is, "Boy, you've got a really hard job." You tell a beach bum you don't envy him, what with having to drink all that beer, smoke all those cigarettes, and hit up all those strangers for spare change, he'll nod and say you don't know the half of it.

Ryan continued. "With all her commitments to Adam, does anything ever fall through the cracks here at work?"

Van Vleet's cheeks puffed out and he exhaled slowly. "I've spent my whole career in academe," he said, shifting in his chair. "The typical professor goes through phases. Sometimes they're a little more absentminded than at other times. And, to be frank, Suzannah does need a little more prodding than some other faculty. You know, routine paperwork, that sort of thing. But the staff all love her—all the things she does for our students—and they make sure to remind her if she's late on something."

"Has this problem ever made it to your desk?"

"I will mention one incident. Six or seven years ago, I think. I wasn't chair at the time, but I know from conversations with the former chair that it did occur. I mention it because many of the other senior faculty know about it, and I don't want you to hear about it from one of them without the benefit of the context. But I'm absolutely confident it was a result of some stresses at home. I'm certain of it—"

"What happened, Professor?" Ryan said, leaning in. He had picked up the scent. He'd realized that Van Vleet's reason for leveling with us about Suzannah was the same as Tiffany's reason for telling us about how she was really in town Sunday night to fuck Austin: since other people knew about it, we might find out, and that wouldn't look too good.

"She was coming up for tenure and promotion—you know what I'm referring to, correct?"

"Absolutely."

"Our process here is quite baroque. We have a department committee that makes recommendations on tenure and promotion. Those recommendations go to the department chair, who sends a recommendation to a college-level committee, which sends its own recommendation to the college dean. He or she recommends to the provost, who issues a recommendation to the university president. The president makes a recommendation to the state board of education." He raised his eyebrows. "Just describing it now, it sounds incredible."

"I think the process is pretty standard across universities," Ryan said. "There's a lot riding on a tenure decision."

"You're right, of course, Detective. Essentially, it's lifetime employment. As you can imagine, the process is spelled out in considerable detail in a number of different documents. When a candidate is denied tenure—which is relatively uncommon—he or she has a right of appeal. That appeal can be based on substance—the university says the candidate's work is substandard; the candidate disagrees—or on a violation of due process."

"That you didn't follow your own rules," Ryan said.

"Exactly—" Van Vleet said.

"What went wrong with Suzannah's case?" I wanted to move things along.

"It was a minor technicality, really. She submitted her portfolio to the department committee a couple of days late."

"And that got whose nose out of joint?" I said.

"It was another member of the department, a guy named Mitch Abrams."

I glanced over at Ryan to make sure he was writing the name down in his notebook. "What was it to Abrams?"

"Abrams also came up for tenure that year. He didn't get it."

"I don't understand the relationship."

"A lot of us didn't understand the relationship. We still don't. But what it came down to was that, a couple of months later, when the tenure decisions were announced, and Suzannah got it but Abrams didn't, he complained to the provost that the system had been compromised because Suzannah's portfolio was late but she got tenure anyway."

"I still don't get it. Was Abrams saying she got the job he should've gotten?"

"No," Van Vleet said. "That would have made too much sense. In fact, there's no quota on tenure. They both could have gotten it."

"So what was his beef?"

"His beef was that if the university bent the rules for Suzannah, they should have bent the rules for him, too."

"What kind of rules did he want them to bend? Were his papers a couple days late, like hers?"

"No, he demanded a complete do-over, with new committees at every stage. He argued that the process was tainted. He said the university violated its own due process because she got more time than he did."

"So what happened next?"

"The chair went to bat for Suzannah. Said it was her own fault. The delay, I mean."

"And the university accepted that?"

"That's right. It was the chair's first year in that position. Mistakes happen. The university decided that the technical violation of its procedures in Suzannah's case did not justify Abrams' demand that his case be re-heard."

"End of story?"

"Not exactly. The university has its own appeal procedure in place, so Abrams brought his case to the appeals board, but they sided with the university. They decided that since there was no violation of due process in Abrams' own case, the fact that there was an irregularity with Suzannah's case was regrettable but not relevant."

"Okay," I said. "A nuisance, but no big deal, right?"

"Abrams didn't go quietly. He went to the *Chronicle*—"

"What's that?"

"That's the trade paper for college teachers. A national paper. They wrote it up. Made us look kind of unprofessional. Then, the next year, Abrams did a lousy job teaching—"

"The next year? He wasn't fired?"

"After you're denied tenure, you get one more year before you go."

"Really?" When I got fired last year, I had till five PM that day.

"Yeah, he sabotaged his classes in every way he could. He was in the student newspaper every other week, writing editorials about how corrupt we were."

"The administration let him do that?"

Van Vleet smiled. "The newspaper's run by students."

"What's the name of the chair at that time?"

"Frances Hamblin."

"We've met her," I said. "She's the Melville scholar, right?"

"That's right. She was new at the job. She didn't want to ruin Suzannah's career, get her fired. Frances understands that we're a family here. Those of us who've been here years and years, people like myself and Frances, we build our lives around this department and the fellowship we find within this community. We live here, grow old here, fight and make up, transgress and forgive. It was a bump in the road. That was all it was."

I turned to Ryan. "Is there anything else you'd like to ask Professor Van Vleet?"

Ryan shook his head. "No."

"We want to thank you very much for talking with us. I know this is a very difficult subject—and you have to forgive us as outsiders—but we appreciate you helping us understand what's going on." The three of us stood up. "We'll be back in touch if we need to talk some more."

"My pleasure, Detectives. Good luck with the investigation," Van Vleet said, with a smile, quite pleased with his successful lecture on sexual politics and the tenure system.

Chapter 22

I looked at the clock on the dashboard in the Charger: 3:47. "Think there's anything there?"

"About the business of missing the deadline on her tenure application?"

"Yeah, that and Austin giving money to the cerebral-palsy group."

Ryan was shifting his cane so he could buckle his seatbelt. "From the stuff my father used to talk about, half the faculty used to miss every deadline. It was a point of pride: you know, their minds were on loftier things. So that was no big deal."

"How about sleeping with students?"

"Like Van Vleet said, I think that's been going on since there've been women in colleges."

"And the cerebral-palsy stuff?"

"That could be a coincidence," Ryan said. "All we know about Austin's background is what Suzannah told us: father walked out, mother died of cancer. He could have brothers and sisters, aunts and uncles. There could be cerebral palsy in his family."

"Suzannah Montgomery is home now, right, taking care of her kid?"

"Unless his seizure was so bad she took him to a doctor or the ER."

"Call the secretary in English, would you? Get her address."

Ryan took his notebook and phone out of his jacket pocket. He punched in the number and got the information. "You want to interview her now? She's probably pretty upset about her kid."

"Yeah, I know, it's a shitty time. But we don't have any other leads to run down, and it's too soon to head back to headquarters and tell the chief we're out of ideas. Besides, if she's wrung out, it might be harder for her to lie to us." I looked at Ryan. He wasn't really buying it. "We'll see she didn't have anything to do with killing Austin, and we'll scratch her off our list, okay?"

He nodded, but he wasn't happy.

"You know where it is?" I said.

"It's up on the Bench: 4204 Table Rock."

I started the Charger and pulled out of the lot slowly. I headed back toward town, then up Larchmont toward Table Rock. "Here's what I want to do. We'll tell her the secretary mentioned she went home because of the kid. That'll give us an opening to talk about the cerebral palsy. I want to hear how she responds when we tell her we know Austin was donating to the charity."

I looked over at Ryan. He was looking out his side window. Giving me the silent treatment was about as close as he came to telling me off. I was okay with it.

We were crawling along in a row of cars doing five miles slower than the limit. Even though the Charger was unmarked, I could tell that the cars around us made us as cops. The big spot light next to my rear-view mirror will do that.

We turned onto Table Rock, winding all the way up, catching glimpses of the city between trees and houses. Up at the end of the cul-de-sac, the houses sat on one-acre plots that looked down on the heart of town. We pulled onto the long, curving driveway, big cement squares with a rippled pattern built-in and bordered by brick. There was no grass out front, just these big river rocks in various shades of greys and tans, interspersed with tufts of tall plains grasses. The house itself was U-shaped, with a four-foot-tall stone and brick wall enclosing the courtyard to make a rectangle. Inside the courtyard I could see high-end outdoor furniture with soft cushions around a fire pit, and, next to the house, a long brick barbeque with an outdoor kitchen next to it. My house would have fit inside the courtyard.

We parked in front of the three-car garage and walked up to the front door. There was something unusual about the front door but I couldn't place it.

Ryan sensed what I was thinking. "No front steps," Ryan said. "Wheelchair." He was talking to me again.

I rang the doorbell. A couple of moments later, Suzannah Montgomery opened the door. She looked like me after I'd had an episode with my own son: wrung-out and weary, a toxic brew of guilt, anger, and regret. The bags under her eyes were puffy, and her eyes were red-rimmed.

"Professor Montgomery, Detectives Seagate and Miner? We talked to you for a couple minutes yesterday, at the grad student's defense?"

It took her a few seconds to place us. "Yes, I remember," she said, her hand still on the doorknob. "Do you need to talk to me?" She was wearing jeans and a sweatshirt, no socks or shoes. But she did have all the silver bracelets and necklaces on.

"I know this is a bad time, Professor, but I'm afraid we do need a couple of minutes."

"Sure," she said, stepping back to invite us in. We stood in the marble-floored foyer, looking straight through the house to the wall of windows, then a wide deck overlooking the city. Suzannah Montgomery led us into a living room off to the left. It had a tan low-napped carpet, like you see in stores, made so it didn't slow down wheelchairs. A wine-colored leather couch and matching armchairs were arrayed around a fireplace bordered in river rocks. She gestured for us to sit.

"We're real sorry to barge in on you like this. The secretary in the department told us you had to come home because your son was having problems."

She rubbed her eyes. "He has seizures. This one was pretty bad. His father took him to the hospital." She put her hands on her hips, like she wanted me to get to whatever bad shit I wanted to deliver.

"Is he all right?"

"He didn't injure himself, if that's what you mean." She shook her head. "But no, I don't think you could say he's all right. He gets so frightened." She pressed two fingers to the corners of her eyes to keep from crying. "This one will take him days to get over."

"I can only imagine," I said. "Does he stay at home during the day?"

"No, he goes to a special school. They called my husband. He works here at home."

On the mantelpiece was a framed photo of her and her husband with the boy and his older sister. "Can I look at your photo?"

"Of course," she said, forcing a small smile. Her jewelry jangled as she waved toward the mantelpiece.

I stood up and walked over to the photo. "Oh, he's such a beautiful little boy," I said. "Was he about, what, eight in this photo?"

"No, that's a recent photo. He's twelve. But he's very small."

She sat on one of the leather arm chairs. I could see she was exhausted, but she didn't want to sit down in the chair, which would signal we could stay longer.

I walked back to the couch and sat down. "As you know, Professor, we're trying to learn everything we can about Austin

Sulenka. Because you were his adviser, we assume you knew him better than most of the other faculty members did."

"Working on a thesis with the student will necessarily bring the faculty member and the student together. Either that," she said, tilting her head, "or drive them completely apart."

"How was that going? I mean, his thesis."

"I've done enough of them to know that you can't really say. The student can be slogging along, making very little progress, and you're absolutely certain it's not going to work—at least, that it won't be ready to defend in time for graduation. Then, all of a sudden, the student makes some sort of breakthrough—finally understands what you've been trying to tell him for months and months, starts to buckle down, whatever—and then he knocks out one chapter after another and finishes in time, and it's first-rate work."

"Was Austin going to finish in time for graduation?"

She shook her head and put on a pained expression. "Like I said, I can't say for sure that he wouldn't have finished, but he hadn't yet made that breakthrough. And as you saw yesterday, with Melissa, other students are already defending."

"Professor, do you know that Austin Sulenka donated over seven-hundred dollars over the last year to United Cerebral Palsy?"

Her head pulled back, almost imperceptibly. "What? No," she said. "I didn't know that."

I looked at her. Her eyes darted out toward the glass wall overlooking the deck, then back to me. I waited for a count of five.

"That's very odd," she said.

"We thought so, too," I said.

"Perhaps he had a family member with the disease?"

I let her comment hang there. "Has Austin ever been here, in this house?"

"Yes," she said. "Several times. Last few years, we've held the Fall department get-together here. He does attend them."

"Did he ever meet your son?"

She furrowed her brow. "You know, I'm not sure. He might have." She nodded her head. "I think Adam was here once or twice during those get-togethers, so it's possible they did meet."

"He might have seen this photo," I said, pointing to the fireplace.

"We have many photos of Adam around the house."

"Do you talk with your students about Adam?"

"Not as a rule, no. I mean, I don't ever mention Adam or cerebral palsy in my teaching. But in small groups, I'm sure I have mentioned it. As you said, the secretaries know why I had to leave campus this afternoon."

"Do you think Austin's donations to United Cerebral Palsy might have had something to do with Adam?"

Suzannah Montgomery exhaled and put her hands out. "He never mentioned anything like that to me. I can say that for sure."

I waited a few beats. "Do you think Austin might have had— I don't know—some kind of crush on you?"

"I really don't think so, Detective." She scratched at her neck with her long fingernails, then smiled. "I mean, look at me. I'm forty-eight. Most days, I look fifty-eight. I'm married, two children, one with special needs. I don't see myself as someone who would attract any man, certainly not a young man." She shifted her weight on the chair.

I paused. "It just seems so curious, the donations to United Cerebral Palsy."

She shrugged. "I'm afraid I can't explain that."

"Did you know he sold his plasma and his sperm?"

"No." Suzannah Montgomery frowned. "I didn't know that."

"There's no grad students in English with cerebral palsy that you know of?"

I caught a glint of anger in her eyes, just for a second. "Not that I know of."

"Professor Montgomery, were you having an affair with Austin Sulenka?"

Her face turned red, and her eyes were blazing. "How dare you even ask me such a question?"

"It's just a question, Professor." My eyebrows went up. "You can give me a yes or no. You were or you weren't."

She stood and walked toward me, her finger pointing like a pistol. "Detective, I am married to a very attractive man who looks ten years younger than me. Every woman in Rawlings who is under sixty and wants to save the salmon thinks that the best way to do that would be to sleep with him. I have a fourteen-year-old daughter who thinks I'm a royal bitch because I won't let her wear a tank-top to middle school. And I have a twelve-year-old boy who weighs forty-eight pounds, has the mind of a five-year-old, and wears diapers. Who *this afternoon* had a seizure that lasted almost three minutes, that terrified him so badly that he was crying hysterically for over an hour—and who for the next week will not sleep through the night without waking up screaming. And you want to know if I was having an affair with a graduate student? Are you out of your mind?"

"Is that a no?"

"I will contact your supervisor tomorrow. In the meantime, you can go to hell. Start by getting out of my house. Now." She strode out of the living room, toward what I assume was her bedroom.

I turned to Ryan. "You want to follow her and get her answer?"

He stood and gave me a dirty look. Then he turned and started walking out of the living room, toward the front door.

Back in the Charger, Ryan put his belt on with a little more force than necessary, then folded his hands in his lap and stared out the windshield.

"What?" I said.

He didn't respond, didn't look at me.

"Listen, I know she's had a shitty day. But I thought it would be useful to try to catch her off guard."

He turned to me. "What do you think we accomplished in there—besides angering a distraught woman?"

"I wanted to follow the cerebral-palsy thing. Ten to one Austin was giving that money to the charity because of her."

"So what exactly does that prove?"

"It doesn't prove anything. But do you see a guy like Austin—a guy nailing multiple women on any given night—thinking that cerebral palsy is really a terrible disease, so he'll let someone tap his arm couple times a week, and he'll jerk off into a plastic cup so he has money to give to the charity—all because his thesis adviser has a kid with cerebral palsy?"

"Why not? You think you know everything about him?"

"Of course not. But I think I've seen enough to know that everything's a transaction to Austin, and every transaction's about sex. He might have had some kind of real feelings about that kid. He might even have had some real feelings about Suzannah. But he wasn't the kind of guy who had an unrequited infatuation with a woman. If he was all dreamy about Suzannah and her sick kid, my money says he was fucking her, too."

Ryan turned to me. "I'm not sure Larry Klein would say that adds up to probable cause."

"I'm not talking about probable cause. I'm just saying, a guy like Austin needs the pussy. That's what he does. It's who he is."

"I'm not there yet."

"Okay, how about this? Did she answer my question about whether she was doing Austin?"

"You're lucky she didn't come after you with the fireplace poker."

"All right, tell me what you know about her marriage to her husband."

"I don't know anything about her marriage."

"Yes, you do. What did she say about him?"

"That he works at home. That he runs this environmental group."

"What's he look like?"

"I have no idea."

"I do. He looks good. Didn't she say she looks fifty-eight, and he looks younger than that?"

Ryan nodded his head. "That all the women who want to save the salmon want to sleep with him, something like that."

"That's right," I said. "She said she couldn't attract any man, let alone a young man. Put it together, Einstein."

He looked at me. "She's sexually insecure. A good-looking young guy comes along, shows some interest in her—or in her kid. However it develops, they end up in bed."

"And once you put the two of them in the sack, there's all kinds of reasons she might want to strangle him."

"Just like the other women we're looking at," Ryan said.

"Until we come up with probable cause for arresting Tiffany Rhodes, Brian Hawser, May Eberlein, or Kathy Caravelli," I said, "we need to look at Suzannah Montgomery."

Ryan was silent. This time I think it meant he agreed with me.

Chapter 23

My fingers were curled around some heavy-duty chain-link fence topped with razor wire. On the other side of the fence was a long line of young guys, hundreds of them, all in orange jumpsuits, the line extending to the horizon. Their ankles were chained together so they were walking with tiny, shuffling steps. Their hands were chained together behind their backs, too, and each kid was attached to the kid in front of him by another chain around his waist. Officers in black uniforms wearing helmets with dark visors that hid their faces were hurrying the kids along, hitting the slow ones on their shoulders and backs and heads with nightsticks. The kids were being led onto a grey bus, dozens and dozens of them struggling up the steps into the door at the front.

Tommy was in chains, and as he walked past me, he glanced up for a second but didn't react. I was crying, out of control, as I watched him in the procession of young guys, hundreds and hundreds of them awkwardly climbing up the steps into the grey bus.

Something pushed against my shoulder, rocking me back and forth. "Karen," I heard a man's voice over the clanking of the chains and the cries of the kids as the guards hit them with nightsticks. "Karen, it's for you."

I began to climb out of the dream. Mac had my cell in his hand. The pale green light from the screen gave his face a sickly glow as he handed me the phone. I looked at the fuzzy orange numbers on my clock radio. All I could make out was that the time started with a 2.

I cleared my throat. "Seagate," I said.

"Seagate, this is Pelton." Rob Pelton was one of the night-duty detectives. "Sorry to wake you."

"That's okay, what is it?"

"Your grad-student case. You're looking at a co-ed, right? A girl named Tiffany Rhodes?"

"Yeah, what about her?"

"She's in the ER."

"Shit. What happened?"

"Looks like domestic violence. A uniform team was called to her apartment."

I pulled my feet out from under the covers and planted them on the carpet. I rubbed my eyes. "All right, Rob, I'll catch up with you at headquarters. Could you get the uniforms to meet me in fifteen at the ER?"

"Got it," Pelton said.

"Thanks a lot." I ended the call.

Mac said, "You need anything?"

"No, I gotta go out. Thanks."

I got up and carried the phone with me into the bathroom and turned on the light. I speed-dialed Ryan. In a moment, his wife picked up. "Hey, Kali, Karen Seagate. Sorry to do this to you."

Her voice was tiny and far away. "That's okay." I heard the phone being jostled.

"Yeah, Karen." It was Ryan.

"Sorry, partner. Tiffany Rhodes is in the ER. I'm gonna head over. Just wanted to give you a head's-up in case you want in. I can do it on my own."

"No, that's all right. I'll meet you there."

Mac had turned on the light on the night table on my side of the bed. It was plenty for me to get dressed. He was lying on his side, his arm holding my pillow over the side of his head.

I was out the door in two minutes. The night was cold, black, and still. With no traffic, I made it to the hospital in eight minutes, then parked in the curved driveway leading up to the ER entrance, far enough away from the big glass doors that I wouldn't block any ambulances coming in. As I was getting out of my Honda, I saw Ryan's Mitsubishi pull in behind me.

He caught up with me as we tripped the big glass doors. He was wearing jeans and a nylon BYU windbreaker over a tee shirt; I'd never seen him wearing anything but a suit. "What do you know?"

"Just that the uniforms thought it was domestic violence."

We walked past the four or five people scattered among the twenty or so blue plastic chairs. There was a homeless guy whose face was bruised and bleeding a little, a teenager with what looked like a dislocated shoulder, and a couple sets of young parents with little kids in pajamas blowing snot all over the place.

We walked over to the two uniforms standing near the desk.

"Detectives," Wilson said, nodding to us. I knew Wilson, a big square-jawed guy with a jarhead cut. Next to him was a short Hispanic woman I'd never met. Her badge said Arroyo.

"Thanks for coming by," I said to Wilson. "Brief us."

He pulled a notebook from his back pocket. "We got the call from a neighbor at 1:47. Went over, knocked on the door. No answer. Forced the door open. Female Caucasian, eighteen to twenty, lying on the floor, unconscious, in front of a bookcase. Finger marks on her upper arms. Face bruised bad, like she'd been popped a couple of times. Pool of blood coming out of the back of her head, and she'd vomited. We called for a bus and notified Pelton and Malone. The paramedics were there in four minutes."

"There was no guy in the apartment, right?"

"Yeah, we cleared the place. The drawers in the bedroom were open and empty, like the guy had thrown some stuff in a bag."

"All right, Wilson, Arroyo, thanks." The two uniforms turned and left.

"Ryan, I'd like you to meet up with Pelton and Malone. They're probably still at the apartment or back at headquarters. I don't know how the chief wants to play this—"

"You mean as a separate case or part of Austin Sulenka?"

"Yeah, but meet with the two detectives—you help them or they help you. Just make sure you get the specs on Brian's car, put out an alert on it. Get his home address—he's from Billings, right?"

"That's right."

"Contact MSP and Billings PD to try to run Brian down. I'll stay here and figure out what's going on with Tiffany. I'll catch up with you back at headquarters, okay?"

He nodded and headed out.

Pulling my shield out of my big leather bag and putting it around my neck, I walked over to the desk. "Rawlings PD," I said. "Detective Seagate. You saw a college girl, Tiffany Rhodes, within the last half hour?"

The woman looked at her computer screen. "That's right." Her expression was somber. I couldn't tell if that was because of what she was reading off the screen or what she did for a living. "I'll call the attending. He'll be out as soon as he can. Take a seat, please."

"Thanks." I walked over to a corner of the waiting room as far as I could get from the sick little buggers. I sat and waited. Except for the occasional whine and crying jag from one of the kids, the place was quiet. Scared, sad, and quiet.

I was zonked. I don't sleep well anymore, and when I have to get up at two o'clock the adrenaline only lasts me an hour at most. Soon as I sit down, if the place is reasonably quiet, I can go out in a couple minutes. I glanced over at the food machines in the corner of the room. A four-year-old boy in Spiderman pajamas was germing up every surface he could reach. I waited for him to move on. A few second later, he was crawling on the floor, picking at something on the underside of one of the blue plastic chairs. I glanced at the adults in the waiting room. I figured it had to be a dad without a mom. There he was, over to the side, reading a magazine. He had long, stringy hair and a droopy mustache, a leather Harley vest with fringes over a sleeveless tee shirt. Not exactly a helicopter parent, but I guess he deserved some points for at least bringing the sick kid in.

I walked over to the machines, a dollar bill in my hand. I fed the bill in and, with my knuckles, pushed the buttons. I waited as the cup filled, then carefully lifted it out of the machine without touching any surfaces.

I burned my tongue on the coffee-colored battery acid, my mind fixed on whether I'd just gotten Tiffany hurt. It was Brian beat her up, no doubt about it. But what did she do to piss him off? It could've been nothing to do with the case. I've done enough domestics to know it doesn't have to be anything real big. Half the time, it's something that's been brewing for days or weeks. The guy gets madder and madder and, since he's likely to be the strong, stupid type, one day he explodes and beats the crap out of her. If she's conscious, she tells me what she did wrong. She bought the wrong kind of ketchup, or she was talking too loud on the phone when he was trying to watch football, or he saw her smile when she ran into the guy from down the street, or some other deadly sin.

I couldn't shake the feeling that we'd done something that got Tiffany in trouble with Brian. The idiot already knew she had traded pussy for a grade with Austin, even though that hadn't worked out quite right from her perspective. Nothing we'd done would've tipped Brian off she was still screwing Austin. We were careful to make sure we asked for her DNA along with Brian's so it wouldn't tip him off we already knew she was at Austin's apartment. The little chat we had with her at the coffee shop shouldn't have gotten her in trouble. Even if Brian knew about it, Tiffany could've said we just ran into her. I wasn't seeing how we could've gotten her beat up, but my gut told me we had.

The metal swinging doors opened and a guy in scrubs came out. The front of his blue shirt was covered in blood, including the mask that dangled from his neck. He was tall and skinny, with thick brown hair and glasses. Even though he looked only thirty, I could see the wrinkles forming around his eyes.

He saw my shield and came walking over to me. He wiped his brow with his sleeve. "David Tristan," he said. "You're here about Tiffany Rhodes?"

"Karen Seagate," I said. "Yeah, what've you got on her?"

"It was domestic violence. Somebody punched her around. Grabbed her, shook her, then looks like he hit her in the face. Broke her cheekbone. She probably fell backward, hit her head on something."

"How bad is she?"

"Fractured her skull, which ruptured the membrane and caused some bleeding. We did a CT on her, but she was swelling up pretty bad. We removed part of her skull and put in a drain. But the lesion was too far inside the brain. The neurosurgeon couldn't control the bleeding."

"What are you saying?"

"I'm saying we couldn't save her."

I got wobbly, then I heard the paper cup of coffee hit the floor. The room grew dark. Someone was grabbing my upper arms, leading me over to one of the plastic seats. In the distance, someone called out "Nurse." Then I was gone for a while. I smelled some ammonia or something and came back. I recognized the nurse from behind the counter. She was holding smelling salts under my nose. Her face was in close to mine. She looked concerned.

She had a hand on my shoulder, supporting me. I saw the doc turn and start walking back toward the big swinging doors.

"Are you all right?" the nurse said to me.

"Yeah," I said. "I'm fine. Just give me a second." I took a few deep breaths. I didn't know why I was reacting like this. I didn't even like Tiffany. "What's your name?"

"Cynthia," she said.

"Call the doc. Get him back here." I closed my eyes for a second. When I opened them again, the doc and the nurse were standing in front of me. I lifted myself up off the chair. Cynthia put out her arm to help support me. "Okay, listen, this is important. We know who attacked her. When we pick him up, we need him to think Tiffany's alive. Do you understand me?"

I looked from the doc to the nurse. They both nodded.

"Doc, what can you say happened to her? A minor concussion?"

"Sure, a concussion and a bruise to her cheek. We're holding her for observation because of the concussion."

"Cynthia, can you make that happen? I mean, on the computer."

"Of course," she said. "What about notification of next of kin?"

"We'll take care of that," I said. "But it's real important you work with me here on the concussion thing. The guy who did this we like for another murder, and I want to be able to work a deal with him on this domestic, okay?"

The doc said, "Whatever." He turned and disappeared back through the swinging doors.

Cynthia said, "Are you okay to drive?"

That's usually a good question, but not so much now I'm on the wagon. "Yeah, I'll be fine. Thanks a lot."

I walked out into the cold air, which helped me sharpen up a little. I got in my Honda and drove over to headquarters. I carded my way in the back door and checked in the detectives' bullpen, but Ryan wasn't there. Neither were Pelton and Malone. I decided to try the incident room.

Rob Pelton, Andy Malone, and Ryan were sitting at the big table.

"Hey, Karen," Ryan said. The two other detectives acknowledged me, too.

"Catch me up," I said.

"Rob and Andy secured the crime scene," Ryan said. "Robin will head over to do the forensics when her shift starts."

"Did you reach out to MSP and Billings PD?"

Rob Pelton said, "All that's done, Karen. We got the guy's ID off some stuff in the apartment. We got his vehicle specs, too."

"Did you do a canvass?"

"Yeah, we did it," Andy Malone said, stifling a yawn. "Only people we got anything from was the couple in the next apartment. They were the ones called it in. Indians or Paks or something. They didn't really know Tiffany and Brian. Some shouting, furniture crashing, then silence. Called 911. They heard tires screeching a couple minutes later. That was it."

"Did you contact the chief, Rob?"

"No, I decided to hold off till five. That's when he wakes up anyway. There's nothing he needs to do now. We've been looking for the guy's car. Billings PD is looking at his parents' house. We've got a unit parked near his apartment here in town in case he comes back for a toothbrush. Let the chief sleep."

"Okay, you want to brief him when he gets in?"

"Sure," Rob Pelton said. "Then he'll decide whether to wrap this in with your case or treat it as separate. Sound okay to you?"

I looked at Ryan. "Got any questions for them?"

"No," Ryan said. "I'm good."

"All right, Rob. Andy. Thanks a lot," I said. The two night detectives stood up and headed out.

"You need me for anything?" I said to Ryan.

He shook his head. "You want to talk about how Brian decided to beat up Tiffany?"

"I'm exhausted," I said. "How about we wait until the chief comes in?"

"Yeah, that's fine," he said, and I turned to head off to the storage room, where we've got a couple of cots for cops who find themselves at headquarters during the wrong shift. "Were you able to talk to Tiffany?"

I felt the stinging in my eyes, and then the tears started. "I'm sorry, Ryan. Forgot to tell you. Tiffany's dead. Brian killed her. Brian did, or we did." I wiped at my eyes.

"Don't do that, Karen," he said. "We didn't do it."

"And how do you know that, Ryan? Tell me how the fuck you know that." I was crying now, tears falling off my chin.

He turned his back to me and stood there, motionless.

"I'm sorry. I shouldn't have talked like that to you." I touched his arm, but he didn't move. I wiped some of the tears away with my knuckles. "I told the hospital to keep it quiet. In case Brian contacts them." I turned and stumbled off to the storage room and the cot.

Chapter 24

I heard a door open, but since my dreams are so full of sounds and sights that don't make any sense it didn't seem unusual that in this particular dream I was stumbling across a high plain full of scrub brush, where there weren't likely to be any doors.

"Karen, the chief's ready to see us." It was Ryan, his voice coming in small from the other side of the room. My eyes stung a little as I opened them and tried to focus. I couldn't quite tell where I was. He hadn't turned on the light in the storeroom, so all I saw was his big shape silhouetted in front of a rectangle of light from the hallway.

"Give me two minutes, okay?"

"I'll be in his office." When Ryan is pissed at me, he speaks in clipped phrases.

I felt my forehead begin to throb. I get that when I don't sleep enough. When I'm upset, which I was about Tiffany, it gets worse. I staggered to the ladies' room and splashed some water on my face. There wasn't much I could do about my red-rimmed eyes. Then I realized that nobody gives a shit what I look like, a realization that comforted me for well over a half-second.

Margaret waved me into the chief's office. He was in his mesh chair behind his desk. Ryan stood, then sat back down on the small couch as I sank into one of the soft chairs.

"Ryan's been catching me up on the Tiffany Rhodes case and his work with Pelton and Malone last night."

"Good," I said. "Sorry I missed that."

The chief waved his hand to tell me it was fine that I was able to get some sleep.

"At least we've got her DNA now." I didn't intend it to come out cruel. And I didn't mean it to sound critical. Not critical of Ryan or the chief, anyway. I was looking at the carpet, my eyes stinging and my head pounding. The two guys didn't say anything for a few long seconds.

Finally, the chief spoke. "Give us your read on what happened to her."

I looked up at him. "Since Brian Hawser skipped, it's pretty clear he did it. Only question is why."

"No possibility it's unrelated to the Austin Sulenka case?"

"Well, yeah, I guess it's possible. Technically. There's a handful of domestics every year in town. Half the time the woman doesn't know what set him off. But it would be a hell of a coincidence."

"What do we know about her whereabouts before Brian attacked her?"

I turned to Ryan. His face was a blank. He was still mad at me. "You get a chance to tell the chief about interviewing her at the coffee—"

The chief interrupted. "I want to hear your version."

"We hadn't followed up on where she was Sunday night, after she screwed Austin. Brian thought she was home in Billings—or at least that's what she told us he thought. So we interviewed her again, at a Starbucks."

"Why'd you go there?"

"It was her suggestion. She didn't want us to come to her apartment because Brian was there. She figured he'd get suspicious if he saw we were still looking at her for Austin."

"You arranged this interview on the phone, right?"

"Yeah, she was in the bedroom. Brian was in the living room."

"So it's possible Brian heard Tiffany arranging to meet with you."

I nodded.

"Then she comes out of the bedroom," the chief said, "and tells him some story about how she has to go out."

"And he could've followed her," I said.

"I was just speculating," the chief said. "So what did you get from her at the coffee shop?"

"She told us she went to her girlfriend's place. Couple guys came over, with weed. She thinks she had sex. She wasn't sharp on the details—whether it was one guy or two, blowjobs or official fucking. Only thing she was certain about was how she didn't get in her car and drive over later to kill Austin."

"And why was she certain about that?"

"She wouldn't drive because she knew she was wrecked and she already had a DUI."

He shook his head. I don't know if the chief has any kids, but his expression told me maybe he did. "Any chance either of the two guys with the weed are involved with the domestic?"

I frowned and shook my head. "A guy gets fucked by some girl he doesn't know her name, that's better than Christmas. The two guys wouldn't even know where she lived. If they found out, it would be to get her to screw them again."

The chief looked over at Ryan. "You see it that way?"

"Yes," Ryan said.

"Any other theories on how Brian killed Tiffany?"

"It's possible she just wanted to break it off with him," I said.

"Go on," the chief said.

I hadn't thought this through, but I started talking. "Think about what she'd been through in the last few days. Austin dies, she has to tell us she was still doing him, she has to tell us she did those two guys in her girlfriend's apartment. She realizes she's out of control. If she's still attracted to Austin because he's a cut above Brian, and she's not even able to be faithful to the idiot when a couple of guys wave a hash pipe in front of her face—it's possible she decides she's taking advantage of Brian, which he doesn't deserve because even though he's basically a shithead, he's a loyal shithead. He stuck with her after he found out about her doing Austin. He trashed Austin's car. He didn't beat her up for it."

"Yes, but that last part doesn't square with him beating her up last night."

I put my palms up. "I have no idea what happened," I said. "Depends how she handled it right before he smacked her around. A few months ago, when he found out about Austin, she was his girl. She made a mistake. He forgave her. End of story—until we butt in. But last night, if she wants to break it off, she might decide to tell him she was still doing Austin—and then did the two dopers for no good reason at all. To show Brian that she's not worthy of him."

"So now she's not his girl," the chief said. "Now she's officially a slut."

"That's right. A slut who's been taking advantage of him. Which pisses him off. Just like Austin was taking advantage of him. But this time he can't just vandalize a car. This time, it's personal. And since he loves her, in his shithead way, he loses control."

The chief and Ryan were silent.

"That's if she and Brian didn't have anything to do with killing Austin," I said. "If they killed Austin, this is her chance to take out Brian."

"And take the kind of beating she took?"

"She thought she might take a few punches but she'd be okay."

"How's that?" the chief said.

"Maybe she had a gun. Thought he'd beat her up, then she'd shoot him."

The chief looked at Ryan. "Brian have a permit?"

"He has a .45," Ryan said.

"The plan didn't work." I glanced over at Ryan, who at least was looking at me. "But the plan was she'd have silenced the only other person who could finger her for killing Austin. And her bruises would back up her self-defense story."

The chief rested his chin on his fist. "Here's what I'd like you two to do. Run down the remaining leads on the Sulenka murder."

"What do you mean?" I said.

"Rule out the two guys with the weed. Get with Robin to see whether Tiffany's DNA matches the DNA on Austin's body. Remember you wanted to see if there was another woman who had sex with him? One is the grad student, May Something. The other, presumably, is Tiffany. If it's not, you need to identify the third woman."

"Wouldn't it be better to put me and Ryan on Brian Hawser?"

"No, we don't know if Brian is part of your case. I'm going to open up a new case file on the Tiffany Rhodes murder."

"Who's gonna work that?"

"For the moment, it's Pelton and Malone."

"They're on night shift."

"I'm aware of that, Karen." His tone was hard-edged. "They don't have any open cases right now. If they need someone to help them during the day, they'll tell me, and if you and Ryan are free, you're up."

"And when we figure out Tiffany was killed because of the Sulenka case?"

"If that's how it turns out, we'll fold the two cases together and I'll decide on assignments at that point." He paused. "You and Ryan make sure the file on the system is complete and current so Pelton and Malone can access everything they need." He paused. "Will there be anything else?"

"Do you want me to notify Tiffany's parents?"

"No," the chief said. "I'll do it. It'll sound better coming from the chief."

"I can say it right."

"I know that, Karen." He paused, his tone a little softer. "I know you can. By the way, when you told the hospital to put a lid on her death, that was smart. That was excellent. But I'm going to notify her parents. I want to check with Larry Klein first to see what we can do with the hospital, then I'll be in a better position to reach out to the parents. For all we know, they might be close to Brian. Might tip him off, and we would lose any leverage we have on him with the Sulenka case."

"Plus we could have a bad PR problem."

He stared at me. "Go home and get some rest." It wasn't a question. "Ryan can work this alone today. You're dismissed."

I shook my head and turned to leave. Since the carpet in the chief's office is pretty thick, I couldn't hear Ryan following me until we were out on the tile in the hall.

Back at our desks in the detective's bullpen, Ryan sat down.

I said, "You got the name of Tiffany's girlfriend, where she screwed the two guys?"

"You not going to head home?" Short for, You're not going to go home, like the chief just told you to do because it's obvious you're not in any condition to work, if work includes talking to people?

"Give me her name."

Ryan pulled his notebook from his pocket and turned the pages. "Emily Johnston."

"Phone number."

"Karen, I have to agree with the chief."

"You do. Why is that? I'm too fucked-up to run the case?"

"If he can put two teams on the case, why not?"

I shook my head. Now he wasn't even leveling with me.

"It doesn't matter who goes after Brian," he said. "As long as someone's doing the liaison with the MSP and with Billings, what difference does it make?"

If he wanted to pretend it wasn't about me, I'd play along. "The difference is we earned the right to take the lead on this case. Obviously, it's Brian killed Austin."

"Or Tiffany."

"Yeah, whatever. It wasn't the two dipshits with the weed, that's for sure. They'd want to wash her car, not beat her up."

"You're probably right, but just let it go. We'll mop up the stuff here in Rawlings. When Pelton and Malone bring in Hawser, I'm sure the chief will let us lead the interviews."

"Dream on," I said. "Just get me Emily's phone number."

He hit the keys for a little bit. "There's three in town, but this one is a CMSU student." He started writing on a slip of paper. "Emily Johnston, 450 Crest Wood, Apartment 3C. 526-7634." He handed me the paper.

I sat down at my desk and punched in the number. My head was still thumping, my eyes still stinging pretty good. I rubbed at them, which made it worse. Someone picked up the phone. "Is this Emily Johnston?"

"Yes."

"This is Detective Karen Seagate, Rawlings Police Department. Do you know a woman named Tiffany Rhodes?"

"Why?"

"It's a case related to Tiffany. There was a break-in at her apartment, someone took some stuff."

"Oh, my God, she didn't tell me about that." Emily Johnston paused. "What does that have to do with me?"

"She came over to your place Sunday night. Couple of guys came over. Can you give me their names?"

"Fred and Larry."

"You have last names?"

"I don't know their last names."

"You got addresses on them?"

"They're here in my building. They're in 3F."

"All right, thanks."

"Wait, you don't think they broke into Tiff's place, do you?"

"No, of course not. We just want to talk to them a couple minutes. It's routine. Thanks a lot, Emily." I hung up the phone.

I turned to Ryan. "You coming?"

He stood up and followed me out to the lot behind the building.

"Take Wilmington west," Ryan said after we'd gotten into the Charger. He was going to let me be miserable for a while. It's one of his better qualities.

He directed me to the apartment building. I parked in one of the visitors' spaces. We walked over to the mailboxes, stacked in rows and columns under a stucco overhand.

"Write down these names, would ya?" I said to Ryan. "3F is Boegland and Edwards."

We walked the three stories up the outside steps. Ryan was slowing down a little as we got up toward three. I knocked on the door.

A pimply guy—small build, slouchy posture, dirty brown hair and a shitty excuse for a moustache—opened the door. I put my shield around my neck. "Are you Boegland or Edwards?"

His eyes were open wide. "I'm Larry Boegland. What's this about?"

"Seagate and Miner. Rawlings Police Department. Can we come in?" I started to walk in before he could respond. He stood back. "Is Edwards here?"

"He's sleeping." His voice was getting high, a little squeaky. "What's this about?"

"Wake him up."

He hurried toward one of the bedrooms, and thirty seconds later a tall, stocky guy with matted hair wandered out behind him.

"You're Fred Edwards."

He nodded.

"We're investigating a break-in at Tiffany Williams' apartment Sunday night." I wanted to see if they knew her last name. "Can you tell us where you were Sunday night, around ten?"

Fred looked at Larry, who looked back at him. Neither of them seemed to know what to say.

"While you guys think this over, let me explain something. I already know the answer to my question. So if you lie to me, I've got a search warrant right here." I tapped my big leather bag. "I'll have a narcotics team over here in ten minutes—with a dog that's got a fuckin' nose on it you won't believe. If there's one pot seed in this apartment, we'll arrest you on possession, maybe possession with intent. Penalty for that starts at one year and goes up from there, depending on the quantity. Do you understand me, Larry?"

I looked at him. He nodded, obediently.

"And you, Fred, you understand me?" He was now fully awake.

"Which one of you brought the pot to Emily's place?"

"That was me," Larry said, his eyes down on the floor.

"The two girls, Emily and Tiffany, which one did you screw, Larry?"

"Both of them, I think."

"And you, Fred, you do them both, too."

"Yeah."

"All right, guys. Good. You've told me the truth so far. We've got an eyewitness puts you two in the lot behind Tiffany's apartment. Around midnight. Admit it and we can work something out on the burglary."

"That's bullshit," Fred said. "We practically had to crawl down the hall. We both crashed here. I was dead till after eleven the next morning."

Larry said, "It wasn't us. I don't even know where Tiffany lives. I don't even know that's her name. What'd you say it was, Tiffany Williams?"

I glanced at Ryan, who nodded slightly.

"Okay, guys. We're gonna do a little more investigating. You two stay in town. We might wanna bring you in for a lineup later this afternoon. You understand?"

Larry nodded. Fred said, "Yes, Officer. We can come in any time. It wasn't us. I swear."

Ryan and I turned and left the apartment.

"Ready to scratch the pot boys off our list?"

"Yes, Officer," he said, giving me a small smile, which I was very glad to see.

Chapter 25

The Way Things Worked Out. It was nothing more than that. Not sexism, not the good-old-boy network. Not that I was a drunk or had fallen apart. Just the way things turned out.

That's why the two night-shift detectives were chasing down Brian Hawser, who packed his gym bag with some haste after he shook the shit out of his live-in girlfriend, Tiffany Rhodes, then punched her in the face hard enough to break her cheekbone, propelling her into a hard, pointy surface, fracturing her skull, ripping the tissue membrane underneath it, and causing the brain bleed that killed her right about the time he was merging onto the interstate toward Billings or parts unknown.

So what we *knew* so far is that four months ago Brian busted all the glassy parts of Austin Sulenka's automobile because Austin nailed his girlfriend, Tiffany, who wanted a higher grade in Austin's English course. Then, the night Austin was strangled, Tiffany fucked Austin. One last time before she killed him? Before she and Brian killed him? It gets a little fuzzy at this point.

But last night we're pretty sure Tiffany told her lover boy she was still nailing the handsome English teacher with the big dick. Plus, perhaps, the two dweebs with the marijuana. Yes, she did them, too. For the marijuana. Or, one way or another, Brian found out about her extracurriculars. Then Tiffany got dead, and Brian got gone.

I'm not the only one with anger issues.

But it's just The Way Things Worked Out: Ryan and I were interviewing the two marijuana morons instead of sniffing Brian's trail. But the chief was right. We should scratch off all the local ladies who liked to straddle Austin Sulenka. We were getting to know them, checking their stories, figuring out which ones were telling us normal little white lies to make themselves feel better about their normal little shortcomings, which ones were spinning tales black enough to make us think, yeah, I could see them maybe wrapping that cloth around Austin's neck, tying a cinch in it, then pulling it tighter and tighter, not stopping when his eyes started bugging and his face turned ghostly blue, his arms grasping at the cinch with some strength at the start but then relaxing and falling to his sides as if he'd just experienced this beautiful, intense orgasm.

The night detectives could do just as good a job coordinating the search for Brian Hawser as we could. And two plus two still does equal four detectives. I was wrong to get pissed at the chief. Murtaugh isn't a sexist asshole. He's just a manager, running his crew.

"You in there, Karen?" Ryan said. I was apparently sitting behind the wheel of the Charger but not, you know, doing anything, such as driving.

"I want to make sure Robin's going to get Tiffany's DNA from the hospital." I reached behind me to the back seat, where I'd just tossed my big leather bag, and fished around to get my phone. I speed-dialed her. She confirmed that she had indeed been told about Tiffany, would be going over there within the hour, and would start to type her DNA. In response to my next question, she said it would take thirty-six hours at least. Then when I suggested that after she typed it she run it through one of her DNA databases to see if there were any surprises, she told me that was a great suggestion and asked me to hold a second so she could find a pen or pencil somewhere to be sure to write it down.

I need to work out some sort of signal with her that says it's my turn to act really pissy now, could she hold off until later?

"Okay," I said to Ryan, "while we wait thirty-six hours on Tiffany's DNA, how do you want to go at Suzannah Montgomery?" She had handed in her promotion papers a few days late, which obviously marked her as a natural-born killer. "You want to track down her husband, the environmental guy?"

Ryan was wearing a pained expression. "No, I don't think so."

"Because he's—what was that word you used about his wife when the kid had those seizures?—he's all disturbed?"

He raised an eyebrow. "I said she was distraught."

"Yeah, that's it. Because he's all distraught?"

"Well, I think he might still be distraught, disturbed, distressed, discomfited. Upset." He paused. He can be a real showoff. "But that's not why I wouldn't go after the husband now. I'd rather run down Van Vleet's story about her tenure case."

"Why's that?"

"We talk to the husband, what are we going to say? 'Could you tell us if your wife was having an affair with her grad student?'"

"I like it," I said. "Then we ask, 'And do you know if she strangled him? Did she mention any of that during pillow-talk?'"

"True, that would make for an interesting interview, and we could get thrown out of whatever room we were in when we asked him, just like his wife threw us out of her house. But we don't yet have any evidence of an affair, and all we'd accomplish is to have another member of that same family call the chief to complain about his two unhinged detectives."

"You're such a pussy, you know that?" But I did appreciate how he said there were two unhinged detectives.

"Let's run down that thing we do know about: the tenure case. If it turns out there's anything to it—the story doesn't add up—then we can go after the husband. But if she turns out to be clean, there's really no reason to pry into their marriage, is there?"

"Really? You've heard of a lot of grad students living on mac and cheese and selling their fluids so they can give money to a disease charity?"

He looked at me. "Not a lot. A few."

"Without getting to screw somebody for their good works?"

"A few," he said again. "Remember, I'm LDS. We've got some real Boy Scouts."

"All right," I said. "Let's find out all the horrifying details about how Suzannah Montgomery submitted her papers a few days late."

"Another way to look at it: by the time we cross Suzannah off our list, Pelton and Malone will have tracked down Brian Hawser, and we'll be sitting across the table from him in Interview 1."

"Then I can get really unhinged?"

"Then you can break him like a matchstick."

I nodded. "I'm gonna hold you to that. Okay, how do we go at Suzannah Montgomery? Frances Hamblin was the department chair who backed her up. Want to interview her again?"

Ryan shook his head. "She's not going to be straight with us. Since she was a player, all we'll get from her is what she gave to the appeals committee years ago."

"Then who?"

"Let's try the provost. I don't know who he is, but if he can't tell us what really happened, he'll know someone who can."

"And you're thinking this guy's gonna dish some dirt on one of his faculty members?"

"We're going to have to figure out a reason for him to be candid with us."

"So it doesn't get into that teachers' trade paper again?"

"That, or because telling the truth is the right thing to do?"
I looked at him.

"Would you like to call me a pussy again?"

"No, you're a child."

"Okay, I'm a child."

"A little, tiny girl child."

"Would you please drive me home?" Ryan said. "I don't think I can go on."

"I have a better idea. I drive us over to the university. You phone the provost and see if we can talk to him about Suzannah Montgomery."

As I turned the Charger over and headed toward campus, Ryan swiveled the computer and started looking stuff up. He opened his phone and made a call.

"Dr. Audrey Miller will be able to see us for a few minutes before her next appointment."

"I feel blessed," I said.

I parked in the lot behind the Administration Building. We made it to the executive offices on the first floor. Inside the glass doors with all the big cheeses' names painted on them stood Audrey Miller, a short, stocky woman of about sixty, with black and grey wavy hair, cut short. She was wearing a severe black dress, a couple of inches below her knee, and office-camo black-tinted stockings over her thick calves. "Audrey Miller," she said, and I introduced me and Ryan. We all shook hands. She didn't bother to smile.

She looked down at her black pumps, which were covered in dust. "Jennifer," she said to one of her assistants, "could you get me a wet paper towel?" Then, to me, "I'm sorry, I just came from a groundbreaking."

I nodded, wondering if it was my turn to tell her where I just came from. I decided not to mention that Ryan and I had just interviewed two stoners who had screwed Emily Johnston and the late Tiffany Rhodes Sunday night.

The assistant hurried back. "Let me do that," she said, bending down on one knee to clean off the provost's shoes. She had two paper towels, so she didn't have to lick the shoes clean.

"Thank you," she said to the assistant. "Come in," she said to me and Ryan. We walked into her big office, which had a massive oak desk with matching file cabinets, a couch, three upholstered chairs, and a conference table big enough for six, all sitting on a deep-plush slate-colored carpet. One wall was reserved for diplomas, plaques, and large, framed professional photos of campus. The other walls had what looked like real paintings on them. Off to the side was a door that I think opened to her own bathroom. Her office was bigger than any room in my house.

Audrey Miller gestured for us to sit. She took her high-backed black leather desk chair and stared at her laptop. She looked at her laptop and hit a few keys, then squinted through her rimless glasses at her watch. "I have a very important meeting in exactly seventeen minutes. What can I do for you?" She looked at me, assuming I was the senior cop.

"Why don't you start?" I said to Ryan. Since I was running on fumes and my head was still throbbing, I thought we'd have a better chance of getting something out of this woman if Ryan led.

He nodded. "Provost Miller, we're hoping you can help us with some information related to the Austin Sulenka case."

She put out her hand, telling him to continue. She wasn't going to waste everyone's time cluck-clucking about how terrible it all was. I liked that. She sat stock still, eyes focused on Ryan, the creases between her eyes sharp.

"It's about an incident from seven years ago. The tenure case of Suzannah Montgomery, in the English department."

Audrey Miller looked puzzled. "What does that have to do with the murder?"

"Well, ma'am, we can't go into any detail about that. But I can say that some questions have been raised about Professor Montgomery in her role as Austin Sulenka's adviser."

"Raised by whom?"

"Unfortunately, all we can say at this point is that we'd like to understand a little more about Professor Montgomery's tenure case and Professor Hamblin. Do you have any knowledge of that situation?"

"I was the chair of the Faculty Senate at that time."

"There was another tenure candidate that year—"

"I knew Mitch Abrams."

Ryan sat up straighter in his chair. "Professor Abrams appealed his denial of tenure. Professor Hamblin supported Professor Montgomery. Do I have this correct so far?"

"What happened is this: Mitch made some allegations about due-process problems with Suzannah's case. Frances Hamblin said those problems were her fault. The appeals committee ruled in favor of Suzannah and Frances and against Mitch. That is what happened." She shifted her weight on her chair to signal that she had spoken and the truth was now established.

"As we understand it, Mitch Abrams argued that he was entitled to a new review of his case because of irregularities with Suzannah Montgomery's case. Apparently, her papers were submitted late."

"That is what appeared in the university's public statements, and in the *Chronicle*."

Ryan looked at her intently for a moment. "Is that not the truth?"

Her gaze drifted off beyond Ryan's shoulder. She was silent for the longest while. "No, that is not the truth."

Ryan looked at her. "Could you tell us what the truth is?"

"Close the door." Ryan rose briskly and did it, then came back to his seat. "Mitch alleged that while it was true that

Suzannah submitted her papers late, the irregularities extended beyond lateness. Much beyond lateness."

"Could you tell us what the allegations were?"

"Would you excuse me a moment?" She stood, walked around from behind her big desk, and left the office, leaving the door open.

I looked out to the outer office, but I couldn't see where she had gone. "Bladder-control issues?"

Ryan said, "I think we're supposed to sit here."

Two minutes later, Audrey Miller walked back into her office. She was holding a plain manila envelope, which she placed on the edge of her desk, in front of where Ryan was sitting.

"You'll have to excuse me," she said, looking at her watch. "I need to get to my appointment. Can you show yourselves out?"

"Thank you, Provost Miller," Ryan said. The two of us stood up.

She walked out of her office.

Ryan picked up the envelope from her desk, dropped it into the leather briefcase at his feet, and clicked the clasp shut.

Chapter 26

Back in the Charger, Ryan said, "Well, what would you like to do next?"

I gave him a look. "Open the damn envelope."

"Oh, yeah, right," he said. He opened his briefcase, pulled out the envelope, opened the shiny tab, slid out the documents, and started reading. And he kept reading. I counted six pages. The sun streamed through the passenger window, highlighting the shape of the writing on the other side of the photocopies. They were letters.

After about three minutes, I said, "I'm not disturbing you, am I?"

He turned to me. "No, not at all. I'm good, thanks." Finally, he straightened the pages and slid them back into the envelope.

This time, it was me who said, "Well, what would you like to do next?"

He smiled. "They're photocopies of three recommendation letters for Suzannah Montgomery. From seven years ago, when she was coming up for tenure."

"Since she did get tenure, I assume they were positive letters."

"Correct, they were."

"Any thoughts on why the provost put those three letters in an envelope and placed them in front of you so you would pick them up?"

"My guess is that she wanted us to read them."

When my son, Tommy, was small, he would occasionally play that annoying kid's game where he repeated everything I said. One day, I'd had enough. We got some quizzical looks in the grocery store, this six-year-old crying hysterically and shouting "Stop it, Mommy," and me, age thirty-two, shouting "Stop it, Mommy" right back at him. Ryan is quite a bit smarter than me in almost every measurable way, but when it comes to infantile behavior, he's not in my league.

I looked at him. "Why do you think that is?"

"To be perfectly honest with you, Karen, I don't really know."

"Can I assume that you didn't see anything in those three letters that would provide a clue?"

"Yes, you can assume that," Ryan said.

"In that case," I said, "I think we have two alternative explanations."

He looked at me, raising an eyebrow.

"One," I said, "is that the provost is mentally incompetent. Or, two: she wanted us to take the letters back to headquarters, read them a few more times, and try to figure out why she gave them to us." I paused. "Which alternative would you think is more likely?"

"I like Alternative Two."

"Thank you." I paused. "If I drove us back to headquarters now, do you think you could start to act like an adult?"

"I'm sorry," he said through an enormous yawn. "The baby's decided that the best way to get a lot of attention from his parents is to cry for five minutes every hour, all night long. When you called me last night in the middle of the night—whenever it was—Kali and I had just fallen asleep for about the sixth time. I'll behave. I promise."

"I'd appreciate it. Because if you're the idiot, I have to be the adult, and I don't want to confuse everyone."

"Got it," he said as I turned over the big Hemi engine in the Charger.

We drove back toward headquarters in silence. I glanced over at Ryan, whose eyelids were drooping, his chin sinking onto his chest.

At our desks, he handed me a letter. I read it over a couple of times. It was from a Robert Harson from University of Nevada at Las Vegas. He said Suzannah Montgomery seemed like she had done useful work in the four articles of hers that were included in the package. Her research was "interesting" and "opened up several intriguing new avenues of inquiry on Crane's 'The Open Boat.'" This other thing she had written about Vonnegut's *God Bless You, Mr. Rosewater* was good, too. And this conference paper about Vonnegut and technology was "a refreshing take on a well-researched topic."

"Ryan, do you know how to read these things?"

"What do you mean?"

"This letter says Suzannah's scholarship is good, intriguing, whatever. What the hell are we supposed to be looking for?"

"Not exactly sure," he said. "Give me another minute to go through these two again."

I read my letter again. Everything looked fine. The professor thought Suzannah was a good scholar. I sat back in my chair, pulled the lever under the seat so I could lean back, and closed my eyes. In a few seconds, I was out.

My head snapped back and I woke up all of a sudden. It took me a few seconds to realize where I was.

Ryan was talking to someone on his cell. He was asking all kinds of questions about what it meant if the letter said this or said that. I couldn't quite follow the conversation, hearing only half of it. Every few seconds, he'd go "uh-huh," "yeah," or "I see." Then, he broke out in a big grin. "That's it. Thanks a lot, Dad. Love to Mom." He ended the call.

"Did Dad tell you who killed Austin Sulenka?"

Ryan laughed and snapped his fingers. "*That's* what I forgot to ask him."

"What'd you get?"

"He was going on about how professors write these letters about other professors. You know, how if they don't like something the professor has written, they'll be snarky, but in a subtle way. They'll say it was "fully satisfactory" or "competent" or "workmanlike" or some other phrase that says it's second-rate. If they like it, they'll use all kinds of over-the-top language, like the book is a breakthrough, or scholars will have to rethink how they approach the author."

"Okay, so what does that tell us about Suzannah?"

"Well, if my dad is right about how to translate these letters, Suzannah is just what Frances Hamblin and that grad student, Melissa, said about her. She's competent. She produces acceptable research, but nothing extraordinary."

"So that's why the provost slipped us the letters? To tell us her faculty member was acceptable but not extraordinary?"

"Nope." He smiled and leaned back in his chair, his fingers intertwined behind his head.

"Why'd you say 'That's it' at the end of the call?"

"Because something my father said helped me figure out why the provost gave us the letters. He said that when three professors study a tenure candidate, they each see a different person."

"So?" I was shaking my head.

"So, your letter, from the professor in Nevada, says Suzannah's okay, not great. One of the two other letters—a professor in Santa Barbara—says Suzannah's okay, not great. But this letter," Ryan said, picking it up and waving it at me, "this professor from Massachusetts, says Suzannah is great."

"I don't get it. The Massachusetts professor likes her more. So what?"

"Like my father said, that professor is seeing a different person."

"We got two different people coming up for tenure?"

"I don't know exactly what's going on, but I'm going to find out right now."

"How exactly do you plan to do that?"

"Not exactly sure, but this professor in Massachusetts is the key. I can feel it."

I nodded my head, telling Ryan to go right ahead. He looked at the letter, then punched in a number on his desk phone, and hit Speaker.

"Frederickson."

"Professor Frederickson, my name is Ryan Miner. I'm a detective with the Rawlings Police Department in Montana."

There was a pause, like the professor needed to process all that. "Yes?"

"Professor, can you give me a couple of minutes to help with a case we're investigating?"

"You sure you have the right person? I'm an English professor at UMass."

"Yes, sir, I do have the right person."

"Okay, go ahead."

"About seven years ago, you wrote a letter about a professor named Suzannah Montgomery, who was coming up for tenure at Central Montana State University." Ryan paused. "Does that ring a bell?"

The professor's sigh came through clearly. "Yes, unfortunately, now I do remember why the word *Rawlings* rang a bell."

"Can you help us understand the situation a little better, Professor?"

"Are you recording this conversation in any way?"

"No, sir, I am not."

"I have your word on that?"

"Yes, sir, you do."

"Can you tell me what this is about?"

"Only very broadly, sir. We are following a line of inquiry about Suzannah Montgomery in relation to a murder case here in Rawlings. We have some reason to think that Professor Montgomery's tenure case might be relevant in some way."

"At the time the incident occurred—you say it was seven years ago now?—our university attorney here at UMass suggested that I not comment publicly about it."

"I can assure you, Professor, that this conversation is completely privileged and that I am not recording it in any way."

"What do you want to know?"

"You wrote a letter about Professor Montgomery, at the request of her department chair, Professor Frances Hamblin, is that correct?"

"Yes, that much is correct."

"I have in my hand a photocopy of the letter from Professor Montgomery's file. It is quite a positive letter, citing her 'extraordinary contributions to the study—'"

"You don't need to quote from that letter, Detective."

"I'm sorry, Professor, I'm confused."

"I am fully aware of what is in that letter. I know it is written on UMass letterhead and that it bears my signature. But I did not write it."

"You did not write it?"

"That's right. I wrote parts of it, but someone else altered many other parts."

"Can you tell me how you know that, Professor Frederickson?"

"Some weeks after I wrote my letter to the English chair at Central Montana, I received a phone call from the Faculty Senate chair at that school—I don't remember her name—"

"Was that Audrey Miller?"

"Yes, that could be it. She told me that she was in possession of some information that my letter had been altered. She read me the letter she had and asked me if that was what I had written. I looked on my computer and told her that, no, I had not written the letter she had in her files. She asked that I send her a copy of the letter I had in fact written. Which I did."

"Did you hear back from Audrey Miller?"

"Some months later I received a phone call from her. She thanked me for my candor but said the university had decided not to pursue the matter any further. And that was that."

"How did you respond?"

"I told her that I was extremely uncomfortable knowing that a letter I had spent some hours preparing had been altered, and that I wished to see the matter resolved fairly. I didn't want a bogus letter with my name on it floating around."

"What did she say to that?"

"She said that she completely understood my position, that she thought the situation at Central Montana was a disgrace, but that someone in the upper administration had made the decision not to pursue it. I asked her what sort of protection she could offer me. She replied that she had written up the situation in a confidential memo to file and that, if I requested it, she would make it available to me."

"How did you respond to that, sir?"

"I went to my own university attorney, who advised that since I possessed a copy of my real letter, I should simply write up the conversations I had had with Professor Miller and file that account here at UMass, which I did."

"Have there been any repercussions for you in the past seven years?"

"Fortunately, no. I have tried to forget the whole incident, and, until your call a few minutes ago, I had succeeded."

"Professor, I want to thank you very much for taking the time to talk with me. I sincerely hope I do not need to take any more of your time."

"I appreciate that, Detective. Goodbye."

Ryan raised his eyebrows and smiled. "Is there anything you'd like to say to me, Karen?"

"Yeah, let's go see if the chief is in."

We got up and walked out of the detective's bullpen and down the hall to the chief's office.

"The boss in?" I said to Margaret.

She picked up her phone and told him we were here. After a moment, she hung up. "Chief Murtaugh will see you."

"Thanks, Margaret." I knocked, and he told me to come in.

Murtaugh remained standing, so we did, too.

"Nothing yet on Brian Hawser," he said.

"Okay, thanks. We wanted to run something else by you."

He gestured for us to sit.

"Suzannah Montgomery, Austin Sulenka's adviser. She got pissed at me when I asked if she was having an affair with Austin."

He nodded. "I can understand her reaction. Why'd you ask her that?"

"Remember I mentioned Austin was selling plasma and sperm so he could give money to the cerebral-palsy charity? Well, that's the disease her kid has, which struck me and Ryan as kind of a coincidence. So, anyway, we've done some more checking, and there's some weird information about her coming out that we want to run by you."

He waved me on.

"She came up for tenure seven years ago. She got tenure, but when we interviewed the provost this morning, she puts this envelope on her desk for me and Ryan to take with us, and she leaves the room."

The chief frowned. "Huh?"

"The envelope contains letters of reference about Suzannah Montgomery from seven years ago. We learned that someone doctored one of the three letters to make Suzannah look a lot smarter than she is."

"The provost gave you those letters?"

"It seemed strange to us, too. I mean, what is she trying to do: get the school into trouble with some kind of scandal?"

"You were clear with the provost you were investigating the Sulenka murder?"

"Absolutely clear," Ryan said. "Either the provost really hates Suzannah Montgomery and wants to embarrass her or get her fired, or she thinks this has something to do with the murder."

"Have you figured out why the provost might have a grudge against Suzannah Montgomery?"

"All we've got so far," I said, "is the provost—her name is Audrey Miller—was the head of the faculty senate when Suzannah Montgomery's tenure case came up. There was another person in the English Department also came up for tenure, a guy named Mitch Abrams, who didn't get tenure. He made a big stink about how there were due-process problems with Suzannah's case, so he wanted a do-over with his own case, but the university told him no."

"What were the due-process problems?"

"That she submitted her papers a few days late."

"That's it?"

"Well, that's all that went public. But it's possible Mitch Abrams told Audrey Miller how the due-process problem was that Suzannah phonied up a reference letter."

"Suzannah Montgomery was about forty years old then?"

"About that," Ryan said.

"Anyone who'd fake a letter—they start doing things like that long before they turn forty," the chief said. "Figure out what's going on."

Chapter 27

"I'll get her name and SS, see if they can fax me her CV," Ryan said.

"Great," I said as I headed off to the ladies', which would be as good a place as any to think about what the hell a CV is.

When I got back a minute later, Ryan had already put a photocopy of her résumé on my desk. Handwritten on the top was Suzannah Montgomery's Social Security number.

"See anything interesting?"

"Not yet," Ryan said. "I just want to be clear on the dates. She was hired at CMSU in 2004, the same year she got her PhD from Delaware. She started on the doctoral work in 1999."

"That sound normal?"

"Yeah," he said. "Five years is normal." He shifted in his chair. "She got her MA from Clemson in '96. BA in '94 from South Carolina."

"So, the question is, where was she from '96 to '99?"

"That is the question."

"Who'd be smarter to ask: Delaware or Clemson?"

Ryan scratched at his cheek. "I'd start at Delaware and work backwards."

"Go ahead," I said. "You do Delaware, then I'll do Clemson."

Ryan went online and got the number for the English Department. He punched it in and put the phone on Speaker. A secretary picked up.

"Good morning," Ryan said and introduced himself. He explained we were investigating a crime that might involve Suzannah Montgomery. He stated the dates she was there. He looked down at the professor's résumé, then added that her last name at the time might have been Suzannah Collins.

"I'm sorry, Detective, information about our students, current or past, is protected by federal law. We cannot give it out without the student's written permission."

"I think there's an exception when it's law enforcement making the request," he said patiently.

We heard the sound of her hand covering up the mouthpiece. There was a little tap, as if her ring hit the phone. I could make out muffled talking but couldn't tell what she was saying.

After a few moments, we heard a man's voice. "This is Jeremy Cox. Can I help you?"

It sounded like a boss. Ryan introduced himself again.

Cox said, "Tell me your name and affiliation, and if you're real, I'll call you back in a minute."

Ryan spelled everything out and hung up.

A minute later, Ryan's phone rang and he picked up.

"Sorry to have to do that, Detective, but I've gotten stranger stories from people who are just making mischief."

"I understand completely, Professor Cox. If I ask you a question about Suzannah Montgomery—I think she was Suzannah Collins at the time, 2004 PhD American lit—do you know who I'm talking about?"

"Vaguely," he said. "I never had her in a class, but the name is familiar."

"Do you have a file on her?"

"Let me get it. You said Collins or Montgomery. She started here in 1999, right?"

"That's it," Ryan said.

A minute later Cox came back on. "Sorry," he said. "The files from the nineties were just moved to another office. What do you need?"

"Could you give me an overview of her career with you? Grades, comps, etc."

"Okay," he said. "Let's see. Undistinguished grades. 3.12 GPA. Low pass on her comps, second time around. Defended in April 2004. To be frank with you, she didn't make much of an impression around here."

"Do you have the name of her dissertation director?"

"It was Frank Forsyth."

"Is he tough?"

"Not anymore," Cox said. "He's dead."

"What was he like?"

"The way I'd put it is, Who did he like?"

"And how would you answer that?" Ryan said.

"Let me phrase this diplomatically. He liked women. Unmarried women. And those married women who took a certain attitude toward their marriages. Do you understand what I'm saying?"

"Yes, sir, I do." Ryan paused. "Professor Cox, I want to thank you very much for this information. You've been very helpful."

"All right, Detective, good-bye."

Ryan hung up. "That's Suzannah. Just getting by."

"How do you read that bit about the dissertation guy?"

"Well," Ryan said, "that could just be snarkiness about the dead guy. Maybe he was attractive, and Cox isn't."

"Or it could be how Suzannah got by."

"Right," Ryan said. "If she was totally pragmatic about it— you know, a kind of grad-school Tiffany Rhodes—that might've been how she got her degree. The university where my father works, there's always one or two active affairs between a professor and a student—a graduate student, I mean. Everybody kind of knows about it, but if the student is over twenty-one and acts like an adult, and the professor doesn't talk about it publicly, the administration turns a blind eye."

"Okay," I said. "Let me see what's going on at Clemson." I got the department number and reached a secretary who transferred me to the chair, a woman named Gould. Unlike Cox from Delaware, Gould didn't want to call me back to see if I was real. I asked her if she knew Suzannah Collins.

"No," Gould said to me. "That was before I got here, but let me see if she's in the system." I heard the clicking. "Yeah, she's here. Your Social Security was correct. Suzannah Collins."

"Mediocre student?" I said.

"Actually, no. She was an excellent student. GPA over 3.9. Honors on her MA exam. She even wrote a thesis, which she didn't have to do because she took the exam."

"She was studying American literature?"

"The transcript doesn't say, but most of her courses were in British and colonial."

"That's odd," I said. "She teaches American. That's what she got her PhD in."

"Not so odd," Gould said. "People change all the time."

"Okay, I see. Do you know where she went after Clemson?"

"Sorry," she said. "Before my time."

"All right, Dr. Gould," I said, "thanks for your time."

"No problem." The line went dead.

"I wonder how she went from an honors student to mediocre," Ryan said.

I shook my head. "It could be a million things. Something that happened in those three years from '96 to '99."

"I don't like it. She's an excellent student as an MA. If she lost her enthusiasm for literature, why would she go on to get a PhD? And do a lousy job at it?"

I leaned back in my chair. "Maybe the MA program was a lot easier than the PhD. She just sank to her natural level."

Ryan was frowning. "If you were talking Harvard or Yale or something, maybe. But Delaware's not in that league. It's fine, but it's not a few notches up from Clemson."

"It could be something unrelated. She fell in love, starting going out with guys, whatever."

"Still don't like it. She falls in love, she might decide not to go on—I mean, if the guy lives someplace where she can't get her PhD."

"She starts the program, then falls in love or gets into screwing. One way or the other, she finds something else to do with her time. She's only a year away from getting her PhD. Hooks up with a dissertation director who likes young women. She figures, what the hell? That would be how I might've done it."

"You don't do an MA exam, get honors on it—do a thesis, too, just for the heck of it—then decide you want to keep going and turn into a weak student."

I shrugged. "How about this? I call Clemson back, see if there's anyone there who remembers her?"

"Yeah," Ryan said. "One more call."

I picked up the phone and hit Redial. I recognized the secretary's voice.

"Hi, this is Detective Seagate again. From Montana? I was just talking to Dr. Gould."

"Let me see if she's available—"

"No, no, I don't want Dr. Gould. I want to talk to you. Can you tell me your name, please?"

"Mary Clark."

"Okay, Mary, do you remember a grad student named Suzannah Collins, got an MA in 1996?"

"I was in grade school in 1996," she said. "Let me get Cynthia. She's been her twenty years."

"Okay, thanks a lot."

A moment later, a voice said, "This is Cynthia."

I explained who I was and asked if she knew Suzannah Collins.

"Oh, yes, I remember her very well. Very sweet girl. And smart as a whip."

"Yeah, Dr. Gould told us she was an excellent student. You happen to know where she went after she graduated from Clemson?"

"It was just terrible, what happened—"

"Yeah, what happened?"

"She was in a car accident. She was very badly injured."

"So, she went back home to recuperate?"

"Well, I'm not sure you'd call it recuperate."

"What do you mean? How bad an accident was it?"

"There were all kinds of internal injuries. Plus, she broke her neck."

"I see." Which would explain the three years between Clemson and Delaware.

"The thing that was so heartbreaking was the leg."

"Excuse me?" I said.

"When she was a little girl, she was a talented dancer. Then, to lose the leg in the accident."

Ryan and I looked at each other. Both of us shook our heads no. "She lost her leg," I said.

"That's right. Above the knee. I think that affected her more than anything else."

"Well, yes, I can understand that. Cynthia, do you have a home address for Suzannah on your records?"

"Give me a second," she said. We heard her typing. In a moment she came back on and read us an address and phone number in Columbia, South Carolina. I wrote it all down. "Okay, thank you very much, Cynthia—"

Ryan interrupted me. "See if she has a photo."

I nodded. "One more thing, Cynthia. Do you have a photo of Suzannah?"

"I don't have one in this office. But I think I can get you one, from her student ID. Would that be okay?"

"That would be terrific." I gave her my e-mail. "If you could get that to us, that would be great. Again, thanks very much."

We ended the phone call. I turned to Ryan. "Suzannah's got a prosthetic leg?"

Ryan shook his head. "I could be wrong, but I've never seen anyone with a prosthetic leg that good."

"I can't even remember if she was wearing pants or showing her legs," I said.

"She was wearing a skirt the day she did that defense. You know, with Melissa?"

"How about yesterday, at her house?"

'No," Ryan said. "Jeans."

I looked at him and raised an eyebrow.

He put up his hands in mock defense. "I'm a detective. I'm supposed to notice things."

"All right," I said. "Good to know, horn dawg."

My computer beeped softly. I looked down at the screen. An e-mail had just come in, from a Cynthia Henley in Clemson, South Carolina. Ryan was out of his chair, moving faster than I'd seen him move since he was shot.

I clicked on the attached file. Up came the photo of a dark-haired woman with a thin face and wide-set green eyes. Her nose was long and narrow. She was wearing an awkward, tight smile.

"Interesting looking woman," Ryan said.

"Very interesting. Kind of looks like she might be a dancer, no?"

"Absolutely," he said. "But she doesn't look a bit like Suzannah Montgomery."

"Not even a little."

Chapter 28

"You want to tell the chief?"

"Not yet," I said. "Wouldn't know what to tell him. There's something screwy with the records system at Clemson? Let's dig a little more."

"Call Suzannah Collins' home address in South Carolina?"

"It's worth a try," I said, looking down at my notes from the call to Clemson. I dialed the number and hit Speaker.

The phone rang four times, then went to voice mail. "Hello," the robot voice said.

Shit. The robot started explaining how nobody was home. I was about to put the phone back in its cradle when someone picked up.

It was a scratchy voice, but at least it was a real voice. "Hello," it said in three syllables, with a couple of throat-clearings in between.

"Good afternoon," I said. "I'm trying to reach the Collins residence. Do I have the right—"

"Whoever you are," the scratchy voice said, "I can't help you—"

"No, sir, please don't hang up," I said. "I'm not asking for money. This is Detective Karen Seagate, calling from Rawlings, Montana. Are you Mr. Collins?"

There was a pause. He was working hard at clearing his throat. "You say a detective? From Montana?"

"Yes, sir, Mr. Collins. That's right. My name is Karen Seagate. You can call me Karen." He sounded like he was seventy, but seventy with an oxygen tank. "We're investigating a case here in Montana, and I need to find out a little more information on Suzannah Collins. She received an MA in literature from Clemson University in 1996. Are you the father of Suzannah Collins?"

There was silence for the longest time. I could hear his phone being shifted from one hand to another. His breathing was labored.

"Sir," I said, "are you there?"

"Yes," he said. "I'm here." It sounded like he was sniffling, wiping at his nose.

"Okay, good. I asked if you are the father of Suzannah Collins."

"Suzi is my daughter. Yes. She went to Clemson. Yes."

"All right, Mr. Collins. Could you give me a couple minutes to help in this investigation here in Montana?"

There was a pause. More sounds of him trying to breathe right. "Go ahead."

"Sir, can you tell me where we could reach Suzannah? We'd like to talk to her."

Now it was obvious he was crying. I didn't know quite what to do. I looked at Ryan. He held up his palm and whispered, "Give him a minute." I nodded.

It was almost literally that long before Mr. Collins could talk. "She can't talk," he said. "She's here, in Charleston, but she can't talk anymore."

"I'm very sorry to hear that, Mr. Collins." I waited a beat. "Is that from her injuries?"

"A few weeks after the car crash, she had a stroke. She's in a coma now."

"Oh, my God, I'm so sorry to hear that. I didn't mean to upset you like this."

"It's not your fault," he said in a thin voice. "What'd you say your name is?"

"Karen, sir. I'm Karen."

"My name is Harold. Everyone calls me Harry."

"Thank you for telling me that, Harry. Here's the thing, Harry. I sure don't want to upset you any more than I already have, but there's something going on here that's confusing me. Here in Montana, I mean. I'd sure like to be able to talk to you a little bit to see if you can help me understand what's going on."

"I'll try, Karen. Not so sure I can help." He coughed. "But I'm willing to try."

"That's real nice of you, Harry. I really appreciate it. Here's where we are. There's this woman in Montana calls herself Suzannah Collins Montgomery. She's a professor here at Central Montana State University. She teaches literature. Married to a man named Montgomery. But she went to Clemson, got an MA in literature at exactly the same time as your daughter. You see what's confusing me?"

"Are you asking me …" He started coughing hard. "Are you asking if there was another woman there named Suzannah Collins at the same time Suzi was there?"

"That's right, Harry. Did Suzi ever talk about another girl with the same name?"

"I think I would've remembered that," Harry Collins said. "I do believe that would have made an impression."

"Do you have any idea who this woman might be? I mean, the woman here in Montana who calls herself Suzannah Collins Montgomery?"

"I don't know anybody lives in Montana," he said.

"All right," I said. "I thank you for that information. Now, Harry, I want to ask you a couple of questions about Suzi's car accident. I know it's gonna hurt you to have to remember it, but I have to ask you."

"That's all right, Karen," he said. "It hurts me every day. Some days it doesn't make me cry, but it hurts me every day."

"I understand that, Harry. I do. Can you tell me if there was another car involved in that accident?"

"No," he said. He was breathing hard. "It was just the one car."

"What happened?"

"It was late at night, maybe eleven or midnight. The car went off the road. It was just a country road, a two-lane near the college. The car went off the road, crashed into a big thick horse chestnut. Crushed the whole side of the car in."

"Suzi was alone?"

"No, no, she wasn't alone. She was with her roommate, a girl named Carol."

"Was Carol hurt, too, Harry?"

"She was banged up a little. Bumps and bruises, but no, she didn't get hurt bad."

"Suzi was driving at the time of the accident?"

There was a pause. "That's what the police report said."

"You don't think the report was accurate?"

"No, ma'am, I don't. I don't think Suzi was driving."

"Tell me about that."

"Both the girls had been drinking. That came out later. I know Suzi wouldn't've drove if she'd been drinking. I just know it."

"I understand, Harry. She'd have known better, is that it?"

"That's part of it. Other part is that her injuries don't match up with her being the driver."

"What do you mean, Harry?"

"The car went off the road and hit the tree. The whole right side of the car was crushed in, starting at the engine and going all the way back past the rear seats. It was a small Japanese car, and it was just totaled. Suzi was the one who got hurt real bad. Her leg was destroyed, had to be amputated. All the internal injuries, the broken neck. And then I think her head got hurt, too, which maybe caused the stroke later on. But the other girl, Carol. Like I said, she was just black and blue. The policeman told me, he took me aside, he told me no way Suzi was the driver."

"But when the police arrived at the accident scene, Suzi was behind the wheel."

"That's right. And Carol was sitting in the passenger seat, squeezed in because half the engine was where your legs are supposed to go. She'd called the accident in on her phone."

"Did the police or the prosecutor or anyone investigate who was really driving?"

"Nah," Harry Collins said. "They asked me if I wanted them to investigate, but I said no. My insurance from the fire department here in Charleston takes care of the expenses for Suzi. The damage was done. My daughter's not coming back. I don't have any interest in chasing down that other girl. She said she didn't do it. I don't believe her, but it doesn't matter what I believe. It's not me she's got to answer to."

"This other girl: Carol. You ever hear from her?"

"Last I saw her she was climbing into the ambulance. The second ambulance, that is. The first one was the one took Suzi away."

"Did you say you know her last name?"

"Used to. Don't anymore. But her first name was Carol, I do remember that. Because that's my sister's name."

"Harry, I want to thank you very much for talking to me. God bless you, Harry, and Suzi."

"Thank you, young lady. I'm sorry, I don't remember your name."

"It's Karen, Harry." But I think he had already hung up.

Ryan came over to me and put his hand on my shoulder. "Are you okay, Karen?"

"I've been better," I said. I looked down at my watch. It wasn't even three yet. "It's just been a long day." I wiped at my eyes. "I'll be back in a minute, okay?" I got up and walked toward the ladies' room.

After I washed my face and tried to pull myself together, I came back to my desk. I saw my notebook was gone. I glanced over at Ryan, who had it open in front of him. He was on the phone.

"Could I speak to Cynthia, please? This is Detective Miner, from Rawlings, Montana. My partner, Karen Seagate, just talked to Cynthia a few minutes ago." When he looked up and saw me, he hit Speaker and waited a moment. "Yes, Cynthia. Detective Miner. Karen Seagate was called away for a minute. Do you have a moment for another question?"

"Of course, Detective."

"First, we want to thank you for helping us get in touch with Suzannah Collins's family in Charleston. Here's what I'm hoping you can help me with. Suzannah was roommates with another young woman, named Carol. I don't have a last name. Could you check and see if you had another MA student named Carol, same time as Suzannah?"

"Can I get right back to you on that?"

"Absolutely," Ryan said, giving her his phone number. He hung up.

"You doing okay?" he said to me.

"Yeah, I'm fine."

"Thought I'd see if I could nail down who this Carol is."

"Great, thanks."

"After we do that," he said, "then we talk to the chief?"

"Sure," I said, struggling to find a smile, "then we talk to the chief."

Ryan's phone rang. He picked up. "Miner."

"Detective, this is Cynthia from Clemson. Carol could be Carol Winters."

"Do you have any contact information on her?"

"Sorry, her records have been purged from the system. I'm sure we have them here somewhere on paper, but they're not with all the other records."

"Do you know why that is?"

"Carol Winters never received her degree. She was dismissed from the program in her final semester."

"Do you know what happened?"

"I'd forgotten it, but I checked with a faculty member who was involved with the case. It was the first year the students took their MA exams on the computer. She was caught cheating. She'd managed to store some cheat sheets on the computer somehow."

"Do you know where she went after she left Clemson?"

"No, I'm sorry. I figured you'd ask, but we don't know. Nobody made a real effort to keep track of her, if you know what I mean."

"I do know exactly what you mean. Cynthia, this has been very helpful. Thank you very much." He hung up.

"Let's take a walk," I said. The chief was standing in his outer office, talking with Margaret about something on her computer screen.

"This a bad time, Chief?" I said.

"No," he said, "go on in."

We walked in but stayed on our feet, in case the chief was in a hurry.

"Sit," he said as he came in a moment later. He took a soft chair in front of his desk. "What've you got?"

"Well, this is kinda weird. Suzannah Montgomery—Austin Sulenka's adviser—we think that's not her name."

"What do you think her name is?"

"Carol Winters."

"You have my attention."

"The woman here in town, she calls herself Suzannah Collins Montgomery. She's married to a guy named Montgomery. Problem is, Suzannah Collins is the name of a woman lives in South Carolina, got in a bad car accident after she got her MA at Clemson in the same class as Suzannah Montgomery, when she was Suzannah Collins. She's in a coma now, in South Carolina. We just spoke to her dad."

"So how do you get to Carol Winters?" His face was screwed up pretty tight trying to follow this.

"What we think is going on, Chief," Ryan said, "is that these two women—Suzannah Collins and Carol Winters, they're roommates, both going for an MA in English at Clemson—were out drinking one night, crashed the car. Suzannah Collins was badly injured, Carol Winters just banged up. Police report said Suzannah Collins was driving, but the injuries say it was Carol Winters. Anyway, Suzannah Collins loses a leg, breaks her neck, other bad injuries, few weeks later has this big stroke. Meanwhile, Carol Winters was tossed out of Clemson for cheating. She never got her degree."

The chief rubbed his forehead. "It's been a long day, guys. Put this together for me."

I said, "My money is that Austin Sulenka's adviser is Carol Winters. Suzannah Collins got a good degree from Clemson, but she was out of the picture because of the car crash. Carol Winters couldn't get her degree. She took the one Suzannah Collins wasn't using. Took her name, too."

"So where'd she get her PhD?"

"University of Delaware."

"And what was her name at Delaware?"

"Suzannah Collins. She hadn't married Montgomery yet."

"So tell me how this makes her a murder suspect."

"Well," I said, "I don't know if it makes her a murder suspect. But it kinda makes her a liar. If she's Carol Winters, we know she got thrown out of grad school for cheating and probably switched places in the crushed car so she wouldn't get a DUI or vehicular manslaughter. Then she grabs Suzannah Collins' transcript and Social Security number, goes and gets a PhD, never makes contact with Suzannah Collins in South Carolina before her stroke, when she could still talk."

"So your point is," the chief said, still frowning, "if she's that kind of person, everything she's told us could be false."

"Like you said earlier, when we thought she just faked a recommendation letter, person like that doesn't start lying when they're forty. So, she's outraged when I ask her if she was screwing Austin. Makes me think maybe that's exactly what was going on."

"What do you want to do next?"

I looked at Ryan. He waved for me to go ahead. "Our approach to the Sulenka case has been, if she was screwing Austin and she doesn't have an alibi, she's a suspect. Does she have a motive? Sure: one day Austin bangs her real good, she's feeling all intimate, she tells him who she really is, and he blackmails her. She told us his thesis wasn't coming together. That was his way of getting the degree."

"Or her husband finds out about the affair," Ryan said. "He kills Austin. Or he and his wife kill him. Same scenario as Tiffany Rhodes and Brian Hawser."

The chief was silent for a moment. "I think you need to talk to her husband." `

Ryan and I stood up. "Want to tell the university about Suzannah Montgomery's identity?" I said.

"No." The chief shook his head. "We don't have any proof yet. And we're working the Sulenka murder case."

"And the Tiffany Rhodes murder."

"That's right," the chief said. "If it turns out Suzannah Montgomery killed Austin Sulenka, that will solve the problem of the identity theft. If she didn't kill Austin but she isn't who she says she is, I'll inform President Billingham. It's a civil matter—"

"Unless she killed her roommate driving drunk."

"It's a civil matter unless the authorities in South Carolina make it a criminal matter. If Central Montana wants to pursue a civil case against Carol Winters, that's their prerogative." He looked at me, then at Ryan. "Talk to the husband. See if he knows who his wife is."

Chapter 29

"How do you want to go at him?" Ryan said as we walked down the hall toward the detectives' bullpen.

"We've already pissed off his wife. You know, asking her if she was screwing Austin. So I assume he knows we're looking at her." We got to our desks and sat down.

"Yeah, he's going to be hostile, or at least on his guard." He paused a moment. "How hard do you want to push to find out about whether he knows his wife is really Carol Winters?"

"He's not gonna know we were in touch with Harry Collins. He's not even gonna know we know about his wife's phony reference letter. I'd like to give him an opportunity to lay down a bunch of lies about his wife so we can come at her with a little more muscle. All we have now is that someone phonied-up a reference letter. We're not even sure she did it—"

"Who else you got in mind for that?"

"No idea, really." I exhaled a long breath. "Maybe Frances Hamblin, the scholar. She was the department chair at the time. She went to bat for Suzannah when she submitted her papers late. Maybe she had some reason to help Suzannah get tenure."

"Or the provost," Ryan said.

"Audrey Miller gave us the photocopies of the letters. It's pretty clear she's got it in for Suzannah."

"True," Ryan said. "But unless we're willing to put a lot more taxpayer time into figuring out why she's holding a grudge against Suzannah, we're never going to get to the bottom of that one."

"You asked me who else might've messed with the letter. All I'm saying is, it could've been the woman put the letter in the envelope for you to put in your briefcase."

"So your point is we don't know Suzannah Montgomery doctored the letter."

"Thank you," I said. "And we don't know Suzannah Montgomery is Carol Winters. My point is, the less Aaron Montgomery thinks we know about his wife—and him—the more bullshit he'll feed us. Make sense?"

"Yup," Ryan said. "You want me to call him, see if he's home? She said he works at home, right?"

"First let's see if she's home. I'd rather she not be there when we talk to him."

"Let me call the English department, see what her schedule is."

I nodded. Ryan looked in his notebook and picked up his phone. I walked over to the north end of the bullpen and into the break room, where I rinsed out an old glazed mug that said World's #1 Dad. The underside said Made in China. I guess that's what they call irony. Kid buys a nice gift for Daddy, maybe ends up giving him a little hit of lead every morning. I poured a cup of coffee. When I got back to my desk, Ryan was finishing up with the call.

"She'll be teaching and in office hours for the rest of the afternoon. I called Aaron Montgomery. He'd be 'pleased' to see us."

"That's what he said? Did he sound really stupid?" I picked up my bag and headed over to the coatrack for my jacket.

We drove out to Table Rock, up the windy road toward the top, where the air got a little cleaner and the houses a lot more expensive. We parked on the street, outside the stone wall enclosing the courtyard of the Montgomery house with its orange tile roof.

I rang the doorbell. Footsteps came quickly. The door opened. Aaron Montgomery was a handsome man, a little over six feet, good shoulders, thin hips. His face was deeply tanned, the crow's feet pale from squinting in the sun. His hair was medium brown, thick, going grey at the temples. He had round lenses in his rimless eyeglasses. His tan chinos were sharply pressed, his wool shirt expensively tailored, the sleeves half rolled up. There was some kind of dish towel over his right shoulder. I'd put him at fifty, but the kind of fifty who would still interest the typical thirty.

"Detectives." He gave us a broad smile. "Aaron Montgomery." He reached out a meaty hand to shake mine, then Ryan's as I introduced us.

"Thanks for taking the time to speak with us." I could be polite, too. It didn't come as naturally to me as it did to a smooth character like this guy, but I could do it.

He repeated our names to make sure he got them, as if that's something he's used to doing and thinks is important, and then invited us in. I remembered how you can see right through the house to the big floor-to-ceiling windows that led to the deck overlooking the city. The view was probably half the price of the house.

He led us into the living room. His son, Adam, looked up at us apprehensively. He was twelve, but he looked eight. He was a cute kid, with his father's coloring and sandy hair, but he was sitting in some kind of wheelchair that I'd never seen before, where the seat was reclined like a hospital bed that bends in the middle. The chair had big pads on either side of his head so he couldn't tilt it too much to the left or right. The boy's arms and legs were all tight, contorted. It looked like he wouldn't be able to stand on his own if he were out of the chair. His eyes went back and forth from me to Ryan. He made some kind of gurgling sounds that weren't exactly words.

Aaron Montgomery walked over to him and put his hand on the boy's shoulder, then leaned down and whispered something in his ear. A crooked smile came over the boy's face, and his muscles relaxed a little. He made a cooing sound.

"This is my son, Adam."

Ryan and I said hello to him, and he smiled at us but didn't seem to understand what was going on.

"Won't you sit down, Detective Seagate, Detective Miner?" I could see Montgomery working to use our names. That was probably his way of imprinting them in his brain. The three of us sat.

I looked at Adam, then at his father.

"Go right ahead," Aaron Montgomery said. "Adam's happy to watch people talking."

That sounded like a phrase he had worked out over the years. I nodded. "As you know, Mr. Montgomery," I said, "we're investigating the murder of Austin Sulenka, your wife's graduate student."

His face took on a serious look and he nodded gravely. "Horrible," he said. "Just unbelievable."

"Yes." I paused a moment. "As I'm sure you can imagine, during an investigation like this, we need to understand all sorts of things about the victim's close associates, things that don't necessarily seem closely related to the crime but might be relevant in one way or another."

He was still nodding. Maybe he wasn't going to give us any attitude about insulting his wife.

"We wanted to ask you about one of those things."

"Please," he said. "Go ahead."

"You're aware, of course, of the situation that arose during Professor Montgomery's tenure case, about seven years ago?"

He shook his head sadly. "What a mess that was."

"It sure does sound like quite a stir about something pretty small."

He held my gaze. "That's exactly how I would characterize it. I mean, Suzannah's papers were submitted a couple of days late. Frances admitted—"

"That's Frances Hamblin? The department chair?"

"That's right," Aaron Montgomery said. "She's a wonderful woman, a real treasure, but it was her first semester in the job. She admitted that she dropped the ball. Frankly, I think it was absurd that anyone made anything of it at all. Suzannah is a superb teacher. The kids all love her. She gives so much to the department—to the whole university, in fact." He put up his hands and shook his head, like he had to stop himself from going on about the injustice.

"Did you know Mitch Abrams, Mr. Montgomery?"

He shifted in his chair. "Yes, we did. Suzannah was quite close to him. They were cut from the same cloth. Both student-oriented, I mean. Lots of thesis committees, active in the grad-student organization, brown-bag lunches on how to get into PhD programs, that sort of thing. It was a shame, his not getting tenure."

"What did you make of his appeal of that decision?"

"Personally, I don't know enough about whether his credentials merited tenure. Suzannah said they did," he said, with a smile, "but when she likes someone, as I know she liked and admired Mitch … well, she might not be the most unbiased observer."

"But about his decision to appeal his case. If I understand the facts correctly, his appeal wasn't based on any allegations of unfairness about how the various committees treated his case. It was about how Suzannah's papers were a few days late—and she wasn't penalized—which constituted a violation of due process. What did you think about that approach?"

"As I say, I'm not that familiar with the details of the situation," he said, his palm out, "but I would say this. If my experience as an environmental advocate has taught me anything, it's that these conflicts are almost never about the strict merits of the case. More often than not, they're a power struggle. They're about setting down a marker for some future case, or payback for something that has already happened."

"Do you think that's what was going on here?"

He shrugged his shoulders. "Like I said, I don't know the particulars. But I do know that when you have a powerful institution judging whether a person meets its standards of quality, deserves to be admitted to the holy circle …" Montgomery paused. "Then, all the power is with the institution, not the applicant. The only protection the applicant enjoys comes from the policy documents. And I have no problem with an applicant holding the institution's feet to the fire on its adherence to its own policies and procedures."

"So you don't think a technical violation of the procedures, like Professor Montgomery's late papers, is necessarily a mere technical violation—I mean, from Mitch Abrams' perspective."

He smiled. "You said that better than I could have. That's right. There is no such thing as a 'mere' technical violation. It's like in law enforcement. If the police obtain evidence without having followed the proper procedures, you can't use that evidence. What's that concept called?" He looked at me, then at Ryan.

"Fruit of the poisoned tree," Ryan said.

"That's it," Aaron Montgomery said, giving Ryan a broad smile. "That's a terrific metaphor, isn't it?" Ryan returned his smile. "But my point is, the law says there's no such thing as a mere technicality."

Ryan said, "If you think there's no such thing as a mere technicality, Mr. Montgomery, does that mean you think Professor Montgomery should have been denied tenure because her papers were late?"

Montgomery's eyes flashed for a second, then he caught himself and switched on his big smile. "That would follow if it were my wife's fault that the papers were late."

Ryan nodded.

"Mr. Montgomery," I said, "do you know a faculty member named Audrey Miller?"

He frowned, then shook his head. "Sorry, no," he said.

Adam started to whimper and shift in his wheelchair, his arms and legs tightening up.

Aaron Montgomery turned to the boy, then raised his nose into the air. "You'll have to excuse me a moment, Detectives. I need to change Adam."

"Of course," I said as he got up and walked over to his son and pushed the wheelchair toward a hallway that extended off to the side of the room.

"What do you think?" I said in a quiet voice to Ryan after Aaron Montgomery was out of earshot.

"I think he's a very good father."

I gave him a look. "About what he said to us."

"Well, I did notice he said he didn't know who Audrey Miller is."

I nodded. "That's bullshit. A woman who was head of the faculty senate during the Mitch Abrams case, who's provost now, who's apparently trying to destroy his wife—no way he doesn't know exactly who she is."

"Would seem to me," Ryan said.

"And by the way," I said. "Don't go pointing out when he contradicts himself."

Ryan smiled. "You mean about how if there's no such thing as a mere technicality, his wife shouldn't have gotten tenure?"

"Yeah, that's what I'm talking about. This isn't a debate. We're civil servants. We want to come off dumber than him. You don't hear me sounding smart, do you?"

He raised any eyebrow. "Not sure how you want me to answer that."

"Good. Then don't answer it."

Aaron Montgomery came back into the room, pushing his son in the wheelchair. "I'm sorry to keep you both waiting." He gave us a small smile.

"Not at all," I said. "Professor Montgomery mentioned to us how much she relies on you in caring for Adam."

He nodded. "She's just being gracious. He's at his school most days. We let him stay home today because the seizure yesterday upset him so much. Most days, Suzannah does much more for Adam than I do."

"Where did you and Professor Montgomery meet?" I said.

"University of Delaware," he said. "She was getting her PhD in English, I was getting my MS in architecture."

"You didn't know her at Clemson, then."

"No. I did my undergraduate work at Cornell. In fact, I've never even been to South Carolina."

"What did you do after Cornell? I mean, before you went to Delaware?"

"I was a junior architect for a man named Lawrence Yu, in Berkeley. He was one of the pioneers in sustainable architecture. He's retired now. A great man. It was one of those lucky accidents in life. Working with him got me into environmental activism, which is the focus of my life now. " He glanced over to

Adam to make sure the boy was okay. Then he smiled at me and Ryan.

"This was in the late nineties, right?"

"That's right," he said. "Suzannah and I are almost exactly the same age. Off by a month."

"What was she doing at this time?"

"After she got her MA from Clemson, she went home to care for her mother. She had liver cancer. The woman's gone now," he said, shaking his head. "Two years caring for her. Suzannah is really a special person. Caring for her mother like that, and then Adam."

"Absolutely," I said. "Amazing the strength some people have. Then off to Delaware? I mean, then she went to Delaware, where you two met?"

Aaron Montgomery smiled. "First, she took a year off. She went to Europe for a year. Her mother had left her a few thousand dollars, so she went off to Europe. She was a big fan of Henry James. Still is. She kind of followed his tracks, you know, visiting the places he went, the places where he set his novels."

"That sounds delightful." Which was more polite than, You are so full of shit.

"I think she really needed that time off. After the experience with her mother. But then," he said, glancing at Adam, "adult responsibilities have a way of catching up with all of us."

"Yes, they do," I said. I glanced over at Ryan. "Do you have any other questions for Mr. Montgomery?"

"No," he said, then turned to Aaron Montgomery. "You've been very generous with your time, sir."

"Yes, Mr. Montgomery," I said. Ryan and I stood.

"It was my pleasure. Detective Seagate, Detective Miner. I hope I've answered your questions."

"Yes, you certainly have," I said. Then I waved and smiled at the boy. "Goodbye, Adam."

Ryan waved and said goodbye, too, but the boy seemed locked in his own world and didn't respond in any way I could see.

I glanced at Aaron Montgomery, who was gazing at his son. It was plain that he loved the boy, and his eyes showed the sadness that he never would be able to make contact with the boy trapped in his ravaged body.

"Thank you again," I said to Aaron Montgomery as we walked out the front door into the bright sunshine.

Back in the cruiser, Ryan said, "That boy's lucky to have those parents."

"He sure is." I started the engine. "Unless they end up in prison."

Chapter 30

I'd slept well that night, finally having gotten rid of the headache. And shaken at least a portion of the dread I'd been feeling for somehow having gotten Tiffany killed. Next morning I was focused and hopeful that today would be the day we wrapped this up. We met up with Chief Murtaugh in the incident room.

The chief pointed to the photo of Suzannah Montgomery taped to the whiteboard. "You two ready to move her into the girlfriend category with Tiffany Rhodes and …" He turned back to the board. "May Eberlein?"

I frowned. "What we got from her husband yesterday doesn't decide it—for me at least." I looked at Ryan.

"Aaron Montgomery is a pretty sophisticated character," Ryan said. "He doesn't let on that he knows we're looking at his wife. He makes a very logical case for what happened with his wife's tenure case. It was the department chair's fault, so the university shouldn't punish his wife."

I said, "And he doesn't say anything bad about that guy Mitch Abrams—"

"Who's that again?" the chief said.

"The guy who didn't get tenure. The one who started all the trouble by appealing the decision, saying it was a due-process violation by the university so he should get a do-over."

"I don't know about Karen." Ryan put his cane down on a table. "But I think Aaron Montgomery's not coming clean with us. He told us he didn't know who Audrey Miller was—the head of the Faculty Senate during this whole incident."

"Yeah," I said, "I agree. Just not sure whether he's a lawyer-type liar—you know, leaves stuff out if it makes his wife look bad—or if he's a bald-ass liar who'll make shit up to keep her out of jail."

"Bottom line," the chief said, "you're not ready to put Suzannah Montgomery in Austin Sulenka's bedroom." He looked at me.

I nodded. "But I'm not ready to say she wasn't there."

"Okay," the chief said. He turned and started toward the door. "Keep going until you run it down or something else turns up."

"So, nothing from Pelton and Malone about Brian Hawser?"

"They briefed me this morning at the end of shift. Nothing." He sighed. "I did talk to Larry Klein. He told me I have to inform Tiffany's parents this morning that she's dead."

"Shit. If they're in contact with Brian, he's halfway to Mexico right now, feeding them some bullshit about how he didn't have anything to do with it."

The chief shook his head. "Maybe so," he said. "Or they could tell us where he's couch surfing in Billings. Either way, we have to inform them. If they find out we've kept that under wraps for more than twenty-four hours, a bunch of us'll be looking for work. Larry put it in writing. Called it our 'ethical duty.'"

"Okay," I said. "So Larry'll still be employed."

The chief gave me a hard look. "I'm calling them when I get back to my office. That way, we'll all be employed. Then he'll show up. We'll get him. We'll bring him in." He reached into his jacket pocket. "Excuse me," he said as he pulled his phone out.

His expression turned grim. "Be right there," he said into his phone, then closed it and put it back in his jacket pocket. "You two come with me."

He wasn't asking.

We hurried along behind him as he rushed out of the incident room, down the hall leading to his office.

Margaret was standing in the outer office, her face ashen.

"Did you notify the Tactical Unit?" he said to her.

"Yes, sir," she said.

The chief waved us into his office. He shut the door behind us. "That was the Substation on campus. There's a gunman in the English Department."

"Like you said, Brian'll turn up," I said.

"The officers on campus have issued the alerts—all the instant messages and e-mails to students. They've locked it down. The Tactical Unit will be ready in twelve minutes."

"Are there any injuries?"

"One of the secretaries reports that the English Department chair screamed a couple of times, but no reports of gunfire." He paused. "You two've been in that office, right?"

Ryan and I nodded.

"Can the Tactical Unit set up for a clear shot?"

"Depends on where exactly Brian is in the office. There's a floor-to-ceiling window—how wide is it, Ryan?"

"Four feet," he said. "Maybe five."

"I don't want the Tactical Unit set up on the quad there," I said. "Brian sticks his head out, he'll see them plain as day. He knows he's hurt Tiffany, and if the department chair was screaming, Brian's probably roughed him up already. He knows he's not walking out of there without doing some serious jail time. So he might as well start firing."

"So what're you saying, Karen?"

"Two things: have the Tactical Unit work with the Substation officers to make sure they set up so Brian can't see them. And let me and Ryan go over there now."

"How do you want to play it?"

"I'll go in, unarmed. You're sure the hospital hasn't leaked that Tiffany's dead, right?"

"I can't vouch for what every doc or nurse might have said off-duty," the chief said, "but yes, they've assured me they've locked down the whole case. Her charts on the system are secured."

"Well, that's our best chance of turning the heat down—make Brian think he hasn't already fucked things up beyond repair."

The chief turned to Ryan. "You on board?"

"Absolutely," he said.

"All right," the chief said. But he wasn't looking happy. "You two get going. I'll work with the Substation officers and the Tactical Unit."

We rushed downstairs to the parking lot behind headquarters and got in the Charger. It's the version with all the emergency lights mounted inside. I flipped them all on, the red, blue, and yellow flashing on the grill, inside the windshield, on the rear deck, and on the rear bumper. I'd never stood on the Charger's pedal before. We were on campus in less than four minutes.

I parked it out behind the Humanities Building, on the other side from the English department's main office. An officer from the Substation was over to my door before we could get out. The badge said Betz.

"What have you got?"

"Male gunman, early twenties, white. Looks like one handgun. In the English department main office. He might have beat up the guy in the office."

"Any other hostages?"

"No, all the staff are out. We've cleared out all the offices and the classrooms in the building."

"Have you had any contact with him?"

"No, we haven't seen him. All we have on him is what I told you. From a secretary."

"He hasn't made contact with anyone."

"Not that I know of."

"All right, Betz. The Tactical Unit will be here in less than ten. The chief is coordinating that. If they park back here, tell them they're not to set up in the quad where he can see them."

"What about the library? They can get a clean shot from the roof."

"What's the distance?"

"Less than three-hundred feet."

"If you have to. My partner and I are going up to make contact with him."

"You know him?"

"Not sure, but we think he's named Brian Hawser. He's a suspect in the Austin Sulenka case—the grad student from Sunday night?"

"Big guy? Two-hundred pounds?"

"Yeah. That what the secretary said?"

"Yeah."

"Okay, thanks."

Ryan and I headed inside the building, up to the third floor. We stood at the end of the hall. I could see the door to the English Department half open. There was nobody in the hall.

"See the glass?" The interior wall of each office had a glass panel from the ceiling down to about seven feet off the ground. The glass was there to let daylight into the hallway from the exterior windows in the offices. "Help me get that table over to the glass outside the chairman's office," I said. It was a small work table, maybe four feet by three, located twenty feet away from the door to the department.

We walked over as quietly as we could, lifted the table, and carried it over to the chair's office.

"Get up on the table," I said to Ryan. He grimaced as he lifted his leg to get up. "Lean on me," I said. He put his hand on my shoulder and hoisted himself onto the table. He stayed crouched down so Brian wouldn't be able to see him through the glass from inside the office.

"Okay," I said. "You got your phone?"

"Yeah," he said.

"Phone the department office. I'm gonna talk to Brian."

Ryan pulled his phone from his inside jacket pocket, opened it, and hit some buttons.

"Give it to me," I said. I heard the phone ringing from inside the office. Two rings, three, four. Finally, someone picked up.

"Brian, this is Detective Karen Seagate, Rawlings Police Department."

I looked up at Ryan, standing on the table, looking through the glass. He nodded to let me know it was Brian who'd picked up the phone.

"Brian, I'm gonna come in. Unarmed."

"What the fuck for?"

"I just want to talk, that's all."

"It's a little late for talking, don't you think?"

"No, Brian, it's never too late for talking. We can resolve this thing. You and me."

"You're right about that," Brian said. "I could finish off this shithead right now, then take myself out before you can shoot me."

"Yeah, you could do that. But there's not gonna be any shooting. I'm coming in. Unarmed."

I shut the phone and handed it to Ryan.

"I don't like it. Wait for the Tactical Unit, Karen. It'll be five minutes, tops."

"No, I got it," I said. "Me going in is our best shot at cooling this down."

"Let me go in," he said.

"No way. You got a wife, two little kids," I said. "Besides, you can't even get onto a table by yourself."

He smiled, but I could see the concern in his eyes.

I looked at his hand, which was gripping his service pistol. "You stay right where you are. You see him come at me—" I held my hand out. I didn't have to finish that sentence. Ryan nodded.

My big shoulder bag, with my holster and pistol, was on the table, next to Ryan. I took off my coat so Brian would see I was unarmed. I walked over to the office door. I looked back at Ryan, who gave me a thumbs-up. He raised his pistol to the window, resting the barrel on the metal flashing that separated the window from the drywall.

It would help things a lot if Brian didn't look up and see that pistol barrel. If he threw a shot at Ryan, the drywall wouldn't even slow it down.

I walked slowly into the outer office, my hands up. The door to the chairman's office was opened. "Brian, I'm coming in. I'm unarmed."

I walked toward the chairman's office. From the doorway, I could see Brian, a .45 in his hand, looking down. I couldn't see the chairman, Jonathan Van Vleet, who was hidden by his desk, but I could hear him breathing, loud and shallow.

Brian looked up at me, then raised the pistol to a firing position. His face was shiny, his eyes red-rimmed, jumpy. Maybe Ryan was right about waiting for the Tactical Unit guys. "I told you," Brian Hawser said. "There's no point."

"Yes, there is, Brian."

He shook his head. "No, it's over."

"Is he dead?" I pointed to Van Vleet.

"Not yet," Brian said.

"He's not shot, is he?"

"I hit him," Brian said. "With this." He lowered the barrel of the pistol an inch, then raised it again, aiming it right at my chest.

"Okay," I said. "There's nothing's happened here we can't work through."

He smirked. "How do you see that?"

"Van Vleet's a simple assault," I said. "I can talk him down from that."

He shook his head. "Really?" Sarcastic. His shoulder twitched so bad I was afraid he might squeeze the trigger by mistake.

"He knows you got a bad deal. He'll want to make that right."

Brian just looked at me.

"I've talked with him about it. The grad student, Austin Sulenka. Van Vleet knows what Sulenka did was wrong. You give me the gun, I promise you, you will not do any time for hitting this guy." I put out my hand, palm up, and started walking toward him.

"Stop," Brian said. "Don't play me. You'll get the first bullet. I'll get the second." He glanced out the window, down at the quad. "Where's the SWAT team?"

"There's no SWAT team. I told my chief I wanted to talk to you. Said I could work this out with you."

"I told you not to play me."

"It's the truth, Brian. I know this looks bad—I mean, from your perspective—but listen to me. I can get the assault suspended."

"You're full of shit."

I shook my head. "Brian, I've seen situations look worse than this, but they ended okay."

"So this fucker," he said, nodding his head toward Van Vleet, "he's gonna not press charges. Tell me all about that," he said.

"Way I figure it, he feels responsible for what Austin did. You know, it was on his watch this happened. He gets a little roughed up, he decides not to press charges. He gets to look like a hero."

He stood there, motionless, for the longest time. "And Tiffany, she wants to look like a hero, too?"

"I was just talking with Tiffany, this morning. She's feeling better. She loves you. You know that. She told me she's not gonna press charges."

"That's what she said to you," Brian said, nodding. "She said that to you this morning."

I was in too far to turn back now. If he knew she was dead, he would probably pull the trigger right now, just like he said. First bullet for me, second one for himself. "That's right," I said. "She knows you didn't mean to push her like that. It was an argument, that's all. An argument that got a little out of hand."

He looked like he was going to start crying. I couldn't tell if he was buying what I was saying. But I was all in now.

"She loves you, Brian. You know she does. You'll work this out with her. I know you can."

The pistol was aimed right at my heart. "I tried to get back to our apartment,' he said. "I saw your squad car."

"That's just routine. Whenever there's a domestic. That doesn't mean anything." My saliva tasted metallic. I could feel my heart thumping in my chest.

"So Tiffany's not gonna press charges. And you've got a squad car in front of my apartment. Two officers in it. Eating sandwiches, drinking coffee, laughing." He nodded. "Because she's not gonna press charges."

"That's right, Brian. That's just a state law, a requirement. Doesn't mean anything."

He squinted, like he was looking down the sight of his pistol. "Tell me what you and Tiffany talked about, this morning."

"Like I said, how she loves you. She knows it was an argument. That's all."

He nodded his head. "What were we arguing about?"

Shit, he knows I'm lying. But there was nothing I could do to change the story now. "It was about Austin. That thing last semester. That's what it was."

He gave me a sad smile. "You didn't talk to her this morning." He began to shake his head, like he was sorry that this was how it was going to end. "She told me what really happened. She was fucking the grad student all along. She fucked him the night he got killed."

"No, Brian," I said. "That wasn't what happened."

His shoulder twitching, he shifted his weight. "I'm done being lied to. She told me about fucking the grad student, then how she fucked those two guys over at her girlfriend's apartment."

He didn't know she was dead. "Don't you see what she was doing, Brian?" I was making it up now, hoping the sentences would hang together. Hang together enough, anyway, to convince this exhausted son of a bitch pointing the .45 at me. "She knows she's made some mistakes, just like you have. Just like we all do. She loves you, Brian. You have to know that. And you love her, too." He squinted, looking down the barrel of his pistol. "She wants to make it right with you. That's what she was doing. That's all it was."

"You've just told your last lie," he said as he started to walk toward me slowly. I closed my eyes, waiting for the sound and the impact.

I flinched at the explosion from Ryan's pistol. Glass shards stung the side of my face. Brian spun around and grabbed at his right shoulder as the gun flew out of his hand and bounced off the glass of the exterior window before falling to the carpet. Brian was hunched over, silent, holding his shoulder.

I rushed over and retrieved the pistol. I pulled out the magazine. It was full. I was slamming it back in when Ryan made it into the office. Brian let out a cry of pain as Ryan pulled his arms behind his back with some energy and cuffed him.

I went over to the other side of the desk, where Van Vleet was crumpled on the floor. He had a couple nasty red bruises on his face. Blood was trickling down from the one above his left temple; the one on the right side of his jaw was the size of a golf ball.

"Van Vleet, can you hear me?" His eyes were cloudy and half-closed, but he made some kind of sound I interpreted as yes. "It's all over," I said. "You'll be okay."

I picked up his desk phone and punched in 911. "This is Detective Seagate," I said. "Send two buses to the English department, on University Drive. Third floor."

Chapter 31

"What's that, involuntary manslaughter, for killing his girlfriend?" the chief said to Larry Klein.

"We call it negligent homicide, for some reason, but yeah, that's what it'll be."

The chief was still getting used to Montana terminology. In most states, *negligent homicide* is used mainly for killing someone when you're driving drunk, whereas *manslaughter* is for punching your girlfriend in the face so hard she cracks her skull open on a cabinet and dies of a brain bleed.

But *negligent homicide* makes sense, too, since Brian Hawser was negligent in not thinking of what her head was going to smack into after he punched her. If he'd taken the time to set up some pillows, all he'd be looking at is simple assault, which is five-hundred bucks and six months—provided the court concluded Tiffany's busted cheekbone wasn't that big a deal. If they decided it was a serious injury, it would be aggravated assault, which would cost him fifty-thousand bucks and twenty years, the same as he'll get for the negligent homicide.

Technicalities aside, if he'd bothered to set up the pillows, Tiffany would be drinking her meals through a straw for a while, but she'd still be alive. Another option: when he found himself arguing with her, he could have turned and walked away without even punching her in the face at all. That way, right around now he could be pursuing his normal routine: sitting on his couch in his living room, playing video games, eating Slim Jims, and leaning over every once in a while to rip a good fart.

Ryan and I, along with the chief and the prosecutor, were standing in the narrow hallway between the two interview rooms, behind the door marked Janitor. From there, we could look through the one-way glass into either of the rooms. Brian Hawser was sitting in Interview 1. He had a shirt draped over his right shoulder, which was bandaged up tight from Ryan's bullet that he'd taken this morning.

I told the doc we were going to question him, so don't dope him up too much. The doc asked me if he'd be okay with some pain. I assured him he would.

Brian was looking kind of wrung out, sitting there at the table with his right shoulder higher than the left. His eyes were about half open, with big black bags beneath them. It had been about thirty-six hours since he popped his girlfriend, then decided to pack a light bag and take a drive. Ryan and I didn't know where he had gone or how he had spent those hours, but it didn't look like he'd spent any of them sleeping.

"That's twenty years, right?" the chief said. "How much of that do you think you can get?"

"With his priors and the restraining order, maybe fifteen. He'd be out in eight or ten." Larry Klein adjusted his glasses. "Of course, it'd be nice if you could get him to sign a piece of paper."

The chief nodded.

"You don't need to assign him a public defender?" I said.

"Not yet. As soon as he asks for one, or when you charge him and I arraign him."

"Well, let's see if we can keep him from asking," I said.

Ryan turned to me. "Mind if I do Tiffany?"

"Fine with me. I'll do Austin Sulenka." I turned to Larry. "Any reason we shouldn't try to get him to go for the two cases at the same time?"

He scratched at his thick, close-cropped hair. "Just make sure you don't officially charge him if you can get a statement on the domestic. Try to get both statements, then break the news that the girlfriend is dead."

"You're assuming he's going to confess on Austin Sulenka," Ryan said.

Larry shrugged his narrow shoulders in his black suit. "I'm not assuming anything. If he admits to it, we charge him. If he doesn't, we don't."

"If we can get him to admit to beating up his girlfriend, then we tell him she's dead, we might have a better shot at getting him to sign off on Austin."

"Because he knows he's going inside anyway?" the chief said.

"Sure," I said. "He might be smart enough to want to deal down the charges on Austin. Package them together, get a discount."

Larry Klein shook his head. "He doesn't look smart enough—or alert enough—to think two or three moves ahead. You'll know he is if he says Tiffany told him she did it. You don't have any forensics or eye-witnesses that put him there at the time of the murder, do you?"

I shook my head. "No. Not yet, anyway."

"You're waiting on something?" Klein said.

"No, sorry. I'm just saying, something can turn up. But we're not waiting on anything that puts him at the scene."

"Give him your best story on how he did it, see if he buys it. If he doesn't admit it, let it be. Either way, he's off the street for a while."

"Yeah, I get that," I said, "but I'd like to wrap them both up this afternoon."

Larry Klein smiled. "I think we all would. But if he doesn't confess, he doesn't confess." He turned to Ryan. "Since you're going to do the domestic, why don't you go in alone now, do some interview questions. We'll see if we can spot any tells."

"Sure," Ryan said and walked down the hallway.

Like most police departments, we use the Reid interrogation method, which calls for some low-stress interview questions at the start to see if the guy shows us anything from his eye movements. They say people move their eyes to the right if they're remembering things and to the left if they're thinking. Which is good to know because if you ask the guy if he owns this particular kind of shotgun that you know he owns and he looks left, that means he's thinking about how he should answer the question, which means he's gonna lie. All of this is supposed to tell you if the guy's guilty, in which case you interrogate him hard.

In my experience, though, people don't look in one direction when they're lying and another when they're thinking. And a lot of times—like this one, with the dead grad student—you're not absolutely sure he did it, but you want to come at him hard anyway. So, like with almost everything else they teach you in the academy, it's helpful most of the time. Some of the time, anyway.

And it's not like I've figured out a better way.

The chief, the prosecutor, and I stood at the one-way mirror and watched Ryan enter the interrogation room. He hooked his cane on the edge of the table, then removed his jacket and put it over the back of his chair. Brian Hawser was seated in the chair facing us, making it easy for us to watch him.

"Where's the bitch?" he said. His eyes were glassy, and he seemed a little groggy, from the lack of sleep and some pain meds. He shifted in the chair, putting his left hand on his right bicep to immobilize the right arm, which was probably throbbing pretty hard around now.

"You're referring to Detective Seagate?" Ryan said.

Brian looked annoyed, like Ryan was going to make him spell everything out just to be a pain in the ass. "Yeah."

"She'll be in soon."

That was a good answer. Part of the strategy is to isolate the guy, making him realize he's not in control anymore.

"Let's talk a little bit, Brian," Ryan said.

Brian gave him a fuck-you look.

Ryan opened up the manila folder he had put on the table in front of him. It had the name "Hawser, Brian" written on the tab in black Sharpie. Brian's real folder was thin, no more than a dozen pages long, but this one was a half-inch thick, full of scrap paper to get the suspect thinking he's Public Enemy Number One, so we're going to do whatever it takes to get him off the street. "You're a student at Central Montana State University, is that correct?"

"I have to answer your bullshit questions?"

Ryan looked up and held his gaze. "That's right. I ask the questions. You answer them."

Brian didn't say anything.

Ryan said it again. "You're a student at Central Montana State University, is that correct?"

Brian waited a few beats. "Yeah."

"Good," Ryan said. "Thank you." He waited a moment. "You're a General Business major, right?"

This time Brian hesitated only a second. "Yeah."

I didn't notice his eyes moving right or left.

"I'm looking at your transcript here," Ryan said, glancing down at the file. "At the end of this semester, you'll have finished twenty-one credits, correct?"

Brian's eyes flicked to the left for a moment. "Yeah."

"And you need 120 to graduate, is that correct?"

This time Brian just nodded.

"So how many is that left? I mean, after you finish this semester?"

Brian frowned. "That would be ninety-nine."

Ryan nodded and jotted something on his pad. "Now, if you have to withdraw this semester—you know, because of this thing—how many credits will you have completed?"

Brian's eyes flicked to the left. "Fourteen."

"And how many credits would you need to complete the 120?"

"What the fuck you wasting my time for? Can't you add up this shit yourself?"

"And how many credits would you need to complete the 120?"

"I'd need 106."

Ryan dutifully wrote this down. "You grew up in Billings, right?"

Brian didn't answer.

Ryan said, "You grew up in Billings, right?"

Brian waited a beat, then said, "Yeah."

The chief said, "You better go in now, Karen. His arm is hurting him. We're not going to learn any more from these questions."

"Yeah," I said. "I didn't see much of a tell. His eyes go left a little when he's thinking, but that could be random."

"I didn't get a clear pattern." The chief shrugged. "Do the best you can."

I walked out of the corridor. Once I was in the interview room, I turned on the recording equipment from the control box on the wall and announced the names, date, and time of the interrogation.

I sat down next to Ryan and nodded to him to begin.

"We're going to start our questions with the assault on Tiffany Rhodes," Ryan said.

He waited for Brian to react, but he was expressionless.

"We know that was a domestic assault incident—and we know you were involved. You must have been arguing with Tiffany. You punched her in the face. You fractured a bone in her face."

Brian looked like he wasn't expecting Ryan to accuse him of it. His expression turned grim, and he began to lick at his bottom lip. "Wasn't me."

"Yes, it was, Brian," Ryan said, his voice soft and level. "The neighbors heard the two of you arguing. Heard Tiffany scream. Heard the door slam. Couple minutes later, the neighbor looked out the window, saw you running over to your car, get in, peel out. The rubber's still on the street."

"Wasn't me."

Ryan shook his head slowly, disappointed. "Yeah, Brian, it was. There wasn't anyone else." Ryan stood up and walked over to Brian's side of the table, half sat on the edge of the table, his side up against Brian's bad arm. Brian started to pull away, then grimaced and grabbed at his arm.

"We have a statement from Tiffany, at the hospital. It was you."

Brian sat there, looking straight ahead but not denying it anymore.

"She said it was you, Brian—"

"I don't believe anything you say to—"

Ryan broke in fast. "You'll get a chance to talk later," he said. "We have the victim's statement. All we're talking about now is how it happened. And here's where you can do yourself some good. We know you didn't mean to hurt her. It was just an argument got out of control."

"Wasn't me," Brian Hawser said.

"We know it was just an argument got out of control. It wasn't like you planned to hit her. We know you didn't mean to hurt her. It was just she said something that got you real angry. What was it, Brian? She say something about how she was still fucking Austin Sulenka? Is that what got you really mad?"

Brian looked up at Ryan with fire in his eyes but didn't say anything.

"Okay, Brian, it's good we're starting to communicate like this. A lot of times judges see guys who just hate their girlfriends so much, they plan how they're going to hurt her, then one day the cops show up and the girl's dead. But it's clear that wasn't what happened with you and Tiffany, Brian. Because you loved each other, right? And then, this argument, she says something that gets you really mad, and you lose your temper. I bet you don't even remember hitting her. Now, judges take that into account. Plus, you have the fact that Tiffany isn't going to break your balls about this. She knows it was just an argument, and she realizes she was out of line. That's the way it happened, Brian, isn't that correct?"

Brian's trunk slumped forward. His left forearm was supporting his trunk, his hand cradling the bad shoulder.

"We've already talked with the professor runs the English department. Man named Van Vleet. He says you hit him a couple of times, but I think he understands what happened. I tell you, he's so embarrassed about what happened with Austin Sulenka last semester, I wouldn't worry about him coming at you over a couple of bruises." He paused. "So I think we can get past this thing with Tiffany, then with the professor. Good news is, nobody wants to make any trouble for you about what happened. So are we good, Brian?"

"What?" He was groggy, still leaning up against the table.

"The argument with Tiffany, you punching her, not meaning to. Then, this morning, in the English Department, hitting the professor with your pistol. You did those things, right? We need you to admit those things. You know, for the paperwork."

Brian made a kind of grunting noise, his chin resting on his chest as he slumped over the table.

Ryan leaned over and pulled him up straight. "We need you to say that. We need to have that on the tape. You got in an argument with Tiffany, punched her. Then, this morning, you hit Professor Van Vleet, twice. We need you to say it on tape so that we can get past all this."

Brian opened his eyes wide, trying to focus. "Yeah."

"No, Brian, we need you to say it. You punched Tiffany, and you hit Van Vleet, right? We know you didn't mean to do those things, but you did them, right?"

Brian took a deep breath, widened his eyes again. "Yeah, I punched Tiff."

"And you hit the professor this morning."

"I hit the professor this morning." His body started to sag again. "Can I go now?"

"Couple more questions, Brian," I said. "About Austin Sulenka."

Brian turned to me, his eyes glassy. "She told me she was still fucking him."

"Yeah, we know that, Brian. I want to talk about last Sunday night."

"What about it?"

"Tiffany was over at Austin's place. Around seven that night. She told you that, right?"

He shrugged. "I don't know when."

"Tell us about how Austin Sulenka died," I said.

Brian lifted his head to look at me. "No fuckin' idea how he died."

"The night Austin Sulenka died. You know Tiffany was over there earlier that night, around seven, having sex with him. We've established that, Brian."

He shrugged, then grimaced and grabbed at his bad arm.

"The way it happened, you and Tiffany were so pissed at Austin because he gave her a lousy grade last semester, the two of you headed over to Austin's place later—maybe eleven o'clock. Tiffany knocked on the door. Austin let her in. But then you came in, too. Once you got inside, you strangled him. That's what happened, isn't it?"

"Never been to that fucker's place."

I shook my head. "Now, we know that's not true, Brian. We know you were over there that night you were drunk and smashed up his car. We know you were there that night."

"Never been in his apartment. Never. You had any evidence puts me there, you'd've arrested me for that already."

Shit. He was a little more pulled together than he looked.

"The way it happened," I said, "you lost control when you saw Tiffany coming out of Austin's place that night around seven-thirty. You suspected she was still doing Austin, even though she didn't admit it, so you followed her, just like you followed her to the coffee shop the other day when she met with us. You followed her to Austin's place. You knew she was in there with him, fucking him, for about a half-hour. She came out. You confronted her. The two of you figured the best thing, the only way to get him out of your lives, to get you back to where you were with Tiffany, was to take him out. So you and Tiffany went back to his apartment, she knocked on the door. That's what happened, isn't it, Brian?"

He shook his head. "Never been in his apartment."

"Now, the judge is gonna see it as you losing control, after you realize Tiffany's still involved with Austin. You know, a crime of passion, just like when you punched Tiff the other night."

"I didn't kill nobody."

"It's not like you planned to kill him," I said. "There was no premeditation. It just happened when you found out about

Tiffany. That's real important, it not being something you meant to do."

"Fuck you," Brian said, and his head slumped forward.

"I need you to say it," I said. "I need you to say you strangled Austin Sulenka."

Brian Hawser looked up at me, his eyes mostly closed, some drool hanging off the corner of his mouth. "Yeah, I strangled Austin Sulenka. I did it. Now I need to go to sleep."

I looked over at Ryan, who was shaking his head. Ryan put his hand on my arm. I nodded for him to go ahead.

"Brian, this is Detective Miner. Look at me."

Brian slowly lifted his head, trying to focus on Ryan. "What?"

"What did you strangle Austin Sulenka with? Was it a rope?"

"My hands. I strangled him with my hands." His head slumped forward and made a dull thunk as it hit the table.

Chapter 32

After it became clear that Brian Hawser had killed Tiffany Rhodes but not Austin Sulenka, we pumped him full of caffeine and Tylenol. We waited an hour, then got him to write the statement about how he'd gotten into an argument with Tiffany and punched her, that she'd fallen and hit her head, and that he then took off. Plus, that he pistol-whipped the English department chair.

After he put his signature on it, we told him Tiffany was dead. He crumpled up and started howling for a good long while. Ryan was right in getting him to show us he hadn't strangled Austin Sulenka, even though I wanted to be done with both cases.

Now Brian Hawser was Larry Klein's problem. I was good with letting Larry figure out how hard to come down on him. The way Brian was screaming and moaning in the interview room when we told him Tiffany was dead showed me he really loved her. Even after she told him about still screwing Austin—and maybe about the two dweebs she fucked for weed—I don't think he intended to hurt her. He just didn't have enough brains or self-control or whatever it is that lets some guys not shout at the woman, not get in her face, not shove her, not punch her. Not kill her.

The irony, of course, is that the one Brian really wanted to kill, Austin Sulenka—well, somebody else killed him.

If Austin hadn't nailed Tiffany when she was his student, Brian wouldn't have gotten drunk and broken all the glass on Austin's car, which brought cops and judges into the picture. Of course, we'll never know whether Tiff would have been quite so skanky if she hadn't gotten involved with Austin Sulenka in the first place. If she hadn't gotten addicted to Austin's neon dick, she might not have felt trashy enough to screw the two jerks for the weed.

But maybe I'm being a wistful idiot. Maybe she was just a skeevy bitch who liked weed enough to fuck anyone who'd give her some, and therefore ran a pretty good chance of getting beat up or killed by a guy sooner or later.

I've known a lot of girls like that. I was one for a while.

"Let me fill you in on where we're going with Hawser," Larry Klein said. He was seated in the chief's office, his toes tapping the carpet. The chief nodded for him to continue. "I reviewed the tape of the interrogation. You two," he said, referring to me and Ryan, "walked right up to the line in that interrogation—"

"How's that?" I said. It came out a little more defensive than I intended it.

Larry smiled at me. "That was a compliment, Karen. He was obviously in distress from the gunshot wound earlier in the morning, and the fatigue had caught up with him. When I showed the tape to the public defender yesterday, she wanted to fight me—"

"On what grounds?" I said.

"She thought it was borderline coercion because he was so beat-up looking, and she was unhappy about how you didn't tell him his girlfriend was dead."

"What the hell?" I said. "We don't have to tell him that."

"I explained that to her. We can lie all we want about the circumstances of the crime. If the suspect didn't do it, he'll know we're lying and he won't admit guilt. No harm, no foul. We can't

threaten him or try to bribe him about penalties, like how if he
confesses we'll give him a better deal or tell him he'll get a stiffer
sentence if he doesn't cooperate. Those lies you told him were
perfectly legitimate." He put up his hands to let me know he
wasn't criticizing me.

"Okay," I said, "so whether Tiffany's alive or dead has to do
with how you're gonna charge him, not with whether he punched
her in the face."

"Exactly," Larry Klein said. "Now that we have a confession,
we're free to charge him, and that means he gets a public
defender. She can do whatever she wants to defend him,
including arguing that the confession was coerced. She could
argue temporary insanity or any other damn thing she wants."

"But you're saying our interrogation was clean, right?"

"I think so," he said. "Whether she agrees is up to her."

"What did we do?"

"She might have a point about how Ryan said Van Vleet isn't
going to press charges related to Brian pistol-whipping him."

"There's nothing wrong with that," Ryan said, his voice kind
of forceful. "That's not lying about how the system is going to
treat him. It's obviously speculation about how another victim is
going to act. It's not a guarantee that if he confesses to roughing
up the guy he's going to get a lighter penalty."

"Easy, Ryan." Larry Klein lifted his body off the chair and
tucked his right leg under his left knee. "I agree with you. Hawser
hadn't been charged with any crimes at that point, and you
weren't speaking on behalf of the prosecutor's office. Besides, I
told his counsel that all we were filing at this time was the
negligent homicide on Tiffany. We don't know yet whether we're
going to charge him with the assault on Van Vleet."

"You could hold off on that one," the chief said. "See if you
could use it as bait for a guilty plea."

Larry Klein nodded his head. "Personally, if I were his attorney, I'd hold out for a better deal, but, yeah, we can file that one anytime we want. I'll offer to throw it in as part of a package—"

"How easy you gonna go on him?" I said. I didn't like thinking that we were going to ease up for any reason.

"I was thinking fifteen years fixed, no early parole, instead of twenty, if he just pleads to the negligent homicide."

"To keep him out of court?"

"Yeah," Klein said. "He'd be thirty-seven instead of forty-two. It'd be worth it to not have to try him."

"That's five more years to kill another girlfriend," I said.

Larry Klein shook his head. "There's no difference in the recidivism rates once they're that old and done that much time inside."

"I don't like it," I said.

Larry smiled. "Well, now you're changing the topic." He stood up. "Bottom line, your interrogation was good. You got the confession. I'll work it out with his attorney."

"Thanks, Larry," the chief said as the prosecutor turned and walked out of the office, waving his hand at us.

The chief turned to me and raised his eyebrows. "Any questions?"

I didn't know whether he was asking me if we had any questions about the legal stuff regarding Brian Hawser or about where we were going to go next with the Sulenka investigation.

I stood there, thinking. I could feel the chief's eyes on me. Ryan's, too. But there was something nagging at me that wasn't coming into sharp enough focus yet. Then it hit me.

"Chief, we know Brian didn't kill Austin."

"The way I'd put it, Karen," he said, "is we don't have any evidence that puts him there, and his statement that he choked her with his hands—we know that's untrue."

"What I mean is, we still don't know about Tiffany."

Ryan said, "Where are you going?"

"Don't know," I said. "I just want to make sure we're not crossing off the two of them just because we think it wasn't Brian."

"She admitted having sex with Austin around seven the night he was killed, right?" the chief said.

"That's right," I said. "Then she went over to her girlfriend's place and screwed the two guys with the weed."

"Do you have a timeline on that?" the chief said.

"Not an exact one," Ryan said. "You thinking Tiffany smokes pot with the two guys, then goes over to Austin's place around midnight?"

"I'm not thinking anything. We know May Eberlein and Kathy Caravelli were doing Austin around ten till maybe eleven-thirty. So it's possible."

"I don't like it," Ryan said. "She's stoned, she just screwed the two guys. She's going to go to sleep."

"Let's go back to motive," the chief said. "Why does she want to kill Austin?"

"I don't know," I said. "Same reason any of his fuck buddies would want to kill him. She fell in love with him? Didn't like it that he was just a pussy hound?"

The chief scratched at his chin. "How do you square that with her doing the two guys an hour earlier? Doesn't that make her the same thing?"

I shook my head. "Yeah, if you're doing it like math. But if you're looking at it from her perspective—she's an average girl, in the worst way. Average looks, average brains. She sees herself settling into an average, boring life with a loser like Brian. Then, all of a sudden, this exciting guy comes along, this intellectual guy, shows some interest in her. She thinks maybe he sees something special in her, so she lets herself think she's special. She falls for him. When she figures out he was just fucking her—realizes maybe he just fucks one or two girls from each of his classes—she realizes Austin sees her as one step up from a hooker. To Austin, she was as special as a used rubber. She gets pissed."

"And you're thinking Brian knew she killed Austin?" Ryan said.

I shook my head. "We'll never know that one. If she told Brian, he's not gonna tell us. He's in love with her."

The chief sighed. "Let's get back to what we can say to Larry Klein. We don't have any forensics putting her at Austin's place after she did him at seven PM. Correct?"

"Correct," I said.

"So we could take his place apart—and her place, too—and anything we find is going to tell us the two of them were sleeping together. Even if you find a blouse at her place with his DNA on the sleeve—it doesn't tell us she strangled him with that sleeve. It tells us the two of them were sleeping together. You get me someone tells us she said she was going to kill Austin, a phone message says she did it, an eyewitness saw her coming out of his place around midnight. Give me something and we'll work on Brian some more to find out whether he knew about it or conspired with her. Until then ..." He just raised his arms, palms up.

"So what do we do now?" I said.

The chief looked at his watch and frowned. "I don't know about you two, but in about five minutes I talk to Tiffany's parents."

"They're here now?"

"In about five minutes," he said.

I shook my head as Ryan and I walked out of his office. The parents were sitting there in his outer office. They looked awful. Both of them were in blue jeans and baggy sweatshirts. The father was a short, stocky guy with a buzz cut. The mother had dyed red hair, pushed off to the side, like she'd slept on it in the car or at the motel. But it didn't look like she'd slept much. She sat there, gazing straight ahead, looking at the wall, a crumpled handkerchief in her hand. The father's expression told me his thoughts were far away, like maybe he was thinking about how he brought his wife and their new daughter home from the hospital right after she was born. He looked like he was going to start crying any moment.

I hurried past them. I didn't want to stop and introduce myself or offer any condolences or anything. Back at our desks, Ryan saw me looking a little the worse for wear. "We didn't do it, Karen."

I shrugged my shoulders. "One way of looking at it." It wasn't me who punched her, anyway.

"Let's get busy," Ryan said. "No sense thinking about Tiffany."

"What you got in mind?"

"We were tracking down Suzannah Montgomery's story. We were trying to figure out—what was that phrase you used?—if the husband lies like a lawyer or a complete liar?"

"That doesn't sound like me." I thought for a moment. "Or a bald-ass liar."

"Yeah," Ryan said, giving me a smile. "That's it. Let's figure it out."

"What was his story?" Now that I'm in my forties, I'm having a little more trouble remembering details from the cases, even if they happened only a few days ago.

"He said he graduated from Cornell, took a job with some architect in Berkeley. She stayed in South Carolina, taking care of her mother, who was dying. Then she went to Europe for a year."

"Yeah, that's right," I said. "He's never been to South Carolina. You got any of that stuff written down."

Ryan tapped at his jacket pocket, where he kept his skinny notebook. He pulled it out and opened it up. "Lawrence Yu, in Berkeley. That should take me the better part of a minute."

I waved at him to go ahead. His fingers started tapping the keyboard.

He picked up the phone, dialed a number, and told someone who he was and what he wanted: Was there an architect named Aaron Montgomery who worked there around the year 2000? "Not a problem," Ryan said after a few seconds. Then, to me, "It's before his time, but he's looking it up." Twenty seconds later, the guy was back. "Hmmm," Ryan said. "Yeah, I can hold. That's quite all right." Another half minute of waiting. "Okay, thanks very much. I appreciate it." Ryan hung up. "The office guy wanted to check with someone to confirm what the records showed."

I frowned at Ryan. "Yeah, that was the question I wanted answered. And did the office guy get that confirmation?"

Ryan smiled at me. "Yes, he did. Indeed he did."

"Why do you break my balls like this?"

"Because it's fun. You're like a sister. An older sister. An overtired, cranky older sister."

"Okay," I said. "Now I understand why you break my balls." I sat there, in my desk chair, just looking at Ryan.

"Come on, you want to know. I know you want to know."

I shook my head. "I really don't give a shit anymore."

"Ask," he said, still smiling. "Please? Pretty please?"

"Never." I got up out of my chair, lifted my bag off my desk, slung it over my shoulder, and started walking over to the coatrack.

"They never heard of him."

"See you tomorrow."

"The office boy said they never heard of him."

I stopped and turned. "Were you talking to me, Ryan?"

"I'm sorry, Karen," he said. He opened his eyes wide and hung his head down on his chest. "It was wrong of me to do that."

I walked back over to the desk and put my bag down. Then I sat down in my chair. "Asshole."

"That was hurtful, Karen."

"All right, you're sure you got the right architect firm in Berkeley?"

"There's only one Lawrence Yu Architecture, LLP in Berkeley."

"So Aaron Montgomery doesn't just lie like a lawyer," I said. "He makes shit up."

"The Montgomerys sound like a perfect couple. She steals her roommate's identity, complete with her MA degree."

"Yeah, lovely. The question is, What's the fastest way for us to figure out if the two of them killed Austin?"

"We don't have probable cause to search the Montgomery house or her office or anything like that. We can't compel her to give us DNA to put her in Austin's apartment."

"The only thing we can do," I said, "is see how many layers of lies they've told, confront them, and see if we can pressure them to work with us."

"Threaten to expose them?"

"He's got this high-profile do-gooder job, she's a tenured university professor. Plus, they've got that sick kid who needs lots of care. You saw the father with him. He loves the kid, right?"

"Looked like it to me," Ryan said.

"So that might be their vulnerability. If we can show them how it can all turn to shit if we expose the lies—going all the way back to the car crash, when she put the other girl in the driver's seat—we might be able to get them to plead to Austin."

"You mean if they both plead to Austin, the court might be able to work out some way they alternate jail time, so one of them can take care of the kid?"

"You got a better idea?"

"Nope," Ryan said.

"Okay, so what other bullshit did he try to feed us?"

Ryan looked down at his notebook. "Two things. She cared for her mother for two years, then she went off to Europe for a year."

"The mother thing could be a pain to track down."

"Because we don't know which mother it is: Suzannah Collins or Carol Winters?"

"I hadn't thought of that. I don't want to call the real Collins father again to ask whether his wife died. And Carol Winters … there must be a bunch of them in Charleston, South Carolina."

"That's if she's from Charleston," Ryan said. "But why should the mother be from Charleston? Every other fact about this woman has been bogus."

"I know who's got accurate facts," I said. "The FBI. Let me call Allen Pfeiffer. He'll be able to tap into the State Department records."

"Of course," Ryan said, smiling and nodding his head. "Passports."

I went to my contacts on the computer and pulled up Allen Pfeiffer's phone. He'd helped us out on a couple of earlier cases. There's a process for local law enforcement to requisition information from federal sources, and it only takes a few days or weeks to find out what you want. But if you know a friendly fed who's willing to tap a few keys, it goes much faster than that.

I dialed. Then I looked at my watch. It would 6:15 in Washington. Shit. The phone rang a few times. Then he picked up.

"Pfeiffer."

"Aaron, this is Karen Seagate, in Montana. You're supposed to be home, having a drink by now."

"Yeah, that's what they told me during orientation. How're you doing, Karen?"

"I'm good, thanks, Allen." We spent a couple of sentences catching up. "Allen, can you tap the State Department database?"

"What do you need?"

"If I give you a name and Social Security—I don't have a passport number, but they're U.S. citizens—can you give me dates of travel, leaving and re-entering the U.S.?"

"We stamp passports only on re-entry, so all I can get is when they come back into the U.S. The only way I could tell you when they left is if you can tell me where they went—I might be able to contact that country and get the date they arrived there. Give me what you got."

I told him the information for Carol Winters, or Suzannah Collins, or Suzannah Montgomery, with the best Social Security I had. I also told him about Aaron Montgomery. I said I thought she or the both of them might have been traveling between 1996 and 1999. He asked where I thought they might be leaving from in the U.S. I told him I thought they might have been living in South Carolina, so maybe they were on an international flight from Atlanta. He said he'd call me back in a few minutes.

I went into the break room and found some pastry I recognized from yesterday and some coffee from this morning. I heard the phone ring from the bullpen and hurried back to my desk.

It was Allen Pfeiffer. I put him on Speaker. "I couldn't get anything on exiting the U.S. There's no centralized database that collates all the passenger manifests from the different airlines. If you had a date and airline, I could do that, but not without the name of the airline."

"Yeah, I understand that," I said. "How about coming back to the U.S.?"

"Suzannah Collins and Aaron Montgomery got their passports stamped in Newark, New Jersey, on June 9, 1998."

"Have you got addresses on those passports?"

"Yeah, they're roomies. At 1400 Evergreen Parkway, Apartment 2D, in Charleston, South Carolina."

I thanked Allen and hung up.

Ryan said to me, "So we don't know when they left the U.S."

"I don't really give a shit when they left the U.S.," I said. "I know that Aaron Montgomery said she went to Europe. He didn't say they went together, right?"

"That's right," Ryan said. "And he said he's never even been to South Carolina."

"So they both have some honesty issues."

"Doesn't mean they killed Austin."

"No, it doesn't." I ran my finger along the edge of my desk. "But it does mean that if one of them did it, the other one was probably in on it—or at least knew about it."

"So how are we going to force them to give it up?"

Chapter 33

"No," the chief said, shaking his head, his mouth set in a frown. "I'm not going to do that. It wouldn't be smart."

"How's that?" I said.

"I'm not going to go to the university to pressure Suzannah Montgomery to work with us. We have no evidence she violated any laws."

"All the lies on her application forms at Central Montana State?"

"That's civil. If the university wants to go after her, they can. But that's for the university to find out. It's not for us to tell them. Certainly not now. Not without proof."

"The car accident in South Carolina?"

"Key words there are 'South Carolina.'" The chief showed no expression. "When it comes time to inform the university, I'll be on the phone to President Billingham. But not yet. He'd tell you the same thing: if we can arrest her and indict her for a felony crime, that's the cleanest way to do it. If we can't, what's he going to do with an allegation that she fudged her papers?"

"I wouldn't call stealing a woman's identity fudging her papers."

"We're a ways from proving identity theft. Right now she's got a U.S. passport saying she's Suzannah Collins, and I bet she has a marriage certificate that makes her Suzannah Montgomery.

We'd have to do a lot of legwork to prove she's—what'd you say her real name is?"

"Carol Winters."

"Carol Winters." He frowned. "Anyway, I don't want to bring in the university. We get them to pressure her—she's a popular teacher—what's that going to look like? A police department that can't make an arrest, so they start harassing an innocent faculty member with a sick kid. If she's guilty, she'd have no incentive to cooperate with us. It might even make her run. You two need to figure out if she—or she and her husband—killed Austin Sulenka. Answer that question yes or no, then we'll talk about what to tell the university. Understand?"

Ryan and I went back to our desks to keep digging through the layers of lies the Montgomerys had assembled. We'd already unearthed plenty, and we could probably keep going for another couple of weeks and come up with a lot more, but what was the point? We already knew she'd been in the car with the real Suzannah Collins when it crashed, and that she'd poured her into the driver's seat to save herself from vehicular manslaughter if the girl died. We already knew that she'd stolen Suzannah's degree, her Social Security, basically her whole life. But we weren't getting any closer to figuring out if she killed Austin Sulenka.

"What do you want to do next?" I said to Ryan.

He sighed. "Well, I guess we could find out if Aaron Montgomery really went to Cornell."

"I bet he was down at Clemson with Carol Winters and Suzannah Collins."

"Could be," Ryan said.

"How about this?" I said. "He's down there, starts seeing Suzannah Collins—"

"The real one, or the one he married?"

"I'm guessing both. He starts out with the real one, but she sounds kinda boring, you know?"

"You mean, a good student, straight shooter?"

"Exactly," I said. "Kind of like you. So he switches over to Carol Winters."

"You figure he makes the switch before the car accident?"

"I don't know," I said. "As long as we're making him a bastard, let's have him switch over after the car accident. Suzannah's all busted up, then she loses the leg and strokes out."

"That would make him a real bastard," Ryan said.

I put my elbows on my desk and rested my head in my palms. "Why are we wasting our time on this shit?"

"I think the chief would call this police work. If you've got a better idea—"

My cell rang. I opened it up and answered. "Seagate."

"Detective, this is Aaron Montgomery."

"Yes, Mr. Montgomery, what can I do for you?" I raised my eyebrows at Ryan as I hit Speaker.

"I'm worried about Suzannah." He did sound scared.

"Why is that, sir?"

"Suzannah didn't come home last night, I mean, after she was finished at the university."

"Is that unusual, Mr. Montgomery?" A somewhat obnoxious question, given that she was the guy's wife and not his girlfriend, but I was okay with him knowing he wasn't exactly my favorite person at the moment.

There was silence, as if he didn't want to lie to me, although I didn't get why that would bother him since everything else he had told us was a lie. "I've tried her a number of times—all through the night—and she didn't pick up."

"She usually keeps her phone on?"

"She *always* keeps her phone on. Because of Adam. In case I need to reach her."

"All right, Mr. Montgomery. Don't let your imagination get away from you. She's probably fine. Maybe her phone's not working."

"That doesn't make sense, Detective. She would've called me. There's something wrong, I know it."

"Let's stay calm, Mr. Montgomery. We get missing-persons calls literally every day, and they turn out to be simple misunderstandings. Where are you now, sir?"

"I'm at home, with Adam."

"All right, you stay there. Detective Miner and I will be out there in ten minutes. We'll take all your information and work out a plan. Does that sound okay?"

"Yes, Detective, thank you. Please hurry, though."

"Ten minutes." I ended the call.

Ryan said, "How do you read this?"

I shook my head. "Not sure," I said. "He's a liar, so I assume there's some kind of lie in what he said. I just don't know what his angle is."

"He's trying to lead us on a goose chase for some reason."

"Why?" I said.

"I don't know. Maybe just to take us off the trail of running down the lies."

"I don't like it. We'll find her, then we're gonna be more interested in looking hard at the two of them."

"She's gone, but he knows where she is."

"Okay, good," I said. "That's it. She's on the run. They've got a destination, but he's gonna make it a missing-persons. We'll go looking for her, but we won't find her ..."

"She's not taking her car. He'll switch cars, too, so we don't know what we're looking for."

"But why tell us? Why not just get in the other cars and head off to wherever?"

Ryan scratched at his chin. "Not sure. But for some reason they want us to think she's a missing person."

"Maybe she is," I said.

"She's going off on her own?"

"Why not?"

"Well, her kid, for one thing," Ryan said.

I shrugged. "She killed Austin. She knows we'll be able to prove that somehow, but we won't be able to implicate her husband. She knows Adam will be better off with him, anyway. So she goes off the grid, leaves the kid with him. Even if he knows she killed Austin, he can't be compelled to testify against her because they're still married."

"And they stay in touch."

"Hey, she knows how to steal identities. He must, too. So next year, they're in Los Angeles or Costa Rica or some other damn place."

"Just one problem with that theory."

"Yeah?"

"They've got this other kid, the girl."

"What's the problem?"

"You see her running away from both the kids?"

"What we know about her? Yeah, I do."

"How do we handle Aaron Montgomery now?" Ryan said.

I stood up. "Let's head out there now. We'll phone the chief, tell him what we're up to."

We hurried to the lot and got in the Charger. I pulled out into traffic, then drove us toward the Montgomery place in the foothills.

"You want to just interview him?" Ryan said.

I thought a second. "If we think she's on the run and he might want to follow her, let's make it a little harder."

"Bring him in?"

"Call headquarters, have them send a patrol car out after us. We'll have the uniforms bring him in for questioning. That way, we're free to chase down Suzannah if we can figure out where she's gone."

"He's not going to like that," Ryan said.

"That's true. But as Larry Klein would say, now you're changing the topic."

Ryan opened his phone and called it in. Took thirty seconds.

"Call the university Substation, have them find out what kind of car she's got, see if it's in the Humanities parking lot."

Ryan did it. "Said it would take five minutes to run down the sticker and check it out."

"Now call the English Department, see if she's scheduled to be there this morning. Find out if they've seen her."

Ryan opened his notebook and found the number. He phoned the department, spoke to the secretary. "Is that unusual?" he said to her. He waited for the answer, then thanked her and ended the call.

"Yeah?"

"She missed her class, and, yes, that's not like her."

"She's on the run," I said. "I know it."

"Let's try to keep him in town," Ryan said.

We were in the foothills, winding our way up toward the Montgomery place.

Ryan got a call on his cell. It was an officer at the Substation. She drives a 2010 Lexus SUV, white. "Thanks," he said to the officer before ending the call. Then, to me, "Her car's not in the lot at school."

"Where'd you go, Suzannah?"

I pulled into the driveway outside the Montgomery house. We walked up to the door and I knocked hard.

The door opened in a second. It was Aaron Montgomery, but not the smoothie we had interviewed a couple days ago. His complexion was almost grey. His skin sagged beneath his eyes. He was wearing old blue jeans and a stained yellow tee shirt. His movements were quick and jittery. "Thank God you're here, Detectives," he said.

We don't usually get a greeting like that. "Hello, Mr. Montgomery," I said, my voice noncommittal.

"Please come in." He led us back toward the big living room with the fireplace. His son, Adam, was in his wheelchair. The boy's eyes followed us, but he didn't say or do anything. That was closer to the kind of reaction we usually get.

When we got into the living room, Aaron Montgomery walked over to his son and started rubbing the boy's shoulders. The boy didn't seem to react, but it looked like it calmed his father down a little. "What's the plan? What are you going to do?"

"We've checked with the English Department. She's not there, and nobody's seen her today. Her car's not in the Humanities lot. It's a white 2010 Lexus SUV, right?"

"Yeah," he said. "That's it."

"Can you tell us when you last talked to her?"

"It was yesterday afternoon, maybe around four."

"And what did she say?"

"Said she was going to be home around five-thirty. I told her I'd work on dinner. She asked me how the kids were doing. You know, absolutely routine."

"She didn't mention the lockdown on campus? A guy with a gun?"

"No, nothing like that."

"Did she say was going to stop and do some errands, anything like that?"

"No."

"When we talked with you on the phone fifteen minutes ago, I asked if she ever stayed out overnight. You didn't exactly answer me."

He frowned. "Like I just said, Detective, we talked and she said she'd be coming home around five-thirty."

"You don't think she could've changed her mind and decided to do something else?"

"I don't know what you're getting at, Detective," he said, straightening up and removing his hands from his son's shoulders. "I've told you what you need to know about our phone conversation."

"Well, there's the problem, Mr. Montgomery. You haven't been honest with us."

"What are you talking about?"

"We'll start with some simple things. You said you've never been to South Carolina. You said you worked for Lawrence Yu, the architect in Berkeley." I paused. He walked over to a cream-colored soft chair and sank onto its matching footstool, his forearms on his legs, his head hung down.

"Suzannah Collins, Carol Winters. You understand where I'm going? So when you say you don't know where your wife is, first question comes to mind, Which woman we talking about here? Next question, why should we think she's missing? Maybe you and her just felt things are getting too hot here and decided to move on. Could that be what's going on here, Mr. Montgomery?"

Adam started looking around, first at his father, then at us. He sensed something was wrong and started to moan.

Aaron Montgomery raised his head and looked at me. "I'm not going to say anything at all about any of those allegations without advice of counsel."

"But you do see how that makes us think maybe you're not telling us the truth, don't you?"

"I don't expect you to believe me or to understand anything about any of those matters. I phoned you for one reason: to ask you to help me find my wife. Are you willing to do that? Are you willing to do your job?"

"Yes, Mr. Montgomery, we are always willing to do our jobs." I turned to Ryan. "Check and see if the officers are here yet." Ryan turned and walked out toward the entrance hallway.

"What are you doing?"

"We want to make sure we have every opportunity to do our jobs—to help you find your wife. So we're going to bring you in to police headquarters and question you about your wife's whereabouts and any other relevant matters that could help us find her."

He stood up. "This is outrageous. I call you, asking for your help, and you're going to bring me in for questioning?"

"That's right, sir," I said. "We can hold you for twenty-four hours, then we have to charge you or release you."

"You can't do that," he said. "What about Adam? What about my daughter? She comes home from school at three-thirty."

I nodded and reached into my shoulder bag and pulled out my phone. I opened it up and speed-dialed headquarters. "This is Seagate. I'm at the home of Aaron and Suzannah Montgomery." I gave the address. "I need you to alert Child and Family Services. We're going to bring in Mr. Montgomery for questioning. He has a son, he's here now, he's handicapped, in a wheelchair. Age twelve. He'll need care. And a daughter, age fourteen, who'll be dropped off from school around three-thirty. Yeah," I said. "Thanks."

Just then Ryan walked back into the living room. I looked at him. He nodded.

"Okay, Mr. Montgomery, there's two officers in your driveway who'll bring you in to headquarters. They'll stay here with you until the people can come for Adam."

"You can't do this," he said, panic on his face and in his voice.

"Can," I said. "And will. We've got two cases we think you can help us with. The murder of Austin Sulenka and the missing-persons. While the child-services people are getting here, you might want to pack a bag with the things Adam is gonna need for the next twenty-four hours or so. You know, clothing, diapers, special foods, whatever."

Aaron Montgomery let out a long, low wail and sank onto his knees on the carpet. Seeing his father respond this way, Adam started crying, first a little bit, then hysterically.

I walked out of the living room. Turning around, I saw Ryan standing there, looking at Aaron Montgomery and his son. "Let's go, Detective," I said to him in a clipped tone.

Chapter 34

"I still don't know who killed that graduate student." Frances Hamblin leaned on her silver-handled cane as she stood in the foyer of her really expensive house behind the gates in the Ravensmere development.

"Good morning, Professor Hamblin, sorry to stop by without calling. Detective Seagate; my partner, Detective Miner."

"Yes, lovely to hear your names again," she said, "but this is not a good time for a talk. Would you be able to stop by my office at the university? I'm available between two and three on Wednesdays."

"I'll be in the Charger," I said to Ryan. "Would you mind helping Professor Hamblin gather her things?" Ryan looked down at his shoes.

"What are you talking about?" the professor said. "What things are you telling this man to help me gather? I am not going anyplace."

"Actually, Professor, you are." I held my gaze. "We're bringing you in to police headquarters for questioning in regard to the murder of Austin Sulenka. If you resist, I will personally put you in cuffs and arrest you for obstruction of justice."

Her expression was puzzled, and then, suddenly, she smiled. "Would you like to come in, Detectives?" She had terrific teeth.

"Why, yes, Professor, if this is a good time for you."

"This is a wonderful time," she said, tipping her head just a little. "Would you please come this way?" she said. She turned and led us into a sitting room, all the furniture mahogany, covered in a pale blue brocaded cloth and sitting on slender, curved legs. Off to the side, a matching mahogany grand piano sat on the same style legs. "Sit, please," she said. "Can I get you some coffee, perhaps tea?"

I glanced at Ryan, who was wearing a small smile. He shook his head no.

"That's very generous, Professor, but we don't want to take up any more of your time than necessary. We have just a few questions."

She gestured to the couch near the large window that looked out over her front yard. She took a high-backed armchair. "How can I help?"

"We'd like to know when you last had contact with Suzannah Montgomery."

"I thought you said this was about Austin Sulenka."

"It is. But at the moment we're trying to learn more about Suzannah's husband so we can help him with a problem. Her husband, Aaron?—"

"Yes, I know Aaron."

"Aaron Montgomery is concerned that she did not come home last night."

"Did you check at the university?"

Now it was my turn to smile. "When did you last have contact with Suzannah Montgomery?"

"If you are asking whether she spent the night here, the answer is no."

Well, okay, I'm nothing if not flexible. "Does she ever spend the night here?"

She sniffed and raised her chin a little bit. "Yes, sometimes she does."

"Would you like to tell us about that?"

"Are you asking me to reveal details of my personal life?"

"My partner and I are trying to figure out who killed Austin Sulenka, as well as where Suzannah Montgomery is. To the extent those details about your personal life could help us with either of those two matters, yes, I am."

"Let me address the second matter first. I have no idea where Suzannah Montgomery is, and I haven't been in contact with her—by phone, in person, by e-mail, in any way—for three or four days. On the question of whether she killed Austin Sulenka, the answer is no. She did not kill him."

"Can I ask how you know that?"

"Because she told me she did not do it."

"I don't want to be impertinent, Professor, but Suzannah Montgomery does take some liberties with the truth."

"Yes, of course. As her friend, I am well aware of that. She is an inveterate liar."

I took a deep breath. "Okay, then, if you admit that she's a liar but you know she didn't kill Austin because she said she didn't … Do you see where I'm going?"

"Rest assured, I see where you're going before you do, Detective, but if you don't mind my offering a critique, you're being awfully reductive here."

"Now, I don't even know what that means."

"Does Suzannah Montgomery lie? Yes, she does. As does everyone. I daresay you lie all the time."

She was right, of course, but I didn't blink. "So what makes you think Suzannah was telling you the truth when she said she didn't kill him?"

"For one thing, she was very fond of him. Since she began the affair, she had enormous verve, tremendous vitality. I tell you, it took twenty years off her age. Austin gave her a kind of sexual energy that I don't see in most of our graduate students."

"Is that what drew her to him?"

"No, I don't think so, although he certainly was an attractive young man. Even a crone like myself could see that. No, I think it was the connection he had with Adam."

"Her son?"

"I don't know what it was, but Austin could communicate with the boy. Not with words. It was something deeper. The smile on that boy's face when he was with Austin was remarkable to behold. I don't think even Suzannah had that connection with him. Her whole body was just filled with joy—that's the only word for it—when she saw her two boys together. That's what she called them: her two boys."

"You said 'for one thing.' You had another reason she didn't kill Austin?"

"Yes. This is very simple, but very profound, and very true. Suzannah is not about hatred. Or pain. She is about love."

"Really?" I prepared myself for the bullshit.

"I know that for a fact. When my husband was diagnosed with Alzheimer's, now some nine years ago, and then passed, five years later, Suzannah was the only one in the department—the only one, period—who made an effort to befriend me. I understand that I have a somewhat prickly personality. Suzannah saw right through that. She made a sincere effort to reach me. I'm not talking about cards and flowers and all the rest of the empty gestures. I'm talking about friendship, about caring. I'm talking about commitment. She befriended me. Our souls are now joined together."

I paused a moment. "So, about those reference letters, when she was coming up for tenure?"

Frances Hamblin frowned and fluttered her hand, as if she were shooing away a gnat. "As a scholar, Suzannah is negligible. I am well aware of that. And if this were a serious university with talented students, she would never have been hired in the first place. But this is Central Montana State, and Suzannah is a terrific asset to *this* university. She is a wonderful teacher, and she does more for our students in one week than I have done in three decades. I feel no remorse at all for my role in that incident."

"You mean that incident when she phonied up a reference letter?"

Professor Hamblin looked confused. "I have no idea what you think she did, and I do not intend to provide you with any more salacious gossip. Suzannah Montgomery is a loving, wonderful person who could never hurt another soul. She is with me now, as I speak, as she is with me at all times."

My phone rang, the muffled sound coming from my big leather shoulder bag. "Excuse me a second." I walked out toward the entryway so I could take the call. I pulled the phone out of my bag and looked at the screen. It said Rawlings Police Department.

"Seagate," I said.

"Detective, this is Sergeant Hamilton. We know you got a possible missing person. We got a message from Montana State Police. They've got a car in the reservoir. And a driver."

"Know what kind of car?"

"Not yet."

"We dispatch anyone?"

"Harold Breen left about five minutes ago. Robin is out at another crime scene. And we've got two uniforms there. We're working on getting the tow truck over there."

"What part of the reservoir?"

"The boat launch."

"Okay, thanks, Sergeant. Miner and I will head over."

I ended the call and went back into the room, where Ryan was chatting the professor up about Melville. He looked up at me to get a read on the phone call.

"We have to go, Professor. I want to thank you for taking the time—"

"Yes, yes, *et cetera*, Detective." She leaned down hard on her cane and slowly rose from her chair. "I recommend you turn your attention away from the trivial matter of infractions of silly rules and concentrate instead on making sure she is safe."

"I appreciate the advice, Professor. We'll let ourselves out."

Getting into the Charger, Ryan said, "What's up?"

"There's a car in the reservoir. Driver inside."

"That all you know?"

"Yeah." I steered us out of Ravensmere, out past the steel gate that swung open at a stately pace. We headed toward State Road 19, which would wind along the river about eight miles, where it connected with the reservoir. The river was running high and fast, the reservoir near capacity from spring runoff. This winter we'd gotten more than our usual snowfall, and the township had opened the irrigation canals a couple of weeks early to take some of the pressure off the reservoir. The Greenpath was flooded in a number of spots, with the river lapping at the tops of boulders that bordered the riverbank and pooling around the cottonwoods and other scraggly trees that lined the banks on both sides.

"Was Professor Hamblin telling us she was having an affair with Suzannah Montgomery?"

I turned to him. "Yeah, I think that's what she was saying. What did she say: 'our souls are joined,' some horseshit like that?"

"That was it."

"Well, if you got a PhD, I think that means you're fucking her."

"Well, now you're just being reductive," Ryan said.

"I still don't know what that means."

"It means you're oversimplifying a complicated situation."

"By reducing the joining of the souls to sex?"

"Exactly."

"But there was sex?" I said.

"As a detective, I'd have to say we have no evidence to draw that conclusion. But if you reduce the complex spiritual relationship—the joining of the souls—to a merely physical relationship, as if they were two dogs or pigs, then you're being reductive."

"So they were getting their rocks off, plus feeling good about themselves because they weren't just a couple horny old babes fucking like they used to when they were young."

"I wouldn't use that vocabulary, but yes, I think that's the point."

"You could've been a professor."

"Thank you."

"It wasn't a compliment."

We passed the Hilltop Inn, perched on the top of a bluff overlooking the western edge of the reservoir, which terminated in the huge concrete wall with the three big circular spouts that fed the river. A half-dozen serious Harleys sat in a row in the parking lot at the Hilltop. There were always a half-dozen serious Harleys there. Inside, the bulky bikers with do-rags on their bald heads played pool and listened to Creedence and Skynyrd on the digital jukebox while they drank Coors and Old Milwaukee. I was fine with them, mostly because they didn't run drugs or girls and when they got cranky they just beat up each other, not any civilians. Plus, the owner was good about not letting them walk out of there shitfaced and get on their cycles.

We made it to the access road that served all the mechanical gear that operated the gates controlling the water that fed the river. We snaked our way along the edge of the reservoir, the water looking cold and black under the cloudy sky. In the distance, I could see a couple of fire trucks with boat trailers half-submerged.

I parked us off to the side, behind Harold Breen's van, and Ryan and I walked down toward the concrete ramp. The ramp was about thirty yards wide and extended fifty yards into the reservoir, with floating docks on either side. But with the water this high, only about ten yards of the ribbed concrete was visible. A dive-team van was parked on the ramp, its boat trailer mostly submerged. Sixty or seventy yards away, the red rubber dive-team raft was bobbing in the slight chop of the water. One guy was in the raft, another in the water nearby, his head just visible above the surface. I saw a line going off the front of the raft, down into the water.

"Good morning, Harold," I said to the Medical Examiner.

"Hello, sweetheart," he said. He was wearing a thin green nylon jacket, his big gut sticking out the front. "And good morning to you, too, Ryan."

Ryan acknowledged the greeting and said, "All we know is there's a car in there. You got anything else?"

"Nothing useful," Harold said. "A guy in a little boat saw the outline of a car, called it in. Said he thought he saw a person inside."

I said, "So the divers haven't told you anything?"

"They just went in a few minutes ago."

A second diver broke the surface near the raft. The two divers flopped their way into the raft, and the third guy started the outboard, pulled in the anchor, and aimed the raft at the ramp.

It took a half minute for them to get to shore. One of the divers and the pilot stayed with the raft, straightening it out and hooking its bow to the trailer winch. The other diver walked over to us.

He had already left his tanks, fins, and other gear in the raft. Still, he walked slowly and laboriously in the heavy-duty rubber dry suit that looked like it weighed at least fifty pounds.

"I'm McDevitt." He was breathing a little hard.

"I'm Seagate, this is Miner. You know Harold Breen, the ME?"

"Yeah," McDevitt said. "Good to see you all."

"What you got down there?" I pointed out toward the water.

"A car and a driver."

"What kind of car?"

"It's an SUV. Lexus."

"White?"

"Near as I can tell."

"Driver?"

"White woman. Middle aged."

"How long will it take to get the car out?"

McDevitt shook one leg, then the other, as if he was trying to get the blood flowing again. "It's sitting right-side up on the bottom. I can attach a cable, run it back here to shore. The truck should be able to pull it out within an hour."

"Harold, how long will you need to tell me how she died?"

"Anywhere from one hour to one week. Depends."

"Can you start this afternoon?"

"I can start this afternoon. Can't say I'll finish this afternoon. But I'll let you know what we're looking at."

Chapter 35

"This is how she died," Harold Breen said, using a pencil to lift the hair off Suzannah Montgomery's right temple.

It was a loose-contact wound: the muzzle was resting lightly against the skin when the pistol discharged. The skin encircling the entry wound was blackened. Outside the circle were the characteristic reddish-brown dots that showed us she was alive before the bullet penetrated her brain. I turned to Robin, the Evidence Tech. "Can I see the gun?"

She shook her head. "No gun."

I paused. "No gun?"

"We tore the SUV apart. And we searched the ramp and the brush on either side."

"Were the windows on the SUV open or closed?"

"Everything was closed except for the front passenger window, which was open about four inches." Robin reached over the corpse and pulled up the upper lip. "Look at this."

"What am I looking at?"

"You see the gums on the right side of her mouth?"

"Yeah."

"Now look at the left side."

"Okay, what?"

"She was left-handed."

"How do you get that?"

"Most people, the gum recedes more on the side opposite their handedness."

I stepped back a little to see what she was talking about. "You mean, they brush harder on the opposite side?"

"That's it," Robin said. "Plus, her watch was on her right wrist."

"Okay, she was left-handed," I said.

"Most suicides use their dominant hand when they blow their brains out. I'd expect her to shoot herself with her left hand."

"Ryan?"

He shrugged his shoulders. "Maybe she was lefty but she used her right hand because the window got in the way." He paused. "I do find it interesting that we didn't recover a weapon."

"The diver said the SUV was right-side-up, right?"

"Yes, he did," my partner said.

"Robin, when you looked at the SUV, did you see any evidence it rolled over once it was in the water? The roof scratched or anything?"

"No, it rolled in, kept going for a while. The transmission was in Drive. I think the engine was on, and it was driven into the water. It kept going for a few seconds until it stalled out, then it kept rolling a little bit. But it didn't flip. If you're asking whether the pistol fell out the passenger window, I don't see that happening."

"If she shot herself," Ryan said, "the pistol would either still be in her right hand or on the seat or the floor. It would still be in the Lex."

"What do you think, Harold?" I said.

"All I know is she was alive until a bullet penetrated her brain. Then, less than a minute later, she was dead."

Ryan turned to me. "You want to ask the divers to go back in? They've got a hand-held sonar that can find a gun."

I paused a moment to think. "Not sure what the pistol's gonna tell us. If it's in the water, not likely it'll have any prints left on it. Let's start by getting the round. Harold, could you pull the round out?" He nodded. "And Robin, you try to see if there are any striations that identify the gun."

"Sure," she said.

"Ryan, let's go upstairs and see if the Montgomerys had any weapons registered." I turned to Robin and Harold. "Thanks, guys."

Back at our desks, Ryan said to me, "The Montgomerys don't have any permits."

"Which doesn't tell us anything."

"Very true," Ryan said.

"What are we missing here?"

"Let's pull back a little," he said. "We're thinking about which hand she used to shoot herself—and what happened to the gun. Why are we ruling out murder?"

"We're not ruling out murder. We're just starting with the most obvious explanation, which is that she killed Austin Sulenka, who she was screwing, and she knows we're onto her. Who do you see wanted to kill her?"

"It's not Frances Hamblin."

"No, what with their souls joined together."

"Her husband," Ryan said. "He finds out she's screwing Austin. Or Frances Hamblin."

"I don't like it." I shook my head. "Aaron and Suzannah have a long history of lying—all the way back to when they lived in South Carolina, where he says he's never been. Her doing some recreational fucking—for all we know, they video it for their private collection."

"Aaron killed Austin, or the two of them killed Austin. Aaron finds out Suzannah is going to plead to it, leaving him on the hook."

"Still don't like it," I said. "Why does he kill her out at the reservoir?"

"So he doesn't leave any evidence at the house. Doesn't have to dispose of the body."

"Aaron's out shooting his wife in the head. Where's Adam?"

"His sister's watching him," Ryan said. "Or he's at his school."

"How does Aaron get home to call us about his wife being missing?"

"In his own car."

"So both the family cars are out at the reservoir? How'd he convince her to drive her Lex to the reservoir?"

Ryan scratched at the corner of his mouth. "You know, it's a lot easier to ask questions than to answer them."

"I repeat my question: what are we missing here?"

"It wasn't suicide," he said.

"I'm listening."

"I get why Suzannah doesn't want to shoot herself in the house. But there are plenty of places within walking distance of campus—right on the river—where she could kill herself and not be discovered for days. Why would she drive out to the reservoir, put the car in Drive, and shoot herself in the head?"

"What's the problem?"

"For one thing, the car's still worth twenty-thousand bucks."

"Nah. You're going to kill yourself, you're not worried about the Blue Book on the car."

"I would if I were trying to make things easy on my husband and my two kids."

We sat there for a while. I was certain we didn't understand how and why Suzannah Montgomery killed herself—or got herself killed. If you've never been a cop, you'd be surprised how often you sit at your desk, knowing you don't understand something but not knowing exactly where you went off track or how to get back on it.

Ryan's phone rang. "Miner," he said. He listened for a little bit, then said, "Thanks very much, ma'am." He stood up and started putting on his suit jacket.

"Where you headed, partner?"

"We're going out to visit May Eberlein."

"Why's that?"

"Because she missed her defense this morning."

I got up and hoisted my big leather bag onto my shoulder. "You don't want to miss your defense, I guess."

"No," Ryan said as we hurried out to the parking lot. "You really don't."

It took us about seven minutes to make it out to the house where May Eberlein rented the apartment upstairs.

"I'll check the apartment," I said as I rushed around the side of the house to the metal stairs. "You get the key from the landlady."

I climbed the stairs and knocked hard on the door. There was no glass on the door, and no window to look into the apartment. I ran back down the stairs and circled the house, looking for her car. There were a couple of spots at the end of an unpaved driveway on the side. All I remembered about May's car was that it was a small red Japanese thing. The dark green Buick behind the house would be the landlady's.

I rushed back out front, where Ryan was finishing up with the landlady. He held the key up. "Doesn't know where she is."

Back up the metal stairs. Ryan opened it up. I called out to May, but the place was empty. Nothing looked out of the ordinary. There were a few dirty dishes in the sink, food in the refrigerator. In the living room, a set of student essays was sitting on the coffee table, next to a few books.

I headed into the bedroom. The closet door was open. I looked in. It was empty, just a couple dozen cheap metal hangers hanging on the rod. I scanned the rest of the room. No shoes. No nothing. "She's gone," I said.

Ryan was down on the floor, looking under her bed. "No suitcases," he said.

"Did the landlady say anything about where she might be?"

He shook his head. "She doesn't know anything."

"Shit."

"Well, you did want to know what we were missing," he said. "I think we figured it out."

"Thanks, Sherlock. Call the lesbian girlfriend, would you? Find out if she's still in Rawlings."

I hurried out of the house, down the metal stairs, and around to the front of the house. I banged on the front door and gave the landlady back her key. Told her we wanted to talk to May. I gave her my card and asked her to get in touch if she ran into her.

I looked over at the Charger parked at the curb. Ryan was already inside. I hurried over and got in the driver's seat. "Get through?"

"Kathy Caravelli is in her studio. Hasn't heard from May since the day we were over there."

"Let's head back to headquarters and put out the alerts on her car." I turned over the Charger and drove us back to headquarters. While Ryan put out a national and a Montana alert for May Eberlein and her red Suzuki shitcan, I went downstairs to check with Harold Breen and Robin about the bullet from Suzannah Montgomery's head. It was a 9mm round, but the striations were too compressed by the impact for Robin to identify a manufacturer.

I went upstairs and checked in with the chief.

"You're sure she's on the run?" he said.

I nodded. "She left her books and shit, but all her clothes are gone. All the shoes."

"Got it," he said. "Now we wait."

Actually, now we write up all the reports, including the domestic that killed Tiffany Rhodes, the boyfriend pistol-whipping the English department chair, and the shot Ryan put in the boyfriend's shoulder. We didn't have an autopsy report yet from Harold about Suzannah Montgomery, but I opened up a file on that one and started to fill it in.

It was a little before quitting time when I got the word from Montana State Police. It was a Sergeant Miller.

"We got your red Suzuki in the O'Day Manor Motel. It's on Old Oak Avenue, two blocks south of State Road 2 in Shelby."

"Great," I said. "Where's Shelby?"

"All the way north, on I-15."

"Up near the border?"

"Twenty-five miles south of the crossing."

"Here's what I'd like you to do. She's a suspect in a murder down here in Rawlings. If she moves, grab her and hold her. If she stays in the motel, don't move in. We'll need a couple hours to get there."

"Okay, we'll sit on her till you get here."

"Thanks, Sergeant."

We gassed up and headed north. Five minutes north of Rawlings, we were out in the country, with nothing to keep us company except the scratching sound of the wind-whipped grit on the side of the Charger. Every little while, we'd see a small herd of cattle and a few farmhouses with barns and some silos. An hour out of town, the sun sank off of my window. I swung my visor over and turned on the heat. We passed through a bunch of small towns, each with a stoplight or two and a John Deere place, a bar, a soft ice-cream stand, and a couple gas stations.

"Shit, you think we should've gotten an arrest warrant?"

"I don't think so," Ryan said. "It's a classic hot pursuit. We're fine."

"Because she's headed for the border?"

"The way I'd see it."

"Hope Larry Klein sees it that way, too."

Ryan and I didn't talk much after that. Cases like this, you want to figure out exactly why the murder happened, but you can pretty much guess the broad outlines, and the details don't usually give you any sense of satisfaction. Where we were right now, May Eberlein and Suzannah Montgomery were both screwing Austin Sulenka, probably one of them was in love with the guy. Maybe both of them. So they got into some sort of competition, which got out of control.

We pulled into the lot at the O'Day Manor Motel, a basic two-story family-run joint. I parked alongside a big Ford sitting near the office. It was obviously an MSP officer. I got out and introduced myself to him, a guy named Reynolds. His Smokey hat was on the seat next to him, but with his jarhead haircut, his dark blue uniform, and his big Ford painted municipal grey, he wasn't fooling anyone.

"She's in Unit 16," he said. "She brought in some fast food about an hour ago. I've already told the girl in the office you'd be by to pick up a key."

"All right, thanks," I said. "Did you scope out an exit?"

"There's a bathroom at the back of the unit with a window big enough for her to crawl out of. Just that and the front door."

"Okay, give us a few minutes, okay? Me or my partner will come out and let you know when we're done."

"No rush," he said.

I got back in the Charger. "Let's get the key, then give me a minute to set up in back. You knock and announce, okay? If she doesn't break for the window right away, I'll come around front."

Ryan nodded. He disappeared into the office as I found the path that led back to an alley lined with scraggly weeds. There were a couple of dumpsters full of broken-down cardboard boxes and ringed by two- or three-hundred cigarette butts. Unit 16 was the eighth unit down from the office. The window was about chest-high. It had frosted glass, so I couldn't see clearly. I put my ear to the stucco wall. The shower was going. I could see the steam curling around the window. I heard Ryan bang on the door and call out "Rawlings Police Department." I waited a minute for him to get inside, then went around to the front.

I turned the doorknob on Unit 16 and walked inside. Ryan was sitting on an armchair near the TV, facing the bathroom. He nodded to me and, just as I sat on the end of the bed, the bathroom door opened, releasing a cloud of steam. Out stepped May Eberlein, nude except for a pale yellow towel wrapped around her head.

She screamed when she saw the two of us. "What the fuck?"

"Hello, May," I said.

"What are you doing in my room?"

"We need to talk."

"Aren't you supposed to knock?" She put her hands on her hips in a gesture of indignation. She was a beautiful woman. In my experience, most people—men and women—look better with clothes on. But not May. Her limbs were long and slender, her waist thin, her hips smooth and rounded. Her breasts were full and high, with the dark nipples I remembered from the portrait of her at Kathy Caravelli's studio.

"We did knock. You didn't answer. We need to talk to you about Austin Sulenka and Suzannah Montgomery," I said. "You want to put some clothes on?"

She nodded, then turned and walked a few steps to the tiny dresser next to the television. She opened the top drawer. When she turned back to face us, she held a 9mm in her right hand.

I started to slide across the bedspread to get some distance from Ryan, making it a little harder for her to hit us both if things went south.

"Don't move," she said, pointing the pistol at my chest.

"Listen, May, you really shouldn't point a gun at cops. We want to be able to help you." I stood and started walking toward her slowly. "I'm gonna take the pistol now."

"No, you're not," she said, settling into a two-handed firing stance. "I said don't move."

I put my palms up and stepped backward. "Okay, May, let's just talk."

She didn't move, didn't say anything.

"Tell me about that night, May. What happened with Austin? Was it a sex game that went bad? That happens."

May Eberlein turned to Ryan but kept the pistol aimed at my chest. "Is she always this stupid?"

I looked over at Ryan. He didn't say anything. His face was a blank, which was smart: it's less confusing to the suspect if there's only one cop doing the talking. Less chance that she'll panic and do something impulsive.

"Tell me what happened that night with Austin," I said.

"I strangled him."

"But you didn't mean to, right? It was an accident. There was nobody else in the apartment with you two. Nobody who could say it wasn't an accident." When someone's pointing a 9mm at my chest, I'm happy to offer helpful legal tips, even though they might not be accurate.

"Of course I meant to," she said.

I had to keep her talking, give me a chance to think of a Plan B. "Why, May?"

"Because he disrespected me."

"How's that?"

"I cared for him. I might have loved him."

I waited for her to say more, but she was silent. "But he didn't love you?"

"Not enough," she said. "He didn't love me enough."

I didn't know what to say next. The best I could do was hope she would keep talking.

"I gave him every opportunity," she said.

Suddenly, Ryan spoke. "How did you get Suzannah Montgomery to drive out to the boat launch?"

Holy shit. I had no idea what Ryan was doing. Someone's got a gun on you, probably not the best time to remind them they killed two people, not just one. Maybe May could convince a jury she accidentally yanked the knot around Austin's neck a little too tight; it would be somewhat harder to convince them she accidentally lured Suzannah Montgomery to the reservoir, shot her in the temple, fired up her SUV, put it in Drive, and watched it roll into the reservoir.

May and I both turned to him. She aimed the nine at Ryan's chest.

"I told her we needed to talk."

"What about?"

"Something Austin said to me. Something about her."

"That's all it took?"

"I might have said a little bit more. About how if she didn't meet with me, her career was over."

"What had Austin said about her?"

"That they were sleeping together."

"And you told her that, at the boat launch?" Ryan asked his questions calmly, as if he was curious about what happened. Not as if someone was aiming a pistol at him.

"Yes, I did."

"What did she do?"

"She asked me what I wanted. Whether I wanted money."

"What did you say?"

"I made it clear she was insulting me."

"So what did you tell her you wanted?"

"Not so much what I wanted as what I was going to do."

"Which was kill her?"

"That's right. I told her I was going to kill her."

"What did she do?"

"She lost control, began to scream. She said she had to take care of her son."

"What did you do then?"

She looked puzzled, as if she didn't realize Ryan was slow-witted. "Then I shot her."

"You're a fool, May."

"I'm holding the gun, and you're calling me a fool?"

"Austin didn't love you," Ryan said. "Not even a little."

May Eberlein shifted her weight back and forth but maintained the firing stance. She didn't say anything.

Ryan said, "He was just fucking you. You're an easy lay, but you're quite stupid."

I felt my stomach drop. I didn't understand why he was goading her.

"Those are your final words," she said.

"What did he tell you? I mean, so you'd keep spreading your legs for him?"

May's expression became clouded, as if she had never considered that Austin was playing her. "Austin loved me. I know that. But Suzannah corrupted him."

"Corrupted?" Ryan said, with a smirk.

"That's what I said. Austin had no future as a professor. He knew that, and I knew that. But Suzannah dangled this big project in front of him."

"The Melville book?"

"That's right," May said. "The Melville book. Suzannah and Austin were going to work on the Melville book with Frances

Hamblin. Austin started to believe that the connection with Frances Hamblin was going to open doors for him. All he had to do was keep fucking Suzannah Montgomery."

"When he should have been fucking you."

"Something like that," May said.

"I don't believe that, May." Ryan shook his head. "And you don't, either. Frances Hamblin didn't need a third-rate scholar like Suzannah Montgomery, and she certainly didn't need a pathetic grad student like Austin, who spent most of his time sniffing out pussy—like yours." He pointed right at May's crotch.

Jesus Christ.

"If Frances Hamblin wanted someone to help her with the Melville project," Ryan said, "she would have picked up the phone and made a call. The first American literature scholar who answered would have given anything to work with her on it."

May's expression got dark, like she'd never had anyone talk to her like that.

"You want to know why you really killed Suzannah?" Ryan said.

May adjusted the aim of the pistol. She was close to losing it. She didn't respond to Ryan's question.

"You killed Suzannah because you knew Austin had a connection with her he didn't have with you," Ryan said. "It had nothing to do with Frances Hamblin or the Melville project." He paused. "He fed you that line so you'd keep fucking him. He knew you were so morally stunted you'd believe he loved you but that he couldn't break it off with Suzannah because he'd lose the Melville project. He knew you'd believe that line because that's exactly what you would do in that situation. But you had to have known, May. Deep down, you had to have known he didn't want to break it off with her because he cared about her. You? You were just one of the women he fucked. You were just pussy, May. Easy pussy."

"Fuck you," May said slowly.

Ryan picked up his cane, which was leaning against his chair, raised himself up, and began to walk toward her.

"Now you die." She squeezed the trigger. It clicked.

"May Eberlein," Ryan said, "you're under arrest for the murders of Austin Sulenka and Suzannah Montgomery. And the attempted murder of a police officer."

He held out his hand for her to give him the pistol. She was frozen there, her eyes wide and uncomprehending, her hands still gripping the pistol. He grabbed the barrel and yanked the pistol out of her hands with a little more muscle than absolutely necessary. She cried out in pain, pulling her arm back like he had broken her finger.

He turned to me. "I'm sorry, Karen," he said. "Didn't have a chance to tell you." He patted the left pocket on his suit jacket. Through the cloth I heard the muffled clicking of the 9mm rounds. "She takes long showers."

"Not anymore, she doesn't," I said.

Chapter 36

I got May Eberlein dressed, and we brought her back down to Rawlings. Since she'd already admitted in front of Ryan and me how she killed Austin Sulenka and Suzannah Montgomery, the interrogation was quick and easy. She signed a confession for the two murders. Now she, like Brian Hawser, would be Larry Klein's problem, which was fine with me.

I don't tend to have any sympathy for people who aim a pistol at a cop and squeeze the trigger, and I didn't feel sorry for May. She was way past shallow, vain, thoughtless, and the rest of those other bad things we'd all admit to if we were being honest. Ryan was right about her: she was morally stunted. Other people were put on Earth to serve her, praise her, and please her. If they didn't, they didn't deserve to live.

I got pretty upset when Larry told me May's attorney was thinking about an insanity defense. I asked him if she would walk. He told me no. Montana law says we charge you with murder and try to convict you, even if you seem to be crazy. If we convict you and then decide you really are crazy, we don't give you the needle. But we keep it nearby, just in case, sometime in the future, you stop being crazy. That made me feel a little better.

I didn't want to see her executed, although she deserved it at least as much as some poor black guy who kills a store clerk when a robbery goes bad. I knew Larry would make sure she'd stay inside long enough she'd look as crappy and busted-up as me when she got out. That would be harsh but legal, just this side of cruel and unusual.

Her two victims? I didn't have any real feelings for them. I never met Austin, of course, but I doubt I would have thought much of him. The women said he gave good value in bed, and I guess that's something, but I'm old enough to know it's not that much. Certainly not enough. According to Frances Hamblin, the old Melville coot, he made some connection with Suzannah's sick kid, which might have been the only truly unselfish thing he did.

Suzannah Montgomery was a puzzle to me. I'm afraid she was one of those people who I'd dislike more after I got to know her history. She didn't do right by Suzannah Collins, the roommate she maybe destroyed back at Clemson. The car crash was one thing, and I'd like to think I wouldn't have put the Collins girl behind the wheel so I didn't have to take the fall if she died. I'd like to think I wouldn't have done that, but if there was liquor involved I can't say for sure.

No, the real sign of Suzannah's character wasn't that, or even how she stole the girl's transcript and the rest of her identity. The real sign was how she never went to see her—before she had that stroke and went into a coma, or after.

Still, I never saw Suzannah with her sick kid or her daughter, just like I never saw her with Austin or with Frances Hamblin. And I never saw her with her husband.

When we brought Aaron Montgomery in to ID his wife, he fell apart worse than I'd ever seen, and I've done that little ritual at least a hundred times. He screamed, he cried, he collapsed onto the floor, all in a way I took to be genuine.

To be honest, though, I'm not that curious about the weird story of Aaron and Suzannah Montgomery. I don't care about the details of their relationship, how they met, what they did to Suzannah Collins at Clemson, whether he knew his wife was screwing around behind his back, whether he was screwing around, whether he was a phony architect like she was a phony professor.

The one I feel the worst about is Tiffany Rhodes, who died of a brain bleed when her idiot boyfriend beat her up and drove off after watching her hit her head and lose consciousness as the blood soaked the carpet beneath her head. She made some stupid choices, the stupidest one hooking up with Brian Hawser in the first place. But she didn't have too many good cards to play. She wasn't attractive or smart or endearing in any way I could see. She was born to just stumble along through life. But with a little luck, she might have stumbled into a job she was bright enough to do, and she might have stumbled along until she found a guy who was fine with her being ordinary because he was ordinary, too. On her own or with someone ordinary, she might have lived long enough to be okay with being ordinary, long enough to learn not to keep doing stupid things, such as fucking your English teacher so he'll give you a higher grade.

There wasn't one specific thing I did that got her killed. But all along I knew it was possible that Brian would hurt her. I knew it, because I've known too many guys like him, and too many girls like her. But I couldn't stop it. I had to work the case. It wasn't my fault. Ryan said so, and the chief did, too. Even Brian Hawser never accused me of getting Tiffany killed. Still, I'm having some real trouble getting past it.

All the betrayals and infidelities—all this lying and fucking—and what did it get anyone? It killed three of them, put another two in jail, and ruined a bunch of other lives. Suzannah left two kids behind, a healthy daughter and a sick son, neither of whom did anything to deserve the heartache they were going to face. The way these things usually work out, the two kids will end up paying the heaviest price. Adam probably won't understand why his mother and Austin were gone. He'll feel bad about it, but maybe he won't feel responsible for any of it. And the daughter? Aaron Montgomery will need to explain things to her.

My head sees all this destruction as the routine wreckage that happens when you do shit so obviously stupid you really can't explain afterwards what you were thinking—if you were thinking anything at all. Most of it comes down to breaking a trust. Sometimes it's hurting yourself by doing something unworthy of the person you already are or the person you have the potential to be. I've cut myself with that particular blade often enough to know how bad it hurts, and that the scars never disappear.

I'm trying hard to see how, behind all this misery, there's something positive. I'd like to believe that the one thing that runs through all these bad decisions is a human longing for connection and tenderness and love. I know it's hard to see it that way when most of what these characters did was selfish and cruel. But if you could ask everyone involved in this case whether they would have done any of the horrible things they did if they could have had just one person they could trust and love—and would love them—well, I'd like to believe I know how they would respond. I know how I would.

I looked down at the key on my coffee table. The key was on top of a note Mac had left me this morning. The test results were back on his wife, he had written. It was Stage III ovarian cancer, and she was coming apart. I thought a good long while about his decision before I reached for the glass of Jack Daniel's on the coffee table.

About the Author

Mike Markel is the author of the Detectives Seagate and Miner Mystery series:

> *Big Sick Heart*
> *Deviations*
> *The Broken Saint*
> *Three-Ways*

He lives in Boise, Idaho, with his wife.

Thank you for taking time to read *Three-Ways: A Detectives Seagate and Miner Mystery.* If you enjoyed it, please consider telling your friends or posting a short review. Word of mouth is an author's best friend and much appreciated.

Fractures:

A Detectives Seagate and Miner

Mystery

Following is the Prologue of *Fractures*, volume 5 in the *Detectives Seagate and Miner Mystery* series.

Lee Rossman shut off the lights as he exited the reception area of his office in the New Century Building, locked the door behind him, and walked down the carpeted hall toward the elevator. He picked up the faint sounds of Mexican pop music drifting into the hall from the open door of the title-company office a few steps farther along. As he stepped around the cleaning cart that protruded into the hall, he glanced inside but didn't see anyone. He would have said hello. He was comfortable with Hispanics from his years in Houston. And he mixed easily with people who came from nothing, people like himself.

The elevator, smooth and almost silent, delivered him to the basement parking garage. The click of his leather soles on the concrete floor echoed in the silent garage. There were only eight or nine cars left. He recognized a midnight blue Lexus, a dark green Jaguar, and a silver Audi that always seemed to be there when he arrived every morning around seven and were still there when he left, usually twelve or fourteen hours later. As he walked toward his BMW 7 series in parking spot 96, he glanced at his watch: 9:25.

He often thought of what his father had told him, his father who quit high school to work the oil fields for two bucks an hour: you got time or you got money. Nobody's got both.

He tossed his wool topcoat onto the passenger seat and started the BMW, the running lights throwing two white circles on the grey concrete wall, just below "Rossman Mining" painted in maroon letters four inches high. He had been so successful for so many years he no longer thought about how far he had come in his forty-year career.

Lee Rossman eased the car toward the exit, tripping the steel gate, which clanged and shuddered as it rose. He saw the blue light flash and heard the buzzer sound out on the sidewalk as he steered the car onto Main Street. The red and green Christmas lights on the light poles swayed in the wind. After dark here in central Montana, when the gusts picked up, the squat old brick and stone commercial buildings provided some intermittent windbreak, but when he crossed a side street he would hear a muffled whoosh and feel his heavy BMW tilt for a moment as the wind barreled through the tiny commercial center of Rawlings.

He drove six blocks, past the holiday lights and decorations on the stores and offices, now closed for the night. He passed a handful of people huddled in their heavy coats, hunched over in the frigid night air. A digital sign on the bank display read 3 degrees. The movie theatre, its bright bulbs illuminating the lobby posters and the V-shaped white marquee extending out over the sidewalk, offered the only attraction in the frozen purple night.

Lee Rossman turned left on Harrison and drove slowly toward the grittier section of downtown, where the storefronts cowered behind steel accordion gates. He slowed down as he approached Johnny's Lounge and put on his blinker. Above the gouged, dirty wooden door, the bar's name was spelled out in cursive letters, garish blue and red neon. To the left of the name was a huge neon top hat; to the right, a giant cocktail glass, tilted slightly.

From the door emerged a tall, thin young guy wearing matching denim jeans and jacket and a white cowboy hat. He pulled a cigarette from his jacket pocket and, cupping his hands, lit it with a butane lighter.

Sizing up the young man's clothing, Lee Rossman concluded he wouldn't be walking, certainly not more than a few steps. The young man moved slowly and deliberately, concentrating on his boots on the sidewalk, as if he were rehearsing walking a straight line in case he got stopped by the police. Rossman scanned the line of parked cars and pickups, trying to guess which one belonged to the young man, before settling on a new black F-150, its sides streaked with mud.

The young man stepped off the curb, momentarily losing his balance, and steadied himself on the hood of the black pickup. Lee Rossman smiled as the young man walked over to the driver's door and struggled to retrieve his keys from the pockets of his tight jeans. He was a roughneck, out on the town in his new denim and his new truck.

Rossman pulled up behind the truck and waited for the young man to turn over the big block engine. The pickup shook and let out a rumble, and the young man pulled slowly out of the parking spot and drove off.

Rossman carefully parked his BMW in the empty spot thirty feet from the entrance to Johnny's Lounge. He let the engine idle for a few moments, his fingers gripping the heated leather steering wheel. Warm air blasted from the vents on either side of the wheel, filling the cabin. He felt the warmth from the leather seat penetrating his wool slacks, which were designed in London and tailored in Hong Kong but never intended to be worn in Rawlings, Montana, in late November.

What did it mean, Lee Rossman thought, that he was summoned here? At nine-thirty at night?

He shut down the engine and cupped his palms over the heat vents. He looked up to see two girls in their mid-twenties walk up to the heavy wooden door at Johnny's Lounge. They were wearing thick down jackets, blue jeans with rhinestones on the back pockets, and cowboy boots with two-inch heels that had never touched a stirrup. One of the girls pulled at the door, then flashed a big smile as a beefy guy, dim in the shadows inside the bar, helped them pull it open.

Lee Rossman didn't recognize these girls, but he knew they were at Johnny's for the first shift. Until about midnight, there was live music from a country band that had both a male and a female singer and therefore could play any of the popular songs on the two country radio stations in town. Some of the girls on the first shift were there for the line dancing, some for the free drinks from any of a couple of dozen guys who walked in with two or three crisp hundred-dollar bills in their jeans pockets and left without a penny. After midnight—after the girls in denim and cowboy boots had selected their guys and left—another set of girls started to work the pole on the platform behind the bar, and the professionals in tight skirts started to work the guys who weren't there for the line dancing.

He got out of his BMW and slipped into his topcoat. He slid his hands deep into the coat pockets and walked toward the bar. As he was passing the battered door, it opened and a couple came out. He felt the vibration from the bass guitar. He heard the crack of the snare drum, as sharp as a gunshot, and the metallic tinkling of women's voices competing with the amplified music. He felt the humidity coming off the young bodies inside and smelled the spilled beer and the cheap, sweet perfume mingled with sweat.

Lee Rossman said "Excuse me" as the young couple, laughing and oblivious to the old man in the charcoal wool topcoat, stumbled into him. He kept walking, past the window with the neon Coors sign, toward the spot where he had been instructed to appear. He turned into the alley that ran along the wall of Johnny's Lounge. He walked toward the floodlight mounted above the two heavy steel doors in the pavement that led down to the basement, where the bar took its deliveries. He stood there, as he had been directed.

It took him some time to make out the objects in the alley outside the cone of light in which he stood. The moon was hidden behind fast-rushing clouds, and there were no other lights to push back the darkness. On one side of the steel doors were a dozen empty beer kegs lined up alongside the concrete-block wall. On the other side were three wooden shipping pallets stacked against the wall, and a big green dumpster on wheels, with trash and cardboard boxes pushing open its lid. Across the alley he saw a three-story brick building, probably a hundred years old, with ornamental stone-framed windows now bricked in, a vestige of a time when the alley was a through street.

Lee Rossman felt the cold penetrating the soles of his shoes. He glanced down at his feet. The alley, its surface rippled, broken, and patched in various shades of grey and black, was covered with dirty ice, crushed paper beer cups, broken glass, cigarette butts, and condom wrappers. Off to the side he saw a frozen starburst of vomit. He caught a faint smell of urine.

He stood there, under the light in the alley next to Johnny's Lounge, waiting as he had been instructed. He glanced to his right when he heard footsteps.

They looked at each other for a long moment. "Why here?" Lee Rossman said.

His killer did not respond.

"You owe me an explanation," Rossman said.

The killer paused. "You don't want to talk about what we owe each other."

"What do you want?" he said.

"I want your answer."

"I considered what you said."

"And are you done considering?"

"Yes." His tone was strong but full of regret. "I am."

"What is your decision?"

"My answer is no. I will not do it."

His killer was silent.

"I'm going to go now," Lee Rossman said. "I expect you not to mention this to me again. Ever." He started to turn.

"You know it's the only way."

He stopped and turned to face his killer. "There's always another way."

"I'm afraid you've made the wrong decision, Lee," his killer said and walked toward him.

Lee Rossman did not realize what was happening when the killer pushed aside his open topcoat. Only when he felt the knife slide into his abdomen and the pain radiate out in all directions like electric charges did he understand.

His eyes were open wide in disbelief. His knees began to buckle, and then he sank to the pavement, his head hitting hard and coming to rest near a patch of ice in which a candy wrapper was frozen.

The killer bent down and reached into Lee Rossman's inside suit jacket pocket and removed his wallet, then lifted the velvet cuff of his jacket sleeve, unbuckled the clasp on the heavy gold watch, slipped it off his wrist, and let his arm fall to the pavement. Lee Rossman appeared to be breathing, but his skin was beginning to pale and his eyes were glassy and unfocused. The killer turned to walk away, then stopped and returned and, pushing Rossman's topcoat and suit jacket aside, lowered the zipper on his impeccably tailored black wool slacks.